UNCUBICLED

UNCUBICLED

❀

Josh McMains

iUniverse, Inc.
New York Bloomington

Uncubicled

iUniverse books may be ordered through booksellers or by contacting:

iUniverse
1663 Liberty Drive
Bloomington, IN 47403
www.iuniverse.com
1-800-Authors (1-800-288-4677)

ISBN: 978-0-595-49783-6 (pbk)
ISBN: 978-0-595-61244-4 (ebk)

Printed in the United States of America

To my wife, who didn't laugh when I told her I
wanted to write a novel.

At least, not to my face.

Acknowledgements

Oh come on. You aren't seriously stopping to read this, are you? The action starts a couple of pages over. Don't feel guilty if you skip this section. I'd skip it if I were you.

I suppose if you are still reading that means you expect to be thanked for helping me with this project. To cover my bases, let me just say thanks. I couldn't have done it without you. Now move on.

Still reading? I guess you're probably expecting a mention. I hope I don't disappoint.

Thanks to:

Jude for the killer cover art (I'm actually writing this before I've seen it, so I'm trusting you here). If anyone would like to see his other work, visit www. judelandry.com.

Cy for being the one person who never tired of me talking about my manuscript.

Taylor for having such a boring summer job that I started writing to keep you entertained.

KC for being surprised that you actually liked the story.

Mom for always encouraging me to write, and then for finally sitting down to actually read a draft.

Pete for plugging the book on his podcast (again, I'm writing before this has happened, but even if he doesn't you all should check out The Bored-Again Christian).

Janet for showing interest in the book when mine was waning.

Katy for wringing out typos long after they had become invisible to everyone else.

Dad for telling me repeatedly that this story would make a great movie. Incidentally, I agree. You don't happen to have Spielberg's number, do you?

Ben for a friendship that translated to the page.

Aunt Susan for reading as I wrote.

Natosha for putting your textbooks down long enough to read this.

Brad for folding down the corners of the pages where you had written feedback. That was awesome.

Megan for being the first person to read the entire thing in less than 24 hours. I'm still amazed.

Shauna (and the whole *Maestro!* team) for living through all of the absurdity with me.

And finally, thanks to all the Gilmores out there that inspired this tale. I'd say that you know who you are, but clearly... you don't.

I have to get out of here.

The words themselves were not new. Joe Tompkins had repeated the phrase in his mind a million times during the past three months. He recited the words while trudging the long hallways that led to his cube, throwing fake smiles and nods at the coworkers he passed, outwardly thanking them for holding open hallway doors while secretly wishing they just wouldn't—wishing they would allow him to avoid the brief but draining social interaction.

I have to get out of here.

Joe repeated the phrase during long afternoons—when watching the minutes tick slowly by—when listening to the guy in the cube next door mindlessly sing along with his headphones, him not realizing that he was perpetually off key, him not realizing that everyone in the vicinity could hear.

I have to get out of here.

Joe repeated the phrase when staring at his empty calendar, the times when he would realize that a trip to the dentist might be the most he'd accomplish in a given week, when he would think of his passport at home gathering dust, when he would think of the friends that had abandoned him to the drudgery of his current situation.

I have to get out of here.

The words themselves were not new. The urgency that they had now taken, however, was. He was now on the run. There would be no going back to the tedium of his life—not after what he had just done. They were most certainly after him.

And they probably weren't far behind.

He had to get out of there.

1

Monday, 3:13 PM

Of the many jumbled thoughts colliding in Joe Tompkins' frantic mind, *"You aren't supposed to physically attack your coworkers"* was conspicuously *not* among them. Maybe the thought had been displaced with a more immediate concern like, *"You're screwed—all they have to do is block all the exits"* or *"Your lungs really aren't getting enough oxygen, could you please stop running?"* Or maybe he had just forgotten some of the unwritten rules of office etiquette.

Well, *that* rule—the one about not attacking coworkers—it probably *was* actually written down somewhere. But, right then, Joe didn't really need a lecture on the finer points of the employee handbook. What he needed was someplace to hide.

He crashed through the door of the fifth floor men's room, already winded from sprinting down two flights of stairs, hoping that no one from the hallway had seen him. He did a quick scan of the room.

Empty.

Joe celebrated this fact by collapsing onto the floor of the last stall and gulping in oxygen through an aromatic blend of cinnamon-apple air freshener and the typical stink of a public restroom—stale urine and worse. He had always objected to food-scented fresheners in places where he would never consider actually eating anything. It was confusing for the nose and upsetting for the stomach.

But Joe wasn't really worried about this at the moment. He had bigger concerns. Like the fact that he needed to get out of the building without being taken into custody. Like the fact that security personnel were probably already looking for him.

Like the fact that he was sitting on a dirty floor.

As a rule, Joe didn't sit on public restroom floors. He'd always had that rule. He needed to get to his feet. Though there wasn't any obvious filth, he knew that the floor was covered with the kinds of colorful microscopic bacteria that wriggled and oozed in all the household cleanser commercials. He pulled himself up using the stainless steel hand railing on the wall and made a mental note: He would sooner burn the slacks than wear them again. Much sooner.

Now standing, coming to terms with the fact that he needed to figure out his next move, Joe leaned against the wall, letting his head roll back and rest on the bluish-green tile. His eyes, strained and watery from staring at a computer screen for the last six hours and the last five years, lifted his gaze upward to the drop-ceiling overhead. Joe blinked as he focused—and then he knew. He had found his path of escape.

All that Joe understood about the intricacies of office building architecture had been gathered from action movies and TV shows. He knew that it was a simple matter to lift a ceiling tile and crawl to a ventilation shaft. He knew that no one would think to look for him there. He knew that he'd be able to exit the building without being seen.

It was a good plan. It was the only plan that made any sense. Though he would have to be quick. There wasn't much time. Joe could already imagine building security organizing a floor-by-floor search. But even now he didn't regret what he had done to Gilmore. He would never regret it. Gilmore got exactly what he deserved.

Joe prepared to execute his escape, carefully visualizing exactly how he would pull it off. He would jump up on the toilet seat and then climb to certain freedom. Well... not jump. There was no reason to actually jump. He would simply step—step up on the toilet seat. But first, obviously, he'd need to cover it with a protective layer of the thin and scratchy bath tissue provided in such a place.

So, with the toilet safely covered and after a quick washing of his hands, Joe climbed onto the seat, braced his hands on the top of the stall and hoisted his body up. Balancing precipitously on the dark blue dividing wall, Joe lifted a yellowed section of ceiling above his head and pushed it aside. Grasping the metal rails, he pulled himself up.

Well, he would have.

But the thin metal of the ceiling support beam was no match for Joe's two hundred pounds and it gave out immediately. Joe came down with it, smacking an eye on the top of the stall door and breathing a quick prayer of thanks that the coat hook was missing. His body hit the white-tiled floor hard and hip-first. A bruise started to show next to his eye as blood started to trickle from the cut in the hand that still grasped the betraying metal rail.

Things were certainly *not* going according to the plan.

He lay there, dazed, wishing he had thought that maneuver through and wondering if he could have possibly avoided the predicament in which he now found himself.

As his mind drifted back to the minutes before, one thing became quite clear. This needed to be the last time that he found himself on the restroom floor.

2

Monday, 3:04 PM

Joe Tompkins was sitting in the exact same spot that he sat every Monday afternoon: in a cube on the seventh floor. He was also there every Monday morning, and every other weekday from 8:30 to 5:00 with the rare interruption to use the restroom or grab lunch from the cafeteria or wander the halls pretending to hurry from one imaginary obligation to the next but really just needing to stretch his legs.

He hated that cube, but attempted to make the long days more bearable by always having a cold Diet Dr. Pepper nearby. It wasn't a perfect arrangement, but Joe had long ago resigned himself to the addiction. Unfortunately even the caffeinated bliss provided by his beverage of choice was beginning to pale in comparison to the fog of boredom that hung thickly in the air all around.

He drained another twelve ounces and stacked the empty can next to its brethren, a white and red aluminum army that was slowly advancing on the little remaining usable desk space that he had left. He would take them to the recycle bin later… maybe tomorrow… maybe Wednesday.

Joe stifled a yawn as his fingers made their way back to their designated spots on his dusty and crumb-ridden keyboard. What should he pretend to busy himself with? Rummaging through the wasteland of out-of-date project documentation on the network drive? Staring at a slide in the long-finished PowerPoint presentation that he had developed before realizing that the boss was going to forget that he'd even asked for it? Checking his personal email for the forty-seventh time that day?

Since he had spent the morning pretending to read old project documentation and liked some variety in his day, Joe decided on the PowerPoint. He pulled up the first slide and mindlessly typed in, "I used to be an engineer, dammit."

A crinkled red line appeared underneath the word "dammit." Apparently Microsoft didn't approve of what Joe thought was the accepted spelling. Being the grammatically responsible member of the digital age that he was, Joe right-clicked the underlined word and selected "damn it" from the dropdown list. The red line disappeared.

Joe didn't know how he was going to survive the rest of the afternoon.

Just another two hours, he tried to reassure himself in a voice that sounded tired and old even in his mind, *just get through another two hours*. Had the thought stopped there it might have actually *been* reassuring. Unfortunately, it continued, following the sentiment to its logical conclusion.

Then there are four more days until the weekend. And then, just thirty six and a half more years until retirement.

A subtle and familiar panic settled in Joe's chest. He tried not to think about it, but had a hard time finding something else to occupy his mind. There were moments during afternoons like this one, when time itself seemed to stop and stare at Joe through the unforgiving digits of the clock displayed in the lower right corner of his screen, in which Joe seriously wondered if his sanity was slowly slipping away. If it was, he felt helpless to stop it.

The sound of approaching footsteps came from the aisle and diverted Joe's mind from its typical afternoon spiral of fruitless introspection. Someone was about to walk by. Joe reminded himself that he needed to keep up appearances. He knew that the people around him were always watching, and figured that the steady stream of those meandering souls that wandered by his cube were constantly peaking over his shoulder to see what he was working on.

Some of the people around him had arranged their desks in such a way that their monitor faced in and couldn't be seen from the outside of the cubicle. Unfortunately Joe didn't have a long enough power cord for this arrangement. And he didn't want trouble from IT for bringing in an extension cord from home. So he was just careful to always look busy.

In that spirit, he deleted the sentence he'd just added, scrolled to another slide, and attempted to look like he was concentrating before the passerby passed by.

But, it turned out, no one was planning on passing by. Instead the footsteps slowed as they grew closer. Joe shut his eyes. He now recognized the casual gait and could picture the posture of the owner of those footsteps: weight shifted backward, legs dangling out front, feet haphazardly slapping at the floor as though actual locomotion was the last thing on their minds.

Gilmore.

Right on cue, the footsteps stopped just behind Joe's chair. Then came the loud and dramatic sigh. Joe knew this sigh. It was the same noise Gilmore always made when stopping by for a chat—one of those turn-around-and-ask-me-what-I'm-up-to-so-I-can-cure-my-need-for-attention-at-your-expense-with-some-inane-drivel-about-my-pathetic-nothing-life kind of sighs.

Gilmore had come to annoy. Joe just couldn't take it anymore. He had had enough. In that moment, Joe Tompkins finally snapped.

Gilmore was going to pay.

Joe had prepared for this, carefully and endlessly rehearsing similar scenarios in his often-idle mind. When the time to act had finally come, he didn't even have to think. He just let his instincts kick in.

In one graceful and sweeping motion Joe sprang from his seat, fingers locked onto his keyboard, and spun on his heels. He extended the keyboard, utilizing his full momentum, and connected full into Gilmore's unsuspecting face. The resulting crack of hard plastic meeting flesh combined in Joe's ears to a wonderful effect with an abbreviated, "So…" escaping from Gilmore's stupid mouth, no doubt his witty beginning to another excruciating story.

Joe was dead sure that the next few words would have been, "did I ever tell you about the time that I—insert brainless monologue here—went spear fishing in the Gulf at night and caught this huge fish, it busted my flashlight—professionally remodeled my kitchen with wood from a hundred-year-old barn without the use of proper tools—set up a deer stand in my backyard and saw two deer (Here! I've got pictures!)—got two packs of Skittles for the price of one from the vending machine down the hall…"

Joe had only been there three months and Gilmore was already completing the second iteration through his repertoire of personal experiences, always barreling through the "story" telling and retelling oblivious to any social cues that the receiving party holds absolutely no interest. It was clear to Joe that, had he actually had something to do, Gilmore would have had no respect for how busy he was.

But what was it that caused Joe to react in violence? He wasn't really sure. It was probably that he had suddenly felt backed into a corner, as if Gilmore represented some kind of warden in the intangible prison that Joe felt his life had become.

Or, it might have just been as much to mark the day as any other reason. Maybe simply to make that day different, to remind Joe that something, *something* in his life could still be unique, in some way unlike the other days that stretched far behind and endlessly ahead into a cubicle future of pointless conference calls and slide shows and mornings that came too early and weekends too short, life too plain, people too ordinary, and purpose—any kind of purpose—ever elusive.

"After all," Joe might explain someday when recounting the incident, "sooner or later, *something* had to happen." It was just Gilmore's bad fortune that that something was directed at him.

Of course, this didn't mean that Gilmore wasn't a valid target for Joe's frustration and fury. For proof of that, Joe needed only to remember the morning's staff meeting. The weekly staff meetings were always the same: the boss starting with a not-quite-brief-enough narrative about his weekend and then directing his twenty underlings seated at the conference table to relate to the group their current self-guided tasks while he pretends to listen.

As this was the only time during the week that anyone was allowed to interact with the boss in person, and because everyone was secretly afraid for him to find out that they don't really know what they were supposed to be doing (the boss secretly afraid that someone would ask for an assignment and thus require him to actually do something only a few short years from retirement), this meeting usually lasted 72 hours straight. Joe still wasn't sure what technology had been developed to slow the wall clock down, but it always only registered an hour or two.

As Joe was the last one into the conference room that morning, he had had to occupy the only remaining seat—directly across the table from Gilmore. And as the meeting dragged on, Gilmore sat there: mouth hanging open, eyes staring into space, and tongue curved up just barely touching his top lip. Maybe he was trying to look like a statue: an ugly, mustached, mouth-open statue with a blank stare, unkempt eyebrows, a receding hairline, and a curved tongue serving no purpose but to stimulate Joe's rage.

But that tongue was licking keyboard now.

Gilmore reeled backward from the impact, tripped on the carpet and landed full on his back with a delicious groan. The lady in the cubicle across the hall screamed. The PC on Joe's desk lurched as the cord to the keyboard tightened and disconnected, causing the tower to tip and crash into the army of cans, scattering them into the hallway. Heads were starting to pop up out of the surrounding cubicles.

Joe stood over Gilmore and looked around with crazed eyes. He only had time for one more blow to the face before he had to make his escape.

It landed beautifully.

3:19 PM

Joe struggled to pull himself off of the bathroom floor. Then he re-covered the toilet seat with paper and sat down. His head and his hip ached and the scratch on his palm was starting to burn. Apparently trying to climb up into the ceiling had been an incredibly stupid thing to do. For a few seconds he sat in disbelief at what had just happened, in that brief hazy period after an injury in which it doesn't quite seem real yet, in which he almost could convince himself that, if he just concentrated hard enough, he had the power to turn back the clock a minute or so and undo it.

A sharp throb of resurging pain from his newly bruised eye and the wince that accompanied it brought him back to reality. He swore under his breath and then hobbled up to the sink in order to get a look at his injuries and plunge his hand under the cold running water.

The water stung as it washed the wound. Joe tried not to think about the germs that surrounded him—even though he knew that they were no doubt determined to infect the cut. He weighed this for a second then, with his free hand, turned on the hot water. He could live with the added pain. The germs, he hoped, couldn't.

Joe twisted his head from side-to-side in an attempt to stretch his cramping neck and then took a moment to look in the mirror. His piercing blue eyes stared back at him, one punctuated with a bright red spot next to the iris—the beginnings of a black eye. His short brown hair was mussed as the morning's hair gel had long worn off. His face wasn't as thin as it used to be, then again neither was his waist. But overall Joe wore his five-foot-ten frame rather well. At least he thought so.

For some reason he then attempted to straighten his hair and his rumpled tan off-brand golf shirt, taking time to tame the left collar that seemed determined to curve upward toward his chin. He had tried to re-invent his image when taking this job by wearing a crisp shirt and tie everyday, but that had lasted less than a week. Spending the first two days on the job waiting for someone in authority to speak with (or for IT to bring him his PC) had rapidly broken Joe's spirit. As had Gilmore, who had been happy to fill the void with uninterruptible hours of brain canceling verbal refuse.

The sudden flush of a toilet from behind straightened Joe's stance and brought back the immediacy of his situation to mind. Apparently the bathroom wasn't empty after all. From his view through the mirror Joe could see movement beyond the door three stalls down from where he had fallen.

He was caught. The first thing this guy would do would be to ask him what had happened. The second thing would either be to insist that he accompany Joe to the on-site nurse or report him directly to building security. Joe knew that either outcome would ultimately land him in police custody.

Quickly, he snapped his head down and buried his gaze in the sink. There was only one option available. He had to take this guy out. Joe's right hand tightened into a fist. He was already past the point of no return. There was no going back now.

The guy in the stall was, however, apparently in no hurry. An endless string of shuffling, zipping, and buckling sounds indicated that he was in the process of collecting himself. Joe continued to wait, seething with impatience. He envisioned himself kicking the stall door open just to get the unpleasantness over with, but even in this state of mind he wouldn't consider invading the sanctity of a bathroom stall. After all, he wasn't an animal. Plus there was the risk of literally catching the guy with his pants down. He couldn't attack someone in that condition. He just couldn't.

So, the plan was to wait by the sink, pretend to rinse his face in the nasty tap water and spring upon the guy as he washed his hands… preferably *after* the soaping phase. Joe stamped down any moral objection to what he was about to do by reminding himself that this guy had obviously heard him fall but had never asked if he was okay.

Joe was careful not to admit to himself that had *he* heard an out-of-place noise while on the commode, he would have just chalked it up as an opportune auditory distraction allowing him to progress with his business at hand with a diminished chance of being overheard.

Finally, the stall door creaked open. Joe scooped some water in his hands and let it drain out before lifting it to his face. How many punches would it take? Surely the guy wouldn't be expecting it, but a twinge of doubt in his ability to knock someone unconscious started to grow in Joe's mind. But there was no time for that. Slow footsteps were approaching.

Just be quick about it, Joe told himself as he turned his body purposely toward the sink next to him while keeping his eyes pointed downward. He drew back his fist and raised his eyes. But there was no man standing there. Instead, Joe caught the last glimpse of the guy disappearing through the bathroom door and it closing behind him.

Gross.

"HOW ABOUT WASHING YOUR FRICKIN' HANDS YOU FILTHY PIG!" Joe screamed in spite of his good fortune. But with the noise of the ventilation and the thickness of the door, he doubted that the man had even heard.

"Ok, what's the plan?" Joe now whispered, forcing himself to focus. "Get the heck out of the building, same as before."

He had to get back to the stairwell and then down to the ground floor. He would worry about security at that point. There was no reason to stay here. He walked back to his stall and picked up the metal ceiling rung that had come off in his hand. Not the best weapon, but certainly better than nothing. He hoped he wouldn't have to use it.

Joe wrapped his cut in a wet paper towel. He then dried off his hands, careful to keep one towel with him to open the door with. He filled his lungs, grasped the handle, and peeked out the door.

The long hallway was mostly empty with just a few stragglers ambling from cube to cube. The nauseating beige carpet showed signs of age and clashed with the light gray burlap fabric pasted over the maze of discount cubicles stretching endlessly to a distant horizon awash with a fluorescent glow.

No security—at least not yet. Joe sprinted toward the stairwell and reached for the door. But just as his hand closed in on the handle, it turned and the door started to open. He stopped short and bit his lip.

A random woman (Joe thought he recognized her from HR) walked through. She threw him a bewildered look as he brushed past her and bounded down the stairs, impromptu weapon still in tow.

They must be waiting at the main exit, Joe's thoughts told him. Unfortunately, that was the only exit he had ever used and the only one he was familiar with. He wasn't even sure what other exits existed, let alone which direction they would lead him from the sprawling office complex. He would still have to quickly find his car in the massive parking lot if and when he made it out of the building.

Out of breath again, Joe slammed into the metal railing that separated the stairs halfway between the second and third floor. He leaned against it, body aching, chiding himself for not utilizing that prepaid yearlong gym membership more than twice. *This* was pathetic.

A tall tinted window ran up along the stairwell allowing the only glimpse of the outside world to those not fortunate enough to merit a windowed office. Joe took the opportunity to gaze out at the sea of windshields sparkling in the afternoon sun. He twisted and pressed his face against the glass in an attempt to see the front entrance. He could just make out the awning that led up to the lobby doors. There wasn't any visible activity. Security was most likely organizing some sort of blockade—best to keep civilians out of the way.

With nowhere to go but down, Joe willed himself on again, this time at a slower pace. And as precious seconds ticked by he reached the ground floor.

As he had never actually taken the stairs before, he was surprised by the second door at the bottom of the stairwell—an emergency exit. Sure, an alarm would sound if Joe used the door, but it was either that or the main lobby exit. He allowed himself another few seconds to catch his breath, tightened his grip on his weapon, and threw his full weight into the door handle.

The alarm immediately exploded in his ears, but that wasn't the first thing Joe noticed. The door hadn't budged. It had, however, reflected Joe's momentum right back at him forcing him backward and landing him on the dirt-covered concrete of the stairwell floor. The metal rung was knocked from his grasp and fell with a clang that was drowned out by the irritating alarm that filled and echoed through the entire chamber.

Something about the event sapped Joe of any remaining will to flee. He knew that he was beat.

Slowly Joe picked himself up and dusted himself off. He left his weapon behind and opened the door to the ground floor muttering something about an anonymous tip to the city's fire marshal.

He was met by the curious stares of the faceless employees that lived there. He didn't care. He just plodded slowly toward the lobby hanging his head; resolved to his fate. But he still didn't regret his actions, just the lack of an escape route.

The lobby was just ahead, behind tall oak doors that only opened with an ID badge on the way in, but allowed anyone to walk out. Joe wondered if the police had arrived yet, or if he would just be surrendering to building security. If so, would he have to sit quietly as coworkers paraded past him leaving for the day while he waited for the cops? Maybe they'd at least let him wait outside.

In fact… maybe… could *that* be his chance to escape? Could he just pretend to cooperate, ask to wait outside, then attempt to bolt? It wasn't like building security carried guns… or handcuffs for that matter.

"Okay, new plan," he breathed, "Just act cooperative."

Joe approached his exit, unable to see what was just beyond. A dull click informed him that the motion detector had sensed his presence and disengaged the lock. He slowly exhaled and reached for the door. It swung open easily.

3

Ned Dyer didn't know it, but after three long years of living in fear and suspicion, the other shoe was about to drop. Tonight the consequences of the threat he had received would finally begin to play themselves out. The outcome would not be pleasant.

Not pleasant at all.

Monday, 5:14 PM

For the past three years there had been a certain apprehensiveness that Ned Dyer felt whenever in a crowd of unfamiliar people, or in a strange or poorly lit place, or even when driving in light traffic as he now was—on his way home from work. The recurring thoughts had originally always been: *"Is my family safe?"* and *"Are my friends safe?"* But after a few harried months they had collapsed into a smaller circle of concern, an almost purely selfish: *"Am I safe?"* as Ned had distanced himself from those around him.

For a long time Ned had lived like that, cut off, turned inward, run by a mixture of worry and disbelief. He had followed his instructions exactly, unsure of their source and sometimes doubting their sincerity, but never risking the penalty of disobedience. And he had waited, unsure of what for, half-expecting some kind of confirmation that he had performed correctly, some kind of lifting of the restrictions imposed, any kind of feedback beyond the continued health and safety of himself and his loved ones.

This had never come and he couldn't help but wonder if he were starving himself of human contact pointlessly. So, after a full year and a half of living this way he had begun to cautiously reengage the world around him, every effort deliberate, continually on guard, always keeping the secret of the threat to his life close to his chest. No one was to know. It was the only way to keep them safe.

But Ned Dyer had another secret too. Though his enemy was invisible and unknown, he had found a way to fight back.

So, as he had begun to re-inflate his life and replace the things he had left behind, his circle of concern had widened again. It seemed that this concern was never far from his mind, and instilled within him a degree of paranoia that he had come to accept as part of reality for someone in his particular situation.

And, as much as he had tried to move on with his life, his thoughts always returned to the same train, riding around the track in his mind to their predetermined conclusion:

Something is out of place. Something doesn't resolve. There has to be more to the equation.

Ned had been trained to think in patterns. The threat to his life three years ago was blazingly out of place, incongruous with the general flow of his days and years, stranger still because of the form in which it had come.

His car happened upon a patch of stiffer rain and the green-yellow-red Doppler image that he had studied before leaving the office appeared in his mind—another batch of isolated thunderstorms, brightly gift wrapped for Southern Illinois' evening commute.

Ned kicked the wipers up to high and leaned forward to aid his navigation of the downtown traffic and signals. This pushed the unpleasant thoughts from his attention as he piloted his black BMW the rest of the way to his cul-de-sac.

As he pulled into his driveway, Ned noticed an out-of-place car through the still pouring rain, parked on the street in front of the Beswicks' house two doors down. It was a light-gray Volkswagen sedan, with two mysterious figures sitting suspiciously in the front seat. Ned's shoulders tensed and he began to absorb every detail about his surroundings with quick flicks of his eyes. He memorized the digits on the Volkswagen's Kansas license plate, registered the rain-soaked newspaper on his front step, scanned the other, more familiar vehicles of his neighbors parked in driveways nearby. Ned imagined would-be attackers hiding behind these cars and ducked slightly, trying to peer underneath them—searching for feet.

As his BMW pulled into the safety of his large unattached garage, Ned watched in the rearview mirror as the two figures in the Volkswagen threw open their doors and ran, umbrellaless, up the Beswicks' yard and into the house. It seemed that they had been waiting, fruitlessly, for the rain to let up before making their entrance. Perhaps they were just ordinary, visiting relatives and not thugs come to rough Ned up after all. Still, he'd enter the license plate into his personal database of potential enemies once he got inside.

Ned stepped through the side door leading to his kitchen, collapsed his umbrella, sending a brief shower of collected rain to the floor, and disarmed the home security system. His modest assortment of keys assumed their position on the dark green marble countertop that connected each top-of-the-line stainless steel appliance that sat on the ceramic tiled floor. Dark oak cabinets hugged the glazed walls, projecting an air of elegant simplicity in the often-empty kitchen.

This house had been Ned's pet project since moving from Atlanta three years back. He lived there alone—for the first time in his life. It had been a difficult adjustment but he hadn't had a choice.

And now his likeability and ambition had replaced most of the things he had left behind. He had found his stride at the new job almost immediately and coworkers had evolved from acquaintances to friends in just a few short months. In fact, he was going to meet his accounting-department fiancée for dinner in just over an hour.

Mindful of the time, Ned changed out of his business-casual-office-attire and descended to the basement living room. Engineered hardwood ran the length of the elongated room of alternating dark and light green walls. Ethan Allen had supplied the brown, leather, over-stuffed chairs and thick, white sofas. A stocked bar at the back of the room stood next to the stone archway that led to Ned's wine cellar.

The pride of the room, however, was the very large off-white industrial-grade theater projector that stuck obtrusively out of the center of the ceiling as if to say, "Don't let the décor fool you. This is the house of an engineer." Ned was fond of informing people of its thirty thousand dollar value, purchased in need of a new circuit board on eBay for less than two grand.

From a closet Ned produced his customized recumbent exercise bike—a testament to an unchecked mixture of adolescence and ingenuity. The seat allowed the rider to lean back while pedaling with his legs more in front than underneath his body. Comfortable handgrips extended directly in front allowing him to push or pull with mild resistance in order to build up arm strength. Each action triggered an input to a modified Xbox controller allowing for a more interactive gaming experience. The entire wireless contraption glided on felt pads as Ned pushed it into the center of the room. And while he enjoyed using the device immensely, he still thought of its construction as "the fun part."

The lights dimmed as the twelve-foot-wide section of wall coated in reflective white paint morphed into the familiar first-person-shooter vantage point of a futuristic world gone horribly wrong. Waves of sound engulfed Ned from the analog vacuum-tube-based sound system recessed into the walls. Ned would insist to anyone who would listen that the modern digital systems destroyed the richness of the sound quality. He was undeterred by his inability to find someone who shared this conviction.

A quick game of online Halo 3 later, he had worked up an appetite.

Ned was one of those guys still blessed with a teenage metabolism a decade after being a teenager. Sure, he exercised a little, but not enough to counter the healthy portions he normally ate. Yet at 6 feet tall he only weighed in around 150 pounds. Some might have considered him a bit scrawny, but the thinness of his face was well balanced with a short, trendy, sandy-colored beard, a comfortable smile, and deep brown eyes behind narrow dark-rimmed glasses.

After a three-and-a-half-minute shower Ned was out the door again, pleased that the rain had now stopped, with shiny new cell phone clipped on one hip and large black pager on the other. He was headed to the local Australian steakhouse to meet his fiancée Sue—and the unpleasant fate that awaited him there.

After giving his name and non-smoking preference to the hostess, Ned Dyer sat down on the long wooden bench that lined the restaurant's lobby and waited for Sue to arrive. His eyes instinctively scanned the room, as they always did, looking for anything or anyone out of place.

His gaze came to rest on a clear plastic fishbowl half-filled with assorted business cards on the counter. The sign taped on the front touted a chance to win a free lunch. Ned didn't care much about that, but he had just had some new business cards printed up and was eager to use one. He pulled his small-bills-and-photos wallet out of his right front pocket and produced a fresh business card. There was his name in bright red print:

Ned Dyer
Abstraction Engineer

He had made up the title, but upper management had approved it, so it was official. He had almost gone with "Abstractionist," but that had lacked the oxymoronic contradiction that made him smile when he read it. This was his dream job, a continuation of the work he had started at his company back in Georgia.

By education, Ned was just another software engineer. True, he had minored in mathematics and psychology, but he knew that this uncommon mixture hadn't really helped him get his first job out of school at the aerospace firm in Atlanta. Though Ned excelled at the job he was hired for, writing code as assigned, he had quickly become bored with this. "Talking to machines is easy," he would often say, "getting ideas across to people is the hard part."

And so, he had quickly moved from coding subroutines, classes, and event handlers to writing requirements and diagramming designs. This was almost considered an art form in the aerospace industry as life-dependant systems were subject to stringent government regulations. This required an ability to produce clearly and consistently detailed documentation that ran counter to most engineers' aptitudes and interests.

Within a year, Ned had redefined the company's approach to technical writing. He had attacked it like he would develop a computer program: breaking down sentences into more elemental constructs, reusing phrases and descriptions in an object-oriented hierarchy, even developing software tools to organize the information graphically. To him, he was engineering systems using human languages rather than software languages. After all, a monkey could be trained to write code.

Ned had been making quite an impression and was on the fast track toward advancement until the day, three years ago, when he had been forced to leave town.

That day was burned into his memory like a brand on his brain.

He had left work early with an upset stomach and arrived at his fourth floor apartment. Both the knob and deadbolt were locked, as usual, due to the insistence of his slightly obsessive compulsive roommate. This being the case, the presence of the large manila envelope that Ned found on the other side of the door was something of a mystery. It hadn't been there that morning, and Ned knew he'd been the last one to leave for work that day.

The envelope was obviously meant for him to find, though, as it had "NED DYER: For your review" written on it in large block letters scribbled in black marker. What he found inside would haunt him for years, eventually forming a kind of mental backdrop in front of which his life would be played out from that point on.

The first in the packet of pages was a mock software requirements document. To most anyone else, this would have appeared odd, unfamiliar, and cryptic. To Ned Dyer, however, there was a beautiful clarity to the framework that the enclosed information was built upon. It exactly followed the standards he himself had developed: requirements uniquely numbered, active tense, keywords in all caps, newly defined terms underlined, at least one input condition and one output condition surrounding the verb "shall"—written in bold type.

The requirements were clear. They were consistent. They were testable. The FAA would have been pleased. But, while the structure of these sentences was flawless, the content made Ned's already upset stomach turn.

---

[1] UPON receipt of this document, Ned **shall** quit his job in LESS THAN OR EQUAL TO 2 weeks.

[2] UPON quitting his job, Ned **shall** relocate to another state.

[3] IF Ned informs ANY person of the receipt of this document, Ned **shall** <u>regret</u> this action.

[4] IF ANY person becomes suspicious of Ned's motives for quitting his job, Ned **shall** <u>regret</u> this.

[5] IF Ned behaves appropriately, Ned **shall** continue his life WITHOUT <u>regret</u>.

*<u>regret</u>—defined as the emotion Ned Dyer will experience as a result of bodily harm enacted upon himself or his friends and family members.

At first Ned wrote it off as an ill-attempted joke by a coworker. Then he looked at the photos on the accompanying pages: a picture of his parents doing yard work in front of their house in central Illinois, a picture of his sister and her kids playing at their neighborhood park in Indianapolis, a picture of his grandmother in the nursing home near Chicago, and a picture of his roommate asleep in his bed—taken from inside the apartment.

Reflexively Ned dropped the envelope and an object slid out from inside. He bent down and picked up the small leather collar—sticky with dried blood and fur. His mom had said that the family cat went missing the previous week.

Ned barely made it to the bathroom to throw up—not sure if it had been a result of the package or the stomach bug. He gave his two-weeks notice the next day.

"I think that he thought that I wouldn't notice!"

Ned Dyer was halfway through a story about his day as he finished his twenty-ounce-porterhouse-and-loaded-baked-potato dinner. His fiancée Sue sat and listened intently, long finished with her meal, saving the other half of her grilled chicken sandwich for the next day's lunch. She wore a simple black dress that complemented her figure. A pearl necklace hung around her neck beneath dark brown hair, recently cut and highlighted.

Ned's mind had registered this as *"Sue's hair is inconsistent from its appearance yesterday"* when he had seen her at work that morning. Out loud he had said, "Oh, I like your hair!" which he had then punctuated with a quick kiss on the cheek.

"I mean," Ned continued with this story about how the new-hire had sought to "improve" upon a document he had penned, "it was obvious that the subject of the sentences in that section had been altered so that the requirements had mutated to the passive tense! Now, the FAA will allow passive requirements," Ned began to chuckle, "but you can tell that they don't like it."

"What was he thinking?" Sue responded automatically.

"I know!"

A momentary glazing over of his fiancée's eyes—an almost imperceptible jarring of her head as she snapped back to attention told Ned that perhaps he was the only one interested in his story—*bless her for trying.*

"Anyway," he continued, "then I looked down and saw a crisp, new twenty-dollar bill just lying on the floor!"

Sue's expression immediately sharpened into a playful smirk as she swatted Ned's arm. She had taught him that trick to allow oneself a quick exit from a story that wasn't holding the listener's attention.

"I was listening!" she pleaded her case, "At least... I was *trying* to listen..."

Ned leaned across the table for a kiss.

"You know, this is the guy you are marrying," he said with a grin.

"All my friends think I'm crazy," she smiled back.

Their waiter appeared. He was young and nervous and had a comical habit of rapidly glancing back and forth to each of them as he rattled off his waiter-speech. Ned's grin widened.

"Would either of you be interested in dessert this evening?" the waiter delivered the line as if addressing the ever moving ball in an invisible high-speed ping-pong match. The question wasn't lost on Ned though, as his arm reflexively reached for the dessert menu propped up on the table.

"Ned, fresh apple pie at my place," Sue reminded, "a-la-mode."

It was a good twenty-minute drive to Sue's apartment. Ned was sure that he could have had room for both desserts, but sensed that this would have been improper.

"Sorry, Tom," Ned read from the waiter's name tag, "her offer's better. Just the check for me and I think the lady would like you to box that up." He pointed to her plate and then snatched an uneaten french-fry.

"Okay, uh, sure you don't need another Dr. Pepper?" Tom asked awkwardly as he handed Ned the bill.

"Yeah, two's my limit for a weeknight," Ned joked. The waiter emitted what might have been considered a forced laugh, but Ned didn't pick up on this subtlety. He knew that he was hilarious. He had been on fire all night.

Even so, Ned thought he noticed Sue roll her eyes as he fished his large-bills-and-credit-cards wallet out of his left front pocket and placed a platinum card on the plastic tray that held his bill. Tom handed Sue her Styrofoam-boxed half-sandwich, slid the tray off of the table, and disappeared to wherever waiters go when they're not milling around amongst the customer-filled tables.

"So," Sue asked as she gathered her purse from its perch, dangling underneath the table from its collapsible hanger, "did you have a chance to exercise after work?'

"Yeah," Ned answered, "but my bike was acting a little sporadic. I was pedaling forward consistently, but it wasn't always registering on the game. So my guy would run forward, pause, start running again, pause, run some more… I got killed a whole bunch of times."

"Hmm," Sue replied remotely as she stowed her decorated purse-hanger, "Can you fix it?"

Ned resisted the urge to grab a napkin and start scribbling schematic diagrams in order to illustrate, in detail, where exactly he deduced the problem might be. He reminded himself of his audience, that she was probably just asking out of politeness, and went with a larger grained explanation. "The problem is somewhere in the hardware. My old roommate built that part. I should probably give him a call… he could walk me through fixing it."

A bald man in a department-store suit walked past their table and was seated across the aisle. Ned registered his face automatically as he did whenever someone new entered his immediate environment and, after a moment, he froze with delayed recognition. He thought that he had seen this man before—most people wouldn't have remembered—but Ned remembered. Ned remembered everything from that day.

As if to destroy any doubt, they briefly made eye contact. The man's eyes darted guiltily away. He was made.

A long-repressed panic started to well up inside of Ned, constricting his throat and moistening his eyes. He had seen this man in the crowded sidewalk outside his apartment the day he had received the threatening package. The odds were too low for this to be a coincidence. For some reason, his life was being intruded upon again. Did he have the strength to fight back this time? Did he have the will?

Sue was too busy accounting for the items in her purse to notice Ned's drained expression. He barely heard as she asked about his old roommate, "How's Joe doing anyway?"

White-faced and wide-eyed Ned snapped his eyes back to Sue's, swallowed, and hoarsely managed, "Um…what?"

4

Monday, 3:29 PM

Joe Tompkins entered the brightly lit lobby, determined to play the part of a repentant, cooperative, surrendering wrongdoer. He would then allow himself to be escorted outside. There, he would overpower the security personnel around him and escape. He wouldn't have a lot of time to get to his car, and he tried to remember exactly where he had parked in the expansive parking lot that morning as the large oak door swung closed behind him with a thud.

Joe surveyed his surroundings.

The receptionist was at her desk reading a tabloid and chewing gum. A kid in a tie was sitting nervously in the waiting area. He glanced up hopefully at Joe, obviously there for an interview, hoping Joe was whom he was waiting for.

Joe avoided eye contact with the kid in order to convey the appropriate message and glanced at the receptionist while continuing a slow stride toward the front door. She looked up, smiled, and muttered a quick, "Have a good evening."

No one was waiting for him: no building security—no police. Joe quickened his pace, too bewildered to respond to the receptionist, and exited through the glass doors at the front of the lobby.

The warm humid air greeted Joe as he stepped into the afternoon sunshine—a beautiful central Illinois Monday in June. The weekend had been damp and overcast. No police cars to be seen. Not even the guy who patrols the parking lot was around. Rage mixed with relief and Joe spun around to shout at the building.

"Nice security team, MORONS!! You know, there's a war on terror going on!"

Frazzled and confused, Joe strode across the hot pavement, found his eleven-year-old green Honda, hit the keyless entry, waited the obligatory two seconds required for the door to unlock, glanced once more at the building's main entrance (where there was still nothing to see), entered the car, slammed the door, battled with the seatbelt as the auto-lock feature combated his efforts to quickly buckle it, and pulled out of the parking space.

He still didn't understand what had just happened. He had left the building *so* very slowly. The realization that he could have just taken the elevator and strolled out was hard to swallow, but couldn't be denied. It seemed that all his frantic attempts at cunning had gained him nothing but the injuries he now carried. He studied his purpling eye in the rearview mirror. His appearance suggested that he'd been in some kind of brawl. How embarrassing would it be to admit that he had sustained the injuries by his own clumsiness?

But to whom would he possibly have to admit this? He was now on the run. A fugitive. He needed to figure out where he was going next. Surely, security was organizing itself by now. Surely it wouldn't be long before his description was radioed to the police. Maybe he had left enough chaos behind to occupy the authorities for a while, but he figured that he had half an hour at most before they caught up with him. His apartment wasn't far. He'd quickly pack a bag and then get out of Dodge.

He was so close to freedom. The prison lay behind, the open road ahead. He pulled up to the exit of the parking lot and looked back at the building one last time, and then he was gone.

Joe didn't notice the average looking blue Toyota that exited the parking lot a few seconds later.

Upon arriving at his studio apartment, Joe quickly unlocked the deadbolt and darted inside.

The place was cleaner than he had left it that morning, the one room that served as living room, bedroom, and (if judging by the usual piles of clothes that sat in heaps between the sparse furniture) laundry room was now straightened, the sheets on his mattress (which sat on the floor with a college dorm room-like simplicity) fresh and displaying crisp corners, his bookcase organized, the home-based contingent of Joe's aluminum Diet Dr. Pepper army vanished from the surface that served as both computer desk and kitchen table and doubtlessly defeated, crushed, bagged, and laid to rest in the recycling dumpster behind the apartment complex's central courtyard.

The sight of this unfamiliar organization coupled with his current flight from the authorities filled Joe's mind with the horror that he had somehow been caught and, forgoing the usual treatment of handcuffs and a ride down to the station, the police had instead opted to dispense justice by messing with his brain in some kind of sick and elaborate mind game. It had taken several seconds for him to come to a more likely conclusion: that his sister (who lived in town and was overjoyed that he had moved back) had stopped by and furiously attacked the mess, tired of her brother living in what she usually called "a swirling cesspool of filth unbefitting his upbringing."

Had Joe ever considered it, he might have found it slightly strange that he allowed himself to live in such a way when he was usually so keenly aware of potential germs around him. But the reality was that he was comfortable with his own dirt and disorder, and anything that could potentially perish and rot was always discarded appropriately and with haste.

"Sometimes I wish she would just leave things alone," Joe now muttered under his breath, attempting to regret giving his sister the duplicate key, but in reality finding it much easier to locate and pack what few essentials he had on hand because of her thoughtfulness. The only item that gave him any difficulty was the large duffle bag he wished to use for his departure from the life that, it now seemed, had been a mistake for him to lead. He had left the bag conveniently resting underneath a mostly dirty pile of socks on the folding chair in the corner. Now, the socks were gone, the duffle bag was nowhere to be seen, even the chair itself had walked away.

Joe tore open his closet as the miniscule dishwasher gurgled and swished from the kitchenette, filling the apartment with near-deafening white noise. He found the chair inside the closet, folded and stacked with the rest of the set, and then began pulling out coats and dress shirts, sending cardboard boxes still full from his move flying, and at last finding the bag he sought on the top shelf next to a clear plastic container that held the contents of his old desk, hastily packed once the announcement of the Atlanta branch closing had been made.

From the dresser that doubled as his TV stand Joe produced seldom worn t-shirts and jeans and stuffed them into the bag. He then retrieved a bandage from his newly discovered medicine cabinet for the cut on his hand, grabbed a half-full ice tray for his eye from his ancient fridge/freezer, and aimed a swift and angry kick toward what he was sure was the noisiest dishwasher in the known world.

He surveyed the newly cluttered room with indignant fury and the slightest pang of regret at undoing the efforts of his sister. He would not think of her though, certain that the thought of her finding him gone amid apparent signs of struggle would unravel his will to run. But he had to run. They would be here for him any minute. Once she learned the whole story, she was sure to understand this.

Joe slung the bag over his shoulder and walked to the door, the slightest limp developing in his stride as he subconsciously favored the hip that wasn't bruised. He peered through the peephole, half expecting to find a team of uniformed officers ready to burst in, but actually finding nothing but his empty front step. Then he peered back at the apartment with distaste, reminding himself that he had never meant to make this his home—that the plan had been to buy a proper house and build a proper life.

Buying a house hadn't seemed prudent though, he reminded himself, as his job had disappointed immediately. He knew that he had no future there and had sent out several résumés in the last month, but had yet to receive a single response. Life, it seemed, wanted to keep him trapped where he was, dealing with the idiots around him, and Joe's somewhat misplaced anger toward Gilmore burned anew.

He wrenched open the door and left the apartment for what he expected was the very last time, knowing that no matter where he ended up, he wouldn't miss the place.

Joe's expectations of finality were challenged immediately. He stepped back out into the sun, struck by the brightness and a new realization. He had forgotten to get money.

So, back through the door, Joe trampled the debris that now covered his mattress and yanked open the particleboard nightstand at the far end. He pocketed the container of generic antacid tablets at the top of the junk-filled drawer and then dumped the remaining contents on the scattered vestiges of his former life that now coated his bed. Sifting through the clutter, Joe discovered two crisp ten-dollar bills. He added these to the eight crumpled dollars that currently resided next to the wallet in his back pocket.

He knew that whatever his next step was in his new life on the run, this wouldn't be enough to finance it. Credit cards would be traceable. He had to get to the bank—and fast.

5

Joe checked the time as he trotted toward the front door of National Neighborhood Bank—thirty minutes had passed since leaving the office. He was on borrowed time and he knew it, but hoped that he could borrow just a bit more. All that he now had sat in a duffle bag in the passenger's seat of his green Civic, "the mighty Honda" his friends had nicknamed it, taunting him for the size and age of the car. But Joe had seized the nickname proudly. He saw no reason to spend more on a vehicle just because he now could. His Civic had been faithful since high school and Joe had always done his part to take care of it. And, sadly, it now seemed that the mighty Honda was his only friend left. Everyone that he'd known in Georgia was busy getting on with lives that no longer included him.

The meager contents of Joe's duffle bag were not worth much, this being the exact reason he had come to the bank in the first place, but a fear of having the bag stolen while he was inside entered Joe's head when he was halfway to the door and stopped him short. He stood frozen for a second or two on the shiny asphalt, arguing with his sudden desire to retrieve the bag before entering the bank.

Though they would have made excellent points, the central pillar of his argument wasn't that he was running out of time or that walking was becoming downright painful and any of it that *could* be avoided should be. Instead his argument against returning to the car rested mainly on the fact that someone might be watching. Maybe one of the children standing near the strip mall across the street, or the woman pulling into the bank's drive-thru lane, or maybe the occupants of the average looking blue Toyota parked a few spaces down… any one of these people might watch Joe reverse course and wonder what he was up to.

Joe didn't suspect that any of them would consider the action odd enough to warrant a call to the police. He just didn't like being watched in general. It was the same reason that he always kept the blinds closed in his apartment and usually ate lunch at his desk instead of the cafeteria. It was the same reason that he sometimes found himself walking all the way across the office building to another restroom because he had seen someone else simultaneously headed toward his original choice.

But even though the force of this instinct not to be noticed made a compelling argument for leaving the duffle bag where it was, images now crowded Joe's mind of some hoodlum smashing the mighty Honda's window and running off with his supplies. It soon became impossible to focus on anything else, so Joe finally relented and hurried as best he could back to the car to retrieve the bag. He then hurled curses at himself under his breath as he again made his way across the pavement to the front door of the bank.

Joe did virtually all of his banking online and therefore had yet to set foot inside the local branch since moving to town three months back. In the rare event that he needed cash he would normally just accost the drive-thru ATM. But today he was there to empty his account. ATMs had withdrawal limits.

The interior of the bank was overly air conditioned and smelled like the interior of a bank. A few customers waited patiently for their turn to see one of the two tellers behind the long wooden counter. Large in-your-face banners hung from the ceiling and walls declaring high interest rate CDs encouraging savers to save. Joe deduced that this meant that interest rates were currently up and that the other banners, the ones proclaiming low rate loans were safely tucked away in storage, waiting for the market's ebb from its current flow.

Joe was keenly aware of the stares of the video cameras and fellow patrons as he took his place in line. With his blackened eye, wrinkled clothes, bandaged hand, slight limp, and large bag he knew that he must be a sight. He reprimanded himself again for bringing in the bag. For two endless minutes he endured the unwanted and silent attention and sly glances of the other customers before he was finally called up to the counter.

The teller was much too cheery as she addressed him. "Beautiful afternoon isn't it? And how can I help you?"

Joe looked at her with incredulity, as if she should have somehow known that it was most certainly *not* a beautiful afternoon, as if she should have known that it was actually shaping up to be the worst afternoon in his life, as if she should have been aware of the line that he had crossed, invisible but unmistakable, barely an hour before.

You really aren't supposed to physically attack your coworkers. The thought appeared suddenly and unhelpfully in his mind, finally catching up with his actions earlier. Joe blinked it back and focused instead on the buoyant bank teller in front of him.

He could have responded to her in kind, brightened her day with a pleasant smile accompanied with some brief small talk. He had recently listened to an audiobook titled *Get People to Like You* in an attempt to become more influential at work. Basically Joe had boiled the book down to one concept: Act interested in people and ask questions about their lives.

At that point he had had one of the great epiphanies of his life. He had realized that his problem wasn't that people didn't like *him*. It was that *he* generally didn't like *people*. He *wasn't* interested in their lives. He didn't enjoy small talk. And, when he was honest with himself, he didn't want them to like him too especially much. It wasn't that he wanted to be thought of with dislike; he just didn't want to be thought of. He might have preferred listening to a book with a title like *Get People to Leave You the Hell Alone*. In fact, maybe he could write it—*"Chapter 1: Other uses for your computer keyboard…"*

The hint of a smile crossed his face and the teller magnified and reflected it back to him, happy that he was happy and patiently waiting for an answer to her question.

Joe provided one. "I'd like to close my account please," he said.

Her response to this was one of such pure elation that Joe concluded that she must be either mentally unstable or a gigantic fake. No one could seriously be that delighted at something so very ordinary.

"Okey-dokey, no problem! I'll just need you to grab a seat over in that area there," she pointed to a set of four brightly upholstered chairs across the lobby, "and wait for the customer service representative!"

A flick of her chubby wrist summoned the next customer in line before Joe could object. He would rather have left the account open than delay his exit—but his social ineptitude prevented any further discussion of the matter. Here was someone in a position of authority, a representative of the bank. His actions that afternoon might have contradicted this fact, but Joe usually submitted to those around him. Generally, he didn't like to rock the boat. So he decided not to object to the woman's request. He plodded over to the waiting area and sat down, slightly humiliated at the perceived rejection he had just experienced.

It was with shock that Joe noticed the moisture building in his eyes while he began to wait. Feelings of abandonment started to well up inside, drawing from deep within him, as if the loneliness he had felt over the past months was taking the opportunity to vigorously declare itself at the worst possible occasion, somehow triggered by the bank teller who had only spoken briefly and hadn't done a single thing to him. Joe's chest began to heave slightly and he fought it, willing himself to calm down, feeling as if someone had accidentally wandered into the emotional center of his brain and started indiscriminately fiddling with the controls.

Five agonizingly long minutes passed before he was called in, giving Joe ample time to regain composure. When called, he entered the glass-enclosed office of the customer service representative, sat himself down in one seat, and sat his duffle bag down in another.

"So, what can we do for you?" the lady behind the desk asked, her cheerfulness equaling that of the teller.

"I'd just like to close my account, please—the sooner the better."

"Oh," she frowned through a patronizing pout that didn't seem to diminish her projected mood one bit, "I'm sorry to hear that!" She then smiled and somehow oozed even more exuberance, as if Joe's indifferent staring was the best thing that had ever happened to her. "Is there anything we can do to change your mind?"

"No." Joe was careful not to break eye contact so that the finality with which he spoke would not be missed.

"Well," she tried, wrinkling her nose in what she probably thought was some kind of irresistible expression, "would you mind filling out this anonymous survey to help us improve our customer service?"

"Yes, I would mind. I'm in a hurry."

"Okay, you can just take it with you. Just drop it in any mailbox in the United States."

In order to speed things up, Joe took the survey card from her hand and gave her his account number. She nodded appreciatively and punched the number into her computer. Then her face twisted.

"Um…is this the branch that you normally go to?" she asked innocently as if the answer to her question wasn't sitting on the screen directly in front of her.

"No," Joe exhaled in frustration, feeling the time slip by—time that he couldn't afford. "I just moved from Georgia three months ago—but that was the same bank."

"Ah, that's the problem," she smiled again in triumph, "The Georgia-Tennessee-Kentucky division is separate from the Illinois-Wisconsin-Missouri division. We can't access that account directly."

Joe barely understood what he had just heard. "What do you mean? The name of the bank is *National* Neighborhood! I've been banking online just fine!"

"Right," she nodded, "through the Georgia-Tennessee-Kentucky regional division. I've just explained this to you." She typed a few more keys. "It looks like I can allow you to deposit money *into* that account, but you'll have to set up a new account with *this* division if you'd like to use this branch for full access."

"Are you hearing me?!" Joe raised his voice slightly. "I don't want to use this branch. I want to close my account!"

Her reply was abrupt and absolute, and she wasn't smiling anymore at all. "Well, the nearest branch of *your* bank is in Kentucky, sir. We can set up a new account for you at *this* bank and you can then transfer the funds online. They would then be available for withdrawal in five business days."

"Listen to me. I want my money now." Joe tried to keep his voice calm and steady. "This is unacceptable."

"Sir, I am sorry but there is nothing I can do. It's a different system. Now, would you like to set up a new account? Surely you can wait five days…"

Joe's blood was starting to boil. He was wasting precious time here. He needed the money; his account would probably be frozen once he was declared a fugitive. He had over six thousand dollars in savings, leftover from the sale of his condo in Atlanta. That money had intended to eventually go toward a down payment on a house. Now its ambition was to become disappear-and-start-a-new-life money.

This lady was standing in the money's way.

Almost of its own volition, Joe's head turned slowly toward the duffle bag next to him. He studied it as a plan began to form in his mind. Providence, it seemed, had given him a solution to his current obstacle. He just needed the guts to act on it. He just needed to cross another one of those invisible lines that had been drawn around him all his life. Those in authority had always commanded him to stay in the circle, always telling him what he could and could not do. Don't act out. Wait your turn. Be friendly with your neighbors. Don't hit people with keyboards.

Don't rob banks.

Joe's mind floated back over the events of the unfolding afternoon. He was already on the run, rejecting the circumstances of his life. It made what he did next easy.

After all, he was already in for a penny.

Any pretext of politeness between Joe Tompkins and the lady behind the desk had been dropped. They were fully declared opponents now, circling one another with probing eyes, daring the other to make the next move, sparring over the prize they both wanted. The money was rightfully Joe's. He was going to do whatever it took to win it.

"I need this money now because I plan to go off of the grid," Joe explained evenly, "I mean to disappear."

"Sir, that doesn't change the situation…"

"Please," Joe said quickly and held up a finger, "I don't like to be interrupted." He took a breath to calm his nerves and collect his faculties.

He exhaled slowly, using the moment to solidify his decision. He was really going to do this. It was her fault. She had backed him into a corner.

"Tell me," he started, his voice slightly shaking, somewhat betraying the aura he was trying to create, "what exactly do you know about explosives?" A tilt of his head directed her attention to the duffle bag sitting quietly next to him.

"Sir," the lady behind the desk said sternly, attempting to defend her position of authority, to maintain the upper hand, "I'd advise you against saying anything that you will regret."

"I know what you're thinking," Joe surprised himself as the words now came quickly and easily. He hadn't even thought this all the way through, but a strange peace had settled over him and the shaking had vanished from his voice. "You're thinking, 'He doesn't have four pounds of C4 in there. He's just a guy that didn't expect to fall victim to the bank's masochistic policies.'

"And you're probably right. I'm probably just another lump-of-crap pedestrian…" *Pedestrian?* He knew that that couldn't have been the word he had meant to use. It didn't really fit. Joe's mouth was apparently unaware of this internal dilemma, as it continued with its rant undeterred. Joe's attention hurried to catch up.

"…an 'average joe' just having a bad day. That I wouldn't hurt anybody, right? But what if maybe, just *maybe*, I really was at the end of my rope? I mean, the appearance kinda fits, right? And what's the deal with the bag? Why would I bring that in here? Is it really only stuffed with assorted clothes and toiletries… maybe a half-eaten box of Cheez-Its and a couple of cans of Diet Dr. Pepper?"

The lady's expression had transformed from stern and irrefutable to falsely pleasant and placating, as if she was trying to mollify the lunatic that had walked into her office merely by the force of her raised eyebrows, strained smile, and patronizingly rhythmic nod. To be honest the result of this was somewhat hypnotic, but the spell was instantly broken when she started to slowly reach for her computer mouse. Joe's left hand startled him as it leapt out and unplugged the keyboard and mouse cords from the PC tower that sat on her desk.

"I'd rather you just kept your hands still, and on top of the desk, dear," Joe said reproachfully, then continued with his explanation of exactly why the bank should make an exception to its ridiculous policies in his case. "The question is: can you afford to take the chance that I'm bluffing? I'll say this again. I'd like to close my account—right now—in cash.

For the first time the woman looked slightly aghast, but in her eyes there remained a spark of disbelief and distrust. They remained locked on his for a few seconds, an awkward pause in the debate during which Joe held her stare, pitting his desperation against her will. Then she glanced momentarily away, toward the line of customers waiting for their turn at the teller.

One corner of Joe's mouth curved upward into a half-smile. He had found her weakness. Above all else, she didn't want to make a scene. It was very important not to puncture the illusion of order and joy that the employees were obviously trained to project.

Joe bored his eyes into hers and aimed his final shot.

"You'll notice that I haven't even been shouting," he began again. "There's no reason why any of these fine people," Joe waved his hand to indicate the lobby patrons behind him, "need to know anything about what's happening in here." He narrowed his stare and lowered his voice. "What's it going to be?"

Joe and his mighty Honda pulled out of the bank's parking lot. His duffle bag rested in the passenger's seat, six thousand three hundred four dollars heavier. It had been almost too easy.

Since entering adulthood, the occasions in Joe's life when he had experienced pure joy had been few and far between. But he felt joy now, it seemed to burst through him: a wide grin that he couldn't contain, goose bumps that ran up his back and spread across his shoulders, happy tears forming in the corners of his eyes. He was victorious. He had won the battle, unlocked the puzzle, and left his rival vanquished inside the building that now shrank in his rearview mirror. It was a great moment, the first time in months that he had really felt alive.

The celebration was short lived.

As if waking from a light sleep Joe's better judgment re-engaged itself and started to sort through the events of the previous ten minutes, coming to realizations that might have been better left unrealized. The steady rate of his heart quickened and beads of sweat started to form on his previously dry brow. Had he just robbed a bank?

Joe's knuckles constricted causing his whitening fingers to grip the steering wheel more tightly as a building air of panic began to dance behind his eyes—blurring his vision. Had he just *robbed a bank!?*

Ignoring the rising chaos, Joe's right foot continued to weigh down the accelerator as his small and mighty Honda tore through the growing traffic of the town's main parkway. A slight shudder began to resonate in his chest, building steadily to near-seizure status. Keeping the car in his lane became more difficult.

"You… have… to… calm… DOWN!" he screamed at himself. "You can have a breakdown when you're in another city!"

An average looking blue Toyota in the next lane slowed down to avoid the erratic driving.

With concentrated effort, Joe gradually brought the shudder under control. He tried to make himself understand that panic would not help his situation. He needed to complete his escape. He needed to get out of town.

With the back of his hand, he wiped his eyes in order to clear the blurriness. He was back in control. But as he blinked the remaining moisture away a sticker in the upper left corner of his windshield caught his attention. His eyes then focused on the odometer and he realized that he had just ten miles until he was due for another oil change.

Stress had always triggered the worst of his obsessive-compulsive tendencies. Joe desperately tried to ignore the mental warning that he would be breaking a perfect streak of just under three thousand-mile checkups that extended for the past eleven years.

"It doesn't matter… it just doesn't matter." But the whispered mantra didn't help. As much as he wanted to, Joe knew that there was no point in fighting it. He spotted the Golden Touch drive-thru ten-minute oil change place on the side of the road. He pulled over, hoping that the stop would only *slightly* delay his escape from town.

This hope would prove to be misplaced.

6

Joe Tompkins nervously munched on Cheez-Its and antacid tablets while he stared at the dashboard clock. The twelfth minute ticked by as the good folks at Golden Touch violated their implicit ten-minute-oil-change contract, rattling around under the car and under the hood. He didn't really know what all went into changing a car's oil (he was pretty sure some sort of filter was involved) but he knew that his father had always said that letting a car go past the three-thousand-mile mark was like playing with fire.

Joe had taken the brief hiatus from his life-on-the-run as an opportunity to reconnect with reality. A slow-forming hypothesis began to wrap its tentacles around his mind: *What if Gilmore had never even reported the incident?*

"I mean," he whispered to himself between crackers, "that would make sense. We weren't on the same project. He had no business spending that much time talking to me. He might have been worried about potential backlash if management discovered how much time he spends buzzing about. After all, he is a pretty skittish guy when it comes right down to it…"

Joe pictured himself smacking Gilmore in the face with the keyboard. Instead of tearing out of there like a spooked rabbit, he saw himself just making a smart comment like, "So, did I ever tell you about the time that I was sick of listening to your mind-numbing stories?" and then sitting back down. Why hadn't he just done that?

Why had he *robbed a bank* instead!? Why had he escalated it completely out-of-proportion?

Now he really was a fugitive. They knew exactly who he was down at the bank—and bank robberies were big stories in the hundred-thousand-person town. The cops would be scrambling to catch him in order to get their names in the paper. He was screwed.

32

A sudden knock on the half-open driver's side window startled Joe back to the moment. A goateed, gum-chewing auto-service-center employee was grinning at him. He had a slightly dirty yellow thing in his hands.

"Just wanted to show you your air filter Mr. Tompkins." The attendant held the yellow thing up, "You might be okay for another three thousand miles, but I'd consider replacing it now to help with gas mileage."

Yep, filter. Joe remembered getting this thing replaced before.

"I'd like to, Mac, but I just don't have the time today."

"Oh, well, we already have it out, Mr. Tompkins; it won't take any longer to slap in a new one than to just put this one back in."

"Oh… okay then," Joe muttered in timid agreement. He wondered if he was being taken advantage of, but had no idea what he could do about it.

"Alright. We'll get you outta here in a jiffy!" Mac disappeared briefly while informing the guy under the hood of the new sale, then reappeared with a clipboard. "That'll be thirty-eight-fifty."

An average looking blue Toyota pulled into the garage behind Joe's Honda.

For a moment, Joe's eyes lingered in the rearview mirror and studied the Toyota. He began to get the slightest intimation that something was wrong with the situation, even more wrong than the large degree of wrongness warranted by the fact that he had just robbed a bank, but in an instant the feeling was gone.

Joe shrugged it off and stuffed a crisp, fresh-from-the-bank fifty-dollar bill into Mac's hand. The change found its way into Joe's pocket next to his cell phone. The phone was now off, Joe fearing that the police could use it to track him.

At six minutes past the ten-minute deadline Joe pulled out of the drive-thru garage and was finally on his way—no looking back. Regrets, he knew, weren't going to help him now.

He was careful to obey the traffic laws as he headed toward the interstate. South seemed like a good direction. He'd move to smaller country roads once he picked up an atlas, but first he had to get out of town.

Joe approached the Main Street intersection at a speed just under the limit as the light turned yellow. Normally he would have just sped on through but this time, out of cautiousness, he hit the brakes hard and fast and stopped his car short. The light then turned red and Joe was careful to keep his head facing forward and his hands at ten-and-two while waiting for the green.

After what seemed considerably longer than the ninety seconds it actually was, the green light came. Joe eased off of the brake pedal and slowly depressed the accelerator. The mighty Honda didn't seem to like this. Maybe it knew that there was something wrong because Joe didn't mash the pedal down as he normally would when taking off from a stop. The Honda showed its apparent displeasure by lurching forward briefly into the middle of the intersection and killing its engine. The car then rolled a bit, ending up diagonal and partially blocking a lane of traffic in each of the four directions. It took the other drivers a second to realize that the car wasn't going to keep moving. Then they began to honk.

Panicked, Joe reached for the ignition but then stopped. There was an out-of-place smell.

Billowing clouds of light-gray smoke started to roll out from underneath the hood. Joe craned his neck to peer out the windshield and caught a glimpse of bright orange at the base of the smoke. The horns of the other cars ceased as their drivers realized the problem. Joe sat stunned for a couple of moments trying to get his head around what was happening. Then he grabbed his duffle bag and escaped the burning car.

A few daring drivers slipped past the scene, but it wasn't long before all traffic had halted, the remaining drivers giving the smoldering vehicle a generous radius. Joe, who knew from the movies exactly what was about to happen, dived behind a nearby vehicle and waited for the explosion.

The street was hot and dirty and, after about thirty seconds or so of nothing happening except nearby motorists increasingly venturing out of their vehicles to stand and stare, Joe peeked around the tire of the minivan he was crouched behind. He saw the hood of his beloved automobile engulfed in sickening reddish flames. The fire seemed to be contained to the engine, leaving the rest of the car more or less intact. A huge whitish-gray column of smoke rose from the spectacle like a beacon— an easy trail for the police that would be there shortly to follow.

Joe had to get out of there. But he knew he wouldn't get far on foot.

The makings of a plan formed quickly in his mind. The downside of the plan was that it required him to get into his car. And he really couldn't wait for it to be done being on fire. That meant risking it. Luckily, Joe was in a risk taking mood that afternoon.

He stood up and pushed past the ring of observers. Cautiously but quickly he approached the back of the blazing car amid shouts of protest by the audience. The smoke was blowing directly toward him and it stunk of burning oil, paint, and rubber. Joe held his breath and lifted his arm to shield his eyes as the haze engulfed him. Once he reached the car, he tested the door handle and found it relatively cool. Then he pulled.

The hatchback sprang open. Joe dropped his duffle bag to the ground beside him and bent down low, searching through the junk that filled the back of the car and trembling with the fear that any moment could be the moment when the Honda finally decided to blow up. Through the pile of bungee cords, garbage, and assorted items that hadn't quite secured a permanent home since Joe's move, his fingers finally found the distinctive shape of the rollerblades he had bought but barely used. He yanked them out, sending junk spilling out onto the street, grabbed his duffle bag, and ran into the crowd, unsure of exactly where he planned to go next but knowing the skates would get him there faster than his dress shoes would.

As he searched for a place to sit down and change into his skates, Joe fought the grim realization that the mighty Honda, his last remaining friend and only practical means of getting out of town, was now dead.

The car never exploded though. Joe decided that, in real life, cars didn't blow up. Just like the fact that a drop ceiling in a public restroom couldn't really support a person's weight.

7

"Um… what?"

Ned Dyer was pretty sure his fiancée Sue had just asked him a question. He was usually a fairly attentive guy, and even though he was sometimes guilty of being lost in thought or television when she was speaking to him, for the most part he heard whatever she had to say. Besides, she wasn't one to nag in the rare occasion when he wasn't listening. And, had she known the reason that this was one of those occasions, that he was attempting to keep an eye on the bald man across the aisle without seeming too obvious (the man who very likely represented an imminent threat)… well, she probably would have forgiven him for the inconsideration without giving it a second thought.

In fact Ned had only asked her to repeat herself so that the scene didn't seem out of place. It was important not to arouse suspicion, and a sudden cessation of their conversation might have done just that. Ned's primary objective was to get Sue out of the restaurant safely and quickly. To do this he would have to confide in her, but knew he didn't have time to explain properly. He was finally about to pierce the veil of silence that he had kept for three long years. Ned's enemy had finally made another move, and this had changed all of the rules by which he had been living. He would no longer be silent about what had happened to him. It was a cruel circumstance that he couldn't explain the situation in a manner of his choosing, but there was no time. For a second he tried to decide what words would most efficiently convey the seriousness of the predicament to her, but he soon learned that he wouldn't have to. The expression on his face did the trick in an instant.

"You mentioned your old roommate," Sue said as she looked up from her purse, "I asked how Joe was—Ned, what's wrong!?"

Again, Ned found himself unsure how to continue. Things were happening much too fast.

He had been on his guard for years, preparing himself for another incursion by the people that had forced him to abandon his life. It was time to utilize this preparation. It was finally time to act. In his mind he had always pictured it as some surreal and romantic moment where he would rise like the archetypical hero and find himself brave and ready to take his enemy on. But there was nothing romantic about the danger Ned now faced. And he didn't feel very brave. He instead found himself nearly frozen with the fear of the thing, staring wildly into Sue's eyes. They reflected a genuine concern and this helped him find the strength to steel his frantic nerves.

He chose his words carefully and spoke in low tones. "Sue, I need you to listen to me now. I'll answer your questions later." Ned discreetly pulled his cloth napkin over his steak knife as he spoke. "I want you to calmly go to your car, right now, and drive to a friend's house. Lock the doors and stay inside until I call you." Ned slowly pulled the napkin-covered knife off of the table and slid it into his left pocket.

"Ned…" Sue's voice shook. Tom the waiter reappeared with the credit card receipt and set it on the table.

"You folks have a good night," he glanced clumsily from face to face and then disappeared again.

"I promise I will explain later—now go," Ned said quietly as he looked down and filled out the receipt, partly because he didn't want Sue to see the fear that no doubt filled his eyes, partly because it was so very difficult to face her, knowing that he was sending her away, knowing that he was about to confront the unknown danger alone and head on.

"Ned…I'm scared…" He glanced up and his eyes told her that neither of them had time for that.

"Just act naturally," he said.

She sat stunned for a second, then blinked and nodded slightly, the fear now vanished from her face as if she knew exactly what the situation needed: a small smile and a large degree of trust. She collected her purse, rose slowly from the booth, gave Ned's hand a final squeeze as she walked by, and was gone.

Ned fixed his eyes directly on the bald man across the aisle. The guy was still trying to look inconspicuous. There was really no reason that Ned would have been suspicious of his presence outside the apartment building three years before. Ned had parked his car on the street and had strolled past several people on the way to his building. He used to have a habit of looking people in the eye just in case he happened upon a neighbor or a potential friend.

Now he took in each face with a hint of skepticism and distrust—apparently well placed that evening.

Ned raised his body in a measured and deliberate fashion, desperate to insert some kind of control into the situation, wishing that he could just follow after Sue, wondering if they could have outrun whatever this man represented, wondering if they could have just jumped into his BMW and driven away to safety, if he could just relocate again, this time with her, both of them hiding together, building another life, using different names, leaving everything behind.

But Ned knew that that was no way to live. He had had enough of the constant fear. It was time to fight back. It was time to get some answers.

Keeping his gaze locked on the intruder and his left hand buried in his pocket Ned crossed the aisle quickly and sat down next to the man at the table before he could react. In appearance the man was unremarkable—everyman—the kind of guy that no one would notice, just ugly enough to warrant a rapid aversion of the eyes but not enough to stand out. Short nose. Wide set and dark eyes. Shiny bald head.

"Excuse me," the man began as Ned sat, "what do you think you're—"

"Don't bother," Ned cut him off, forceful and to-the-point. "I know who you are. I just don't know why you're here. I've done everything that was asked—*required*—of me. Everything."

The man stared back in apparent disbelief, waiting a couple of seconds before deciding to feign neither offense nor denial. He grinned briefly as pretense fell. "You know, I had a slight feeling you might recognize me…I had shrugged it away of course. I mean, it was two seconds on a sidewalk almost three years ago…"

"Over three years ago," Ned corrected, "Three years, two months, and six days ago."

The man's smile returned and was accompanied this time with a slight chuckle. "You're good, I'll give you that. Are you sure you aren't some sort of robot?"

The guy was showing Ned exactly how much he knew about him. Ned had earned the nickname "the robot" in high school, owing partly to his photographic memory, partly to an innate familiarity with the ways of the computer.

This guy had an advantage over him. Ned needed to level the playing field. He pretended to react to the man's joke and chuckled along with him while discreetly sliding the knife out of his pocket.

Ned shook his head as he laughed. "You wouldn't believe how many times I've heard—" his tone immediately changed to a menacing whisper as he produced his weapon under the table. "I don't want to hear your *jokes*!" he fumed as he made the knife known. "What you are currently feeling against your lower chest is my steak knife pointed directly below your sternum. One move from you and I'll shove it up and in! Confirm to me that you will not move!"

"Ned my boy," the man said with a straight face, as if he wasn't the least bit intimidated, as if he believed that Ned was about as capable of carrying out his threat as he was of teleportation, "there's no need to behave rashly. I'm not here to threaten you…"

"I said, confirm that you will not move." Ned repeated calmly as he pushed the knife through the man's tie, his shirt, and started to break the skin underneath.

The man recoiled involuntarily from the sharp metal. Ned kept the knife against flesh. The man's face reddened as his stone-clad demeanor started to fracture.

"I won't move!" he said quickly and quietly. "I won't move." The man was clearly used to being on the other side of the knife and not enjoying this expedition to the pointy end.

"I had to walk away from my job, my friends, my *family*!" Ned spat, allowing his anger to gain momentum, "My mom *loved* that cat you sick *freak*!"

"What's the problem?" The man grunted, still trying to project an air of apathy but not doing a very good job of it. "You have it all back. Your mom even got a new cat. Heck, you've even got a fiancée now, uh, Sue Bish–Ah!"

"Don't you dare say her name!" Ned seethed and pushed the blade another millimeter deeper. Three years, two months, and six days worth of pent-up frustration, of never having a target at which to direct his aggression, was seeping its way slowly out the sharp end of a stainless steel restaurant chain steak knife.

"Easy, man! Just take it easy! Answer your phone!"

On cue, the cell phone clipped on Ned's belt began to vibrate. He snatched it up with his right hand, keeping the knife in its place. The caller ID indicated that it was Sue.

"Honey, are you on your way to a friend's house?"

"Ned…" she was sobbing, "I'm sorry…"

The line went dead.

Ned knew it was pointless, but he couldn't stop himself shouting her name into the inactive phone as his panic returned.

"I thought summer break was supposed to be a time to relax, or at least gain some real-world experience," Tom complained to Amy, a fellow college student attempting to make some extra cash waiting tables for the summer.

He leaned against the wall behind the wait staff's soda-refilling station. "What are we doing stuck here?"

Tom Rigsby's awkward tendencies extended beyond his professional life. He was, of course, trying to woo the waitress and every opportunity for a venture into casual conversation was aggressively seized. Unfortunately for Tom, his preferred form of communication with the fairer gender consisted almost entirely of complaints about his life. There were only a handful of girls in the world that knee-weakened from this approach and Amy, unsurprisingly, was not one of them.

"At least you seem to get the good tippers… but that's probably because you're hot," Tom whined through the poorly aimed compliment. For him, this was actually a fairly bold attempt at flirting.

"Thanks… that's sweet," she replied with a dismissive you-seem-like-a-nice-guy-but-I'm-looking-for-something-a-bit-more-exciting-than-a-needy-nervous-communications-major-with-no-real-ambition look on her face. She was just waiting for her last table to leave and was pretty much Tom's captive audience until it did.

"Case in point," he continued, not reading her expression correctly, "the table of mine that just finished: I was prompt, was careful to make eye-contact with both of them, laughed at the guy's jokes, and busted my hump the whole evening. I'll bet I get less than a ten percent tip. The guy seemed like a bit of a cheapskate. And then he didn't even leave with his date! He sat next to a guy in Gary's section. Am I supposed to bus the table with him sitting right there?"

"He tipped me twenty-five percent last time I waited on him," Amy said with her attention focused mainly on her own table.

"Well… like I said…" Tom stopped short as Amy vanished. His eyes followed her as she walked away—short blonde ponytail bobbing as her petite figure darted its way between tables to drop off her last check of the night. His eyes then wandered back to the two guys in Gary's section, who were no longer there.

Tom's face lit up.

The two men had been sitting oddly on the same side of the booth, but now there was no sign of either of them. Tom's odds of being able to time his exit to coincide with Amy's (a perfectly normal thing to do) had just improved dramatically. He grabbed a light-blue plastic bin and headed over to bus his final table of the evening.

When he got there, Gary was standing nearby with a glass of iced tea and a puzzled expression. "This guy just sat down, ordered an iced tea, and then left before I got back."

"Good luck with that," Tom replied with mock concern. He collected the remaining items on his table, wiped it down with a fairly clean damp towel, and trotted back to the kitchen.

After depositing the load with the dishwashers in back, Tom returned to his Amy-adjacent perch behind the soda fountain. He removed the receipt from the plastic credit card tray he had picked up and pressed it to his forehead in a not-quite-comedic manner.

"The spirits tell me... a buck-fifty even!" Tom failed to get any more than a brief smirk out of Amy as she waited to pick up her customer's credit card. Undeterred, Tom ceremoniously lowered the receipt and read its contents.

"Amy."

"What, Tom!?" she seemed to be getting a little annoyed.

"This guy just gave me a two hundred dollar tip on a thirty-six-eighty-seven bill! Two hundred bucks!"

That got her attention; maybe something in his voice told her that this wasn't another lame joke attempt. She spun around and faced him directly.

"Let me see that."

She grabbed the slip from his hand and studied it. "Well, it looks like you have a secret admirer," she teased with a smile that made Tom forget all about his newfound wealth. "What's this he wrote at the bottom? It's some website." She turned the paper back toward him.

"What's it say under the web address?" Tom squinted, "'Click on the can of Dr. Pepper. Please!!' What's that supposed to mean?"

8

Monday, 4:53 PM

It is a difficult thing to skate down a cracked and crumbling sidewalk on a hot June day. This fact, however, did not deter Joe Tompkins from doing just that. Nor did the fact that he was desperately out of shape. Or that he was still wearing his work clothes, nursing a severely bruised hip, suffering from just a *teensy* bit of smoke inhalation, lugging around a large and heavy duffle bag, and dodging curious pedestrians. He was also dealing with the anxiety that came with carrying a large amount of cash, a newly minted fugitive status, and a fresh mental image of his getaway car's destruction.

Though, through all of this, Joe felt strangely proud that, if nothing else, he was at least getting some exercise.

Had he taken the time to reflect on and evaluate his current plan-of-action, he would most likely have questioned its sanity. Not that there was anything unusual about wanting to get away from the scene of the car fire, but some might have found his choice of direction a bit odd. He was heading directly back to Golden Touch.

They had just destroyed his car and he wanted to give them a piece of his mind. Besides, he'd only driven a mile and a half after the oil change. It really wasn't that far.

That didn't stop it from *feeling* far though. Joe hadn't skated regularly since… well… high school? *Had it really been that long?* His ten-year reunion was scheduled for next week. Joe was planning on skipping it. He didn't need to relive high school, even for a night.

The nearly new skates glided along easily, provided that he didn't find too many cracks or rocks or sticks or garbage on the concrete path that led back the way he had come. Fortunately much of the slope was gently downward.

Still, Joe felt like he was melting when he arrived back at the Golden Touch parking lot ten minutes later. Streams of sweat trickled down his brow, drenching his face. In fact, every sweat gland in his body was working overtime, trying its best to appease the stifling humidity's ravenous thirst.

Now there had been times in Joe's life when he had pondered the concept of eternity. He had sometimes wondered; if he could pick one moment out of his entire life to relive, over and over again forever, which moment he would choose. It would have to be an experience of such pleasure and joy that it would sustain his soul in a lasting peace and a satisfaction so complete that no other desire would ever come to mind.

He had found that moment in the instant that he opened the lobby door to Golden Touch and felt the sweet, sweet conditioned air waft over his face, his arms, his chest… Heaven itself could not have been better.

The thudding of Joe's heart in his ears all but drowned out the shouts of the attendant, insisting that skates were not allowed on the premises. Joe collapsed into a metal-framed waiting-room chair and drank gallons of oxygen, eyes rolled back, face reddened, and arms sprawled out—letting the valuable duffle bag drop to the floor without care. If he had allowed himself, Joe could have drifted off into the deepest sleep of his twenty-eight years.

Well, Mac the attendant would also have had to allow Joe to drift off. This is something he didn't do.

"Hey, buddy, what do you think you're doing? I said no skates in here!"

Joe's eyes labored to roll forward and focus on the intruder to his celestial refuge. He blinked methodically in slow recognition. It was the guy from Golden Touch.

Exhaustion had lulled Joe's anger to sleep. This guy now woke it up.

"The window…" Joe hoarsely panted, "look… look out the window."

Mac looked confused.

"Smo… smoke!" Joe coughed as his voice started to return a bit, "Do you… see the smoke out the window?"

Mac strained to see. A faint pillar of smoke was visible in the distance.

"That's my car!" Joe shouted, his strength starting to return. "You did that to my car!"

His bloodstream was pumping the anger through his entire body now— the sun-sapped energy replenished by waves of rising ire. Joe rose to his still-skate-clad feet. The extra height they afforded him gave him a sense of control of the situation.

"I trusted you with my car! You blew it up! I need that car! DO YOU HEAR ME?!"

Mac began to cower away from this sweat-saturated lunatic. No more was said about the skates.

"Sir, please calm down… tell me what happened." Mac assumed a safe place behind the customer service counter.

The same strange peace that Joe had encountered at the bank returned and washed through his insides. Words began to form quickly and evenly in his mind. His mouth calmly took over.

"I just had my oil changed here. I drove away. Within a mile-and-a-half, my car was on fire. Now, granted, I don't know a whole lot about cars, but I'm pretty sure that isn't supposed to happen… or is that what you mean by 'the golden touch'?"

"Sir, your sarcasm is uncalled for… now –"

"GET YOUR MANAGER OUT HERE NOW!! HE OWES ME A CAR!!" It wouldn't have seemed possible, but Joe's face adopted an even redder shade.

"Sir, there's no need to shout… I am the manager…"

"THEN YOU OWE ME A CAR!!"

Mac should have seen that coming.

"Sir, please let me explain." Mac's voice took on a pacifying tone, "First let me just say that we at Golden Touch sympathize with your situation and understand your frustration. However, policy forbids us from compensating the customer in these kinds of circumstances until a licensed investigator has submitted a report. Any compensation would be seen as an admission of guilt in a court of law…"

Joe didn't know exactly how, but he had anticipated this response. The practiced delivery took him off guard though—was this a common occurrence at this place?

Joe's words became suddenly controlled and exact, "This is unacceptable. Call the regional manager—now." He bent down and began to unbuckle his skates. He wasn't exactly sure why he chose this moment to do so—maybe he just was making it clear to Mac that the discussion was over.

Mac stood stunned for several seconds, and then decided to comply and make his way to the office in back to make the call.

"Just give me a moment sir."

"Of course," Joe graciously waved Mac on as he fished his tennis shoes out of the duffle bag and pulled them on.

Still on autopilot, Joe watched as Mac left. When he was safely out of sight Joe's left hand picked up the shoulder strap of his duffle bag while his right hand palmed something on the counter. His feet then turned and walked him out the door.

Curious as he stepped back into the sun, Joe looked down and slowly opened his right hand. Mac's car keys looked back up at him.

9:25 PM

Joe had never put any stock in having a high quality sound system in his car before. However, he was quickly becoming a believer in a good subwoofer. The kicking sound system in his new, light-blue Scion tC mini-sports car beautifully converted the *former* owner's mp3 collection to a fluid three-dimensional sculpture of sound that bathed its *new* owner from head-to-toe. Joe was somehow actually enjoying himself, the first time in months.

A stop at the gas station on the way out of town had gone a long way toward lifting Joe's spirits. He was now feeling the effects of the five ibuprofen tablets that he had taken. The stop had also yielded an *almost*-believable temporary license plate tag constructed out of orange construction paper and black marker. He had thought about also making a crude bumper sticker that would declare, "My duffle bag is my copilot."—but that would have just been silly.

The acquisition that had gone the furthest toward putting the smile on Joe's face, though, sat in the cup holder next to the hip, customized gear shift: a cold, twenty-ounce bottle of *regular* Dr. Pepper. He had switched to diet the previous year and, while he found the difference in taste to be small, his body missed the sugar.

At that moment, life was good. It was very good.

The stolen car raced over the cracked southbound country roads while the setting sun gave pause to observe the sight. The sliver of a moon was already in the sky, hovering larger-than-life near the eastern horizon above the cornfield-clad ground that reflected the red sun's glow. Joe took in the scene with renewed vision. He had never found beauty in the prairie land before.

Joe didn't know where he was headed, and he didn't care. He wasn't even being cautious with his driving anymore. He had finally escaped his hometown and he felt alive. He felt untouchable. And he was.

9

Monday, 3:11 PM

The lady that sat across the aisle from Joe Tompkins' cubicle was on her feet watching Joe tear down the hallway at full speed. She then looked back toward Gilmore, who was slowly picking himself up off of the floor. Blood was starting to trickle from his nose where Joe's keyboard had struck.

Cautiously, she asked if he was okay. He didn't reply. He just glared at her in quick annoyance and then stomped off down the hall. She figured he was probably just headed to the men's room.

She was wrong.

5:09 PM

A large plume of darkening smoke rose above the cars ahead of the average looking blue Toyota. Traffic had been at a standstill in all directions for twenty minutes at the town's busiest intersection an eighth of a mile ahead. A fire engine raced to the rescue down the left-hand side of the road. Maybe traffic would be moving again soon.

The Toyota driver's girth had been testing the strength of the bucket seat for a few months now. His affection for cigarettes had yellowed the interior and ruined the car's aroma. He also annoyingly insisted on always having the A/C on its maximum setting, but that didn't stop the man's massive amounts of back sweat from seeping into the seat's cloth upholstery.

The guy in the passenger seat was a little better—he appeared to be in charge. But just that afternoon his bloody nose had dribbled on the floor mat when he had entered the car mumbling something about how he had "apparently laid it on a little too thick." He had been rough with the glove box while in search of the hoard of fast-food napkins (which were now bloodied and lying in the back seat)—all this *and* an entire afternoon of mulling aimlessly around the city streets.

The Toyota was not built for city driving. Sure it could handle it, that wasn't the issue. But the stop-and-go existence of the past few months had been a waste of its not-so-average abilities. There hadn't been a good car chase in a while. The plain blue exterior was just for show. The car wasn't supposed to be noticed. The engine, however, was built for speed.

But the afternoon hadn't been *entirely* uninteresting. One of the gadgets built into the dash had been tracking a transmitter. The large LCD screen between the driver and passenger displayed a map of the town. An overlaid red dot had been bouncing from location to location. The Toyota's job had been to inconspicuously follow the Honda Civic that the dot represented. The driver usually kept a few cars between it and the Honda. This had become easier since the thickening rush-hour traffic had picked up.

As the car sat idling, the red dot on the screen suddenly vanished. The car's computer searched for the expected incoming GPS coordinates that it had been receiving all day to no avail. Something was wrong at the transmitter's end. The driver's heavy pounding on the screen was entirely unnecessary.

The guy in the passenger seat swore and stepped out to investigate. He had been becoming increasingly agitated as the traffic hadn't moved, but the continuing existence of the stationary red dot *had* kept him in his seat. Now the guy ran ahead through the temporary parking lot of cars.

The driver picked up the two-way satellite radio's microphone. He spoke briefly into the handset, "Be advised, we may have lost contact with our subject—over."

The atomically accurate dashboard clock measured as five minutes elapsed before the passenger was on his way back, jogging and waving his arms. He rounded the hood, resumed his seat, and slammed the door much harder than required.

"He's gone," the guy breathlessly explained, "his car is on fire, blocking the whole intersection, but he's nowhere to be seen. He gave us the slip. That confirms that he's onto us! Give the order!"

This news apparently flustered the driver and he picked up the microphone again. His thick voice reflected a decisive, no-nonsense tone, "Make a move on Subject Dyer! Repeat, take Subject Dyer! Subject Tompkins is missing. He set his car on fire and escaped on foot. Current whereabouts unknown! Our tracking measures have failed."

The radio produced a static-filled response, a question. The driver replied.

"Of course, the information is credible—Agent Gilmore is the source! He visually confirmed the burning car! Move on Subject Dyer immediately!"

Two hundred and fifty miles south of the average looking blue Toyota, Subject Ned Dyer's black BMW was, at that moment, driving him home from work through a patch of isolated thunderstorms. He was looking forward to a pleasant evening: a couple of rounds of online Halo 3 and then dinner with his fiancée.

But the evening was not going to be pleasant. Although it would certainly be an evening that Ned wouldn't soon forget.

10

Monday, 9:42 PM

Tom Rigsby might have been having the best night of his life as he pulled his old and battered bluish-purple Plymouth up to the curb outside his house. Even though his parents were on a Caribbean cruise that week, he wasn't allowed to park in the driveway. His car had been known to leak oil.

Amy's white Grand Am parked behind him. Tom could feel his ears throbbing with his heavy heartbeat. This was uncharted territory—Amy had *asked* to come over. The cryptic message on the receipt had apparently captured her interest and she wanted to find out what it meant.

He had done his best to destroy this opportunity with an attempt to explain the message away, "He's probably just some religious freak. The website is probably full of warnings about the end of the world or something."

"So, when are you going to check it out?" she had asked.

"Oh, I'll probably just ignore it," he'd said, intending to play it cool, mistakenly believing that sharing her curiosity would be perceived as a sign of weakness.

"Tom," she had delicately explained in a slightly patronizing quit-trying-so-hard-because-you're-not-good-at-it tone, "*I* would like to check this out. I don't currently have internet access at my apartment, but I'll be on campus tomorrow and *could* check it out then. But, I'll be up for a few more hours *tonight*. Would it be okay if I came over now so that we could see what it's all about together?"

"Uh… well… I guess that would be all right… ya know… if you want…" he had stuttered casually, obviously not learning the lesson that her tone had been trying to teach.

She had exhaled forcibly through an aggravated groan. "Fine, let me change and I'll follow you to your place."

Tom got out of his car. The recent storms had knocked the humidity out of the air leaving it sweet and cool. The damp ground provided a nice balance to the clear, darkening sky that hung over his childhood home on the outskirts of town. Tom had spent many-a-summer mowing the two acres of maple-dotted lawn that surrounded the modest ranch.

The crickets' noisy rhythm was safe and familiar. It helped him to relax a bit as he headed up the driveway. An electric blue bug zapper crackled at the farmhouse next door.

Amy stepped into the light of the streetlamp as she followed quickly behind. She had changed from the unflattering earthy-hued steakhouse standard-issue slacks, shirt, apron, and tie into low-riding faded jeans and a fitted black t-shirt. She had obviously attended to her hair and make-up after her shift. Tom's heart rate sped back up and he fumbled with his keys a bit before opening the front door.

"The, uh, computer is in my room," Tom said as he flipped on the lights. He had never really noticed that his mother's living room décor was quite a bit out of date. It was familiar and clean and nicely cared for though, and Tom didn't mind the wood paneling, dark brown carpet, or patterned furniture. He therefore didn't feel any embarrassment at Amy seeing it. In fact, it wasn't often that he felt embarrassment.

"Just give me a chance to change first," he told her, never having seen the point in bringing a change of clothes to work. "Help yourself to anything in the kitchen."

Amy wandered toward the kitchen while taking in the house. She came across a wall of photographs, neatly hung in wide dark frames.

"You were a cute kid," she observed while looking at a picture of eight-year-old Tom standing between his parents.

The socially appropriate response to this comment is, of course, just a simple, "Thank you." Always unorthodox, Tom decided to go with, "I know…what happened, right?" Compliment fishing was another mainstay in his cache of relate-to-women strategies. Amy didn't take the bait, instead choosing to give him a pained and slightly confused wince while an awkward silence filled the room.

In a rare flush of self-consciousness, Tom excused himself from the awkwardness. "I'll be right back."

He disappeared into his room and quickly changed into baggy jeans and a loose t-shirt and then frantically collected dirty clothes and garbage from around his small bedroom. The collection was tucked into his closet, the bedspread was straightened, and the air was moistened with a fine mist of Febreze. He then stuck a Wint-o-green Lifesaver in his mouth and used an ingenious combination of his tongue and lips to rub the mint against the fronts of his teeth. This was, in his mind, just as good as brushing.

A brief check in the mirror told Tom that his spiky blonde hair was still saturated with mousse, his eyes were still a comfortable light brown, and his height still aspired to reach five foot six. But Amy was only an inch taller... *maybe* an inch-and-a-half.

Amy knocked softly on the bedroom door. "You ready?"

Tom pulled the door open to reveal Amy and two glasses of red wine. He tried to hide his mild surprise as he let the three of them enter.

"I hope this is okay," she said, indicating the wine. "It was in the rack in the kitchen."

"No... sure... yeah, that's fine." Tom stammered as he swallowed the rest of his mint. His heartbeat quickened in his ears again. He'd never actually had wine before, or any kind of alcohol for that matter. This was kind of rare for someone who had just completed freshman year living in the dorms, but he didn't have much of an interest in the stuff and hadn't really been invited to all that many parties.

Well, it's just another liquid right? his mind reasoned, *You should just be able to drink it. Ignore the taste if you have to.*

With that he raised the glass and poured a manly amount into his mouth, determined to make the right impression, confident in his mind-over-matter prowess. But Tom didn't account for his gag reflex as the taste bud poison filled his Wint-o-green flavored mouth. He did manage to swallow some, but the rest dribbled down his chin and onto his shirt during a small fit of muffled coughs.

Smooth. Real smooth.

"Are you okay?" Amy inquired with real concern.

"Uh... yeah..." Tom sputtered as he wiped his chin with his t-shirt in a laid back fashion. "I'm just used to the, uh, clear kind of wine."

"You mean white wine?"

"Yeah, white wine... I'm more used to that."

"Tom, I didn't mean to make you nervous. I'm sorry. If you want, go ahead and change and then let's check this thing out."

Amy McKay set her glass of wine down on the desk next to the computer monitor. She was embarrassed for Tom. After all, she didn't *not* like the guy. He just had some annoying tendencies. Amy had only met Tom about a month ago when he had started working at her restaurant, but she had been around him long enough to be able to categorize him in the unfortunate group of guys that could always be depended on to say the wrong thing around women.

He's just not great under pressure, she thought as she snuck a quick look over at Tom as he pulled on a fresh shirt. He was definitely in shape. She remembered that he had once mentioned that he ran three miles a day. It was obviously something he was passionate about; the walls displayed a couple of runner-themed Nike posters.

So that was something at least mildly interesting. Maybe if she asked him about his favorite running shoe or something she could trick him into a normal conversation for a change. She missed having normal conversations. Staying in town for a couple summer-Gen-Ed classes before her junior year had seemed like a good idea, but her friends had all gone home and her new apartment was lonely.

Amy wouldn't admit it to Tom, but this was the closest thing to a night out she had had in weeks. If he would just keep the annoying quirks to a minimum… she *might* not regret the choice in evening activities. The *Dr. Phil* rerun waiting at home could just keep itself company.

Amy's eyes glanced at another poster on the wall that displayed brightly colored images captured from the Hubble Space Telescope. She made another mental note of possible conversation topics—but best to save them until they were absolutely needed.

"Ok, all set," Tom said as he sat down next to Amy at his desk. "Let's try to check this out before I make another mess."

Amy smiled in hopes that the matter was now behind them, however she did notice that Tom's face still carried a pinkish hue. Tom moved the mouse in order to cancel the screensaver and opened a fresh web browser. He pulled the photocopy of the receipt that he had made out of his pocket and typed in the URL that his customer, one Ned Dyer, had written.

The three-year-old PC whirred and crunched and finally displayed the page's contents. A light gray background framed "Dyer Consulting Services" in large bold letters. A description of the firm accompanied the title.

"Let my patented document organization software aid your aerospace product development, saving your enterprise budget and schedule and helping to ensure your success…" Tom's reading of the mundane company description was perfectly monotonic and might have put Amy to sleep if she hadn't interrupted him before he read the entire page of text.

"Oh, it's just the guy's business. It's odd that he wanted you to go to it so badly."

"Yeah," Tom continued to study the screen, "he's got quite a customer list… I'd say he does pretty well for himself."

"Uh-huh, no sign of the Dr. Pepper can then?"

Tom scrolled down to the bottom of the page. A small caption in the corner read, "DCS is fueled by the life-giving power of Dr. Pepper." It was accompanied with a small picture of the beverage's trademark maroon can.

Amy's excitement started to return. "There! Click on that!"

"You can't," Tom said in a slightly defeated voice. "The pointer doesn't change to the hand like it does when over a hyperlink. It just keeps the arrow. It's just a picture—not a link."

"Oh… well can you click on it anyway?"

"Yeah… I guess… why not, right?" Tom moved the pointer over the picture of the can and clicked the left mouse button. Nothing happened.

"Oh well," Amy sighed, "we had to at least try it."

As she spoke the contents of the webpage faded slowly until the gray background was all that was left. A large picture of a man's head with a thick, black uni-brow then appeared over an empty text box and graphical numeric keypad. The head split at the jaw like a poorly made puppet and began to erratically mouth silent words.

"Well, that's something," Tom reacted as he reached to turn on the computer speakers.

"…code! Enter the code! Enter the code! Enter the code!" the floating head declared in a high-pitched nasally voice. Tom turned the volume down to a barely audible level and then stated the obvious. "I guess it wants us to enter a code."

After half-an-hour of failed code breaking, Amy found herself at the front door of Tom's house, headed back to her car. She had tried to hint that she'd be up for a DVD or a board game or something, but Tom had dismissed these options muttering that he didn't think he had anything she'd be interested in.

"Well, we'll get 'em next time," she said and patted Tom's arm as she stepped past him into the cooling night air. She tried to convince herself that she *wanted* to go to bed early, as it appeared that her other options were limited.

The sky was a deep purple and beginning to reveal its multitude of stars. Amy paused to look up.

"I bet you get a pretty good view of the stars out here," was her last ditch effort.

Apparently Tom was unable to find a self-deprecating response to this and was forced to say something more normal, "Yeah, summer nights are the best. Sometimes I just lay out on our trampoline in the backyard and just look up for hours."

Amy turned back and smiled at him, "Now that sounds like fun. Lead the way."

11

Tom Rigsby was still mildly confused as to how his night had turned out so good. He had apparently invited Amy to do some stargazing in his backyard. And although it hadn't been his intention, he was certainly not complaining.

Initially Amy had jumped up onto the trampoline and challenged him to a seat-drop war. As anyone with more than half-a-brain knows, a seat-drop war is played by two contestants on a large trampoline. From the word "go," each contestant must jump from a standing position and land on his or her backside, bounce from this position back to his or her feet, and repeat the process over again. The first contestant unable to alternate between feet-to-seat or seat-to-feet position loses.

Tom considered himself an expert seat-drop warrior. He had perfected the technique of landing just after his opponent and thereby stealing his or her momentum. The resulting larger bounce for Tom usually caused a bounce for the poor challenger-to-the-throne that was barely able to lift him or her back to his or her feet.

The unintended effect of this genius technique is a not-so-gradual wearing down of the opponent's energy and good spirits. Tom might have been well advised to allow his fair friend to win a few rounds that evening in order to maintain an air of fun with the proceedings. However, he did not.

Amy had been a good sport about it though. After losing five straight rounds she had admitted defeat and had collapsed, breathless, on the smooth surface of the trampoline. Together they had gazed at the star-filled sky. Tom had pointed out planets and constellations and had described various space probes that were currently whizzing around the solar system. She had then somehow gotten him talking about running and he was currently explaining the finer details of his favorite lacing technique.

Conversation started to feel more natural as they continued to chat about the things Tom was most interested in. Amy listened attentively and encouraged elaboration. He had just finished telling her how he was hoping for iPod enabled Nikes (that could track your run electronically) for his upcoming birthday when he realized that he had been completely dominating the conversation. It was rare that a girl would have listened to him for so long without excusing herself for a more-pressing matter. So, Tom again found himself in uncharted territory.

"So… how are you liking your new apartment?" he ventured.

Amy startled him by bolting into a sitting position. "Tom Rigsby!" her face took on a wicked smile, "Did you just ask a question about *my* life?!" She started poking playfully at his arm, "There might just be some hope for you yet!"

A few awkward pauses in the conversation later (during which Amy had forcibly guided Tom into asking appropriate follow-up questions) the night was starting to run long. The crescent moon was high overhead, adrift in the ocean of stars.

"Well, Tom, this was fun. Thanks for a nice evening."

Aware that the evening had to come to an end, Tom suppressed his instincts to say, "Hope I didn't ruin it too much," and instead went with a simple, "Thank *you* for a nice evening." He did manage a subdued, "Sorry the website thing was a bust."

"Yeah… but the two hundred dollars is nice, right?"

"Actually," Tom pulled the copy of the receipt out of his pocket, "It was two-hundred two dollars and six cents."

"What?" Amy asked, "Are you serious?"

"Yeah… why?" Tom was puzzled.

"What did that make the total?"

"Um," Tom squinted to read, "Two thirty-eight ninety-three, why?"

"The code!" Amy squealed, "what if that's the code?!"

Back at the computer, Tom fed the floating head the number. The head froze and faded away. At the top of the page a new title appeared:

Initiating Contingency Plan Gamma… Sending Text Messages…

A black rectangle emerged at the center of the page. It then faded to show a man with deep brown eyes behind narrow dark rimmed glasses, a thin face, and a short sandy beard.

"That's the guy from the restaurant," Tom announced proudly.

"I wonder if we get something for figuring out his clues!" Amy excitedly grabbed his arm, sending electricity throughout his body, momentarily diverting his attention away from the computer.

The image of the man on the screen began to speak as the movie played. Subtitles appeared at the bottom of the screen to coincide with the audio.

"Hello. My name is Ned Dyer," the voice was calm and even, "Please listen very carefully as you will only be able to view this once."

The alarm had been raised.

Men that Ned Dyer had been forced to put his trust in were being called to answer the call. Their objective was simple and their haste imperative. They were to secure his family. They would go, now, in the middle of the night. To the home of his parents, his sister, his future in-laws. They would pound on doors and then unlock them without waiting for them to be answered. They would disable security systems using the codes Ned had provided them. They would carry with them portable video players and show footage of Ned explaining the danger, explaining the need to get them to safety. They would not be particularly polite. They would not attempt to persuade. They would intimidate. They would get the job done. That is what Ned had paid them for. These were not the sort of men his family would try to resist. It was for their own good.

One of these men, however, would not find his charge. He would gain access to Sue Bishop's apartment and find her missing. He would then ignore his further instructions—to track her down. He would simply go back home, indicate his failure on the secure website that had given him his orders, take his pay for services rendered, and go back to bed.

This was unfortunate, but not all-together surprising. Men of high character might not have been willing to accept an assignment of this sort, especially one shrouded in so much secrecy. So Ned had been forced to find men of a lower character, men who wouldn't ask questions—men who might very well let him down.

12

Sue Bishop heard the side door of what she guessed was a conversion van slide open. The tear-soaked blindfold was still tightly in its place. Several hours had passed since she had been taken from the restaurant parking lot on her way to her car. The last image she had seen was the masked man's gun. The blindfold had gone on immediately afterward.

Two sets of strong arms had carried her into the vehicle and bound her hands. Within a couple of minutes she had been told by a computer-altered voice to talk to her boyfriend and had felt her cell phone pressed to her ear. She had only gotten three words out before the phone had been snapped shut. No more had been said to her despite her pleading for information.

For hours she screamed and sobbed. For hours she was met with silence. Eventually she had given up, numb with the shock, both fear and denial balanced in equal proportion.

It had been too difficult to stay seated on the vehicle floor as it would suddenly move or stop unpredictably and without warning. So Sue now lay flat on her stomach, hands tied behind her back. All night she had existed like this, somewhere between the fuzzy dreams of an exhausted mind and the terrifying realities of an adrenaline-fueled hyperawareness.

Time had ceased to have much meaning, but her bladder was now telling her that morning must be near. This had actually calmed her a little and she had broken the hours-long silence with a polite request to use the bathroom. The van had since stopped moving and the door had opened. Sue could feel cool air rush in. It made her sweat-soaked body shiver.

Her hands were then lifted slightly and she could feel the zip-ties that bound them being cut. The stripes they had left on her wrists would take days to heal. Her hands fell limply to her sides and, for a moment, she had an urge to fight—to punch and slap and bite at the unseen men. But then she remembered their guns and let the urge pass. She was broken. She would remain limp and still until directed to do otherwise.

She didn't have to wait long for this direction. The same strong hands grabbed her shoulders, lifted her, and carried her to the door. The computer altered voice spoke again and sounded harsh and foreign to her ears, as if she'd forgotten all sounds other than those of her own screaming or the subtle noises of the van.

"Know this," the voice said, "we have your boyfriend. If you go to the police he *will* die."

With that Sue felt herself pushed backward out of the door. She landed hard on a slope of what felt like long wet grass and rolled backward into what felt like a ditch. She then heard the door slam and the vehicle speed away.

She lay on the cold ground in the fetal position, shivering and sobbing, her body scratched and bruised from the fall. Sue allowed this to continue for another minute or so, then sat up slowly and pried the blindfold from her eyes. Her vision was blurry and it took her a while to focus. When she did she saw the moon, barely a sliver, hanging a quarter of the way above the western horizon. The sky was dark and clear and filled with stars. She guessed at the time—maybe four in the morning.

The ditch she found herself in was next to a country road. A field full of short new corn stalks was at her back. No lights were visible. A nearby sign indicated that she was ten miles out of town. Sue made her way to her shaky shoeless feet and stared in the direction that she guessed the van had gone.

"Fiancé!" her cracked voice screamed at no one, "He's not my boyfriend… we're engaged!" It felt important to her that she set the record straight. She clearly didn't have control of anything else in the situation, but she wasn't about to let them—whoever they were—mischaracterize her relationship with the man she loved.

The shimmer of an object a few feet away then caught her attention. She investigated and found her glittered black purse lying in the grass. Her cell phone was still inside. Quickly she picked it up only to find that the battery had been removed. No way to call for help. No way to check to see if Ned was okay.

And it looked like she would be walking back to town.

As much as the hard pavement of the crumbling country road hurt her nylon covered feet, Sue found it preferable to the random sticks and rocks her feet discovered hidden in the grass. She was moving slowly, too slowly, but she didn't know what else to do. The wind whistled by and kept her cool and shivering. The eastern sky was just barely starting to lighten.

Her head was swimming with confusion and fear. The night air had just started to clear some of this away when a pair of headlights crested a hill in the distant road ahead.

Sue froze with the shock of it, her tired mind trying to comprehend what she was seeing, initially suspecting it as a hallucination but then dismissing this. Maybe the headlights represented help. She took a hesitant step forward and then stopped again.

The realization that it was very likely her captors returning presented itself in Sue's mind. She weighed this possibility against her need for help, but the risk proved too great. She quickly left the road before the headlights were close enough to see her and then waded back through the thick wet grass toward a lonely oak tree at the edge of the field. She would crouch here and wait for the car to pass.

It didn't.

Instead it slowed to a stop only a few yards down the road. From her vantage point Sue could see that it was a large vehicle, possibly the size of a van. Panic pulsed through her as she huddled lower behind the tree.

A door opened and she heard a voice ask for a flashlight. Slow steps began to come toward her as a light illuminated her tree. Tears began to fall again as she trembled with fear. The light was getting closer.

A man's voice called her name. It sounded vaguely familiar.

13

"It's not real, Tom. He's putting us on." Amy McKay had a finality in her voice. The game had gone too far. She struggled to shore up her crumbling belief that the website's message was a joke. "It's just a test to see how gullible we are. Tom, we are *not* doing this! It could even be some kind of trap! There are a lot of sickos out there!" Her voice cracked and her eyes began to moisten. She blinked furiously. There was no need to cry. She was stronger than that.

"It felt authentic to me," was Tom's subdued reply. He was clearly not in favor of an argument—that seemed to be a recurring theme with him. She had been playfully bullying him all evening. Amy wouldn't have guessed that he was capable of any intensity of conviction, especially if it meant offending a pretty girl. Apparently her assessment had been wrong.

Tom sat still, staring a hole into the web browser on the screen. It now glowed with a dull gray background, an unbroken blank page save for the large and simple black text that declared, "Please hurry!" She could tell that he was resolving his inner struggle more quickly than she was. It was as if she was seeing past Tom's awkward exterior into a solid core underneath. There was an unexpected depth of character here.

"Then we should just call the police. Don't look at me like that, Tom, you know that's the responsible move—the *right* move. *Tom, you know it.*" She was holding his gaze now, their faces twelve inches apart, her green eyes staring directly into his. Two tears slipped past her guard and dampened the makeup on her cheeks.

"Amy, he begged us not to. He was obviously scared for his life, for the lives of his family. He thinks the police are being watched." Tom stood up, turned away from her, and faced the wall. Amy knew that the gesture meant that he had made up his mind.

"If you don't hear from me in two hours, call them then." From behind, she could see his head just barely nodding. He turned back toward her, surprising her with the tears in his eyes also. "Tell the police everything then."

"Let's at least wait until daylight. It's already after one… the sun comes up in, like, four hours."

"It's already been hours since he gave me this note," Tom held up the copy of the receipt, "We may already *be* too late!"

"Alright then," Amy said as she resolved herself to a course of action, "but we're taking my car. Yours is a piece of crap."

Tom tried to convince her to just go home or wait for him at his house, but Amy wasn't about to let him play the hero alone. *She* had pressed him to check out the website. *She* had cracked the code. She would feel responsible if something happened to him.

A little more than half-an-hour later, Amy's Grand Am pulled into the narrow parking lot that weaved back-and-forth through the maze of rental storage units. The lot was open to the public and well lit. The dark green rollaway doors looked out at them, carefully guarding their hidden treasures. Amy slowed as they searched for the appropriate row.

"Row F, there it is," Tom pointed from the passenger's seat. He looked a little ridiculous with the BB gun resting on his lap. He had said that he didn't expect to be able to do much with it, but hoped that in the dark it might resemble a rifle enough to make a point. Amy desperately hoped that it wouldn't come to that.

She turned down aisle F and crept along looking for number thirty-two. Things looked innocent enough. She chided herself for being so emotional earlier—the guy in the video had just been so fervent. She could tell that he had been fighting back tears as he filmed it.

Amy parked the car in front of the storage unit. Tom opened his door, but leaned over and gave her a quick kiss on the cheek before stepping out.

"Tom, come on," Amy rubbed her cheek with her hand, "quit being so dramatic."

"Nice… she wiped it off," Tom threw her a grin. That one actually made her smile. She silently hoped that his jokes were getting better and not that she was getting used to his humor.

Tom left the car door open and Amy stayed in her seat with the engine running—ready for a quick escape if needed. She watched as Tom walked up to the keypad, BB gun ready, and punched in the code that Ned's video had given them. A small green light came on and the lock clicked open. Tom bent down and carefully lifted the green door.

4:12 AM

Sue Bishop held perfectly still behind the tall wet grass and the fading protection of the oak tree. The flashlight was fixed on the trunk in front of her. Her trembling right hand felt behind her for something with which to defend herself from the approaching attacker. The search produced a tree branch that had recently fallen, a stout but sturdy club as thick as her wrist. Certainly no match for a gun, but maybe he wouldn't be expecting it.

"Sue! Are you there?" the voice called again. Sue tried to imagine what the voice would sound like distorted by a computer. Why had they let her go just to recapture her a few minutes later?

The light bobbed as the steady footsteps grew closer. Sue planted her feet beneath her huddled body, ready to pounce. A woman's voice called to the man from inside the idling vehicle, "Do you even see her? I don't think she's here."

The flashlight turned back toward the vehicle. "She's supposed to be right here," the man replied. "I thought I saw some movement behind this tree." During the brief darkness, Sue picked up the tree branch and held it at her side, ready to strike. The flashlight came back toward her, moved forward, slowly rounded the tree, and shined directly into her eyes. "Sue?" the voice asked.

She let out a scream as she sprang from her hiding spot. A swift blow from the branch landed on the flashlight-holding hand. The light went out as it crashed to the ground with a crack of plastic that accompanied its startled owner's yell. Sue immediately turned and ran into the field of new corn, confident that they wouldn't be able to shoot her in the dark.

"Sue wait!" the voice called after her.

Unfortunately the bright light had destroyed her built-up night vision so that she was also running blind. Large white blotches hovered in front of her dilated eyes. The thick, damp mud clung to her feet, slowing her pace. She heard more shouting behind her: a brief argument between the two voices.

A false step caught a small corn stalk and sent Sue crashing face-first into the slick earth. Heavy breaths forced their way in and out of her aching lungs as she lay flat beneath the surrounding plants. The smell of fertilizer burned in her nostrils. Wet sticky soil coated her hands and arms. Her head felt light and dizzy. Mud had plastered her recently done hair to her cheeks and neck.

Sue hoped to rest there to clear her mind and regain her sight.

"Sue!"

The owner of the still vaguely familiar voice was now steadily trotting after her. She began to fear that the lightening eastern horizon would soon betray her position. She had to make another run for it. One final breath escaped slowly as she prepared herself for one final race toward freedom.

Sue's mud-caked body shot up off of the ground and sprinted anew. Her feet and legs burned with panic and exhaustion. Her steps were unsteady. But she would get away—*she had to.*

Unbeknownst to Sue, however, her pursuer was an amateur runner and not only had the benefits of shoe-clad feet, but also those of a superior lacing technique. He caught up easily and assumed a path parallel to hers, out of reach of the muddy branch that she still carried.

"Sue, stop!" he called, "Ned Dyer sent us!"

She continued to run. It had to be a trick.

"He said to tell you that he found twenty dollars!" the man called out. Then, softer, "whatever that's supposed to mean."

The rhythm of Sue's footsteps gradually slowed and then halted. The man approached cautiously as she bent her head down, dropped her tree branch, and gracefully collapsed back onto the mud, saturating it with warm thick tears.

"Amy McKay, I'd like you to meet Sue Bishop," Tom Rigsby called up to the silver SUV idling on the country road as he led the bruised, muddy, and still sobbing woman up the slick grassy slope. The wrist on his right hand was tender and displayed a bright red stripe where Sue had hit him with the tree branch. "She was kidnapped right from the restaurant's parking lot! They just dropped her off here like a half-an-hour ago."

"I am so sorry," Amy's voice was rich with concern, "Come on, Tom; let's get out of here."

Amy handed Tom a thermal blanket and he wrapped it around Sue's shivering shoulders. Sue whispered a "thank you" as Amy helped her into the back seat of the SUV. Tom sat up front alone. He executed a u-turn and drove back in the direction from which they had come.

Tom had never driven a brand new vehicle before. And while the Mitsubishi Endeavor was technically a year or two old, the odometer showed less than two hundred miles. The ten-inch touch-screen computer monitor in the middle of the dashboard had listed several of the car's enhancements earlier. This Ned guy had spent a *lot* of money on the thing.

The doors were unlocked and the keys in the ignition when Tom had found the SUV in Ned's storage unit. Upon turning it on the first time, the touch-screen activated and displayed the familiar floating head asking for a code. Tom punched in the two-three-eight-nine-three combination from the receipt and the screen morphed into the computer's main menu. A green indicator at the top of the screen informed him that the wheel locks had been successfully released.

Another indicator then blinked in red text, "Contingency Plan Gamma Has Been Initiated… Assessing Progress…" Tom selected the blinking text and in response the menu changed to the "Potential Threat Priority" screen. Ned's voice startled Tom over the speakers, "Highest priority threat identified! Please follow the instructions on the computer screen."

The item at the top of a short list of operation names was blinking. It read, "Recovery of Sue—Operation Compromised."

From Ned's video earlier, Tom had some idea as to what this meant. Contingency Plan Gamma was apparently Ned's fallback plan, the last resort in a web of overlapping measures he had taken to ensure the safety of his family and friends. Those that he had hired to provide this service had in some way failed, and he was forced to seek help from another source.

The video had implored Tom and Amy to seek out the SUV in order to monitor the progress of his plan and, if necessary, act in order to help it succeed. Tom had made Amy a deal: they would try to help if things didn't seem too dangerous. Picking up his fiancée hadn't seemed like too big of a deal.

So Tom had acknowledged the blinking message on the Endeavor's screen and this caused a street map to be displayed. A moving purple icon marked "Sue" had been displayed on a road outside of town. A silver icon marked "You" showed the Endeavor's position at the storage unit facility.

"Transmitter Located… Routing Shortest Path… Please Secure Sue…"

Tom and Amy had been attempting to close in on the purple icon for almost an hour when it had finally stopped moving on a seldom-used road ten miles outside of town. The computer had displayed the "Trust Phrase" about finding twenty dollars. Tom still didn't understand what that meant, but it had gotten Sue to stop running from him.

He entered into the prompt that the recovery of Sue had been successful. "Phase One of Contingency Plan Gamma Complete… Thank You" was the displayed reply. The menu page reappeared with a new blinking indicator: "Play Explanation Video: Sue Specific." Tom asked if she was ready to watch. She was.

A video similar to the one Tom and Amy had watched at his house played. Sue watched one of the monitors built into the front-seat headrests from the back seat. Ned's face explained the story about the package he had received three years earlier, his contingency plan preparation, and that the purse hanger he had given her for her birthday actually contained a small homing transmitter that had allowed her rescue.

Tom was not driving very fast as he was still a bit shaken from the night's events and was starting to fight back a fit of yawning. The clock read 4:25 a.m. He neared the end of the obscure country road and slowed to a stop at the T intersection. His right blinker waited patiently as a vehicle approached quickly from the left. The large windowless rusty brown conversion van slowed and turned right without the courtesy of a turn signal. Tom hated that.

As the van passed and as Tom pulled out, it illuminated the interior of the Endeavor. Sue gasped when the reflection of the van's headlights shined back briefly onto the driver. He was wearing a black ski mask—just like the man that had abducted her. In fact, it was the same man.

"DRIVE!" Sue screamed with a shrill and panicked voice, "IT'S THEM!!"

It took a second or two for Tom to comprehend what was happening. A loud squealing noise from behind was accompanied by a pair of bright headlights rounding the corner. He stomped on the gas and yelled to the back seat, "Hang on!"

The sudden power exerted by the Endeavor's engine surprised the three occupants as it accelerated down the country road. It appeared to be no ordinary van behind them though, as it kept pace. In fact, it was gaining.

Sue paused the playback of her explanation video and yelled up to Tom in a shrieking and thoroughly unhelpful manner.

"They're getting closer!"

A loud beeping noise suddenly began filling the vehicle. This also wasn't helpful. It appeared to have accompanied a new message on the computer screen in the dash, but Tom was too focused on getting away to attend to it. He shouted to the backseat instead.

"Amy… I could use some help up here! Aim the gun out the window and shoot at their tires!"

As if on cue, a loud crack thumped against the Endeavor's rear windshield. A divot indicated where the bullet had struck. Amy screamed and assumed her place in the passenger's seat, "They're shooting at us with *real* bullets, Tom! I don't think the BB gun is going to do much!"

"At least do something about that beeping!" Tom yelled. He glanced at the screen. Bold letters read, "Potential Pursuing Vehicle Detected. Deploy Countermeasures?" He looked up at Amy and she looked back. Then she grinned slightly and pressed the "Yes" button on the screen.

The van's headlights flooded the interior of the Endeavor. Two more shots and two more divots. The reinforced glass of the rear windshield was beginning to crack.

"Deploying countermeasures," Ned's calm voice declared over the SUV's speaker system. A loud clank preceded several smaller clanks on the road behind them. The van's headlights wavered. Three pops in rapid succession were immediately followed by a loud screeching noise as the van swerved and tipped and slid. It rolled violently with a sickening array of crashing and scraping sounds, sparks flying, and then finally left the pavement and slammed into a telephone pole on the side of the road. Tom glanced at the speedometer. He was going well over a hundred miles per hour. The guys in the van didn't stand a chance.

"Thank you, Ned," Tom whispered through nervous laughter as he slowed to ninety. A large orange flash lit up the sky behind him. The van had exploded. Tom pushed the realization that lives had just been lost from his mind. He could wrestle with that later. More pressing matters still needed to be attended to. Where were they supposed to go from here?

Amy was busy interacting with the computer screen, "Guys, there's a menu option for directions to safe houses. The nearest one is in Kentucky— sixty three point eight miles from here."

"Lead the way Ned," Tom was still nervously chuckling, "But I'm going to need a nap when we get there."

Sue leaned forward and handed him a cold can of Dr. Pepper. "Here. This was in the refrigerator in the back."

The sun was cresting the horizon when the silver Endeavor pulled into the driveway of a small ranch in a random subdivision somewhere in Kentucky. The garage door opened automatically, triggered by the SUV's computer system. Tom pulled in and shut the vehicle down. His exhausted body began to tremble from the recent trauma. This was more than he was used to handling.

The trio entered and took stock of the modestly appointed home—three twin beds in two bedrooms, bottled water in the refrigerator, non perishables in the pantry, assorted clothes and toiletries, and a large first aid kit.

"Go ahead and crash, Tom," Amy said and motioned toward the bedroom with the single bed, "I'll make sure Sue's taken care of. You did good tonight." She kissed her hand and touched it to his cheek, "Thanks."

Tom nodded appreciatively and then collapsed onto the bed and slept hard.

14

Tuesday, 10:06 AM

Tree-filtered sunlight poured through the windshield of the light-blue Scion, bringing the humid air inside to a light boil. The windows were, of course, shut tight for safety and Joe Tompkins' sleep had been fitful since sunrise—but he hadn't given it up. The hot stale air now teamed up with his aching bladder to finally rouse him from his slumber in the reclined seat.

He had driven randomly until almost two in the morning, mostly south, turning east or west occasionally as the opportunity had presented itself, on the obscure country roads that crisscrossed downstate Illinois. Finally unable to keep his eyes open any longer, he had pulled into a dirt path through a small patch of woods near a sprouting soybean field.

Joe struggled to sit up and rub the fog out of his eyes. He fished the cell phone out of his pocket in order to check the time. It was switched off. Gently the events of the previous day began to unfold themselves in his recollection, taking care not to cause undue alarm. After all, he was just waking up.

Keep the phone off, Joe, he told himself. *They can't track you with it off.*

Drearily he inserted the stolen key into the ignition and turned it halfway in order to engage the dashboard clock. Joe read it through blurry eyes: 10:07. He was just about to react to this with a comfortable sigh and grin when the mp3 player resumed operation causing an explosion of heart-thumping sound to fill the car. Joe reacted by momentarily leaving his seat. He then swore and slapped at the stereo's power button.

Now fully awake, he got out of the car and attended to his aching bladder.

Joe stretched and cracked his neck with gentle opposing pressure on his head from his hands. He took in the landscape from the edge of the woods, the flat farmland stretching in all directions to the tree-lined horizon. A few oil wells clanked rhythmically in the middles of a few short green fields.

The outside air was cooler than in the car, and a refreshing breeze swept past. Joe's throat was dry and tender. His eye and his hip were as sore as ever. A deep breath filled his lungs and then slowly escaped.

It was time to get moving.

Another five ibuprofen tablets went down hard—barely aided by what little saliva Joe could summon. He then engaged the engine and pulled out of his hiding spot. The car sat at the edge of the road waiting for its driver to pick a direction. Joe had reached a point past the end of the plans he had made. An important decision was looming.

Okay, Joe, now what are you going to do? Move out west? Head to Mexico?

It was too early in the day to tend to long-term plans. First, he decided, he'd at least need to find a place to clean up and get a cold Dr. Pepper. Joe pulled onto the gravel path and stopped at the intersection of two long-forgotten roads. He opened the road atlas that had come with the car and searched for the nearest town.

He found it and plotted his course. Loose rock popped under the tires as the sports car turned and sped away.

Taking a shower at the truck stop had been about as unnerving for Joe as all of the events of the previous day combined. The bottoms of his feet still felt contaminated as he walked into the small town library. He was there to check the hometown news, but his next stop would definitely be to pick up some shower shoes and new bath towels.

The library was brightly lit from the sunshine coming through the large windows that lined the 60's era building. Joe stared in mild horror at the airborne dust swirling in the sunlight. The place *smelled* dusty too. He decided not to stay any longer than necessary.

The fiftysomething librarian directed him to the "multimedia center" separated with a collapsible curtain from the single room of books. The two computers that constituted the "multimedia" part of the "center" were ancient and sat side-by-side on a low brown folding table. One of the two metal folding chairs in front of the table was occupied by a local.

"Mornin'," Joe tried to sound genuine and not-at-all conspicuous. The man nodded his head in agreement. Apparently no more needed to be said.

Joe took the other seat and clicked the internet icon. The high-pitched grinding indicated that the PC was happy to oblige, but required the tiniest bit of patience while it executed the task. When able, Joe browsed to his local newspaper's site to read journalistic coverage of his growing criminal résumé—assault, robbery, grand theft auto.

But after twenty minutes of searching he could only find a small story about the snarled evening commute. A car had apparently burned for forty-five minutes in the town's main intersection before the fire department was able to stop the blaze. Joe skimmed the article and stopped on the second-to-last paragraph. He reread it. He reread it again.

"The regional branch of Golden Touch auto service centers took full responsibility for the fire, saying that a recent customer's poorly secured air filter appeared to be to blame. An issued statement detailed the company's response: 'Golden Touch prides itself in its dedication to customer service. We have already provided this customer with a loaner car, free of charge, and will be presenting him with a check for the sticker price of a brand new Honda Civic. He will also enjoy free regular maintenance for two years at any Golden Touch service center in the region. Customer satisfaction has always been our number one goal.'"

Joe knew his mouth was hanging open. His left eye started twitching. "They turned it into a commercial," he told the computer screen. The man in the seat next to him shifted his weight in his seat in disapproval of the taboo. There was no need for talking.

Joe ignored the man and decided to recklessly follow a hunch and opened another browser. He was going to check his work email account. This would leave an electronic trail to the small town library for law enforcement to follow, effectively destroying the result of the hours of erratic driving the night before. But he didn't care. He could spend the day driving again if he had to.

There were only two new emails in his inbox once he had sorted out the droves of useless informational messages that come with belonging to a large corporation. One was a meeting announcement from HR.

Joe Tompkins,

You have been selected to attend the upcoming "Handling Office Conflicts" lunchtime seminar on Thursday. Please indicate if you will be able to attend and if you have any specific dietary requirements.

More information is available on the Human Resources intranet page.

The other email was from his bank.

Mr. Tompkins,

We apologize for the difficulty you may have experienced during your recent visit. We wanted to inform you that you have successfully closed your account with the Georgia-Tennessee-Kentucky regional division of National Neighborhood Bank.

Also, to further express our gratitude for your years of patronage, we have opened a new account in your name for the Illinois-Wisconsin-Missouri regional division with $20—our gift to you.

Have a great day!

Please take a minute to fill out our anonymous online customer satisfaction survey…

12:05 PM

Joe Tompkins' blood was on fire. The lady at the bank the day before hadn't taken him seriously. He had just gotten off of the phone with her as he headed toward the interstate that led back to town. Apparently she hadn't even informed her superiors of the incident. She had just used "manager's discretion" to bypass the bank's policies and give him his money.

Funny that she couldn't have just used that discretion in the first place. The prospect of the bank receiving the bad publicity of a fake bank robbery by a patron trying to withdraw his own funds had apparently changed her mind. Joe had ended the call by yelling, "You can keep your bleeping twenty dollars!" He had forgotten to tell her what she could do with the customer satisfaction survey. It was almost worth calling her back…

Some corner of his brain was attempting to plead the rational case—that this was a good thing. After all, half-an-hour earlier he had been a multiple-count felon on the lam. Now he was just guilty of playing hooky from work. Joe figured that he'd probably escape punishment for that also.

He calmed down a little and began to consider the prospect of re-entering on Wednesday the life that he had rejected and fled from on Monday. The promise of a new car did little to counter Joe's rising feelings of despair. He was going back. Had he really thought that he could escape?

Joe pulled into a fast-food drive thru to grab some lunch. A loud beep from his recently-switched-on cell phone lying in the passenger's seat informed him that a text message was waiting in his inbox. Joe flipped the phone open and displayed the message. It was from his old roommate, Ned Dyer. Joe had barely heard from him since he had up-and-gone three years ago.

"911**Pizza Time Everybody!**911" the note read. Joe threw the phone back down. It had been too long for him to appreciate Ned's sense of humor. Plus, that stupid message just cost him fifteen cents on his phone plan. "Not a good time, Ned," he sighed.

Joe was still bitter about him leaving—sticking him with the apartment's full rent, tossing their friendship aside. He and Ned had been best friends since middle school. They had attended the same college and had gone to work at the same company afterward. Joe had dual degrees in electrical and computer engineering, which complemented Ned's software engineering degree. They had been a great team—in school and on the job—the two of them usually accomplishing more than most five-person teams. They were well on their way to changing the way their company did business when Ned left.

Joe found out later that he had started his own consulting business using some concepts that Joe had helped develop. He had never received any percentage of profits even after he heard about the company's success. In fact, Ned had been gone for a year and a half before Joe had even heard from him for the first time—via email. Joe had long given up on trying to contact him at that point. Ned had apologized for being so distant—explained that he had been and continued to be really busy. Joe had half-heartedly replied that it was okay. Since then Ned had attempted to reconcile the friendship, but Joe had decided to quietly hold onto his anger instead.

"…elcome to… ould you… try our… meal?" The static produced from the drive-thru intercom aspired to take on the quality of human speech. It mostly failed.

"Yes, I'd like a number seven with a Dr. Pepper and that's all please," Joe carefully enunciated.

"That's… mber seven wi… cter Pepper. Anything else?"

Rage coursed though Joe's body. Had he not just told the stupid box that that was all? "You just lost a sale, PUNK!" Joe shouted at the intercom. Then he peeled out.

Renewed anger coursed through his body as his car sped down the road. A minivan up ahead pulled out of a parking lot right in front of him. Joe slammed the brakes and mashed the horn, screaming obscenities that no one else could hear. He was being boxed in again. He was being forced to slow down. He had tried to break free, but was caught like a marble in a labyrinth, the ground tilting suddenly underneath him, forcing him back the way he had come, forcing him back to his cubicle. It seemed his only recourse was to experience the fury that trembled through him like earthquake, searching for a target toward which to unleash his wrath.

He would get around the minivan, one way or another. Joe clamped his hands on the steering wheel and wrenched it to the right, hopping the curb and gunning the engine. The world blurred around him as the small car leapt onto the thin strip of grass the ran alongside the road, caught pavement as a tire grazed the sidewalk, and fishtailed away from the street, heading directly toward a bright red fire hydrant. Joe stomped on the brakes as the car slid, coming to a stop just inches from the hydrant.

Then everything was still.

His breaths were coming out in short bursts, his eyes staring in the distance, his mind in sudden and horrid confusion. What was he doing? This was not who he was. He followed the rules. He controlled his temper. He didn't recognize the person that had guided his actions since yesterday afternoon.

Somehow he'd found himself on a path of self-destruction. Now he had been granted a reprieve. The consequences had been erased. Why was he starting down the path again?

Joe blew out another short breath and made a decision. He would let go of the anger. He needed to deal with some of his unresolved issues. He needed someone to talk to.

Ned was obviously trying to make an effort. Maybe it was time to let him off of the hook.

People were starting to approach the car. Joe looked up at them, waved, and pulled back onto the road before having to explain himself. Once he was a good distance away, he picked up his phone and looked through his contacts directory to find Ned's new address. A check of his atlas revealed that he was only fifty miles away. He approached the highway and turned south toward his friend Ned's place on the off chance that he would be home.

As Joe continued to retreat from the brink of consuming anger and frustration, his mind drifted to what he had done to Gilmore the previous day. He wouldn't have thought it possible, but a genuine regret began to rack his conscience. The guy hadn't deserved that. What kind of person was he, attacking people without any provocation?

As Joe pulled into the neighborhood where Ned's house was supposed to be, his eyes were instantly drawn to one address. He desperately hoped that it was not Ned's, but soon read the street numbers off of the mailbox out front and this hope was dashed. Joe pulled his "loaner" car up to the curb and stared at the scene before him.

There, nestled among the large and shiny homes that gathered around the quiet cul-de-sac, was a scene of destruction—right where Ned's house should have been. The entire structure was now little more than a burned out shell. It looked as if a bomb had demolished the place. The smell of burnt wood and plastic permeated the air. An authoritative band of yellow police tape stretched around the charred remains. No one appeared to be around, but a blue Toyota sat in the driveway.

Trembling, and with a mixture of concern and disbelief, Joe got out of his car and started slowly up the yard to investigate.

15

Tuesday, 4:24 AM

"Beeeeeeep! Beep!"

The single dash-dot signal issued from Ned Dyer's pager in the cardboard box in the corner of the dingy white room. His captors had emptied his pockets and believed that they had turned off his cell phone and pager when they had led him, blindfolded, to the metal folding chair where he now sat. Zip ties bound his hands behind his back and to the chair.

The blindfold had been removed and Ned had found himself in the center of the room facing a large one-way mirror. Fluorescent bulbs filled the chamber with a dirty yellow light. Ned guessed that the time was about 4:30 in the morning. He hadn't seen anyone come through the grimy white door in hours.

Ned smiled when he heard the pager's signal. He knew that it meant that Phase One of Contingency Plan Gamma had been enacted and was complete. He now had a bargaining chip with which to negotiate with the men who had taken him, but more importantly, his family was safe.

"Thank you, Tom," he whispered to himself. He hadn't been entirely comfortable trusting the fidgety waiter with such an important mission. It wouldn't have been necessary at all if Ned hadn't become complacent. He had just gotten a new cell phone the previous week and had yet to install the software that would have allowed him to initiate the contingency plan himself.

It had been a sizeable risk letting Sue leave the restaurant alone while he confronted the thug. Ned had hoped that he could have controlled the situation, but the bald man had been wearing a wire and his buddies knew he was in trouble immediately. Ned had traded his own freedom for Sue's. The fact that they had lived up to their end of the bargain indicated that they had no idea that he had prepared so extensively for this situation. They didn't know that he was beating them at their own game.

Ned's smile widened—then transformed into a wince. A large welt was growing next to his right temple—his payment for the steak knife episode. He struggled to stretch his back without forcing the plastic to cut into his hands. He only needed to wait… it wouldn't be long now.

A door slammed behind the mirror. Ned heard shouting.

Guess it isn't entirely soundproof then, he thought. The mirror shook as something banged into it from the other side. Someone was not happy. The grimy white door burst open and produced the bald man. He was wearing a fresh shirt.

The man walked rapidly and directly toward Ned, pulled a 9mm from his shoulder holster, and pressed it against Ned's forehead, forcing his head backward. "Now this is the second time that you've violated our agreement tonight, Neddy! The first time it only cost you this," Baldy slapped Ned's welt with his left hand, "This time it's gonna cost you more!"

"Do what you're going to do," Ned's voice was cold and even—he had left his fear behind upon receipt of the signal from his pager, "but don't you dare try to rewrite history to me. We never had an agreement. It was a threat."

"Well *excuse* me," the man's mouth poured sarcasm as he took a few steps back and leveled the gun anew between Ned's eyes, "you've violated the *threat* then –"

"Shut up," Ned's tone took on a commanding quality, "It's my turn to issue the threats." He took a long look up and down the man, pretending to size him up. "I shouldn't be wasting my time talking to you. Let me talk to your superior. The police will be on their way within a few hours. Get me someone I can actually negotiate with." Ned's thoughts did not carry the same level of confidence as his voice. His thoughts were hoping that he knew what he was doing.

The man clearly did not appreciate being talked to like this by someone that was tied to a chair and supposedly his prisoner. Ned steeled himself as Baldy raised the gun in preparation for another bash to the head when the door opened again. A tall man in a gold tie walked slowly in.

"You are excused, Fuller," Gold Tie said in a low voice. His short graying hair was slicked back. Fuller's hand stopped mid-swing and he turned, reluctantly, toward the door.

Ned couldn't resist. "See ya later, *Fuller!*" he sing-songed after him, "Take care of that cut on your chest!" Fuller spun back around and landed a hard blow across Ned's left cheek, opening a small gash. Blood started to trickle. But it was worth it. Ned had successfully gotten under the man's skin. He knew that he was controlling the situation much more than his captors had intended, even more than they yet realized.

"That will do, Fuller," Gold Tie pulled another metal folding chair from its place against the wall, set it directly in front of Ned, and sat down. "Mr. Dyer, we seem to have a situation here. It appears that you have taken steps to protect your family." He gestured with his large hands as if sharing an intimate concern with an old friend. "I have reports that say your parents, your fiancée's parents, and your sister and her children all disappeared in the middle of the night."

"They're safe," Ned stared directly into the man's gray eyes, "You won't be able to touch them."

"Ah, that may be true, Mr. Dyer. But unfortunately for you we never lived up to our earlier bargain. We still have your fiancée. We can still control you with threats to her."

"There... right *there* was your mistake, buddy," Ned was starting to gloat, "You've underestimated me. I know that she was released. I also know that she is safe from you. But, for argument's sake let's pretend that I'm wrong. It shouldn't be any problem at all for you to confirm to me that you still have her. Why don't you just have her give me another phone call? No? I even know that my mom's *cat* is safe! You can't even get to *him*!" Ned was enjoying the situation a little too much. It was probably a combination of exhaustion, adrenaline, and the culmination of a painstakingly laid out plan playing out with clockwork precision. The man looked surprised and a little perplexed at Ned's revelation, but he allowed Ned to continue. He was clearly a different class of thug.

"The way I see it, you've only got two ways to threaten me left—but I don't think that you'll use either of them. Option one: you could go after my acquaintances or coworkers. Big problem there is that I'm not really that close to anyone." This was actually a slight lie, Ned had indeed formed several friendships at the office, but it was true enough for his current purposes. "You see, I've been careful over the last three years not to form relationships with anyone that I haven't put security in place for. So going after those people will mean little more to me than if you just started picking people at random. I resolved in my mind a long time ago that, if it came down to that, the blood would be on your hands—not mine.

"Option two: you can threaten me physically. Let me tell you right now that this doesn't scare me near as much as potential harm to my family. But that doesn't mean that I haven't taken measures against this as well. The pager I was wearing should have tipped you people off. Why the *hell* would I need both a pager *and* a cell phone? It doesn't make any sense! It's a fake! The real device is encased inside! You only turned off the shell. It's been transmitting my location every seven minutes to a series of three redundant servers in three hidden locations. One of them is mobile! The best part is that it's been recording and transmitting audio in bursts too. Say hello to the police! The whole digital package is being compiled as we speak! That's my insurance. It's scheduled to transmit the entire thing to the cops in about four hours. Also, it will lead the police to the sealed threat envelope that you people gave me three years ago. I'm sure that their forensics team would love to check that out.

"So, here's the offer," Ned was confident as his rehearsed speech reached its dramatic conclusion, "I walk out of here, *right now*, and I never hear from you people again. In return I'll keep the evidence from the police. Remember, *your* voice is on the recording. Plus, just for a show of good faith, I'll give you some free advice: Don't send anyone to my house tonight."

This got the man's attention. His calm demeanor had been fading slowly as Ned had talked. Now his eyes were wild and his voice animated, "What do you mean about your house!?"

"Beep! Beeeeeep!" the pager in the corner sounded again—this time with a dot-dash signal.

Ned closed his eyes. "Any blood is on your hands, not mine," he repeated quietly. "You shouldn't have sent them to my house."

Ned's mind was flooded with images of the reinforced safe in his guest bedroom. It was a decoy, rigged to blow up if there was any attempt to breach it during the first few hours of a contingency plan's activation. Even Ned had scolded himself for taking such extreme measures, but he had figured that if he had been captured or killed and someone had broken into his house that would mean that an all-out-war had been declared on his life. He wasn't going to go down without exacting a toll on the faceless enemy.

Gold Tie jumped out of his chair, picked it up, and threw it against the wall with a scream. The combination of sounds echoed in the room as he took four long strides to the door and slammed it behind him.

Ned's heart was pounding in his chest. He had done it. They had to release him now. Next he just had to face Sue and his family. How would he get them to understand his need for secrecy? What would be their reaction to all of this?

After a few minutes, the door to the white room opened again. Mr. Gold Tie stepped calmly back in. He picked up the chair off of the floor and placed it back in front of Ned. He sat down again.

"So, do we have a deal?" Ned asked him. His consulting business had taught him the art of making the sale. This was a pitch that he had landed perfectly.

"Mr. Dyer, let me make two apologies. First, let me apologize for losing my temper just now. I assure you that it does not happen often. Second, I apologize that my organization has underestimated you. It seems that seven of our agents have needlessly lost their lives in the last hour. Four were in your house attempting to gain access to your safe and triggered an explosion. And three died in a car accident while attempting to recover your fiancée, which as you are already aware, we had in fact released as agreed. Let me also promise you that I will never lie to you again. I believe in respect—that you are a man worthy of respect, Mr. Dyer, and the attempt to trick you was not a respectful thing to do.

"Now as for your offer… I'm afraid that there is indeed a problem. You have, in fact, underestimated my organization in two—make that three— very important ways. First, you mistakenly believe that a brush with law enforcement would deal this organization a crushing blow. In reality, it is little more than a nuisance—one that we would rather avoid to be sure, but simply a nuisance nonetheless.

"Second, you believe that you have taken your loved ones out of our reach. The truth is that my organization has a much greater wealth of resources than we have utilized in your case. Now that you have escalated this matter, my superiors will simply employ more sophisticated means in locating your family.

"And third, you indicated a belief that you would be walking out of here without having to endure any more physical mistreatment. Let me personally assure you that this is not the case," the man displayed a sudden bone-chilling grin. "You've underestimated your importance to us. After all of your preparation and planning, Mr. Dyer, the only real success that you will be able to claim is that you have become a greater drain on our resources than anticipated. Rest assured that you *will* pay for that."

"I've taken steps to allow myself to withstand torture," Ned struggled to maintain the tone of his sales pitch. "Morphine caplets will release into my bloodstream in response to a series of facial twitches." It was a blatant and ridiculous lie, but Ned was attempting to adapt at this point. The man's response to his proposal had completely thrown him.

"My dear Mr. Dyer, didn't I just promise that I would no longer lie to *you*? Did I not just explain that I believed in respect?"

Ned didn't have much of a chance to panic at the new revelations. He barely managed, "Who *are* you people?" when the man with the Gold Tie produced a nightstick, raised it, and brought it down hard on the top left side of Ned's head.

The dingy white room went black.

A calm, rich tone with measured cadence: "My dear Mr. Dyer, didn't I just promise that I would no longer lie to *you*? Did I not just explain that I believed in respect?"

Four seconds of little input—just a low buzzing most likely due to fluorescent lighting. No signals of interest detected. Discard.

An emotional, slightly panicked, and breathy voice: "Who *are* you people?"

One-point-three more seconds of little input. Discard.

The sound of an object striking another.

Brisk footsteps—the clack of a door handle—a squeaky hinge—the slamming of a door.

The audio signals were sorted and compiled with the recording of the previous seven minutes. Updated GPS coordinates were packaged with the data. The device hidden inside Ned Dyer's pager transmitted the packet to the cell tower off to the northwest.

It would be its last transmission as it was smashed to bits a minute later.

The data packet was then relayed to the broadband transceivers in three redundant servers in three different locations. These computers were each hidden, and were each running Ned Dyer's custom-built contingency plan software.

Forty-two minutes later the software registered that the receipt of six consecutive transmissions had been missed, signifying that the homing device hidden inside Ned's pager was no longer functioning. This caused the program to exit its current loop of execution and drop into the *transmit_ Evidence_Packet_To_Police* subroutine three hours earlier than expected.

The primary server computer hummed lightly in the darkened enclosure of the storage locker. It transmitted a message informing the other two hidden servers that it was capable of carrying out the current task and went about collecting and compressing the last several hours of data that it had received.

It zipped this up, attached it to an email that detailed the location of a sealed envelope ready for forensic analysis, and transmitted it to the designated email address. A few minutes later a "confirmation of receipt" message informed the primary server that it had successfully completed its function. It passed the message along to the redundant servers. They would not be needed. The valuable payload of data was on its way to the authorities.

The evidence-laden email bounced around in cyberspace for an eternity of almost six seconds, brushing past billions of bits of data all hurrying to their intended destinations. The message eventually found its way through the black coaxial cable that led up to a workstation at an obscure local twenty-four hour office support company.

A dreary operator sat behind the grubby computer under dusty yellow lighting. A popup window blinked on the screen heralding the email's arrival. The attachment, compressed as it was, still contained a large amount of data. It took the PC a few minutes to display the message:

Instructions:
1.   Burn contents of attached zip file onto a DVD.
2.   Print attached document.
3.   Deliver to the local police station immediately.
$200 has been wired to your account to cover the expenses.
Please hurry.
Ned Dyer

"Steve! You won't believe it," the guy sitting at the email's destination computer said. "I just got an email from that weird guy that paid all that cash for us to 'wait to be contacted' last year! It looks like he wants us to hand deliver something to the police."

Inside the desktop PC's DVD burner a tiny laser burned a couple of billion tiny indentations into a spinning disc as it transferred the evidence data to the tamperproof physical medium. Another laser inside the networked printer transferred black ink to a plain white page—a summary of evidence against the mysterious organization that had so disrupted Ned's life. It would now be impossible for a hacker to prevent delivery of the information to the authorities.

The summary printout and data DVD were dropped into a plain manila envelope. A black Sharpie was used to write just one word on the outside of the envelope: "**POLICE.**"

A messenger was dispatched to deliver the pre-dawn package. The officer at the front desk of Ned Dyer's hometown police station received and opened the envelope with greasy fingers. After skimming the data enclosed, the officer strolled over to the high-grade office shredder and placed the envelope and its contents into the slot.

A high-pitched whirring noise ensued while hundreds of small metal teeth devoured the package, reducing the precious information to meaningless shreds of paper and plastic. The officer then walked back to his desk while placing a call on his cell phone.

"Don't worry, it's taken care of," was all he said.

16

Tuesday, 12:54 PM

Joe Tompkins couldn't believe what he was seeing as he climbed the slight incline of Ned's yard toward the charred wreckage of Ned's house. The frame was mostly intact, but blackened and crumbling. Melted vinyl had seeped into the lawn and hardened. The large unattached garage was, however, untouched by the fire.

"They pulled four bodies out of there this morning," a cantankerous voice came from behind. This startled Joe and he turned to see a retiree, one of the neighbors, standing close behind him, dangerously close to invading Joe's personal space bubble. Joe wasn't sure how this guy sneaked up without him noticing. His attention must have been drawn to the carnage of the house.

The man had a bitter look on his face that was slightly betrayed by the glimmer of excitement in his eyes. Joe correctly guessed that the man took pleasure in complaining about his neighbors and was overjoyed to have a grievance so concrete.

"Did they identify them? Was anyone able to make it out? Is Ned okay?" Joe was panged with sudden concern for his friend's wellbeing. The man seemed to relish the attention and drew his response out in order to savor it.

"Is that the guy's name that lived there? He barely ever even nodded to me. *You've* already said more to me than he ever did."

Joe interrupted before the man could get both of his feet up on his soapbox. "Is Ned okay!?" he repeated.

"No idea… I couldn't get the police, the firemen, or the paramedics to give me the time of day. I've been paying *their* salaries with my taxes for over forty years! But they can't tell us what's going on when the house next door blows up? There's something wrong with that…"

Joe felt bad about it—he really did—but he turned back toward the house and dismissed the man with a wave of his hand. He needed more information than the guy was going to be able to provide. He stepped up to the remains of the house and slowly walked the perimeter. An indistinct feeling of foreboding began to creep up Joe's spine. Something didn't fit here.

As he rounded the back of the house and passed the blackened staircase that still jutted up from the crater, the driveway again became visible. Joe's eyes locked onto the car parked there. It was just an average looking blue Toyota—but it looked vaguely familiar. Something in the recesses of his mind told him that it had special significance… that he should be on his guard.

Joe continued to survey the damage as he approached the still intact garage. He glanced back to the front yard where the neighbor was now shuffling away, muttering loudly about "common decency" or something. A chilling tingle began to dance on the back of Joe's neck.

"Don't freak out, Joe," the calming thought appeared in his mind from nowhere. Joe found this odd. He wasn't even thinking of freaking out. He had no reason to freak out.

The sudden movement of Joe's right arm was not the result of a decision to act by his conscious mind. It was as if the arm knew what it was doing all by itself. Of what this was, Joe had no idea. His legs were apparently in on the plan though, a quick step toward what *had* been Ned's kitchen allowed the rogue hand to close on a loose section of lead pipe. Joe didn't even feel the resistance as the crumbling joints gave way, releasing the weapon from its plumbed holster.

Joe's mind was still puzzled, but his entire body was in on the act now. He spun quickly on one heel with the pipe extended. He was shocked when it connected with a fat man's forearm behind him. The guy's arm was just coming down holding… *a gun?* It looked like he was trying to hit Joe from behind.

The gun went sailing through the air and into the ash and debris of the house. The fat man's fat face wore an expression of sudden confusion, his mouth agape, his eyes opened to their maximum capacity. Joe didn't understand the fear reflected in those eyes until he noticed that his right hand was raising the pipe for another blow.

An authoritative voice boomed from a spot near the garage, now behind Joe's back, "Drop it, Tompkins!" Joe thought that he recognized the voice, but its tone was out of place. "Drop it now!" the command came again—the voice now unmistakable.

It couldn't be him… it didn't make any sense… Joe's hand released the pipe and it dropped to the ground with a thud.

"Turn around now, *slowly*."

This doesn't make any sense! Joe's mind repeated. *I don't think that I can even accept this!*

"I just told you not to freak out, Joe," the calming foreign voice re-entered his mind and seemed to fracture his thoughts. It became hard to focus on what was happening. Joe began to suspect that he was losing the grip on his sanity.

Joe turned around to face the man behind him. It had been the previous day—a lifetime ago—since he had seen this man last, more than two hundred miles to the north of the cul-de-sac where he now found himself. But there Gilmore was, not more than ten yards away, with a handgun leveled directly at Joe's chest.

Joe thought that he was perfectly justified if he decided to freak out a little.

He slowly raised his trembling hands above his head. He had never had a gun pointed at him before. His mind was still attempting to reject the image of Gilmore being there at Ned's burnt house. His eyes closed tightly and reopened in an effort to make the image go away. It didn't. Gilmore really did have a gun aimed at him. He had apparently picked the wrong guy to hit with a keyboard.

"G-Gilmore," he tried hesitantly, "Man, I am so sorry about yesterday… I've just been having a hard time with the new job… and I got frustrated. I just snapped and you were the closest person around. I am so sorry…"

Gilmore had turned his head to one side and now glared at Joe with a look of disapproval and contempt. "Do you think I'm *really* that stupid, Tompkins? You can cut the act."

Joe didn't know what that was supposed to mean. He didn't know how Gilmore had found him. And he didn't know where Gilmore had gotten a gun.

"Put your hands behind your back," Gilmore commanded.

"Seriously, Gilmore," Joe tried again, "I really feel bad about it. I don't know what got into me. They already have me signed up for this seminar at work… I'm definitely going to utilize the employee counseling hotline too. I swear!"

"Put your hands behind your back, Joe," Gilmore repeated.

Joe blinked one last time in an attempt to make Gilmore vanish. He opened his eyes slowly and Gilmore was indeed gone. But so was everything else. It was as if the sun had suddenly gone out. It was as if Joe had suddenly been struck blind.

Other senses had faded also. There was only silence… and an unusual weightless sensation, as if he was falling.

The experience should have been terrifying. But strangely, he was perfectly calm.

Joe knew that, in that perfect darkness, some amount of time was passing. It might have just been a few seconds. Or it might have been several days.

There was no way to tell how long it had been when a blurry hint of an image began to appear in front of Joe's eyes. The muffled hum of a speeding engine started to grow in his ears. He began to feel his weight again. He felt as if he were sitting.

All at once, Joe's senses sharpened. Images now of the highway speeding toward him, the sound of the car and the horns of angry drivers, the feeling of his fingers gripped around the Scion's steering wheel, the smell of... *gunpowder?* Joe was back in his loaner car, zipping down the interstate at close to a hundred miles an hour. The clock told him that about ten minutes had passed since he had blacked out. He had an unsettling feeling, as if someone had just edited out a part of his life.

He didn't like it.

Joe's eyes darted toward the passenger's seat. The handgun that Gilmore had pointed at him now sat on the floor mat. The smell told Joe that it had been recently fired.

What just happened?

Joe's mind was now frantic. No blood—no pain (other than the injuries received the previous day)—*he* hadn't been shot. Had he shot someone else?

A fast approaching sign told him that he was headed south. He had no idea how he had kept control of the car while unconscious. Joe decided to at least slow down and tried to ease off of the accelerator. His foot, however, kept the pedal pressed down. His hands were still locked onto the wheel. They weren't listening to his brain's commands either. A deep and dangerous sense of panic swelled inside of him. Joe no longer had any doubt that he was losing his mind.

"Stay calm, Joe," the foreign voice was back in his head, "everything is under control. Pay attention."

"I am paying attention!" he screamed, "I'm losing my sanity! Are *you* paying attention?!"

In a fit of desperation, Joe twisted his neck and aimed his open mouth at his right shoulder. It was the only way he could think to fight back. And he would draw blood if he had to. Just as his teeth made contact however, Joe felt his head twist back to the forward-facing position and slam—hard—into the headrest behind him.

"Pay attention, Joe!" The uninvited thoughts now took on a bitter and commanding tone. "Stop fighting!"

Joe was determined *to* fight against whatever was happening. He could no longer move his head, but he could still fight for control of his mind. He focused all of the concentration he could muster at resisting the intruding voice. And, for a second or two, he was successful at blocking it out.

Then a kind of pressure began to build in his skull. He fought to maintain his resolve. Sweat started to form on his forehead. His arms began to tremble, then shake.

Soon the building pressure became too much to withstand and resistance slipped from his mind's grasp. A fleeting thought of despair at the defeat was soon swept aside as the pressure quickly vanished. Panic subsided. Calm returned.

Vague impressions now gently began to seep into Joe's mind like coffee dripping slowly through a filter: a sense that his situation was far more complicated and dangerous than he had been aware, a sense that *something* had been guiding his actions, a sense that he could trust its guidance.

In addition to these impressions, Joe began to gain some insight into what had happened during his blackout. He now knew that he had somehow wrestled the gun from Gilmore, fired two shots, and fled to his car. Details beyond that were fuzzy.

One thing wasn't fuzzy though. His need to find Ned was now overwhelming. He still didn't know if Ned had been one of the bodies removed from his house. Joe was sick with the possibility that he might have been.

The influx of information inside Joe's brain suddenly halted. He had apparently learned enough for now. Joe didn't immediately realize that he had regained control of his right foot. He kept it on the accelerator. He had to get to Atlanta. There wasn't much time.

17

Three Years Ago…

"So… I think Ned invited Schultz," Dan Curtis was hesitant with the information—Joe had just chewed Schultz out earlier that day. Joe stopped short on the steep incline of the sidewalk that led up to his apartment near downtown Atlanta and looked up at the sky. Dan halted also. "I just thought you should know before we get up there."

Joe seemed to study the heavens—a few cumulus clouds; the ones closest to the southwestern horizon were coloring the February sky with shades of orange and pink. The setting sun was already hidden by the hills and the trees. He looked back at Dan and let out a sigh of acceptance, "That's Ned for ya, arms wide open to anyone. It's fine… I'm used to it. I'm not apologizing to Schultz though."

Dan had been delighted to see this kid (who had been out of school for less than two years) take on Schultz (who was well into his forties) in the code review meeting that afternoon. Schultz had been brought on as a contract engineer six months ago and hadn't contributed to the project yet. Finally he had been nailed down and forced to develop some software. Ned had already written requirements and design documentation for him to follow and Joe had overhauled the coding standard. These two kids had taken most of the planning work out of the job; the contractors were just being brought in to pound out the code.

But Schultz seemed to have a knack for following the plans just enough to make his work defensible, but not enough to make it useful. He had to be dragged through reviews and told each and every item to fix. In reality it usually ended up taking longer to review and repair his initial submittal than it would take a halfway decent contractor to just do it over from scratch. But management always seemed to have a soft spot for these guys. And guys like

Dan were used to picking up the slack. It was a bit frustrating, but he was compensated well for his efforts.

Dan had been there over a year now, also as a contract engineer. Eleven years in the industry, the last seven as a contractor, had given him perspective enough to classify fellow contractors within a few minutes into one of two categories.

Category one was comprised of people like Dan—sharp, efficient, hard working, and good communicators. The engineers in this group contracted themselves because they saw it as the best way to make the most money. Company loyalty was a thing of the past. Dan had often seen situations where direct employees would suffer at the hands of a layoff before contract employees would.

He knew that job security was an illusion, especially in this industry. Projects and capital ebbed and flowed with the cyclical lifecycle of government spending. Huge downsizing and huge staffing initiatives were often separated only by a few months time. Category one people counted on this. Category one people worked for themselves.

Category two people, however, were the engineers that were contractors out of necessity. These guys usually made their unfortunate employers painfully aware that they would be willing to accept a direct position—*any* direct position—but were unable to convince any company to commit to them long-term.

These were the guys that knew it all—until asked something specific. These were the guys that could do it all—until required to perform. These were the guys that had no understanding of the importance (or the mechanics) of personal hygiene. These were the guys that everyone avoided. And with the violent swings in staffing levels in the aerospace industry, these were the guys that happily slipped through the cracks in budget, in schedule, in management.

Many of the category two people eventually got exposed and shipped out…only to wait for the next tide to come in: taking on the form of another company in dire need of staff, another community to infect. And then there was always the lucky few that were able to finagle a direct position, dig in, and eventually worm their way into management—their qualifications consisting mainly of seniority.

Schultz was *firmly* in category two.

This was probably most apparent in the occasional all-hands meetings that the company held. As the division had several locations working on the same large project, these meetings consisted of an hour-long conference call across four offices, three states, and two time zones—with well over one hundred fifty engineers in attendance.

The management of the high-tech company should have been ashamed that it took a good ten minutes at the beginning of every one of these meetings to get everyone on the phone, logged in to the presentation, and quieted down enough to proceed. Dan had once conservatively figured that the average delay wasted well over two thousand dollars of the company's money in paying engineers to sit and wait.

Inevitably, one or two aspiring comics (usually those that are unaccustomed to having any kind of audience—especially such a large and captive one) used the "Are there any questions?" portion of the meeting as their own personal open-mike test-bed for new material. The attention-grabbing ordeals usually consisted of obscure and poorly timed joke attempts or inappropriate and unnecessary questions.

Dan had seen this phenomenon in other companies also, but Schultz was exceptionally gifted in the discipline. He added an extra dimension to the act by mumbling and stuttering through his presentation while persistently pursuing completion of his not-quite-thought-through comment—the hope of laughter as his reward. His goal of invoking laughter was, however, *always* realized—if only a result of Schultz's own brain-scrapingly irritating guffaws that echoed through the four crowded conference rooms of more than three hundred rolling eyes.

Even worse, Schultz had recently picked up a new category-two friend: Fischer. And this guy apparently thought that Schultz was pure comedic genius. So now there were two sources of the out of place guffaws that echoed through the four crowded conference rooms.

When most people met Fischer, one of two words usually came to mind: *gross* or *disgusting*. Dan was sure that there were some that would have taken the time to come up with something more poignant like *repulsive* or *a-walking-sack-of-sweat-and-flatulence-covered-in-old-ketchup-stains*. But most wouldn't take the time; they'd want to get away from him immediately.

Fischer was also the guy who thought that his recently-divorced classification gave him license to descend upon each-and-every unfortunate female in the office, regardless of relationship status, and soak up every ounce of attention and pity that the rules of politeness required that they give to him.

"At least Ned didn't invite that Fischer guy," Dan offered as he and Joe continued up the sidewalk, groceries in tow.

"Yeah, could you imagine *both* of them *in* my apartment—*at the same time?*" Joe gave an exaggerated shudder as he unlocked the apartment building's front door and held it open for Dan. They took the elevator to the fourth floor.

I shouldn't have come. I should have just stayed home tonight, the thoughts were now repeating endlessly in Meg Trotter's mind. She was cornered in the crowded living room, listening to Fischer recount his recent excursions into the world of online dating, a painful smile plastered on her lightly freckled face.

Her gray eyes glanced hopefully at Ned across the room as she started transmitting "Come rescue me!" messages via ESP. It didn't work. He just stood there talking to Schultz about analog sound systems or something.

Hey, you chose this field, Meg. You knew the social risks going in.

Meg looked down at her half full glass of water. Could she down this inconspicuously and then excuse herself to get another drink? She dismissed the idea. She didn't want to spend the evening making trips to the one bathroom shared by the twelve guests.

Okay then, fake a sudden illness it is.

A rare pause in Fischer's ear-bleeding agony of a story informed Meg that he was waiting for a response to the last thing that spewed from his bloated face. She replayed the last sentence, stored in the section of her memory that she reserved for things that she heard but had consciously ignored. He was still apparently talking about his attempts at online dating: "So I got plenty of responses initially, but once they see my picture they stop talking to me."

How the hell was she supposed to respond to that? She was frozen for a second or two—caught in the glare of the two beady eyes barely poking out between Fischer's large sweaty forehead and his bulbous sweaty cheeks. Frazzled dirty-brown whiskers covered his jaw and were threatening to overtake the rest of his face, which, in Meg's humble opinion, would have been an improvement.

"Well… that just goes to show you… women are as superficial as men," she said.

The thinly veiled insult glanced off of Fischer's dull head, apparently escaping his comprehension. He sucked in another lung-full of perfectly good air and prepared to contaminate it with the foul odor that lived in his mouth while laboring on to the second leg of his self-absorbed anecdote.

Luckily, the door opened and provided a potential distraction. Joe Tompkins and Dan Curtis walked in with a few sacks of groceries.

"We've got meat, and we've got beer!" Dan's booming voice proclaimed over cheers from the small crowd, "Joe, time to fire up that grill!"

Meg saw her chance and took it. She had only arrived ten minutes ago, but they might have been the worst ten minutes of her life. She jumped up from the secondhand couch with a halfhearted "excuse me Fischer" and crossed the room to the kitchen. Joe was sorting through the groceries and preparing to step out to the grill on the small balcony.

"You didn't forget the zucchini did you?" Meg called out as she approached Joe. A glance over her shoulder showed her that the slightly baffled Fischer was making movements to follow. Meg grabbed Joe's hand—hard—and pulled him toward the balcony. "I'm going to make sure you grill it right. It isn't like grilling meat you know."

Once the sliding glass door was safely closed behind them, Meg turned on Joe, "You didn't tell me Fischer would be here! I've been successfully avoiding him at work all week!"

"Do you think that *I* would be here if I had known he was coming?" Joe replied with wide eyes and the hint of a smile. "I thought you were going to bring a friend anyway."

"She couldn't make it. Besides, I wouldn't want to subject her to *that!*" Meg tilted her head toward the inside of the apartment. "He's still wearing that shirt that he wore to work! I didn't know they made fabric that thin. *It's almost see-through!*"

"Well, at least he doesn't know where *you* live." Joe countered. "I guess Ned invited Schultz and Schultz invited Fischer. I'm not going to let it ruin my evening. Wait until you see this table we built."

"Yeah, um, you're going to have to do better than some computerized poker table to make up for the last ten minutes." She poked him in the arm, "Did I mention his breath? I doubt he'll be hungry for one of those burgers. I'm pretty sure he ate a dead skunk on the way over here."

Joe shouldn't have been taking a drink of his beer. Meg smiled as he nearly choked at her last comment.

"Okay," Joe responded after regaining control of his respiratory system, "just follow my lead."

He opened the door, stepped inside, and called to Dan, "Hey man, can you come out here and take over? Turns out we got the wrong *kind* of zucchini—whatever that means. This one," he pointed to Meg, "is going to show me what we were supposed to buy. We'll be right back."

As they walked back down the sidewalk to Joe's mighty green Honda he turned to her and asked, "So, what are you in the mood for? Mexican? Thai? Seafood?"

"Italian," Meg laughed. "How about Italian?"

"Anyone else need something to drink?" Dan Curtis asked as he vacated his seat at the computerized poker table that Ned and Joe had built. Anyone could tell that these kids had yet to take on any real financial responsibilities. Dan took a long glance around the fairly new two-bedroom apartment as he stepped back into the kitchen: hardwood floors, new appliances, and a view of the downtown skyline. He hadn't ever lived like this when he was in his twenties.

No one looked up from the table in response to his inquiry. They were all too focused on the game at hand. Dan pulled another beer from the fridge and paused at the blue marble countertop. A large black charred spot caught his attention.

"Hey Ned, what's this on your counter?"

Ned was busy staring at the seven inch LCD screen recessed beneath smoked glass into the table in front of him, displaying his current status in the multi-player computer war game playing on the custom-built table. "What, the burn mark? Yeah, Joe thought that, since it was marble, it would be a good place to light the junk mail." Ned looked up with a grin, "We're pretty sure it'll come off."

Dan noticed the lighter next to the kitchen phone. "Remind me never to have you guys collect my mail if I go on vacation." He shook his head slowly and resumed his seat.

The once-ordinary poker table still had the same basic look and feel as it had a few months earlier when Ned had borrowed Dan's pickup to bring it home. Polyurethane-coated maple made up the base and ran along the edge of the octagonal top. Rich green felt still covered a portion of the surface and still sported the four images of each of the four suits in four of the eight corners. Oversized cup holders and chip trays sat at each potential player's position.

In the middle, however, in full manifestation of these kids' "savings accounts are for wimps" attitude sat a Plexiglas covered cutout that displayed an eight-sided section of the large plasma TV that was buried into the tabletop. This was in addition to the eight small LCDs at each side that allowed only the player seated there to view the screen. Each display was connected to the rack of small, networked computers in the table's pedestal.

The screen in the middle showed an overhead view of the entire game map. Battles could be seen from the high altitude view as their explosions lit up the ground. Each player's screen showed their territories in detail and allowed them to manage their resources and armies. The graphics left a lot to be desired, after all it was just a prototype, but the game play was top notch.

The prototype multi-player war game was one of many planned uses for the system. Ned had talked about a type of operating system he had architected—tailored especially to promote software development for the contained network of the table. All kinds of multi-user, multi-perspective applications were envisioned. In addition to gaming, Ned and Joe intended this to be the preferred system for typical household use. "Let's get families interacting around tables again," Joe had once said while explaining the product's vision to Dan.

Tonight had been the unveiling of the project to some people from the office. Dan was certainly impressed with the ingenuity, but remarked that the cost of such a system would be prohibitive for most working families. Ned had replied that that was true of the personal computer twenty years ago.

Ned had also complained that they hadn't gotten the full effect of the presentation since Joe had skipped out on the party. The guy had left with Meg for "the other kind of zucchini" hours ago. Dan didn't blame them; Schultz and Fischer had made it a tough evening to get through. Even Ned appeared to be tiring of their company.

Schultz was scrawny and twitchy. He employed a loud "kehhh" sound when speaking to more than one or two people (the result of him forcing air through his nose and mouth simultaneously in a kind of half coughing, half laughing manner). It was starting to grate on Dan's nerves.

He had had one-on-one conversations with Schultz and had observed that it was only when the guy was trying to entertain a group that he had trouble getting the words out. Dan braced himself as Schultz was obviously gearing up for another comedic assault.

"Yeah... kehhh... r-r-r-re... kehhh... remind me not... not to... kehhh..."

"Your turn, Schultz," Ned politely reminded. Schultz continued to labor through his comment *without* taking his turn at the game.

"Ri... right... kehhh... but remind me.... not... kehhh... not to a-a-ask you g-guys..."

"Come on, Schultz," Ned tried again, raising his voice, something Dan had rarely ever heard him do, "talk while you play. Talk *while* you play!"

"O-okay... kehhh... I know... kehhh... but remind me n-not to ask y-you guys to w-w-watch... kehhh..."

There was nothing for it. Dan watched in thin amusement as Ned resolved himself for the thousandth time that night to wait for completion of the pathetic joke attempt. Schultz of course made no movements to take his turn.

"...watch m-my mail when... kehhh... I'm on va... vacation either!" Schultz rewarded himself for the expertly timed one-liner with a series of "kehhh" sounding laughs. Fischer joined in. Schultz glanced from face to face in an endeavor to evoke reassuring smiles from his audience. The audience had abandoned its role in the exercise much earlier in the evening.

"That's great. We won't," Ned seemed to have regained control of his temper, "Now go."

"Okay…kehhh…where should I put my new armies?" Schultz started clicking the mouse on the shelf just below the table's surface.

"That's not what I meant, Schultz," Ned's voice remained cool and controlled. "Go. It's time for you and Fischer to leave. It's been real." With that Ned hit the switch that cut power to the table and the screens all went blank.

Dan watched as Ned got up, walked slowly to the door, and held it open for the pair. "Have a good weekend," he said with an insincere tone. "See ya Monday."

Fischer labored to his feet. "Why do I have to go? He's the one taking forever to take his turn!" The whining pitch of Fischer's voice was high and squeaky. His puffy lips curved and twitched in a disgusting fashion as if trying to mimic those of a pouting child.

"*You* weren't even invited," Ned's voice was still calm. "Schultz barely was. You two have already scared away forty percent of the other guests. Or hadn't you noticed?"

Dan smiled at the accuracy with which Ned spoke. He figured that the situational mathematics had been calculated in a subconscious background in Ned's mind. He was probably unaware that normal people would have just said "half of the guests." But Dan could easily see Ned objecting to that. *Half* was an exact mathematical term. It should be used with precision.

In fact, Dan had noticed that most everything Ned said or wrote had a degree of precision and efficiency. This kind of obsessive quirk usually accompanied a degree of social maladjustment. Not with Ned though, everybody liked Ned—other than the recent exception of Schultz and Fischer.

With an array of indignant grunts the two annoying guests gathered themselves and stomped out the door. Ned closed the door behind them and turned to Dan, "Never again… go ahead and call Joe. Tell him its okay for him and Meg to come back. Let's get a real game going."

"Well, we're trying to focus on the computer table right now. But the lawn mower is next." Joe Tompkins sipped the last of his now lukewarm coffee and set it back on the chessboard table. The deep orange décor of the coffeehouse was dimly lit and smelled of steamed milk and coffee beans.

"I think I've heard of automated lawn mowers before… I'm pretty sure you can already buy those," Meg Trotter replied as she studied the board, contemplating her next move. She wasn't much of a chess player… but neither was Joe. She was sure that if anyone halfway decent at the game had been watching them he or she would have been appalled at their mutual stupidity.

"Sure, other systems exist," Joe said with a slight hint of defensiveness in his tone, "but none of them have decent navigation systems. The mowers just drive around randomly within a defined boundary. Eventually they're supposed to hit all the grass. Most of those systems need a guy to pick the thing up and carry it to each section of the lawn. Some of the mowers even need to be chased down and switched off manually. And none of them can cross a sidewalk by themselves.

"We want to build something that's smarter, something that takes the human out of the picture completely. We don't want people to have to even *think* about their lawns being mowed."

Meg continued to listen as Joe laid out the concept: A small shed would house the mower. Moisture sensors on the shed would combine with weather data from the internet to feed the algorithm that would determine when it was a good time to mow. The mower robot would be battery powered and quiet enough for night use.

GPS, local relay stations, and onboard accelerometers would allow the mower to know its position in the yard (hopefully to the nearest centimeter). If needed, a series of waypoints could be buried in the yard to allow the mower to periodically correct any drift that had crept into its navigation solution. Armed with this information it could follow a preset path around the yard allowing for efficient mowing and could even cross boundaries like sidewalks or driveways.

Joe said that he eventually saw this branching into a more complete lawn care system with another robot that dispensed fertilizer acquired from a hopper attached to the recharging shed and maybe a sprinkler-bot that could replace costly lawn irrigation systems.

"Anyway," Joe concluded as his hand hovered from pawn to knight and back, "we could really use some help with the software development. *You* know those GPS and strap-down attitude solution algorithms backwards and forwards."

"Anyone ever tell you guys that you try to take on too much at a time?" Meg grinned. "Just implementing the applications that you two have envisioned at work would keep our team busy for another two or three years." She separated another forkful from the large piece of cheesecake they were sharing.

Okay, that was definitely the last bite, Meg, her mind scolded.

Joe finally decided to move his knight and captured one of Meg's bishops. Meg could tell that he expected the move to set off a bloody sequence that would mean the death of his knight, a couple of her pawns, and possibly a rook or two.

"Management won't authorize half of that stuff. Ned and I probably have another year or two to prove ourselves before they give us that kind of budget," he replied. "Your turn."

Meg decided to forego the knight-initiated bloodshed and instead moved her queen. "Check. I guess that I could probably lend a hand, but don't expect me to spend all of my free time working. I'm not like you guys."

Joe studied the board in front of him. "Um… I think that's check*mate*." He looked up at her, "That wasn't nice."

Meg peered over at the predicament that her opponent's king was in. She smiled, "Okay, check*mate* then."

Joe started to move the pieces back to their starting positions. His right hand abruptly stopped and shot into his pocket. It produced his vibrating cell phone. He took the brief call.

"That was Dan. He says Schultz and Fischer have cleared out. Want to check out this table now?"

"Sure. But don't cry if I beat you at that game too." She laughed and gathered her purse as Joe put the chess pieces back in their box.

"You won't," he said, "Ned and I know all the cheat codes."

18

Monday

Meg Trotter sat in another requirements review meeting trying desperately to keep her heavy eyelids open. Was this why she moved from Georgia to this frozen state?

The thought wasn't entirely fair. June in West Michigan was very beautiful. The snowfall in late April had been a bit much to take, but the weather had warmed up since then. There was even a beach within driving distance.

At least, it was what the locals *called* a beach. The perpetually cloudy sky took much of the enjoyment away from lying out on the sand. And while Lake Michigan was windy, the waves were nothing compared to those of the Atlantic. She missed Georgia.

The office that she had been working at in Atlanta had been closed down by corporate a few months back. Project mismanagement had caused an exodus of talent from the company and a departmental budget crisis at the same time. Eventually closing the office was the only move that made any sense.

So, in a pinch, Dan Curtis had helped Meg find contract work in the aerospace field in Kalamazoo. But while she was an avionics software developer with more than eight years experience, she found herself stuck in a bottomless abyss of requirements review meetings. This was just another company trying to make their way through the certification process by brute force. The requirements were crap, but management was applying considerable pressure to "show progress" and pass the reviews.

She had been dismissed when she suggested buying document development and management software from *Dyer Consulting Services*. She had just recently started talking to Ned Dyer again via email. It sounded like he was doing really well—nice house, profitable business, fiancée...

She still wished Ned hadn't left when he did though. Their design team had been forced to scramble to fill the hole. Joe had to take over project documentation management—and was pushed out of the actual software development and hardware design that he loved. Meg had watched as Joe became much more frustrated at work and less bearable to be around outside of work.

She had intended to keep in touch with him, but hadn't. Their friendship was just another casualty of the layoff. At least *Joe* had gotten away from Schultz and Fischer though. Dan and Meg were still working with them. Schultz was even in all of the same review meetings as Meg. It really was a fairly small industry after all.

She had originally hoped to help the new company streamline their product development and certification efforts when she had taken the job. Now she realized that it wasn't worth the battle. Instead, she had her résumé newly polished and available online.

Meg was sometimes tempted just to move back home and find a job when she got there. She could certainly afford a few months off. But the thought of slowing her rate of savings terrified her. She was making very good money at this job, and had become somewhat addicted to amassing wealth. But this wasn't out of greed. She just never felt secure. She was always sure that something bad was just about to happen. The money was her safeguard against whatever this would be.

But even with the pay, more and more Meg had started to question her decision to go into the industry she was in. She had always been a problem solver, and really felt that she was able to do anything she worked at. With her natural aptitude toward math and science, everyone had always told her that she should be an engineer. What they didn't tell her was that she was dooming herself to a life of tedium in the process.

The last couple of years it seemed that all she did was study minutia. She wondered if the time and effort she spent learning the newest development environment or performance monitoring software could instead be spent learning culture—filling the space with art or literature or music, the things that actually added richness to one's spirit, the things that actually enhanced one's soul.

Meg was beginning to feel as if she was missing her chance to leave her mark. She certainly wasn't changing the world one requirements review at a time.

The meeting finally progressed through the last of the horrible requirements and pulled Meg away from her thoughts. The review packet was passed to her for a signature that would indicate that she agreed that the contents were up to the standards the company had set forth.

She brushed her brownish-red hair out of her face and signed her name. She had given up the battle for the integrity of that signature two months before. She was sick of arguing with Schultz about the way things should be.

There's no way they'll pass an FAA audit, she told herself for the thousandth time. But she wasn't totally convinced of that. Things like this got overlooked quite often.

Monday afternoon eventually gave way to Monday evening. Meg finished playing Xbox online at about seven (she had destroyed Ned at Halo 3—he had tried to make the excuse that his controller was broken). After that she was out the door with her bike. She'd been riding for about two hours a night when the weather was dry enough. At least her boring new life had allowed her to drop those eight pesky pounds that had snuck up on her in the past couple of years. She was glad about that since she was going home for her thirtieth birthday in a few weeks and wanted to look good.

The next morning Meg was awoken early and repetitively by a loud beep that sounded every three minutes. It echoed from the living room of her one-bedroom apartment. She twisted in her sheets and peered at the green LED numbers displayed on her alarm clock. Waking reality mixed a bit with the fragments of a soon forgotten dream as she stared—confused as to what the numbers could mean. "5:13," the clock stared back.

Meg had forgotten what had woken her as she won her struggle to comprehend the numbers. *It's too early… go back to sleep, Meg.* Another loud beep sounded from the living room. She recognized it as her cell phone. She didn't really get many calls, so she usually left it on all the time. She wanted to just ignore it now, but realized that she had to at least turn it off to stop the beeping.

She swung her legs over the edge of her mattress and walked with bare feet across the worn carpet to her bland living room. Her purse hung on one of the two empty kitchen chairs propped up against the lonely drop-leaf table. She retrieved the offending phone, flipped it open and glanced at the screen to determine what was so important as to rouse her from a comfortable sleep. She had a new text message from Ned. She swore.

Without checking the contents of the message she tossed the phone onto her sofa and shuffled back into the bedroom. Ned could wait. She was entitled to a good hour and a half more of sleep.

Unfortunately, sleep didn't return. There was something nagging at her mind about the last time she had seen Ned three years before. A ten-minute battle ended with Meg once again staggering out to her living room in her pajamas. She flipped the phone open again and browsed to the unread message.

"911**Pizza Time Everybody!**911" it read. A vague recollection tried to assert itself in her brain. This was supposed to mean something.

What was it again?

Her head jerked up as she remembered. Half an hour later she was showered, dressed, packed, and headed to Dan's apartment—cell phone at her ear.

"Come on, Dan… pick up the phone," she said to herself, "We need to hurry."

19

Three Years Ago…

Joe Tompkins had abandoned his jacket (a light windbreaker) for the season a month before. He still smiled at the native Georgians that donned full winter coats at fifty degrees. And should it actually snow in the winter (or should the weathermen predict a chance of snow) it seemed like the city would virtually shut down. He had seen it snow only once in the two winters he'd lived there, and that light overnight dusting had evaporated by mid-morning.

The daily highs were into the low seventies in Atlanta's late April but most of the townies still wore some form of outer covering. Joe shook his head with an unyielding disbelief as he looked out the window of his mighty Honda at the pedestrians, imagining the horror they'd experience if they ever moved to the Midwest. They had no idea what cold actually was.

Joe parked his car near the university where he and Ned had taken classes during their internships the summer before they had graduated. They had both then accepted full time jobs at the same company and had been with the aerospace firm for almost three years now.

He was a bit early for dinner, so he decided to take a walk through campus. The school was nestled among the rolling Italianesque hills on the east side of Atlanta. Among the many magnolia and evergreen trees, buildings adorned with marble trim, red-tile roofs, and tall archways towered impressively above the foot paths that zigzagged through campus. Joe took in the aura of secluded elegance as he wandered the sidewalks admiring the well-tended landscape.

He checked the time as he completed a loop through campus. He then made his way to the pizza place across the street. It had been Ned and Joe's favorite hangout during their internship. Joe was mildly curious as to why Ned had insisted that the team meet for dinner. Ned had been acting strange and secretive the last couple of weeks. Tonight he was apparently going to make a "big announcement."

Joe strolled up the brick steps that led up to the outdoor patio of the pizza joint. Meg Trotter was already seated at one of the outdoor wooden tables under the bright red awning. She was sipping a glass of water and tearing through the latest paperback action-packed bestseller. A lemon wedge sat on the table in front of her. Joe smiled. He and Meg shared the conviction that the seldom-washed fruit had no business floating in their beverages.

Classifying his relationship with this woman had become more difficult in recent months. She was a coworker and on the same development team, and she was certainly a *friend*. But lately the two of them had been spending quite a bit of time together outside of work. They hadn't ever actually *talked* about it, but Joe figured that it was safe to say that they were, in fact, dating.

Meg gave him a wide smile as he arrived at the table and sat down. "Hey. Where's Ned? Didn't he ride with you?" she asked.

"Dan was giving him a ride. They were finishing up a design meeting— said that they might be a few minutes late. Ned seemed really intent on finishing the design tonight," Joe replied.

"Well, we might as well get comfortable then. Let's order some breadsticks with that spinach and artichoke dip."

Joe suppressed his urge to make a face.

Some forty minutes later Ned Dyer and Dan Curtis arrived with apologies and four software design documents, hot off the presses. This was apparently going to be a working dinner. They did manage to order drinks and pizzas before Ned launched into an enthusiastic presentation of the finer details of the new software design.

Ned had completed a staggering amount of work in the last couple of weeks. It seemed as if something had lit a fire under him.

Finally when Ned's presentation drew to an end, Joe verbalized the thought that was pacing through the other three minds. "This all looks great, Ned, but why can't this wait until tomorrow at the office?"

Ned finished chewing his latest bite of pizza. His face took on a grave and sunken look—and then a weak smile. "Well, because tomorrow is my last day. I start a new job in southern Illinois on Monday."

The words punched Joe in the face. He sat stunned.

Ned continued, "I just wanted to let you three know that these last two years have been the best in my life and that it has been a privilege and an honor to work on this team."

Joe didn't say much during the rest of the meal. He listened as Ned answered questions about the "great opportunity" he had been presented and that he just missed the Midwest and was ready to go back. It all rang false to

Joe though. He knew Ned better than anyone. Ned was the one driving the plans for them to start a side business selling some of their hobby projects. Ned was the one gunning for a management position within the next couple of years. Ned was the one who kept talking about how much he loved living in Atlanta. He had *never* mentioned wanting to move back to Illinois.

Joe decided to wait for the drive back to the apartment to ask his questions.

The evening wound down with Dan and Meg giving Ned warm congratulations and reminiscing and saying how much he'd be missed. Ned was, as ever, the gracious social participant: accepting and dispensing praise with poise, promising to keep in touch, wishing the team well.

As they prepared to disband for the evening though, Ned's carefully polished demeanor seemed to fade. Joe could detect a subtle nervous tone entering Ned's voice.

"Thanks again for coming. We should get together like this again sometime…for a reunion next time I'm in town." Ned's smile lightened and his voice softened to a whisper, "Promise me you guys will meet me here again if I set it up. Meet me here at midnight."

This puzzled the rest of the team, but they each seemed to notice the sudden seriousness in Ned's voice.

"You got it, Ned," Meg responded for the group, "Of course we'll meet you next time you're in town."

With that, the party left a large tip and broke up. Ned and Joe walked to Joe's Honda under the darkening April sky. Joe turned and glanced at the illuminated sign that hung above the restaurant.

"Everybody's Pizza" the red letters glowed.

Ned Dyer stared out the window of his roommate's mighty Honda at downtown Atlanta's illuminating streetlights. Joe had barely spoken since the announcement and was now driving back in silence. As much as it pained Ned to keep the silence unbroken, he knew that any attempt to explain would invite questions that didn't have satisfying answers.

Ned knew that he couldn't risk letting *even* his oldest friend into his confidence about the threat he had received two weeks prior. *Joe is in danger too,* he told himself. The threat had warned against telling *anyone*. Ned still had no idea who these people were or how they gathered their information. He would have to be very careful from now on.

He had secured the new job immediately—hired as a contractor through a consulting company he had recently set up. The plan had been for the consulting company to evolve into a side business for him and Joe. Now it functioned as a convenient way for Ned to keep more of his pay without sharing a cut with a contract house. It also allowed him greater access to tax breaks available to small businesses.

The fact that the job was in Illinois satisfied the threat's requirement that he get out of Georgia. The threat had also required that no one suspect his motives. Most southerners had no idea of the size of Ned's home state. Joe and Ned had both tired of attempting to explain that the terms "Chicago" and "Illinois" were not interchangeable. The misconception aided Ned's attempt to sell the reason for his departure as homesickness. No one in Atlanta had realized that his new job was a good four-hour drive from where he grew up.

"Going back to Chicago, eh?" Ned's boss had said when Ned told him the location of his new job. Ned had never even lived within one hundred miles of Chicago—and his new job was, in reality, just about halfway between Atlanta and Chicago.

"Yep, all my family is up in the area," Ned had replied.

Of course, *Joe* would know that the homesickness excuse was flat. They had grown up in the same town. Luckily it appeared that Joe was resolutely pursuing a campaign of silence. It made things easier.

But then Joe abandoned the campaign and spoke, his voice thick with betrayal, "So, you realize that by not giving a two-weeks notice, you can never be hired by any other division in the entire corporation, right? They red-flag you for a stunt like that."

Ned now had to face a decision whether to admit to Joe that he had, in fact, given his notice but had asked that management not tell anyone, or to lie and say that everything happened so suddenly that he didn't have a choice but to leave without notice. The lie might spare Joe's feelings a bit by allowing him to believe that Ned hadn't kept a secret of this magnitude from him for so long.

"I did give two-weeks notice, Joe. Two weeks ago." Ned figured that the truth would aid his other goal of inserting some distance in their friendship.

Joe's slamming on the brakes in response to this was unexpected and Ned struggled to brace himself as the Honda swerved to the side of the road.

"Why didn't you tell me!?" Joe demanded, "Why did you wait until the night before you left!?"

A deep breath filled Ned's lungs as he prepared to launch into the speech that he'd been perfecting over the last two weeks. It was, without a doubt, the most difficult thing he had to endure in the process of leaving his life behind. He had to end this decade long friendship.

"BECAUSE I NEED SOME SPACE!" Ned exploded back at his friend, "Do you have any idea how sick I am of you following me around!? It's just *so* constant! You're always *right* there! I'm doing it to get away from *you!*"

The pain reflected in Joe's eyes stabbed at Ned, threatening to puncture his resolve to continue the lie. Joe's voice was softer now. He had abandoned his harsh tone and adopted a puzzled and hurt expression. "You've never said anything. I thought you wanted us to start a business... I thought we were a team... What about all of our plans?"

"Keep the bloody computer table!" Ned shouted. His recent affection for British comedies was starting to introduce some new words into his vocabulary. "I'm taking the exercise bike."

"Ned... what's going on? Where is this coming from? Is there something wrong?"

"Yeah, it's getting late and I've got to pack. The movers are coming tomorrow afternoon. Can we *please* get moving?"

In apparent defeat, Joe pulled back out onto the street and drove the car the rest of the way back to the apartment. They barely exchanged any more words that night or the next morning at work or at Ned's big going-away lunch. Ned slipped out of the building in the early afternoon, unannounced and undetected. He and his belongings were gone before Joe got home from work.

20

Meg Trotter pulled into the apartment complex's vast parking lot. A small pond and fountain were in the center of the maze of asphalt and attracted most of the Canadian geese that lived on the Northern Hemisphere—evidenced by the goose droppings scattered over the sidewalks, cars, and long rows of identical mailboxes.

She had never actually been to Dan Curtis' apartment before, so Meg's new orange Mustang was inching around the complex looking for Building J. The car had been an early birthday present to herself. Meg figured that the six-figure yearly contractor rate she was now earning allowed her an occasional extravagance (not to mention the fact that she was nearing thirty, single, and could count the number of friends she had in Michigan on half-a-finger).

Dan still hadn't answered his phone. It was probably turned off. As she searched for his building, Meg tried again to reach him with no luck. She lowered the phone and read Ned's text message again: "911**Pizza Time Everybody!**911"

Meg thought about the last time she had seen Ned three years prior. It was a Friday in April, Ned's last day of work. They had ridden together to his going-away lunch. Ned had oddly insisted that it be just the two of them. He had said that he needed to talk with her.

"Ok, Ned, what is it that you wanted to talk about?" she'd asked, mildly curious—especially after his unexpected announcement the night before at Everybody's Pizza.

"Well, I'm not sure if Joe and Dan really understood last night," Ned replied, "I'm serious about getting back together if I set it up."

Meg was confused by Ned's insistence on the matter. "Right, Ned, we'll get together for pizza at midnight… I think we all understood that."

Ned's expression was firm as he drove the car toward downtown Atlanta's Underground. He had selected a fifties style burger joint as the location of his last lunch while employed at the aerospace company. Meg remembered how Ned had always enjoyed the singing wait staff. Last time they had been there, the staff had broken out into a rousing rendition of *My Kind of Town*, Sinatra's tribute to Chicago. Meg was pretty sure she remembered that that was Ned's hometown.

She sensed hesitation in Ned's voice as he continued the conversation.

"I just need to know that if I ask, you'll all meet me there—no matter what. Meg, I need you to make sure everyone shows up."

"Ned, what are you talking about?" her confusion turned to concern as he kept pressing the point, "Is there something I need to know?"

The maroon sedan pulled into a spot in the parking garage and stopped. Ned turned to face Meg. His succinct and serious tone told her that she wouldn't be getting any more information from him.

"Just promise me that you'll make sure everyone is there… I may need to see some friendly faces."

"Okay, Ned, I promise," Meg still held her concern, but realized that Ned had an implied desire for a degree of secrecy. She understood that she was not to repeat this conversation (as brief and vague as it was) to anyone.

"Make sure Joe is okay too… the news last night hit him pretty hard."

With that they had exited the car and attended the party. It had been a year and a half later when she had heard from Ned again. They had been emailing off and on ever since.

Apartment Building J now loomed ahead and Meg refocused her mind on the task at hand.

At just after six in the morning, most of the parking spots still housed residents' vehicles. The Mustang found the nearest spot to park, still a good distance from Dan's building. Meg hopped out and walked briskly up to the front door.

She buzzed the appropriate doorbell and waited for a reply. None came. She pressed the buzzer again.

"Well good morning!"

The nasally voice startled Meg from behind. She spun and found herself facing Schultz, her scrawny coworker. His bright red jogging shorts clashed with a loose orange muscle shirt and a red, yellow, and blue headband. The outfit appeared to be a random mixture of workout apparel from the last three decades.

Lovely.

"Schultz, what are you doing here?"

"Well… kehhh… I-I've got to… kehhh… keep my physique in top… kehhh… sh-shape. P-power walking is th-the… kehhh… key!"

"But why are you *here*, Schultz—at this apartment?"

"D-didn't D-Dan tell you… kehhh? We live in the same building! You need me to… kehhh… l-let you in?"

"Uh… okay," Meg was hesitant to accept help from this perspiring personification of personal and professional incompetence, but she figured that Dan would be more likely to respond if someone were banging on the door of his apartment.

Schultz reached into the front of his shirt and pulled out the lanyard that held his building key. Instead of just taking the lanyard off or removing the key from its clip, he chose to bend down awkwardly in order to insert the key into the waist-high keyhole. Meg counted silently as twenty-three seconds ticked by before the lock finally clicked open. Schultz held the door open triumphantly and motioned her inside.

"Thanks, Schultz," Meg enunciated with forced politeness as she entered the building. "Oh, and could you tell management that Dan and I won't be in today?"

Dan Curtis' bedroom was pitch black—no thanks to the cheap light gray mini-blinds that had come with the apartment. One of Dan's most firmly held beliefs was that one shouldn't be able to catch even a glimpse of light from the outside world from inside a bedroom. So, he had covered the bedroom windows with cardboard salvaged from some moving boxes and attached it to the wall with duct tape around the edges. Not the most stylish solution to the problem, but it *was* practical.

After a few beers Dan might have remarked that his solution to the problem of the bedroom window was a microcosm of his approach to all of life's problems: functionality before flashiness. This philosophy had served him well as a contract software engineer. It was a rare occasion that he was tasked to build an application from scratch, so an abundance of creativity and style was normally unnecessary. Usually he was just brought in to fix some other engineer's (or team of engineers') barely functioning code. The first step was always the same: strip the program down to its core functionality—no pretty buttons—no flavor-of-the-month coding techniques—no fluff.

Of course, the last three months had been spent wading through an enormous sea of code review meetings. Dan hated being forced to "review" poorly written code developed by poorly skilled engineers. But this job was just a safe place to sit while he waited for the music to start again in the game of *Musical Chairs* that he called his career.

Dan buried his head back into his pillows and shifted his position on the bed, intending to drift back off into a comfortable doze, always sweetest in the hour or two before he had to wake. The annoying buzzing of his doorbell had ceased. An enchanting silence blanketed the cool dark room.

His mind was tired and found sleep again easily. Dan made sure to keep himself mentally exhausted most days, trying never to be alone and sedentary with his thoughts. Inevitably, they would dwell on a part of his life that was now over. And regret made a lousy companion.

Dreams began to quickly form, and Dan was thankful as he always was for a break from the real world. More and more he had recently found himself convinced that his dreams were reality, more and more willing to accept strange fantasy as a replacement for the stark and unyielding world around him. Dreaming was usually a pleasant escape, one without the ill effects of the alcohol.

But sometimes, the dreams were far worse than the reality. Sometimes, the dreams forced him to relive what he was most eager to forget.

This morning was to be one of those times.

As he slept, random images seeped out of Dan's subconscious and began to form pictures around him. He was floating through a long white hallway, brightly lit. He was weightless and free, but being pulled somehow toward the end of the hall. There were shadows there. Figures, silhouettes that he couldn't quite make out.

He drew nearer. Dan could now see that it was a woman… and two children. They were blurry and out of focus. But he knew who they were. He knew their faces better than his own.

Dread. Guilt. The enchantment of his sleep was now broken, invaded by the familiar and unwelcome emotions that always accompanied this dream.

The same thing always happened next. He fought to find an escape. But he couldn't stop it. He could never stop it…

The silence of Dan's bedroom was shattered by a sudden and persistent pounding on the front door. It echoed painfully in his head, saving him from the recurring nightmare, reminding him again of the practical solution he had come up with to his boredom and loneliness the night before. He had kept himself company with network television's horrible excuse for a summer lineup and half a bottle of Jack Daniels. Sure, it wasn't the prettiest solution to the problem, but it was simple. And it was effective. And it wasn't as if he had a problem.

The pounding on the door continued incessantly. Dan groaned and pulled himself out of the bed and onto his feet, shaking his head to clear away the last remnants of panic from the dream. He grabbed a discarded t-shirt from the floor and stumbled out of the bedroom. The tall counter that separated his living room from the kitchenette was piled high with empty cans, bottles, and fast food containers. The garbage had been overflowing for a solid week. Dan let out a slow breath. At thirty-seven he was still living like a college kid. It was probably time to grow up a bit.

More knocking on the front door reminded Dan why he had gotten up. He shuffled over to attend to the bothersome visitor. A check through the peephole revealed an impatient-looking Meg Trotter.

Dan didn't know what she was doing there. And he didn't have any idea what she could possibly be wanting at that particular hour.

As her metallic orange Mustang crossed the state line into Indiana, Meg Trotter finally convinced herself that she needed to try to call Joe Tompkins. The Tuesday morning sun had risen a couple of hours before, but it was only 7:30 in Illinois. Still a tad early for a phone call, but this was important.

It had taken the better part of half an hour to convince Dan Curtis to join her in a mid-week trip from Michigan to Georgia to fulfill some offhand promise made to an old coworker three years prior. Meg suspected that the only reason she had been able to get him to come along was that he had been dreading finishing out the long workweek as much as she had been.

Meg had also made several concessions in bartering for his company on her voyage: they would take *her* car, she would pay for gas, she would let him sleep when he wanted, she would let him drive when he wanted, and they wouldn't come back until the weekend.

Missing four days of work and paying for the trip would eat into her savings for the month. This fact brought with it some anxiety. Meg resolved herself to a month of peanut butter and macaroni to atone for the extravagance.

True to their agreement, Dan was sprawled out in the Mustang's passenger seat, eyes closed, breathing rhythmically, right arm draped across his face. Meg could not imagine how the six-foot-two black man was able to sleep in that position, but she suspected that the various empty beer cans and liquor bottles in his apartment might have had something to do with it.

When awake, Dan had bright, friendly eyes and usually wore a wide smile. At least, when Meg had known him in Atlanta he had usually worn a smile. He had left for work in Arizona at another division of the corporation a couple of years back and had just moved to Kalamazoo a few months before Meg had. She wasn't sure if the change in his demeanor had been gradual over the last couple of years or if it had come all at once, but Dan was certainly no longer the fun-loving friendly guy that she had known. He barely spoke to her at work—he no longer tried to organize office get-togethers outside of the office—he seemed resigned to a career of just sitting through reviews, resigned to not creating anything anymore.

Joe had once told her that he had gone through a messy divorce some years back and that he had a couple of kids that he never got to see. He had also warned Meg against ever bringing it up. Dan had briefly mentioned it to Joe at drinks one night after work—apparently it had been his daughter's sixth birthday. Joe had tried to ask more questions at the time but had been waved off. Joe told Meg that he had brought it up again on a different occasion and that Dan had reacted poorly—that was all she knew on the matter. And she had no intention of prying.

The phone call attempt went directly to Joe's voicemail. Meg was tiring of these men that turned their cell phones off at night. The deadpan tone of Joe's familiar outgoing message straddled the border between his bone-dry sarcastic wit and a serious disdain for all human life.

"You've reached the voicemail of Joe Tompkins. If you have reached this number by mistake or if you are trying to sell me something, do us both a favor and hang up now. If you insist on leaving a message, it should be between ten and forty seconds in length. Do *not* just leave your name and tell me to call you back, my caller ID already provides me with this information. State a brief *reason* for the call.

"Conversely, do *not* leave a long and rambling multiple minute message. The purpose of this technology is not to provide a substitute for the actual conversation you wish to have with me, it is just to inform me of your wish to converse. Adherence to these rules will substantially increase your chances of receiving a return call. *BEEP!*"

Meg flipped her phone closed without leaving Joe a message. Theirs was a complicated friendship—it had toyed with romantic overtones for a long while, until Joe had flatly rejected any potential romance a few months after his roommate Ned had moved back to Illinois. Meg had been sure she hadn't misread his original intentions. It was just as if something had suddenly changed his mind about her. Their friendship had been unsteady ever since. Strangely, however, it had been good to hear Joe's voice, the first time in the months since their office closed, even if it *was* just an old recorded message.

Meg decided to quickly try Ned's cell phone for the third time that morning only to get the same result: instant voicemail. She hadn't left a message for him earlier and decided against it again. The brief and cryptic nature of his text message coupled with his odd and secretive insistence that she round up the old team had told her that he was concerned about talking too plainly and communicating too much via electronic means.

She set the phone in the cup holder next to her empty French vanilla gas station cappuccino. Questions still swirled around in her head about this trip south. Chiefly: *What kind of trouble has Ned gotten himself into?* and *What was their old design team supposed to be able to do about it?*

Maybe Ned really did just want to meet for pizza…

The West Michigan forests had given way to Northern Indiana's rolling fields of corn next to the interstate that Meg's car cruised down at seventy miles per hour. They expected to arrive in Atlanta several hours before the midnight rendezvous, barring any unforeseen complications.

However, clinging to the underside of the Mustang's orange rear bumper, a small electronic unforeseen complication was blinking a small blue LED and radioing the car's location to the two men following Meg Trotter's vehicle—a comfortable five miles behind.

21

The air conditioning hadn't been on when they arrived at the safe house in Kentucky. But, since it was early in the morning, no one had really noticed. Amy was now waiting for Sue to get done in the shower so she could help her attend to the various scrapes and scratches from her hellish night. Tom was already dead asleep—still in his mud-caked clothes on top of the blankets of the inexpensive twin mattress that occupied one of the two small bedrooms.

Amy, however, was wide awake—she had never been shot at before and coming to grips with the events of the past few hours had proved a better stimulant than caffeine. She had been longing for some more excitement in her life—but this was just too much. What were they supposed to do now? She had class in a few hours and was scheduled to work that evening. Severe doubts that she would make either appointment took root in her mind.

Amy didn't know if she and Tom were now fugitives. This Ned guy didn't seem to have much of a plan beyond making sure everyone survived the night. She and Tom would have survived the night just fine if they hadn't been roped into Ned's mess.

She scolded herself for being so selfish. They had very likely saved a woman's life. That was worth the intrusion upon hers. Hopefully things would be back to normal in a day or two.

Two hours later, Sue had been taken care of and was asleep. Amy was taking the first watch—sitting on the lumpy sofa watching the thirteen-inch TV that only got four fuzzy local channels. Her mind was now starting to drift as the excitement of the previous night slowly gave way to fatigue.

The growing stuffiness in the house due to the rising heat of the day woke Amy a little after ten. Initially she was angry with herself for dozing, but no harm seemed to have come from it. The house still seemed secure, still seemed quiet.

She calculated that Tom had been asleep for a good five hours at that point. That meant that it was his turn to keep watch. She turned on the A/C on her way to his room. Tom was still in the exact same position, lying on his stomach on top of the blankets. She lightly kicked one of his still shoe-clad feet to wake him.

He shot up immediately—apparently he had been on his guard even through the deep sleep. "Is everything alright?" he asked in a hurried but tired voice.

"Yeah, I just need to sleep now. You don't mind staying awake do ya?"

A minute later she climbed into the third bed and was out again despite the lingering stuffiness of the house. Much needed and dreamless sleep engulfed her as late morning progressed to early afternoon.

The air was now nice and cool—so much so that Amy had pulled the covers over her to keep warm. She was enjoying the perfect sleeping conditions. Even though the day outside was bright and sunny, the bedroom was almost completely dark.

The pleasant environment, however, made her abrupt waking all the more unpleasant. Her slumber was interrupted when a hand was placed firmly over her mouth. Amy's eyes shot open and locked onto Tom's face. His other hand was giving her the signal to be quiet. She nodded to signify her understanding. He removed the hand from her mouth.

"What is it?" she whispered.

"They've found us. A car just pulled into the driveway. We've got to go, *now*." Tom whispered back. "You and Sue are going out the back. I'm going to try to get the SUV out of the garage. If I can, I'll meet you on the street behind this one. If I'm not there, find somewhere safe and call the police."

"No!" Amy's whisper was now fierce, "just come with us. Forget the car!"

"We need that thing if we're going to get away–" Tom and Amy froze at the sound of the garage door opening. Their safe house had been breached. Amy could now feel her heart beating. How had they known the code? She figured that Ned must have been forced to give them up.

Sue rushed into the bedroom; she'd apparently been awake for a while. She now wore a jogging suit and tennis shoes taken from the safe house closet. He eyes were full of the same terror Amy had seen the night before. "He's in the *garage!*" she hissed.

Tom was on his feet immediately, "You two, out the back! Now!" Amy grabbed her shoes and followed Tom out of the room. She watched as he picked up the BB gun and made his way to the door that led to the garage. "Go now!" he shouted under his breath, "I'll hold him off with this!"

Amy didn't like the plan, but she didn't have much time to argue, Sue was still shaken from the night before. Amy needed to make sure she made it out. It was important to protect Sue.

Or was it?

An unraveling thread of doubt began to cause Amy to question whether this was even someone *worth* protecting. *Sue* had somehow gotten herself wrapped up in this business. Amy and Tom had just been caught up in it trying to do the right thing. No one would have been chasing them if it weren't for her.

Honestly, they really didn't know anything about her…and from what Amy could tell, this Ned guy hadn't known her that long either. In fact according to Ned's video, it had been well *after* Ned had received the threat to his life that he had met this woman.

Amy turned and stared Sue in the eyes as they approached the sliding glass door that led out the back of the house. "It's you they're after," an indignant anger was now growing in Amy's chest, her voice sharpened, "not Tom and me!"

Tom spun around from his perch at the door to the garage. "Amy! What are you doing!? Get out of here!"

She turned toward him, "Tom, has she been alone at all since you woke up?"

"What? Um… yeah when I was in the shower, I guess. Will you just get out of here!?"

Amy surprised herself as she turned on Sue. Her small hands reached out and grabbed the woman's throat. Amy was screaming now, "You led them here! You gave them the code to the garage!" She was now sure that the look reflected in Sue's eyes wasn't terror after all. It was guilt.

Tom had abandoned his whisper also, "Amy! Stop it now! *Get out of the house!*"

"Tom! She's part of this! She led them here!" Amy shouted as she kept her hands locked around Sue's neck. Amy wasn't ready for the swift knee to her stomach. She doubled over as Sue shoved her to the ground, landing hard on the thinly carpeted concrete floor, coughing, and watching Sue tear out of the backdoor.

"Amy!" Tom's voice was strained and panicked, "Get out of here!"

Amy turned over and watched as Tom unlocked the deadbolt, flung open the door, leveled the pump-action BB gun at the unseen intruder, and starting firing as rapidly as the gun allowed, yelling the entire time. Amy could tell that Tom was hitting his mark from the man's startled screams that echoed from the garage.

She rolled back over, struggled to her feet, and stumbled out the sliding glass door into the stifling heat. Halfway across the backyard a noise from the house—a gunshot—from a *real* gun—stopped her in her tracks.

22

Two Years Ago…

It was a tough Saturday. Not that *any* Saturday spent working at the Pretzel Hut in the local mall was very much fun, but this one was worse. Sue Bishop knew that several friends from her high school class were graduating from the local university that day.

It had been her plan too. But her father had gotten laid off when the factory he worked in was closed. The money that had been set aside for her schooling was now needed to pay the mortgage. She was even working two jobs to help out. She had taken a few night classes at the community college, but one semester off had turned into five—the extra hours at work were needed too badly to give up.

Her parents had insisted that she cut back at work and continue with her schooling, but Sue knew they needed the help, at least until her father found decent work again. Everyone said that the local economy was improving everyday. As soon as that translated into more jobs Sue's life would be back on track.

Although that was hard to keep in mind as she dealt with yet another rude pretzel patron on the day she should have been wearing a cap and gown. In contrast she wore a stupid paper hat and bright orange apron with a smiling cartoon pretzel on the front. She had planned on going into accounting. Instead she had a cash register with an automatic coin dispenser. They couldn't even count on her to count out change.

The carbs and nacho cheese in her break time meal did little to help her self esteem. The night before she had counted her fifteenth pound gained since starting this job a year ago. Sue blinked back the tears as she sat alone in a plastic chair in the mall's food court. *I'm just ready for this day to be over,* she thought to herself.

She began to lose the battle with her tears as they started to descend her face. She looked around for a napkin with no luck. Her hands attempted to compensate as she brushed the moisture from her cheeks.

"Here, would this help?"

The voice startled her. She looked up to see a man in his early forties holding out a short stack of napkins from the pizza place across the food court.

"Thank you," she said softly and accepted the gift. "I'm really sorry; I don't know what's gotten into me today."

He sat down in another plastic chair and scooted up to the table. "Today was supposed to be your graduation day… right Sue?"

Her head shot up and she stared at his face—receding hairline, short mustache, unkempt eyebrows… there was no recognition. She had never seen this man before.

"How did you know my name?!" she demanded.

"I know a lot about you, Sue," the man replied. "I know that you aspire to obtain an accounting degree and get a better job than this." He used his index finger to lift her paper hat that was sitting on the table. "I know that your father needs a good job too. I also know that I can provide those things."

"Who are you?" she asked, her voice revealing skepticism and distrust.

"You can call me Gilmore," he replied in a slick style that reminded Sue of a telemarketer. "And there's someone else I'd like you to meet." He produced a file folder, opened it, and showed her a picture inside. It was of a smiling man in a tie. It looked like a blown up ID badge photo.

"This is Ned Dyer," Gilmore continued. "I think that the two of you would really hit it off."

23

Amy McKay was a statue near the back of the small sunlit backyard, frozen by the gunshot she'd just heard from the house behind her. Wooden privacy fences walled off the three yards adjacent to that of the safe house. There was, however, an opening to the yard cattycorner to that one—a gap that allowed access to the light green electrical boxes that stuck up out of the ground.

Amy's mind swam in an ocean of confusion and panic. She didn't understand why this was happening to her. She had helped rescue a woman who had ended up betraying them. She had been shot at and had fled the state. And now she was meant to be running through some random subdivision somewhere in Kentucky from a man with a gun that had in all probability just shot Tom. And to top it all off, her body was now refusing to move.

Come on Amy, you have to get out of here! she pleaded with herself, *Move your feet... one in front of the other.*

Slowly her legs began to obey and she crept slowly toward the opening to the next yard.

"AMY! RUN!!"

Tom's shout from the house startled her. She glanced back and saw a dim image through the sliding glass door: a man with a gun advancing on him. Relief mixed with resolve. It seemed that the man had no intention of killing Tom—at least not yet. That meant that it was up to her to save him. But she first needed something of value to trade.

The plan solidified in Amy's mind. She briefly saw the gunman in the house turn toward her, but she was off running before he could react to her presence. On the other side of the electrical boxes, three large fir trees stood blocking the passage into the next yard. Amy's hands protected her face as she darted though the prickly, sap-soaked branches.

She emerged from the sticky barricade and stopped. She was looking for any sign that would show her the direction Sue had gone. There wasn't any. Amy continued jogging toward the street that stretched in front of the gray two-story house that now loomed in front of her.

The chase brought memories of her childhood to mind. She had grown up in a similar neighborhood and summer nights had been spent playing *Kick the Can* with all the kids on the block. Of course, they had usually used a soccer ball in lieu of an actual can as it was much more comfortable to kick. The games would last for hours, the field of play spanning multiple yards. It was one of her fondest memories.

Amy longed for the carefree spirit of those days to return. There was nothing fun about being chased by men with guns. She wondered again how she had been caught up in all of this. It didn't seem fair.

She brushed the unhelpful thoughts aside as she crossed the street into the next yard. She was following a direction more or less straight away from the opening that led out of the safe house's backyard. The diagonal path seemed the most natural—likely taken by the fleeing Sue as the way to put as much distance behind her as possible.

Amy trotted into another backyard and stopped. Tall wooden fences lined the three sides of the yard with no opening. A dilapidated storage shed sat near the back fence. Amy rounded the yard and prepared to run back to the front of the house, feeling that she was wasting precious time and that her chances of finding Sue were slipping away.

"Amy! In here!" the hushed voice from behind called out. Amy spun and glared at the storage shed. The door was now slightly open. Sue's head was poking out and her hand was beckoning Amy inside. "Hurry!" she called.

The same fury that caused her to grab Sue's throat back in the safe house overtook Amy again. She marched slowly toward the storage shed, determined to regain the upper hand.

Sue had taken a risk welcoming Amy into her storage shed hiding spot. The girl had just tried to strangle her. Amy had somehow gotten the idea in her head that Sue was working with whoever had captured her. It was absurd. Red marks on her face and wrists still gave witness to the kidnapping she had endured the night before. Amy had helped her bandage up the scratches and cuts that a navy blue exercise suit now hid. Did she think that those were fake?

But Sue had reminded herself that her fiancé had asked a lot of these two college kids. They weren't used to all of this: kidnapping, high-speed car chases, running for their lives… Of course, Sue wasn't used to all of this either. *She* still had no idea what was going on. Sure, she had watched Ned's explanation video in the Endeavor, but it was all so vague. All Ned seemed to know was that he had been threatened. He didn't know anything beyond the fact that someone (or some organization) had wanted him to quit his job and leave Georgia.

Sue couldn't imagine how Ned had carried the burden of all of this alone for the last three years. Not to mention all of the preparation for the possibility that the threat would actually become reality. The video in the SUV had said "Contingency Plan *Gamma.*" Sue figured that meant that there were at least three separate contingency plans. She imagined that others were to handle situations with slightly different specifics. In fact, she realized that she had no idea what had set the ball in motion last night. They were just finishing up a pleasant dinner when Ned had suddenly told her to leave. She figured that he must have seen something that tipped him off.

A minute later she had been kidnapped from the parking lot.

Amy was approaching slowly, and Sue now noticed the menacing look in her eyes. She began to panic. It looked as if Amy was out for blood. Sue retreated back into the shed and pulled the door closed. The dark hot stuffy air closed in around her.

A thought accompanied her rising claustrophobia. *Amy could hold the door shut. She could trap me in here.*

A thin beam of sunlight streamed through the small crack in the door and fell on a rusty old garden rake that was leaning up against the shed wall. Sue didn't have a choice. She *had* to defend herself. Gingerly she picked up the dry and dusty wooden pole that served as the rake's handle. Slowly, she used the end of the rake to apply pressure against the door to the shed. It creaked as it began to swing open.

SLAM! The door was suddenly forced back on her from the outside, all of Amy's hundred pounds were devoted to holding it closed. Luckily the rake handle was still wedged in the opening. The inch gap in the door provided the only lifeline of fresh air and sunlight to the frightened woman now trapped in the dark and dirty garden shed.

"Amy! What are you doing?" Sue shrieked frantically, her voice echoing dully inside the enclosure. "Let go of the door!"

"Your friend has a gun on Tom!" Amy's voice seethed through the opening. "Call him and tell him to release Tom or I'm not letting you out of here!" The door groaned with the impact of a renewed shove from Amy.

"I swear I didn't call anyone!" Sue pleaded from her cage, "Why would I? You rescued me from the middle of a field last night! Do you really think that this was all just an elaborate plan to get to you and Tom? I was taken from your restaurant parking lot. How hard would it have been for them to get to you *there?* No one is chasing *you two!* And if I wanted to go with this guy, why would I have run? Amy, *you* saw my cuts and bruises. If I were in on it we wouldn't even *be* here!"

"Nice try, but I can still feel where your knee hit my stomach and where you shoved me down, Sue. You *attacked* me." Despite the tough words, a hint of doubt began to creep into the wrath of Amy's voice.

"You were choking me, Amy!" Sue was pushing back on the door now. The opening widened briefly, causing the rake to slip and fall a few inches. Sue immediately stopped pushing in fear that she would lose the wooden wedge.

"It doesn't matter. *You're* the one they're after. Like you said, no one is after Tom or me. If you are innocent then I am truly sorry, but either way I'm trading you for Tom." Sue heard the sound of a cell phone flip open. Amy was going to call Tom's phone and give away their position in exchange for his release.

Sue couldn't let that happen. This girl was putting them both in needless danger. If these people really were after her, there was certainly no reason to trust that they would honor any kind of agreement. Sue might have been willing to trade her life for Tom's, but that wasn't the option here.

Her fingers tightened around the handle of the rake, preparing to pull it away from the door. She took a quick breath and then slammed her shoulder into the door while pulling on the rake to aid her momentum. The unexpected and greater weight was too much for the petite twenty-year-old on the outside of the shed. The door burst open and knocked Amy away, onto her back, onto the warm thick grass. The cell phone sprang from her hand and fell a few feet behind, snapping closed in the process.

Sue caught herself mid-fall, still tightly holding the rake. She swung the weapon toward the surprised girl on the ground and held the menacing metal teeth only inches above Amy's neck.

"Don't move!" Sue shouted. "I'm not going to let you turn us in!"

Amy's green eyes were now streaming with frightened tears. Her chest began to heave with panicked sobs and wheezing shallow breaths. The girl was terrified.

"Heeeeeeey Yaaaa!" the cell phone in the grass broke the dim silence, belting out OutKast's most popular ringtone.

Sue lifted the rake and held it ready. She would never actually hit this girl with it, but she needed Amy to believe that she would, at least until Sue got her calmed down. "Tell me who it is," she said, "but don't answer it."

But Amy was just shaking—tears still running down either side of her face. "Please," the girl whispered through sobs, "please don't hurt me."

It was plain to see. Amy was beaten. Sue lifted and heaved the rake in the other direction causing it to sail through the air, bounce, and land on the ground several feet away. Amy brought her knees up to her chin and rolled to her side, still sobbing. Sue walked over to the friendly sounding phone and picked it up. The small liquid crystal display indicated that Tom Rigsby's cell phone was calling.

24

The driver of the blue car was following a hunch. He pulled into a seemingly random driveway attached to a seemingly deserted house in a seemingly uneventful subdivision somewhere in Kentucky. The scene seemed quiet: a typical suburban community watching a sunny summer afternoon float by. However, the man was still unsure of what to expect. He would bring the gun just in case.

Joe Tompkins shut off his car and hobbled up the short driveway, Gilmore's handgun tucked awkwardly under his t-shirt and stuck into the back of his blue jeans. He wasn't exactly sure what he was doing at this house, but he had felt compelled to drive there before continuing on to Atlanta. One vague thought had persuaded Joe that the detour was worth the time: *Ned might be here.*

He approached the keypad next to the white garage door and flipped it open. Four digits were needed. Joe didn't even think, his right hand just punched in the numbers: one, six, one, two, ENTER. A low rumble accompanied the rising garage door. It revealed a new-looking silver Mitsubishi Endeavor with what appeared to be three bullet holes in the rear windshield.

Upon seeing the car Joe wondered if he should have rang the doorbell before just opening the garage—but it was too late now. Besides, he wanted to inspect this vehicle. Had Ned been shot at? Joe was still on edge just from having a gun *pointed* at him.

He approached the SUV and took a closer look at the bullet holes, only to discover that they weren't actual *holes*. They didn't go all the way through the glass. Long cracks branched out from each divot though. It didn't look like the window would withstand another shot.

Joe's eyes were then drawn down to a recess in the vehicle's rear bumper. A compartment had been hollowed out. Inside an object glimmered in the afternoon sun. Carefully Joe picked up the metal sphere. It was a little smaller than a golf ball and had sharp inch-long spikes radiating out from it like a miniature metallic sun. Joe guessed that the compartment had probably been full of the tire shredders.

Ned must have had an eventful night.

A noise came from inside the house. Joe put the tire shredder back and slowly rounded the SUV. Inside he could see a large computer display in the center of the dash. It reminded him briefly of the computerized poker table that he and Ned had built while living in Atlanta. The table now sat with most of Joe's other possessions in one of his two rented storage garages up in central Illinois.

Muffled shouting now could be heard through the door that led from the garage to the house. Joe took another step toward the plain white steel door and heard that a male voice was saying something. He was still a few paces away when the door suddenly burst open.

"Ned?" Joe called out and then saw instantly that he was wrong. A short, scrawny college-age kid in dirty loose-fitting jeans appeared in the doorway. He didn't look happy. His pump-action BB gun didn't look happy either. Joe didn't have time to realize what was happening when the first copper-plated steel pellet struck him in the forehead. It hurt. Joe decided to inform his attacker of this fact by loudly screaming, "OW!"

Joe wasn't sure if his message had just failed to deter this kid from continuing the attack or if it had actually provided him encouragement in the pursuit. Either way another BB stung Joe's cheek a second later. That one hurt too. It warranted another, "OW!"

Apparently both participants were willing to continue the experiment to determine if *every* BB that struck Joe would cause him pain. The kid at the door was more than willing to keep providing the high-velocity, air-powered stimuli and Joe (who was simply too confused to move) kept taking it on the chin, the chest, the arm, and another one on the forehead. The experiment was a complete success: one hundred percent of the projectiles produced pain upon impact.

The realization finally dawned on Joe that the BB barrage probably wouldn't end until the kid's supply of ammo was depleted. He turned and took cover behind the SUV.

"NOW GET OUT OF HERE!" the kid screamed from the doorway, still firing shots at the wall just behind him.

"I give up! I give up!" Joe yelled back, his hands now raised in the air. Slowly he began to rise from the safety of his crouching position. Evidently this kid was unfamiliar with standard rules of engagement—another shot landed directly on Joe's outstretched left palm, striking the thinly bandaged cut that he had received the previous afternoon.

Joe had had enough.

He resumed a position of safety behind the vehicle and pulled out the handgun from its blue jean holster. The pellets were still flying above his head. Joe disengaged the safety and took aim at the ceiling of the garage. He had only fired a gun twice before in his life—about an hour before at Ned Dyer's burnt house—and that had been during a blackout. He squeezed the trigger.

The deafening roar echoed in the small garage and combined with the gun's recoil in a successful attempt to liberate the gun from Joe's grip. The pistol clattered on the concrete floor as Joe furiously shook his stinging hand. Luckily the kid in the doorway didn't notice. Joe scooped the weapon off of the floor and rose in dramatic fashion aiming Gilmore's gun at his attacker.

"Drop it," Joe commanded. The pump-action BB gun landed with a loud crack on the concrete. It was probably busted. "Hands up," Joe said as he rounded the SUV's hood and approached the trembling kid, "Now back up slowly. What's your name, kid?"

"T-T-Tom R-Rigsby," the kid replied as he slowly backed into the house. Joe got the feeling that Tom had been trying to be brave. He could now tell that the kid was terrified.

"Listen, Tom," Joe said in an unsuccessful attempt at calm, still a bit angry from the multiple BBs that had collided with his face, "when someone says that they give up, you STOP SHOOTING AT THEM!"

Joe was now stepping into the house as Tom continued to back up toward the half-open sliding glass door the led to the backyard.

"AMY! RUN!!" Tom shouted out the opening. Joe turned and saw a petite blonde girl sprint through an opening between wooden fences and into the fir trees beyond. Tom's relentless attack with the toy gun now made sense. He was trying to protect this girl.

"I'm looking for Ned Dyer," Joe explained evenly, "I'm not here to hurt anyone."

"H-Hard to believe when y-you've got a gun pointed at m-me."

Joe didn't think that was fair. He hadn't initially had the gun out. But he probably shouldn't have opened the garage without knocking on the front door first either. The kid was still trying to be brave. Joe decided to make a gesture of good faith.

"Okay, Tom," Joe's voice remained calm, "I'm putting the gun away." He clicked the safety back on and re-stowed the handgun in the back of his blue jean waistband. "Let's just relax. Do you know where Ned is?"

Tom lowered his hands and spoke with a slight sense of relief, "I thought you people already had him."

This response initially confused Joe and then sparked a degree of fear. "Tom, I'm not *after* Ned! Ned is my *friend!* My *oldest* friend!" Joe stamped down the conflicting emotions that this last statement stirred up and continued, "Has Ned been taken? Taken by whom?"

Joe then listened as Tom hesitantly related his story, starting with an average night waiting tables and finishing with arriving at the safe house early that morning. Joe was taken aback by everything that had transpired, but one part of Tom's story stood out in his head, screaming for clarification.

"You said Ned was threatened and forced to leave Georgia?"

"That's what the video said," Tom explained. "He was warned not to tell anyone. They were threatening his family if he did. Last night something must have happened that caused him to initiate one of these 'contingency plans'. He went to great lengths to secure his family before these guys got to them."

This news hit Joe hard. Three years of thinking that his best friend had abandoned their friendship. Three years of resentment. Ned had been in trouble! Pangs of regret and guilt at not being more supportive, at not allowing Ned to reconcile the friendship racked Joe's body. His throat felt dry.

"Is… is there anything to drink?" Joe asked in a soft voice.

"Yeah, um, there's bottled water and Dr. Pepper in the fridge."

The news of the Dr. Pepper made Joe smile; Ned had done a very good job of setting up this place. Joe walked to the small kitchen, still nursing a bruised hip, and bent down to examine the contents of the refrigerator. Twelve beautiful maroon cans stood neatly in two lines, ready to be of service. Joe reached in and grabbed one.

The sudden movement against his lower back startled him. He straightened up quickly and wheeled around. Tom was now backing slowly away to a safe distance. Gilmore's gun was in his hands and pointing at Joe's chest for the second time that afternoon.

A small click sounded as Tom disengaged the safety.

It had proven a difficult feat to safely duct tape the disheveled-looking intruder to the wooden kitchen chair. But the man who claimed to be Ned Dyer's oldest friend had not struggled. In fact, he had even helped when ordered to. Tom tried not to admit to himself that, had his captive *wanted* to fight back or try to escape during the procedure, there had been several opportunities.

But none of that now mattered. The self-proclaimed "Joe Tompkins" was now secured, his legs held firmly by the ankles to the front legs of the chair, his arms at his sides with wrists attached to the chair's back legs. He would not be getting up without aid.

Now... Tom asked himself, *What do I do with him?*

Tom's thoughts still mainly centered on his own getaway. Even though this man had continually proclaimed his innocence, Tom could not discount the strong possibility that this Tompkins worked for the men that were after them and that backup was on its way. He had to get Amy away from there. He picked up his cell phone and dialed the number she had given him the night before.

"Hello? Tom, are you okay?"

Tom had expected Amy's voice. Sue's voice was a surprise. He still wasn't sure what to make of the confrontation that had occurred as the two women fled the safe house at the arrival of the now duct taped intruder. Had Sue really given away their position... or was she just trying to run away? Tom decided that it wouldn't have made any sense that she was in on whatever had happened to Ned. Not after the car chase the night before.

"I'm fine, Sue. Are you with Amy? Put her on."

"She's here, we're both okay... but she's not really in any condition to talk." Sue's voice sounded a bit odd, as if she was trying to conceal something. Tom's recently paranoid mind shifted into a higher gear. He felt a renewed panic swell in his gut.

"What are you talking about, Sue?" he demanded as anger crept into his voice, "Put Amy on now!"

"Okay, Tom... that's fine," Sue's voice now employed pacifying tones, "here she is."

Tom heard a rustling and a soft, "It's Tom. He wants to talk to you," and then Amy's voice—quietly sobbing.

"Amy! Are you all right? What's wrong?" Tom's mind now shifted from paranoia to dread. The panic scrambled up his esophagus and lodged itself in his throat. He would not forgive himself if something had happened to this girl.

"I'm fine, Tom," Amy's hushed voice breathed, "I was wrong about Sue. She's not one of them." With some difficulty, Tom swallowed. His panic slid slowly back down his throat and dissolved in his stomach. There was a loud sniffle, after which Amy's voice sounded a little stronger and more solid. "Tom, what happened? Are you okay?"

Tom assured her that he was and that the intruder was now safely restrained. Amy seemed to calm down a bit after that. This girl had obviously been frightened that something had happened to him. This caused a degree of self-consciousness to mix in with the flood of relief that accompanied the knowledge of her safety. Amy McKay had been concerned about him.

Tom chided himself for wasting time with the foolish thought while more pressing matters required his attention. *Besides,* he told himself, *knowing me, I'll find a way to screw everything up long before any kind of relationship actually develops.*

Amy and Sue were not far from the safe house. They would be back in a couple of minutes. Tom hung up his phone and stared at his captive. The guy looked as if he had been in a fight long before arriving there. A long purple bruise was displayed over his bloodshot left eye and he had been walking with a limp. Tom wanted to believe his story, but he was determined not to trust anyone who had attempted to sneak into the house brandishing a handgun.

But if he really was some kind of 'secret agent' or something, Tom didn't think he was much of one. After all, the guy had allowed himself to be disarmed and taped to a chair.

Joe Tompkins' dry voice startled Tom away from these thoughts. "Any chance of getting that Dr. Pepper now?"

It was a bit of an understatement to say that Joe Tompkins was now regretting his decision to let down his guard in front of his new acquaintance, Tom Rigsby. The news about Ned being threatened three years ago had distracted him. Tom's story had gained Joe's trust and Joe had taken for granted that the good faith gesture of stowing his gun had gained Tom's.

Apparently, he had been mistaken.

Joe had fortunately (and oddly) been wearing long pants on the hot June day, so that the duct tape surrounding his ankles was simply serving its purpose of restraining his legs to the chair. The tape on his wrists, however, was going above and beyond the call of duty by taking on the additional task of painfully pulling at his ample arm hair. This was causing Joe to rethink his previous strategy of cooperation with his captor in the hopes of proving that he was not a threat. But, as was the case with several of his actions so far that week, it was too late now to remedy the mistake.

At least it appeared that Tom was going to honor his drink request. Joe's throat was now painfully dry. He watched Tom circle back to the refrigerator to retrieve the beverage. This would be a minor relief though; Joe knew that he was wasting precious time here. Ned had called him to a midnight meeting in Atlanta, and from what he had gleaned from Tom's story, it sounded like Ned could be in serious trouble. With the guilt of rebuffing Ned's reconciliation efforts over the past couple of years still fresh in his mind, Joe resolved that he would make every attempt to be waiting for Ned at Everybody's Pizza that night—even with his nagging doubt that Ned would have the opportunity to show up himself.

Tom straightened back up with the pop can in his hand and made motions to pull its tab.

"Could you run that under hot water first!?" Joe asked quickly, his voice sounding more panicked and rushed than he had hoped it would, but it was necessary that he make the request before the aluminum seal was broken. In an attempt to increase the likelihood that his appeal would not go unfulfilled, Joe hastily added a quick (but reasonably polite), "Please!"

Tom looked puzzled, but Joe knew it was just an act. No one in their right mind would place their mouth on an unwashed aluminum container like that. There was, of course, nothing peculiar whatsoever about what he was asking for.

Tom eventually gave in to this perfectly ordinary request, opened the can, and held it to Joe's mouth. The crisp, refreshing, fructose-infused liquid hurried greedily down his throat, seeking to impart the benefits of caffeine to Joe's weary muscles and mind. Twenty-three flavors partied happily on Joe's tongue—stimulating his tired brain with their dance.

The temporary euphoria was interrupted by the abrupt noise of a sliding glass door opening. This caused Tom to jump slightly, jarring the can, slopping the carbonated medicine down Joe's shirt, and cutting Joe's top lip upon the sharp and rapidly retreating container opening. The sting of the new wound blended with a deep throbbing pain from Joe's black eye and a tender soreness from his hip. Joe sucked on the dribble of blood escaping from his fresh cut.

Blinking against the reflected daylight illuminating the recently opened door, Joe made out the figures of two women. The petite young blonde wearing a black t-shirt and jeans fell upon Tom (who had just enough time to turn around) and gripped him in a fierce embrace. Joe's eyes averted respectfully and made brief contact with the hazel eyes of the other woman. She was a brunette and a bit taller than the blonde girl and wore a navy blue jogging suit that didn't seem to quite fit. An odd expression of disbelief was on her face.

"Tom, what happened?" the blonde asked, wiping tears from her cheeks.

Tom apparently elected to recount the Cliff's Notes version of the ordeal. In a matter-of-fact voice he muttered, "I got his gun… and tied him up." Tom indicated Gilmore's handgun now lying harmlessly on the kitchen counter and then stared at his own feet. Joe got the impression that the blonde girl's hug had befuddled the young man. He kicked gently at the linoleum and mumbled, "He says he's a friend of Ned's. He says that his name is J–"

"Joe Tompkins," interrupted the brunette definitively. "He used to be Ned's roommate."

Joe's shocked eyes shot back to study this woman again. He was sure that he had never seen her before. She bent down and looked him in the eye.

"Hi Joe, I'm Sue Bishop, Ned's fiancée. I've seen old pictures of you. You look better without the black eye. Meet Amy McKay," the brunette said as she motioned toward the blonde girl, "and I guess you've already met Tom Rigsby."

"Nice to meet you all," Joe replied with a weak smile, "you'll forgive me if I don't shake hands."

A few minutes later Joe sat of his own volition on the kitchen chair that had so recently served as his temporary prison. He was no worse for wear—save a small cut on his lip and a couple of wrists that sported slightly less hair than usual.

Sue had vouched for him, even though they had never met, and that had finally earned him the trust of the other two safe house occupants. Though, Joe had a vague feeling that the two college kids still clutched a bit of apprehension about this Sue woman and, by association, him as well. The group had elected that Tom be the keeper of the gun while they decided upon their next course of action. Joe noticed that the blonde girl, Amy, had seemed reassured by this decision.

Joe had briefly summarized his experiences of the last twenty-four hours and the group listened with thinly veiled apathy until he reached the news of Ned's burnt house and the bodies that had been pulled from within. At this point Sue had burst into tears. Joe had quickly pressed his opinion that Ned *couldn't* have been one of the deceased. If the goal had simply been to kill Ned, there were simpler and more effective means than arson. Above all, this organization seemed to value secrecy. Setting fire to Ned's house deliberately would have attracted a lot of unwanted attention.

Sue didn't seem to share Joe's conviction about Ned's wellbeing and tearfully excused herself to the restroom. The other three waited at the table in an awkward silence. It was time to decide what to do from here.

"I'm supposed to be at work in a couple of hours," Amy announced coolly. "I think Tom and I are ready to go home."

Tom nodded in slow and silent agreement. The kid hadn't said much since the arrival of the two women. He had been out in the garage consulting the Endeavor's computer while Joe had finished his drink and cleaned himself up and had only just come back in the house during Joe's story.

"I'm supposed to work tonight too," Tom said. "I think we'll be safe. No one knows that we're involved in any of this."

"Okay," Joe agreed, "What about Sue? Has she said what she's planning to do now?"

"She hasn't said anything to me," Amy answered softly, "but we haven't really had much chance to talk since last night."

"Well," Tom offered, "according to the computer in the SUV, her parents are in a safe house in Indiana. I'm guessing that's where she'll want to go." He turned toward Joe and continued, "The computer also had a screen that described you. Your story checks out. It sounds like Ned has complete trust in you." With this Tom pushed Gilmore's handgun across the small wooden table toward Joe. "There's even a specific explanation video waiting for you."

Joe's eyes moistened involuntarily as he accepted and stowed the gun. "Can I watch it?" he asked.

"You can try, it's asking for a secret phrase before it will play. It's supposed to be the answer to the question, 'Where's the best place to burn junk mail?'"

Joe smiled.

"Why, right on the kitchen counter, of course."

25

Amy McKay was in the back seat of the Endeavor. Sue sat next to her. She had calmed down and joined the group in the still-open garage. The guys were watching the computer monitor from the front seats.

Ned's "Joe specific" explanation video went into a little further detail than the other two Amy had watched the night before. It seemed that Joe was part of a small team of engineers that Ned wished to assemble to investigate the mysterious organization and either find a way to stop them or pacify them while Ned's family was safe. Apparently Ned's plans didn't stop with just ensuring that everyone survived the night after all.

Amy was glad that matters were now being handed off to more competent and deliberate hands. She was proud that she and Tom had been able to do their part to help, but was ready for them to get back to their lives. Lives that didn't seem quite as dull as they had the night before. Boring, she decided, wasn't all bad. At least it was safe.

Although, in the midst of the danger Tom had surprised her. He had to be proven much braver than she'd have thought. Amy now admitted to herself that, had she alone received and deciphered the cryptic note on the credit card receipt, she would have just called the police.

A wave of embarrassment washed through Amy as she thought about her own attempted bravery. She had turned on the woman that they had rescued. She had threatened to undo all that she and Tom had accomplished the night before. When the chips were down, she had proved a coward. Tom hadn't wavered even when he had a gun pointed at him. Amy hoped that she hadn't ruined her chances with him.

She reached up to the passenger seat and touched Tom's shoulder. Her hand ran down his arm. His hand reached back and lightly held hers behind the back of his seat.

The video had now progressed through all of the redundant information that Amy had already heard (she noted that Ned had seemed much more emotional when talking about being forced to leave Georgia than he had been in the other two videos). He briefly mentioned that, in a dire case, there might be someone following instructions to help secure his family in a silver SUV and that their paths might cross. Ned now began to talk about the tools that Joe would have at his disposal for his efforts.

"If you come across my silver Mitsubishi Endeavor, or in the unlikely event that you are watching this video from inside of it, there are a couple of handguns stored in a secret compartment in the console between the front two seats. The driver of the SUV will probably be unaware of this—I am not sure who that will be and can't risk arming a stranger. Joe, I pray that you will not need them, but please take them if you get the chance.

"Also, there is thirty thousand dollars in cash stored in the false bottom of the refrigerator in the back. Again, the driver will probably not be aware of it. Tread carefully if you meet him, but use the money if you can. The locations of additional stores of cash and arms are noted on your tablet PC."

Joe shifted in the driver's seat and muttered softly, "I never got a tablet PC."

In the video Ned continued with an air of desperation, "Joe, I have racked my brain since leaving Atlanta trying to figure out why I was singled out and forced to leave. Unfortunately I can only offer you my guesses. Everything that follows is based on a few assumptions and I urge you to pick up the trail here unless you've come across any additional information that leads you elsewhere.

"The most likely scenario that I can come up with is that the threat was meant to remove me from my job. I must have been working on something that this organization didn't want me to. Now, since neither you nor the rest of the design team were forced to leave, I must assume that it was something I was working on alone. That doesn't leave many options…"

Amy started to lose interest as the video described another project Ned had been consulting for at the same company he and Joe had worked at. He had discovered a flaw in some software that was part of a "navigational package" for military aircraft. His recommended fix would increase the avionics sensors' accuracy by more than twenty percent or something. Amy's eyes and head drooped as she began to drift off. When she nodded violently and jerked herself back to consciousness, the video was still going.

"I have full confidence that if anyone can get to the bottom of this, Joe, it's you. Hopefully Meg and Dan are with you, but since you're watching this it appears that I was unable to make the midnight meeting. If anything has happened to me I just want you to know how much I regret the wedge this nasty ordeal has shoved between us. I take comfort in knowing that you are finally aware of the truth. Good luck and Godspeed, Joe."

With that the video concluded and the LCD screens transitioned back to the SUV's main menu. Amy surmised that Ned had not intended Joe to get this video until this mysterious midnight meeting in Atlanta that Joe was headed to. She assumed that there was a tablet PC there waiting for him if not Ned himself.

Joe turned around in the driver's seat and faced the rest of the inhabitants of the Endeavor. Amy knew that he was accepting Ned's charge to take control of the situation. "I'm still going to Atlanta, I still think Ned might be there. I doubt the other two will be, they don't live in Georgia anymore. Sue, if you could take Tom and Amy back home on your way to the Indiana safe house that would help. I'm already running late. I'll take the Scion; you can continue to drive the Endeavor. I think we should give Tom and Amy each two thousand dollars for their troubles from the money in the back. Sue, you can have six, if that's okay, and I'll take the rest. Thank you all for your help and," here he grinned at Tom, "hospitality."

Sue spoke for the first time since she had returned from the restroom, "I'm not going to Indiana, Joe. I'm coming with you. If there's a chance that Ned will be there tonight that's where I plan to be too."

Amy could tell that Joe hadn't expected this. He tried to deflect Sue's intrusion into the plan by explaining in what Amy thought was a fairly patronizing voice that it had been Ned's intention to keep her safe.

"I don't care, Joe," Sue was firm in her response. "I am *going* to Atlanta tonight. I'd prefer if we rode together but I'll go alone if need be."

Joe ended up giving in, but this presented the group with a dilemma. Sue and Joe were already running late if they hoped to make Atlanta by midnight and Amy and Tom lived in the opposite direction. Understandably Sue felt that the Endeavor would be best suited for the mission and Joe's Scion was technically stolen. He didn't feel comfortable either leaving it or letting the college kids take it.

"It's fine," Amy said, realizing that her getting to work on time needed to take a back seat to the more important events unfolding before them. "Just drop Tom and me off at a bus station. We'll be okay."

The group agreed on this and Joe and Sue began plotting a course on the Endeavor's PC. Amy excused herself to grab some supplies from inside before they set off. She entered the kitchen and collected a couple of bottles of water and an unopened box of Wheat Thins. She deposited these on the counter and called back into the garage, "Hey Rigsby! You want to give me a hand in here?"

Tom appeared at the open door and stepped into the kitchen. "What do you need?" he asked.

Without giving him warning she grabbed his shirt and pulled him close. "Thanks for keeping me safe," she whispered, leaning in for a kiss. Tom, obviously caught off guard, took a step backward. Amy persisted and pulled him near again.

Five minutes later the party was off. Joe would take the lead alone in his Scion while the Endeavor followed behind. They would head to the nearest bus station, drop off Amy and Tom, and then continue the journey southward. And though Amy was glad her part was now finished, she was concerned for Joe and Sue. She hoped that they would be okay.

The garage door to the Kentucky safe house slowly closed and the two vehicles disappeared around a bend in the subdivision. It was a good thing that they left when they did. A small herd of mysterious but average looking Toyotas descended upon the house minutes later.

26

Tuesday, 3:37 PM

Ned Dyer felt a pinching sensation in his left wrist—and something felt tight around both of his forearms. The haze in his mind began to lift, leaving behind a throbbing pain radiating from both sides of his head. Ned attempted to lift his right hand to massage his temples. He couldn't. Something was holding his arm down.

His eyes shot open. Brown leather straps tightly bound his arms to the arms of what looked like a dentist's chair. He was reclined slightly. An IV tube ran down his left arm, attached to his skin with tape and a large metal needle. Leather straps also held his ankles and waist in place. His peripheral vision could make out the two thick white wires extending from the sensors taped to his temples.

Ned could feel his mind sharpening as it left the fog of unconsciousness behind. He attempted to focus and recall the events that had led him to this place. He was unsuccessful. For some reason, the filters of his conscious mind were not functioning. He was entering a state of hyperawareness. An induced hypnotic trance was stripping Ned's subconscious mind bare, subjecting it to potential suggestion and tampering.

If he *had* been in control of his brain, the feeling would have reminded Ned of a more intense version of a daydream—like when driving a long distance on autopilot or being engrossed in a good book. Literally *lost* in thought. Ned felt his body relax and let go of the fear that had gripped him when he first woke. It was, after all, a *very* comfortable chair.

His head dropped back to the cushioned headrest. A large computer monitor was now hovering above him. It drew Ned's meandering gaze to the images flashing quickly on the screen—images of breathtaking landscapes: mountains, waterfalls, forests. They seemed vaguely familiar.

Ned's dilated brown eyes were now fixed on the illuminated pictures. Strange sounding words began to form in his mind. He felt as if they were associated with the images. He had never been to the places shown, but somehow he knew their names. *Rangitoto Island… Rotorua… Tongariro Crossing…*

The images began to seep further into Ned's mind—increasing his impressions of calm and security—confusing his senses of loyalty and morality. A fleeting, long-suppressed memory revealed that Ned had been in this chair before, seeing these same images.

Mount Ruapehu… Routeburn Flats… A list of IP addresses… Fjordland…

A voice was now inside his head navigating through the flurry of unfiltered thoughts. *"Solve the problem, Ned. Find the pattern."*

Doubtful Sound… A computer network diagram… Matamata… Source code from a web page with embedded PHP… Huka Falls…

The brilliant New Zealand landscapes continued to mix with technical diagrams and snippets of code. Ned's raw subconscious organized and pieced together the data revealing a new image in his mind. He was being shown some sort of computer virus.

And the virus was on the attack.

There was danger here. Ned began to feel threatened, trapped. He needed to fight back. He started probing for weak spots in the virus' structure, and this led him to discover that he was somehow familiar with the virus' basic design. This gave him an edge.

Instinctively Ned began to test potential counterattack strategies in his mind. Surprisingly, the rapid images on the screen began to change in response. Apparently the computer was somehow tapped into his brain.

The constant flickering landscape images now served as an invisible backdrop to Ned's poking and prodding the crippling virus. Long minutes passed as he battled the digital foe, not understanding why, essentially reduced from human being to some sort of soulless machine that would do the will of the omnipresent voice in his head. Victory against the virus was close, but so was a realization. Ned knew the virus' author.

The voice inside Ned's mind attempted to conceal further the explanation for his familiarity with the code, but it couldn't. That familiarity was the only reason that Ned was equipped to beat this bug and he needed to be aware of this knowledge to continue. Instead the foreign voice began to repeat a single thought on a loop: *"The virus is attacking you, Ned. You must crush it!"*

But it was too late. A growing doubt in his desire to continue now held Ned's attention—fueled by a deeply held guilt. The architect of this virus had been a trusted friend. The snippets of code before him, the basic strategy of the virus' attack… this had to be Joe's code.

He had abandoned Joe three years ago; he would not betray him now. He did not know what Joe's goal with this virus was, only that he wasn't going to stand in his friend's way.

Ned's mind now turned its struggle from the virus and directed the fight toward the intruding voice that was still shouting commands. His suppressed moral compass was reasserting itself despite the hypnosis. He would not allow himself to be used in a fight that he didn't understand.

The technical data on the display dissolved back into the rapid slideshow of photographs. Confusion still surrounded him, but Ned had resisted the voice. He was certain that he had made the right choice.

The voice in his mind now adopted an angry, but smug, tone. *"Just as I suspected Mr. Dyer, you are unwilling to help without proper motivation. You seem to have developed a foolish opposition to following the path of least resistance. Trust me when I say it will continue to cause problems for you.*

"Fortunately for you, however, I've just been informed that your services are no longer needed in this matter. Unfortunately for you, this does not mean the end of today's unpleasantness. Get comfortable in that chair."

Ned *was* comfortable. If nothing else, it *was* a comfortable chair.

27

Tuesday, 12:01 PM

Pale blue eyes, darkly circled, gazed at the syringe resting lightly in Agent Gilmore's right hand. It was rare that someone of his stature would stoop to use the Agency-approved stimulant, but the responsibility for fixing what was already being termed as the "Ned Dyer Fiasco" currently rested solely on his narrow shoulders. This was no time to let pride deprive him of a tool that would facilitate containment of the situation. Seven lower level field agents had been lost during the sleepless night.

He didn't want to deal with the paperwork required if any more peons went and got themselves killed.

Gilmore tightened his left fist causing a vein to show itself and inserted the needle with medical precision. The chemical coursed through his bloodstream and carried the nerve-motivating molecules to his brain. Gilmore closed his eyes as the pain from his tender nose began to recede. It had been extremely difficult to allow the keyboard to the face the day before—*twice*. He had, of course, seen the initial blow coming with time enough to react. He could have incapacitated Subject Joe Tompkins before Tompkins knew what hit him, but that would have involved breaking cover. It was important to find out what exactly Joe knew first, and this had forced him to stay in character. Letting Subject Tompkins "escape" had been the right move, even the Division Head had agreed with that. Of course, losing his quarry due to a car fire was a black mark against Agent Gilmore—there was no way around that. The only thing to do was to rectify the situation. That meant bringing Tompkins in.

The morning had been spent assessing the extent of the "Fiasco," evaluating tips and hunches, and briefing the new field agents on loan from Reserve Division. If the ordeal hadn't been so potentially destructive to the organization as a whole, the shuffling of interdivisional resources would have involved a myriad of jurisdictional conflicts and red tape. But in every corporate establishment (however loose the interdepartmental affiliation) there exists the potential for that remarkable agility and efficiency that arises when all the members are united with a common goal. This unity is seldom stronger than when faced with a common and lethal enemy.

And so the stars had aligned for Agent Gilmore. He found himself in command of the team charged with containing and recovering from the largest direct threat the organization had ever encountered, every necessary resource at his employ. Hedging their bets, Gilmore's superiors were granting him a wide berth in the matter and allowing him to run the operation as he saw fit. Glory and promotion waited to rain down on him if successful, blame and ruin if not.

But this situation agreed with Gilmore. He was always eager to prove himself and he thrived under pressure. His ambition had driven him to take on the mundane but vital assignment to oversee Tompkins, something that would usually be reserved for a much lower level agent. But Gilmore had always preferred a hands-on approach to such things.

With his drug safely administered, Gilmore discarded the needle, removed his elastic vein-constricting armband, and stepped out of the single-occupant bathroom into the hallway of the Southern Illinois branch office. Agent Clemens was busy being fat and leaning against the unfortunate and loudly papered wall.

Gilmore resented being partnered with the large low-level field agent. It was the biggest drawback to the Tompkins assignment—even counting the keyboard to the face.

Clemens had been trusted with the supremely challenging task of following Subject Tompkins around for the past few months, real tough considering Joe mostly just drove back and forth between home and the office. Gilmore was sure that it was about all Clemens was capable of.

The wall creaked noisily in protest as the fat man pushed off of it to resume an upright stance. "Ready to go, boss?"

Gilmore refused to give the obvious answer and brushed past his partner, out the clearly marked exit, and into the small sunlit parking lot. Clemens, hurrying to catch up, approached and unlocked the average looking blue Toyota.

Several minutes later they pulled into the driveway that led up to Subject Ned Dyer's large unattached garage. Agent Gilmore had wanted to inspect firsthand the scene where four agents had lost their lives. Subject Dyer was in custody and currently being interrogated, but the Agency's first priority was to halt the crippling computer virus that had attacked the Division's systems the previous week. Joe Tompkins was under **suspicion** for potentially authoring the virus, but that suspicion wasn't **confirmed until** the decoy car-fire that allowed him to escape. The Division **Head insisted** that Subject Dyer's capture first be exploited in the efforts to **defeat the** virus. It was thought that Ned's familiarity with the author's work **would enable** him to stop the attack if so persuaded.

It had been widely agreed that the threat of harm to his family would provide the best motivation for Subject Dyer to assist in the removal of the virus. Unfortunately the Agency had been forced to bring Dyer in without proper preparation. Losing Tompkins had made them desperate. And in the time it took to process Dyer and arrange a workstation for him to use, he had initiated some sort of complex contingency plan that resulted in removing his family from the Agency's reach and removing the life from seven of its field agents.

Worst of all, somehow Dyer had arranged to receive communication upon successful completion of his plan so that lies about his family's wellbeing were worthless. Arrangements were now being made for hypnotic stimulation of the captive in hopes of enlisting Ned's help by convincing him that the virus was his enemy, but it was doubtful that this tactic would be successful. Outright torture might be the next step, but that was usually undesirable when the situation required that the captive perform some complex task. Physical pain tended to make it difficult to concentrate.

Of course, none of this mattered if the Agency was successful in capturing the virus' author. Gilmore now regretted his defense of Subject Tompkins. He had insisted after months of close surveillance that Joe was completely ignorant of the Agency's existence and that the plans for him should move forward without modification. It now appeared that Joe had not only been aware of the Agency's influence in his life, but had been actively working to disrupt it for some time. This realization had been hard for Gilmore to swallow. He had stood gaping in disbelief at Tompkins' burning green Honda the previous afternoon for three straight minutes. But, he had recovered quickly after that and was now desperately trying to pick up the trail.

Although, after a night full of surprises and hard work, the fact was that the Agency had no idea what had happened to Subject Joe Tompkins.

Agents Gilmore and Clemens exited their car and approached the three-stall garage that sat next to Ned's bombed-out house. Local authorities had been dismissed from the scene and the property had been cleared by bomb-sniffing dogs. The lock on the garage's side door had been picked and the garage had been searched. There was no threat of another explosion. Gilmore stepped through the half-open door into the stuffy darkness. His hand found the light switch and nine ceiling-suspended incandescent bulbs sprang to life, illuminating the space. It appeared that the garage was on a separate electrical circuit from the demolished house.

The dank garage spread out before the two men. The far bay sported a large workshop area lined with two long workbenches. One bench was littered with various electronic components, soldering irons, wire spools, and static mats. The other contained a more garage appropriate array of hammers, saws, ratchet sets, nail bins, and the like.

The middle bay held an old yellow pickup. Gilmore had studied the random notes that had been compiled by Subject Dyer's surveillance team over the past few years. He remembered a reference to Ned purchasing the used truck a couple of years back. It didn't appear to have seen much action since.

The bay closest to the house was empty, obviously where Dyer usually parked his black BMW. The car had been retrieved from the steakhouse parking lot during the night and was currently sitting back in the office garage. After a thorough examination it hadn't provided any useful clues.

Gilmore circled the garage, unsure of what he was even looking for. He supposed that he could have the items in the workshop collected and studied, but something told him that it would be a waste of time. He had hoped that inspecting the site of the bomb blast might inspire him to follow some new direction in his pursuit of Subject Tompkins, but it now appeared to be little more than a waste of time.

He lingered another moment at one of the workbenches and then resumed a brisk pace back toward the door. Clemens was frozen in his stance next to the old pickup, a vague and ignorant expression on his face. Gilmore made a motion to brush past him and continue the inspection outside, but Clemens stupidly decided to impede his boss' exit. Gilmore came to an unexpected stop—Clemens' chubby fingers pressing against his chest.

This was too much.

Coolly, Gilmore took a step backward. Calmly, he grabbed Clemens' outstretched wrist and elbow. And in the blink of an eye Clemens was on his knees; his face pressed against the concrete of the garage floor, his arm twisted behind his back, and his ears receiving the fierce obscenities issued from his superior's mouth.

Gilmore forcibly punctuated the string of insults with a simple command, "You *will not* touch me again!" and then a follow-up question, "DO YOU UNDERSTAND!?" He gave Clemens' arm another twist and dug a knee into the fat man's back.

The muffled voice of the man on the floor was thick with fear as he responded. "Sir, I'm sorry… please… I was just going to ask if you smelled that!"

Indeed Gilmore had now noticed the pungent odor emanating from underneath the old truck. He released his partner and bent down to inspect the concrete floor. The dusty outline of a metal trapdoor could be seen.

There appeared to be a hidden compartment beneath the garage.

Agent Gilmore hoped that Subject Ned Dyer wouldn't mind him borrowing his large hydraulic jack. The old yellow pickup was now propped up at the front end in order to allow access to the metal hatch underneath. The hatch was itself a fairly plain, rust-colored square. A thick iron ring rested on the top and served as its handle.

Gilmore slid the lid away and revealed the two-foot-by-two-foot earth-walled shaft that extended eight feet into the ground. The air inside reeked of alcohol. Dim daylight was reflected in the liquid pool at the bottom. The shaft was obviously too narrow for his portly partner, so Gilmore approached and sat on the edge of the hole, braced his feet against the crude two-by-four ladder that lined one of the shaft walls, and slowly descended. He stopped on the last step, a few inches above the pool at the bottom.

One of the walls of the shaft became the back of an empty wooden wine rack about halfway down. Through it Gilmore could see into Ned's damaged wine cellar. Most of the racks were in pieces. Broken glass and spilt wine covered the floor. A small push easily swung the hinged wooden wine rack into the cellar. The purpose of the shaft became obvious. It was an escape route—another facet of Subject Dyer's reaction to the threat he had received from Agent Fuller three years ago.

That had been a botched operation. Gilmore still wasn't sure how Fuller had managed to hang on to his job after that. The plan to forcibly guide Ned away from his activities in Georgia and relocate him in Southern Illinois had barely been approved when Fuller, led by a false sense of urgency and misplaced bravado, had developed and delivered the threat. And, while the intended effect had been achieved, it had been at the expense of the Agency's precious veil of secrecy. By the time it was known what Fuller had done, Subject Ned Dyer had already given his employer his two weeks' notice. It was decided that any modification to the plan at that point would potentially have caused more exposure by inviting more questions. The Agency had then scrambled to accommodate Fuller's folly and arranged the new job for Ned Dyer in Southern Illinois. Gilmore had then spent the next year and a half tying up loose ends in the matter.

Now the full effects of Fuller's mistake were laid bare. The direct contact with Subject Dyer had caused Ned to dramatically react to the Agency's intrusion. Ned had in all likelihood warned Subject Tompkins as well. The way Gilmore saw it; all of the current problems were the result of Fuller's incompetence. If it had been his operation, Agent Gilmore would have gently massaged *external* circumstances, invisibly guiding Subject Dyer into position. Dyer would then have landed in a position of unknowing assistance to the Agency and open to a high degree of manipulation. Tompkins would still be ignorant too, no computer virus would have been written, and Gilmore's nose wouldn't have been bruised. His jaw and his grip on the ladder both tightened with the thought. He was now wasting his time in a dirty smelly hole while the operation he was responsible for fell apart around him.

He took one last look down into the wine cellar and then began to climb the ladder. But as he did, a muffled sound caught his attention. It sounded like an engine running, and it was coming from one of the dirt walls in the shaft. Gilmore stopped to listen, and then kicked the wall. A large rectangular section of the earth shook slightly and shed some dirt. He kicked it again, harder. More dirt fell and began to reveal a smooth surface. It looked like plywood.

Gilmore's fingers found the edges of the rectangular covering and pried it away. He let the dirt covered plywood drop into the pool of wine and glass that covered the bottom of the shaft. A narrow stainless steel door was now revealed in the wall. The sound of the engine was still quiet, but louder than before. Gilmore pushed on the metal door. It was thick and heavy, but it swung open easily.

A gust of artificial wind swept past Gilmore as the air pressure equalized between the shaft and the chamber behind the door. The air was stale and warm, but a welcome relief to Gilmore's assaulted nostrils. The effect was momentary however, as the aroma of muddy wine quickly reasserted itself as the shaft's dominant odor.

As much to distance himself from the smell as actual curiosity, Gilmore climbed into the dark hole that he'd uncovered. The now deafening noise from some kind of engine echoed through the darkness but was still welcomed in comparison to the stink of the shaft.

The floor of the chamber was smooth and solid. Gilmore imagined that his footsteps would have echoed loudly if not for the sound of the engine. The ceiling was tall enough to stand upright and he proceeded into the blackness with outstretched hands. After only a few feet, the passage took a sharp left and then a sharp right a few feet after that. Gilmore continued to creep along slowly, wondering if he was about to encounter something that the bomb-sniffing dogs would have missed—wondering if he was right where Subject Ned Dyer would want him.

A flash of light pierced the darkness and blinded the intruder who was now beginning to regret his uninvited venture into the secret sanctuary.

Gilmore blinked his eyes in an attempt to regain proper pupil dilation when another flash blinded him anew. Had he set off another trap?

The overhead fluorescent light's third attempt at ignition was finally successful and the soft white glow now shone over the small cabinet-lined room. The loud engine noise was coming from behind a bright red cabinet marked "Generator." Other cabinets were labeled too: "Currency, Armory, Fuel, Servers, Communications, Shower, Toilet, First Aid, Pantry, Bottled Water, Refrigerator, and Dishes." A couple of cots leaned up against some of the cabinets. The walls, floor, and ceiling were made from the same thick metal as the door. The room almost reminded Gilmore of a space capsule. This was a panic room…a bomb shelter… *a fortress.*

On the only section of wall not covered in these descriptive cabinets sat a small but practical desk with a computer monitor sitting on top of it behind a keyboard and mouse. The monitor came to life and displayed a picture of a man's head floating and bouncing off of the edges of the screen in front of a plain gray background. He appeared to be mouthing something erratically like a poorly made puppet. He had a thick uni-brow. He was asking for a code.

A smile crawled leisurely across Gilmore's thin face. Finally he would have some good news to report. This appeared to be Subject Dyer's command center. All he needed was a code… and the man who knew the code was, at that moment, being prepped for interrogation.

Gilmore made the call back to the office after climbing out of the hole and back into the garage. His superiors had sounded pleased. Access to the secret command center would certainly aid in cleaning up and containing the "Ned Dyer Fiasco."

Agent Clemens was having difficulty hiding his excitement at the discovery. No doubt he expected partial credit for the find that, very likely, just broke their case wide open.

Yeah, right, Gilmore thought, *it was his discovery. I'd like to see him try to climb into that hole.*

Gilmore hadn't shared the content of his phone conversation with his partner and Clemens was now visibly curious. He ventured a question, "So… are they going to get the code from Dyer?"

The recent good news had improved Gilmore's mood enough to allow him to respond to his partner without another exhibition of his physical superiority. "Not right now," he grumbled in reply with a slight but still-present annoyance at his partner's continued existence, "first priority is still the inoculation of the computer virus. They've got to keep Dyer happy while they still need him to help with something that complicated. After that they can just torture a simple code out of him."

The lower degree of hostility in his boss' reply evidently encouraged Clemens to venture further down a path of friendly conversation. "I still don't understand why they don't just perform a system restoration to kill this virus. Didn't a report come out within a couple of hours of the initial attack saying that was possible?"

Gilmore's newfound patience was receding fast. He attempted to relieve his partner of the impression that the recent discovery meant that they were now chummy. "Try not to be such a moron! The goal isn't to recover from the current attack! The analyst team says this is just a test version of the bug attacking a single division's systems. We need to figure out how to kill it in case of a large scale assault! The team says we're on borrowed time already! This test virus implanted itself into our Northwest systems months before it was activated. Who knows how many more have been incubating quietly? Are you *completely* incapable of carrying an idea in your head that isn't associated with a deep fat fryer?"

Clemens had been steadily backing away as the volume of the tongue-lashing had been steadily rising. Gilmore, confident that he had successfully put an end to the stupid-question-asking portion of the afternoon, strolled out the side garage door back into the sunshine. The phone in his pocket vibrated to announce an incoming call. It was from headquarters.

"Gilmore here."

A nervous-sounding young man answered. "Uh… yes sir, this is Simmons from Tech Services. There's been some activity in the attempt to track Subject Joseph Tompkins, and you asked to be notified if anything developed." Simmons paused—waiting for acknowledgement. Gilmore's thin patience grew thinner.

"*Yes*… AND?!"

"Uh… well, it appears that he checked his work email from a small-town library and then turned his cell phone back on about an hour ago…"

Gilmore roared into the phone, "AN HOUR AGO!!? Why am I just being told about this now!? WHERE IS HE?"

The kid on the other end of the line was apparently having some difficulty deciding which question he was meant to answer first. He stuttered through his responses, "Um… y-yes… an hour ago… I-I was at lunch a-and the new guy was s-supposed to be watching… but–"

"WHERE IS HE NOW!?"

"A-Actually, sir… that's the… that's the thing. He's in range of the same cell tower that y-you are. We can't pinpoint his location any more than that."

Gilmore backed toward the doorway of the garage as a light blue Scion tC pulled up to the curb in front of the burnt house. He stared in disbelief as

Subject Joe Tompkins casually exited the vehicle and began to approach what was left of Ned Dyer's home.

Could it be that with all of the resources being thrown at locating this guy, blind dumb luck would prove to be the most effective of them all?

"I'll call you back," Gilmore whispered into the phone, "And, for the record, his name is Joe—Subject *Joe* Tompkins. That isn't short for Joseph." He flipped the phone closed and backed into the garage and out of sight.

Now, he wondered, *where did Clemens run off to?*

Gilmore's eyes scanned the scene outside and then located his fat partner. He was standing in a small patch of trees on the far end of the property with his back to both the garage and the front yard. It was obvious that he was urinating.

Idiot.

All Gilmore could do was wait and hope that Tompkins got a sufficient distance away from his vehicle before noticing the not-quite-hidden field agent. Luckily it appeared that Joe's attention was focused mainly on the demolished house.

From the safety of his hiding place, Gilmore watched as an elderly neighbor approached and talked to Joe. This conversation finally caught Clemens' elusive attention and he responded by crouching behind the foliage. Tompkins then left the neighbor and began to walk around the wreckage of the house, past the barely hidden Clemens, and toward the garage—eyes still fixed on the destruction. Joe was now in the perfect position: the house between him and his car with an Agency employee on either side. Agent Gilmore was about to put the lid on the whole "Fiasco" in one fell swoop.

Tompkins appeared to be lost in thought as Gilmore prepared to leave his hiding place. A quick check of his partner's position, however, revealed that Clemens had the same idea. Gilmore's blood began to boil at the thought of his inferior taking the credit for Tompkins' capture, but his pride wasn't foolish enough to put the mission in jeopardy. After all, there'd be credit enough to go around. He stayed hidden and watched Clemens, with gun drawn, approach Joe from behind.

Gilmore drew his own sidearm while Clemens neared his target. Tompkins seemed none the wiser as the agent behind him raised his weapon in order to deliver an Agency-trained blow to the back of the neck. Gilmore doubted that Clemens had ever used the technique against a live target. He also doubted that he would be successful in rendering the subject unconscious, but he'd probably at least knock him down.

Joe's quick movement came as a shock to Agent Gilmore. Even more of a shock was that it took him only a second to turn the tables on Clemens. In that second Tompkins had obtained a weapon in the form of a lead pipe, turned the element of surprise in his favor, and used the pipe to disarm his would-be attacker. Gilmore was out into the open immediately. He took aim at Tompkins and shouted just in time to prevent another collision of pipe and partner. Gilmore secretly wished he could have allowed Clemens to receive a good knock on the head, but that would be irresponsible. This was too important.

"Drop it, Tompkins! Drop it now!"

The command had its intended effect. Joe froze and dropped the pipe in mid-swing. His back was still turned. Gilmore shouted again, "Turn around now, *slowly*."

Tompkins obeyed, saw the gun pointed at him, and raised his trembling hands above his head—a look of disbelief stamped across his face. The disbelief was a bit of a surprise to Agent Gilmore. He figured that Tompkins should have known that the Agency would have a presence staking out Dyer's house. Maybe Joe wasn't quite as bright as Gilmore's bosses thought.

"G-Gilmore," Tompkins spoke hesitantly, "Man, I am so sorry about yesterday…"

The agent turned his head to one side in amused confusion as Joe continued. Tompkins was apparently trying to bluff his way out of the situation by pretending that he didn't know what was going on. It was an odd tactic, but Gilmore figured that the guy was desperate. He'd probably have tried something similar in the situation.

He decided to do Tompkins the favor of dispelling any notions that the mind game would work. Just because he had been acting the fool for the past few months while observing Joe at the office didn't mean he really was a fool.

"Do you think I'm *really* that stupid, Tompkins? You can cut the act. Put your hands behind your back."

Joe, however, apparently decided that he didn't need to cut the act. He kept his hands raised and tried to sell the deception again, "Seriously, Gilmore, I really feel bad about it. I don't know what got into me. They already have me signed up for this seminar at work… I'm definitely going to utilize the employee counseling hotline too. I swear!"

Clemens had recovered from his shock and was now preparing a set of plastic zip-tie handcuffs. Gilmore's patience was now exhausted. His finger tightened slightly on the trigger of his handgun. He wasn't allowed to seriously injure Subject Tompkins unless absolutely necessary. Whether a bullet to the leg constituted serious injury, however, was open to interpretation. Gilmore calmly issued the command a second and final time, "Put your hands behind your back, Joe."

Impressions of wild confusion and terror still played on Tompkins' face. His hands began to fall slowly as he tightly closed his panicked eyes. With his hands halfway down, Joe's body swayed, went limp, and collapsed to the ground. Clemens looked down at the spectacle and then looked up at Gilmore with a blank stare. "Guess he fainted," Clemens shrugged.

"Don't be a fool! Back away from him!" Gilmore shouted as he cautiously approached, gun still outstretched and aimed at Joe's sprawled out body. "Get up, Tompkins! We're not falling for it."

But Joe didn't get up. He just lay awkwardly in a lump—his arms and legs at unnatural angles, his face half pressed against the debris covered ground, his eyes rolled back in his head. He didn't move.

Gilmore was still skeptical, but he wasn't too worried. No matter how aware of the Agency Joe might be, he still was no fighter. He was just another soft American engineer that was steadily allowing his waist to expand and his health to decline.

Gilmore ventured another few steps forward and then kicked Joe gently with his foot.

This turned out to be a mistake.

It apparently gave Tompkins a frame of reference, allowing him to pinpoint his target. Gilmore felt the blinding pain before he realized what had happened. Joe had flung the lead pipe he had fallen on directly at Gilmore's face. A dull clang resounded as it ricocheted off of his forehead, causing him to temporarily lose both his sight and his aim. Before he could even react Gilmore felt his gun wrested from his grip and a swift downward kick connect with his right calf. Gilmore fell forward, aided by another kick to his back.

Clemens stood uselessly nearby.

Gilmore's chin slammed into the ground before he could get his hands in front of him. Tompkins had surprised him again, but Gilmore's training and instincts now reasserted themselves. He turned over and immediately scrambled to get his feet back underneath him. He was halfway up from a kneeling position when the cool steel of his gun barrel found its way to the fresh bruise on his forehead.

Subject Joe Tompkins was standing over him and glaring with unfocused eyes. It was as if he was staring at something some distance behind Gilmore… or some distance in front of him. Tompkins' mouth dropped open loosely and two slurred words spilled out, "Gedt lowwn."

Gilmore was now frozen in sincere confusion. It almost sounded like Tompkins had forgotten how to talk. Joe swallowed loudly. Apparently he was going to try again. This attempt was louder, "GEDTT DLOWN! Puhhh… ON LAA GOUND! MMNOW!"

Gilmore really didn't care what Tompkins was trying to say, his attention was instead focused on the fact that Joe's eyes were still drifting aimlessly and that his legs were within reach. If he was quick enough, Gilmore knew that he could trip the guy—sending him backward before he managed to fire the gun.

Tompkins shouted another, "GEDTT DLOWN!" as Gilmore's left hand flexed and then sprang at Joe's nearest ankle. But the ankle was no longer there, it had been raised in lightning reaction to Gilmore's reach. Joe's right leg now came down hard and fast, crushing Gilmore's hand underneath a sneaker-clad foot. Joe shifted his weight and twisted his heel, successfully breaking a couple of Gilmore's trapped and surprised fingers. The gun retreated from Gilmore's forehead, only to return swiftly as Joe struck him on his right temple. Warm blood began to spill from the fresh wound as Gilmore fell over beaten—beaten and furious.

He pulled himself back up to his hands and knees just in time to glimpse Subject Tompkins disappear around the edge of the house. He couldn't let him get away. *He couldn't.* Gilmore fought to clear his swimming head and struggled to his feet. He ran forward staggering—leaving his worthless partner behind.

Gilmore's steps were unsteady as he rounded the corner of the house. A gunshot sounded. Startled, Gilmore half-dove and half-fell into the well-manicured lawn. Another gunshot pierced the suburban silence while the bloody field agent cowered on the ground. But there was no new pain. He hadn't been shot.

The sound of footsteps indicated that Tompkins was running again. Gilmore lifted his head to reveal his Agency-provided blue Toyota leaning sideways with two flat tires. Subject Tompkins was almost to his car. He was going to escape, and Gilmore wouldn't be able to follow.

Desperately, Gilmore stood once again and lunged for the Toyota. He wrenched the driver's side door open and slammed his left hand against the trunk button—newly broken fingers writhing in agony. The trunk popped open just as Tompkins slammed his door shut. Gilmore staggered to the back of his car and grabbed the special-purpose rifle from inside the open trunk. The Scion's engine screamed as Joe peeled out and began to accelerate toward the entrance of the cul-de-sac.

Gilmore balanced the barrel of the rifle against his left forearm and aimed at the back of the shrinking car. He pulled the trigger.

In response, a small, electronic GPS tracking dart rushed out of the barrel, flew through the air, found its mark, and dug into the metal of the escaping automobile. Then the device's blue LED slowly began to blink.

28

Meg Trotter had spent the entire day in the car and was ready to be out of it. Fortunately Dan had taken over driving after their long stop for lunch. He had been pleasant enough company since waking, and he did share her curiosity about Ned's text message. But they had exhausted that topic of conversation long ago and they were still staring at four more hours on the road before arriving in Atlanta.

A large colorful sign welcomed the southbound passengers of the orange Mustang to Tennessee. Meg's thoughts returned to Joe. She hadn't tried to call him since early morning, but it had been nagging at her all day. Ned had entrusted her with the task of making sure Dan and Joe made it to the midnight meeting at Everybody's Pizza. She had almost called Joe several times since morning, but something had always kept her from it. And the more time she spent sitting and dwelling on the prospect of talking to him again, the more nervous she became.

She had reasoned that Joe would have received Ned's message and understood what it meant. If he was going to respond to it, he would. A phone call from her probably wouldn't convince him to drop everything and drive to Georgia. It was the middle of the workweek, and Joe didn't live in Atlanta anymore. The only reason she and Dan were making the trip was that they were bored at their jobs and, as contract employees, they had more flexibility in taking time off without pay.

But still Ned's insistence that she be the one to gather the group weighed on Meg's mind. She hadn't heard from him since the text message and was starting to get concerned that something was seriously wrong. She could no longer justify not making another attempt to contact Joe. She dialed his number.

He answered on the third ring. "Meg?"

It took some effort for her voice not to shake as she answered, "Hey, Joe, do you have a minute?"

"Sure. I'm actually glad you called. I'm heading to Atlanta. Did you get a text message from Ned this morning?"

A wave of relief washed over Meg at not having to explain herself. A wave of cautious excitement came next; she hadn't seen Joe in months. Now they were heading to the same restaurant.

"Yeah, Joe, that's why I called. Dan and I are on our way to Atlanta too. Do you have any idea what this is all about?"

A worried tone started to creep into Joe's voice, "I have some idea, Meg. There is a lot going on that I don't understand yet. Ned is in trouble. I just came from this house in Kentuck– What the–?"

Meg heard a thump that sounded like Joe's cell phone hitting the floorboard of his car. She continued to listen in voiceless horror as loud crashing, scraping, and squealing noises followed. They were silenced after a few seconds by the line abruptly closing.

3:12 PM CDT

Tom Rigsby had been through a lot of trauma in the past twenty-four hours, but the memory of all of it had been pushed aside. The only memory now present in his consciousness was of an event that had happened only a few minutes before. Amy McKay had kissed him.

The thought kept a smile permanently affixed to his face as he drove the silver Endeavor toward the nearest town with a bus station. Amy sat next to him, gently holding his hand and munching on Wheat Thins. Sue was in the backseat counting and separating the money that had been hidden in the onboard refrigerator.

The Endeavor lazily followed Joe's light blue Scion down the lonely Kentucky highway. They were, of course, exceeding the speed limit, but not by enough to draw suspicion and there wasn't much traffic on the two-lane road anyway.

A large yawn escaped unexpectedly from Tom's mouth. He was still fighting fatigue from the night before. He and Amy had decided to call in sick to work when they got to the bus station; they figured that they deserved a night off. They were also unsure about the bus schedule and doubted that they'd get back in time for work anyway. Joe and Sue had agreed to stay with them until they had their tickets, and if they wouldn't be able to make it back that night, they'd just head to a car rental place. The two thousand dollars that each of them would be receiving would more than pay for it.

A car appeared on the horizon in Tom's rearview mirror and he slowed slightly. He certainly didn't want to risk getting pulled over if it was a cop. Joe, however, didn't seem to notice and the distance between the two caravanning vehicles started to lengthen.

The image of the approaching car was growing rapidly in the mirror causing Tom to scowl and slow a bit more. A hint of suspicion began to grow in his mind. The guy was flying.

What's he after?

The car was now revealed as a dark gray Toyota. It drifted into the left lane in order to pass. Tom attempted to catch a glimpse inside of the car as it zoomed by, but the afternoon sun reflected brightly off of the dark windows and concealed the interior from view.

The Scion was now a good distance ahead. Tom watched with his mouth half-open as the dark gray Toyota approached and drew alongside Joe's car. The Toyota hesitated a second and then swerved, slamming into the driver's side of the Scion and forcing it onto the shoulder.

Tom's Endeavor lurched as he stomped on the brakes, attempting to come to a stop before being caught up in the car accident playing out before him. White smoke began to billow from the squealing tires of the two cars. They were moving as one—and starting to enter into a slow spin as they drifted further onto the shoulder.

The women inside the SUV were both screaming.

The cars ahead had now spun through half of a revolution and were facing the direction from which they had come. Tom watched helplessly as the cars crashed into a guardrail.

The sound of twisting and scraping metal filled the air until the two cars finally halted—the Scion now facing backward in the right lane, the Toyota facing backward on the shoulder. The two cars were still pressed together. Tom managed to come to a stop on the highway's left-hand shoulder about twenty yards behind the wreck.

He strained to see through the Scion's windshield. Joe was slumped over a deflated airbag and steering wheel. He did not appear to be moving. The driver of the gray Toyota was difficult to see, but the movement inside his vehicle was clear. The door of the Toyota, now over the edge of the road, sprang open and the driver climbed out. He was wearing a suit.

Joe had been attacked and needed help. Tom's decision to act was automatic. He unfastened his seatbelt and slid open the secret compartment next to the Endeavor's driver's seat that Ned's most recent video had mentioned. Inside, two black handguns sat next to each other. Tom took a breath and grabbed one. Over Amy and Sue's objections he opened his door and jumped out.

Circling the front of his vehicle Tom saw the driver of the Toyota round the wreckage and begin to open the Scion's passenger door. Tom quickened his pace, closing the distance easily as he headed directly toward the man in the suit. He held the handgun before him and shouted at the man, fierce and full of righteous anger, "Back away from the car! *Now!* I'LL SHOOT!!"

Tom wouldn't have much of a chance to regret this mistake. The man in the suit spun around to face him, locked his cold blue eyes on Tom's handgun, revealed that he also was holding a gun, and rapidly fired two shots at the approaching nineteen-year-old. The white-hot bullets buried themselves in Tom's chest and knocked him backward off of his feet. He landed back-first on the pavement, his head slamming hard against the road with a loud crack. The gun flew from his hand and clattered as it landed elsewhere on the road and slid away.

Pain was everywhere.

Tom tried to talk, but couldn't. He tried to breathe, but couldn't. Thick blood began to pool in his throat and pour from the wounds in his chest. The asphalt was hot against the exposed skin of his arms and the now bloody wound on the back of his head.

His eyes found the sky. It was a radiant blue, streaked faintly with wisps of cloud.

With great effort, Tom turned his head to the side and the idling SUV came into view. The pool of blood now drained from his mouth and onto the highway. His blurry vision made out the image of the man in the suit stepping over him and walking briskly toward the Endeavor. Tom's vision then faded and failed as he struggled to hold to consciousness and life. Darkness now surrounded and chilled him.

He no longer felt the road, but he heard two more gunshots.

It was for nothing.

The thought burned and then faded in Tom's mind. Despair and death raced each other to be the first to close in and overtake him.

Death won.

"Tom!!" Amy shrieked as he collapsed on the road in front of her. Sue was momentarily paralyzed in the back seat of the Endeavor as the man in the suit turned back to Joe's Scion and crawled into the passenger's seat. A couple of seconds later he climbed out again, gun still drawn, and began to walk directly toward the SUV. He stepped over Tom's body and aimed his gun at the silver Mitsubishi.

This cured Sue's temporary paralysis. She scrambled over the divider into the vacant driver's seat just before the first shot hit the center of the windshield. It bounced off of the reinforced glass, adding another divot to the Endeavor's exterior. Sue struggled with trembling hands to shift into drive as the man outside continued to approach and aimed the gun directly at Amy through the passenger's side window. Amy was screaming and crying and staring directly into the cold blue eyes of the man that had shot her would-be boyfriend. He was only a few feet away when he fired again.

The close range shot shook and cracked the passenger's side window, but it didn't go through. Sue finally found the accelerator and the Endeavor sprang forward away from the attacker. She slowed as she passed Tom's body, uneasy about leaving him but desperate to escape. Another bullet to the rear windshield settled her internal debate. The rear window finally gave way and shards of reinforced glass began to fall as the SUV sped from the scene. The flashing lights of arriving emergency vehicles could be seen through the shattered back window.

Amy buried her tear-streaked face in her hands and rocked violently in her seat. Sue's frantic emotions were suspended in her state of shock. Out of necessity, a thin blanket of calm had wrapped itself around her, enabling her to be the pilot for their flight from the danger behind them. But this blanket of calm didn't stop the war of thoughts in her mind. One in particular stood apart from the others—battling for dominance: *You've seen that man before, Sue. You know him.*

A loud sob from Amy brought Sue back to the moment. She looked at the girl that had now been through and lost so much. A new and resolute conviction formed in Sue's head, determined to end the chaos: *This has gone too far.*

"Amy," Sue spoke gently but loudly over the rushing wind while keeping her eyes on the road and her foot on the gas, "can you give me your phone? I'm calling the police."

"NO!" Amy screamed as she lifted her head and glared wildly at Sue, "Ned thinks they might be in on this! Tom thought so too! We *have* to meet Ned in Atlanta now. Otherwise we did all this for nothing!"

Sue was surprised at this response. She had figured that Amy would be ready to stop running at this point. The girl was understandably emotional—obviously trying to salvage some meaning from Tom's sacrifice, but Sue wasn't going to let that influence them into doing something stupid. It looked like the police were already at the scene of the accident anyway.

"Amy, I know this is hard… but I already saw the police coming. The cover is already blown. We need their protection."

"How long were we there, Sue?" Amy's sobbing had stopped now; the argument had temporarily lifted her out of the pit of her grief, "Five minutes? *Three?* Do you really think that the police could have responded that quickly? They must have already been on their way. This *must* have been planned."

Sue considered this for a minute. If that were true, going to the police could be the exactly what "they" wanted. If that were true then the safe move would be to run and hide—to continue to follow the plan. The only thing to do was to resume the trek to the midnight meeting in Atlanta, though Sue was nursing a vague apprehension that she and Amy would be the only attendees.

"Okay, Amy, we'll go to Atlanta. But if that turns out to be a dead end, we *are* going to contact the police there. After all, *everyone* can't be in on this."

An uncomfortable and sorrow-filled silence settled in the SUV—crowded by the sound of the rushing wind from the fractured back window. It was a silence that would remain more or less unbroken during the rest of their journey southward.

This gave Sue a chance to collect and organize her frenzied thoughts and emotions. She compartmentalized her grief and despair—they were useless at the moment and could be dealt with later. Currently, her mind was busy trying to place in her recollection the face of the man that had attacked Joe and Tom—receding white hair, jet-black and unkempt eyebrows, short gray mustache, soulless pale blue eyes… But no matter how hard she concentrated, no memory occurred to her mind—only a name—a last name.

She whispered it aloud, still unsure of how she knew it, "Gilmore?"

Even more confusing than this was the vague impression that this Gilmore was her friend. A significant part of her wanted to turn back and turn herself in.

29

Agent Gilmore watched as the silver pockmarked Mitsubishi Endeavor disappeared over a hill. He hadn't counted on the infamous SUV (that had caused the death of three field agents early that morning) being anywhere near Subject Joe Tompkins. And when he realized that it was *that* SUV, he hadn't counted on the bulletproof glass. He thought that he had killed Sue Bishop in the driver's seat with the first shot to the windshield. After all, his aim was dead on. He didn't know the blonde girl that had been in the passenger's seat, but now she needed to be eliminated as well.

Gilmore looked down with sick satisfaction at the motionless body lying in the center of the street.

You don't pull a gun on me, boy, he thought with a sense of pride, *at least, not if you want to live.*

His superiors might not be thrilled that a few civilians had been roped into the "Fiasco," but that was Subject Ned Dyer's doing. It didn't really bother Gilmore, his work was too important… and there was always collateral damage in war. But Gilmore didn't need to dwell on all that "greater good" stuff. He knew his purpose within the Agency, and he was good at his job. That was all that mattered.

And while things had taken a messy turn that afternoon, his primary objective had been accomplished. Subject Tompkins had been captured. Gilmore had checked Joe's pulse and handcuffed him to his car before going back to deal with the women in the SUV.

An ambulance arrived at the scene with lights flashing and siren blaring. It was followed conspicuously by two more of the Agency's average looking Toyotas. The whole scene could have been dealt with more discreetly if not for faulty equipment from Tech Services. The GPS tracking dart that Gilmore had attached to Subject Tompkins' Scion had only worked intermittently. By the time he had called for backup to come to Dyer's house and gotten his broken fingers and bleeding temple bandaged, the tracker had stopped transmitting.

Half an hour later it had resumed operation and showed Subject Tompkins' car parked at a house in Kentucky. Of course the Agency then wanted to arrange a large contingent of forces to raid the house and this had taken more time for organization and travel. The GPS tracker had stopped transmitting again while they had been on their way and they had found the house empty when they arrived.

When the tracking dart had begun transmitting again it showed Subject Tompkins southbound on a two-lane highway. Gilmore hadn't waited for authorization. He'd just commandeered the nearest vehicle and taken off—determined to end the chase once and for all. He had already been embarrassed by Subject Tompkins: once when Joe gave him the slip with the car fire, and again with the confrontation at Subject Dyer's house. Gilmore would never have lived that down unless he had corrected his mistakes before they had time to take root in his superiors' minds.

Fortunately, that was no longer a problem. Agent Gilmore now ruled the day. He would be on record as the agent that had discovered Dyer's secret command center and secured the elusive Subject Tompkins. And he did that last bit *completely* alone. He had radioed headquarters to provide the ambulance and backup since he was planning on using the risky maneuver to force Tompkins off the road. But the technology had performed perfectly; small metal spikes had deployed from Gilmore's Toyota and attached to Tompkins' Scion upon contact between the two vehicles. Then it had just been a matter of applying gentle pressure to the brakes and wearing Tompkins down. The ambulance was just there in case of injuries.

Gilmore took a deep breath and sat down on the hood of his recently wrecked dark gray Toyota. Lower level field agents could deal with cleaning up the scene. He deserved a bit of a rest while he waited for the inevitable phone call from headquarters.

He didn't have to wait long. He took the call and confirmed the good news. They would no longer need Subject Dyer to kill the computer virus. The author would be ready for interrogation soon. They could now begin the much simpler task of extracting the code to Dyer's panic room command center. If he chose to be uncooperative, Ned was in store for a very unpleasant evening.

The call ended and Agent Gilmore now turned his attention to the last loose end in the whole matter: the silver Endeavor headed south. He was fairly certain that Ned's code would allow them to track it via the command center buried underneath his garage, but maybe the Agency wouldn't even need that. Tech Services had intercepted an automated text message from

Dyer to Tompkins during the night, "911**Pizza Time Everybody!**911." It was obviously some sort of code worked out between the two of them, but Joe had seemed to be heading somewhere in response to the message—probably some sort of cloak-and-dagger rendezvous in a deserted dark alley.

Gilmore had a feeling that the two women in the SUV were still headed to this secret meeting. They would be surprised when they got there though. Tech Services had intercepted the same text message sent to the cell phones of two of Dyer and Tompkins' former coworkers: Meg Trotter and Dan Curtis—and they were already being tracked. All of the fugitive parties were now headed south, probably going to Atlanta. The secret gathering of friends of Ned Dyer was probably supposed to provide them some means of fighting the Agency. Instead it would allow the Agency to bring the "Ned Dyer Fiasco" to a prompt and tidy conclusion.

Joe Tompkins lifted his barely conscious head a couple of inches off of the steering wheel where it had been resting. A fresh bruise throbbed on his forehead. Blurry images of flashing lights and men in suits swam outside of his car. Something cold and hard was pinching his right wrist.

His watery eyes strained to focus on his wrist's assailant. It was a metallic ring—one side of a shiny pair of handcuffs. The other end was clamped on the steering wheel.

Joe's head felt light and it floated gracefully back to its resting place. His heavy eyes drooped and closed halfway. The promise of sleep snuck in to spring Joe from the prison of his new and harsh car-crash-and-capture reality. His weary consciousness welcomed the escape. His sore chest began to rise and fall rhythmically and steadily.

His left hand, however, was a little more active than the rest of his exhausted body. It was busy with its own pursuits. These included retrieving Joe's cell phone from the floor mat, punching in a sequence of buttons, and sending the sequence as a text message to his old friend Meg Trotter. The phone was taken from him a few moments later.

30

Amy McKay had remained mostly quiet as the pleasantly sunlit hills and mountains of Kentucky and Tennessee slowly passed by her window. The red sun dipped below the horizon as the Endeavor entered Georgia, weaving back and forth through the last of the Appalachians.

A stop outside of Nashville had provided a stopgap solution to the problem of the busted rear window in the form of a packing tape and cardboard structure. This had decreased the sound of the wind considerably, but a significant degree was still present for the rest of their journey. Amy was thankful, the pervasive sound dissuaded conversation. She had no desire to talk about what had happened or what they would do next. She just wanted to get to this meeting and find out where it was going to take them.

Her resolve had solidified considerably during the trek southward. She knew that Tom was very likely dead. He had been shot twice in the chest. If he had died, he would have died attempting to be noble—attempting to do the right thing. Amy was certainly going to carry on for his sake. Anything less would cheapen his sacrifice.

It was just before midnight when Sue pulled the SUV into the small parking lot of Everybody's Pizza. The onboard computer had led them directly to the spot—every turn, every side road. Amy was sure that they never would have found the place otherwise. Neither of the women had ever been to the fast-growing city before and the winding Atlanta streets didn't exactly follow the grid pattern they were used to.

They parked next to a metallic orange Ford Mustang and walked up to the lighted doors of the pizza joint. A bell jingled to announce their arrival. Amy followed Sue into the restaurant. Amy would let her do the talking.

The place was mostly empty, only two tables held customers. One table hosted what looked like a study group of summer students from the nearby university, but neither Amy nor Sue even glanced in their direction. They immediately saw the table they were looking for and approached it directly.

An attractive woman with reddish-brown hair and gray eyes was sitting next to a tall black man with a bandaged right hand. Amy recognized them from the Endeavor's computer as Meg Trotter and Dan Curtis, both on Ned's list of trusted friends. In further confirmation of their identities, the pair was leaning over and studying a tablet PC. It had no doubt been left for them by Ned.

Meg looked up as the two women approached the table. She was wearing a slight look of surprise and confusion. "Sue?" Meg tried hesitantly, "Sue Bishop?" She stood and offered her hand in friendship. "We weren't expecting you to be here, we've been waiting for Ned and Joe."

Sue took the woman's hand gracefully and with tears forming in her eyes, "I don't think either of them is going to be able to make it. I'm afraid it's just Amy and me." Sue directed Meg's attention to Amy and they also shook hands.

"Well, if you don't already know, I'm Meg. This is Dan," Meg pointed at the black man who, in addition to sporting a heavily bandaged hand displayed a dark bruise on one cheek. "We both used to work with Ned and he 'summoned' us here." Meg then pointed to the third occupant of the table, a scrawny man in his forties with short curly hair and a bad sense of fashion. "And this is Schultz. He used to work with Ned too. We picked him up on the way down here."

Amy nodded politely at the two men and then turned her eyes back toward the floor. She didn't feel like being very sociable. It had been a hard night and she was really just starting to wonder when she'd be able to sleep.

A jingle from the bell over the door gave her an excuse to divert her attention elsewhere and she looked over her shoulder to observe the new arrival. A disheveled looking man with dark-rimmed glasses, deep brown eyes, and a short sandy beard appeared at the doorway. He had various scrapes and bruises on his face and he stepped gingerly as he walked. Sue gasped as she also noticed him, ran up to the man immediately, fell upon him, and hugged him violently. Her loud sobs could be heard throughout the restaurant.

Ned Dyer had arrived for the meeting. He was right on time.

31

Tuesday, 8:05 PM

Ned Dyer had drifted back to sleep, still held tightly by the restraints of the otherwise comfortable dentist's chair. His brief period of hyper-consciousness had been dizzying and exhausting. The encounter with Joe's virus had left him drenched with sweat. However, the room he was in was cool and he was starting to shiver—but still he slept.

The filters of Ned's mind were slowly rebuilding themselves as the hypnosis-inducing drugs receded from his sleeping consciousness. The memory of the terrifying events of the past 24 hours were no longer repressed and now swirled freely through his vague dreams.

He dreamt that he was being chased by a faceless gang of department-store suit wearing hoodlums through the streets of downtown Atlanta—unable to get to his midnight meeting at Everybody's Pizza. As he ran he tripped and found himself falling into a deep and dark pit brimming with glowing lines of source code. IF and FOR statements crowded around him, guarding their secrets and suffocating Ned's weary brain with recursive calls and infinite loops. A paralyzing fear gripped Ned as he thrashed against the mental onslaught—a fear that he wouldn't be clever enough to escape the chaos.

A sudden splash of water landed on Ned's face and yanked him awake—away from this nightmare of the typical software engineer. Ned reflexively tried to sit upright, but the leather restraints around his waist and wrists kept him down. He was confused. He didn't know where he was but a faint familiarity of his surroundings seemed to retreat from his mind. As he took in the room he struggled to remember how he had gotten here, but the last thing he clearly remembered was being strapped to a chair in a dingy white room. There, his pager had informed him of the completion of Phase One of Contingency Plan Gamma. He remembered the discussion with the tall man in the gold tie—his failed sales pitch for his freedom—the signal that the bomb had detonated at his house—but then there was nothing. He felt as if that had been several hours ago, maybe days.

The man who had been wearing the gold tie the night before stepped from behind Ned's chair into view. He now wore a white button-down shirt with the sleeves rolled up and no tie. He was smiling at Ned with a familiar and sickening look of glee that engaged his whole face. In his large hands he held a small aerosol can with a short red straw sticking out of it.

Ned's heart began to quicken as he remembered the last time this man had spoken to him. He had promised that Ned wasn't finished enduring "physical mistreatment." Ned's throat was painfully raw, but he felt that he needed to try to project a calm demeanor in order to not give in to his fear entirely.

In a hoarse voice he attempted a joke, "It's the molar near the back, Doctor. It's been bothering me for a few weeks now. Before you say anything, I know I don't floss as much as I should, but I do use that toothbrush that sends out the micro-pulses."

The man sat down on a wheeled stool and rolled over the tiled floor—coming to a stop next to Ned's chair. There was an unmistakable note of joy in his voice when he spoke, apparently ignoring Ned's attempt at humor, "You know, Mr. Dyer, it occurs to me that with all of the excitement last night I neglected to properly introduce myself. I feel that it is important that you know a little bit about me before we begin this process." He rolled his stool to the foot of Ned's chair, set his aerosol can down on a table, and continued, "My name is Conroy and I have been with this agency for fifteen years."

Ned felt the laces on his right shoe being undone and responded by shaking his foot furiously against the restraint in order to impede his captor's efforts. Agent Conroy's only acknowledgement of Ned's resistance involved him firmly grasping the toe of Ned's writhing shoe and forcing it painfully downward. Ned clenched his jaw against the sensation and let his foot fall limp. He tried to comfort himself with the rationale that they wouldn't be resorting to these measures if they had access to his family. That meant that his loved ones were still safe.

The thought didn't help as much as he had hoped.

Agent Conroy now had removed Ned's right shoe and sock and then spoke again, "I'll be honest, most of the time my job is rather boring, Mr. Dyer. You know, performing surveillance, preparing reports, the occasional hypnotic interrogation... Rarely is this kind of activity warranted, and even more rarely is it authorized. You, Mr. Dyer, have made my week. Personally

I'm hoping that you won't cooperate immediately. I'd like to draw this out a bit."

Ned closed his eyes and attempted to lower his heart rate. He started to debate about what information he would be willing to give up if need be. He didn't think he knew very much that could possibly be of interest to this organization and, as long as his family was safe, he didn't really care about much else. He would try to resist for as long as he could, but there was no need to be a hero. If they just wanted his help with something, that was fine with him. Ned re-opened his eyes and saw that Agent Conroy had picked the aerosol can back up and had wheeled over to the head of Ned's reclined chair.

"Now, *technically* I am supposed to give you a chance to cooperate before we begin, but I'd rather you just get a taste of what you are dealing with first. You do, of course, know what this is?" Conroy brought the can into Ned's field of view. Ned inwardly groaned. It was a can of diagnostic freeze spray. He had seen it used to test the electrical signal response of flight-hardened circuit boards to rapid temperature change. A small discharge would instantly freeze the surface of whatever it contacted. The can's purple label was crowded with warnings against contact with skin.

"Don't worry; I'm going to start with just a little spray on the top of your foot. We'll move to the bottom or the toes if need be. Oh, I should also mention that this will hurt more than it normally would. I've injected you with a nerve sensitivity enhancer. It is perfectly safe; just think of it as the opposite of aspirin. Now, try to hold still."

With that Agent Conroy rolled back to the foot of the chair and applied the spray to a small spot on the top of Ned's foot. Frost formed immediately as the top layer of skin hardened. Ned closed his eyes and gritted his teeth against the pain. Because of this he didn't see Agent Conroy grab the rubber reflex mallet and use it to deliver a swift blow to the freshly frozen flesh. A painful scream escaped Ned's tender throat before he could stop it.

In only a few seconds the warmth of the room thawed the thinly frozen skin—but the soreness remained. Ned couldn't help his eyes beginning to water.

"That was a fairly small amount of the chemical spray, Mr. Dyer. I am personally very curious about the effects of a larger amount. I am hoping that you will give me the opportunity to find out."

Ned blinked back his tears and stared at Agent Conroy, "Just tell me want you want."

"Just a simple code, Mr. Dyer. We just need access to your 'contingency' systems to make sure that we haven't left ourselves overexposed. You see, the event that triggered the action we took against you last night will be resolved soon. If not for all your extensive preparation, any matters concerning you would now be closed. But now that we have discovered your efforts, we need to dismantle them. We have already gained access to your bomb shelter command center. We just need the code.

"Once our technicians are satisfied, you and your family will be free to go. What's more, I offer you this additional consolation: you won't have any memory of our encounter in this room. All of this will be over and you won't hear from us again. We will provide you with a convincing cover story to tell the people that have been inconvenienced by this mess and then we can all go on with our lives.

"I'm also supposed to tell you that the Agency regrets its intrusion into your life three years ago. My superiors have even suggested that they are open to offering some kind of monetary restitution if you cooperate quickly. But again let me stress that, personally, I'd like to continue down our current road for a while—so please don't answer my next question." He leaned in close to Ned and his deep voice became a whisper, "The system is asking for a five-digit code. What is it?"

It was a convincing pitch and Ned longed to believe it. But he knew that the code they wanted would give "the Agency" full access to his systems, including the locations of the safe houses he had set up. His family would no longer be protected. Telling them the code would unravel everything he had worked so hard to protect.

But Ned was afraid that this process would be too much to withstand. He knew that in the end he would probably give in. Maybe he *could* believe Agent Conroy's story. Maybe he could trust these promises. Maybe it would be better to give in now and avoid any more "physical mistreatment."

Ned swallowed in an attempt to moisten his throat enough to speak again, "I'm terribly sorry, *Mr. Conroy*, but I have no idea what code you are talking about."

Agent Conroy's smile widened and there was glee in his voice. "Thank you, Mr. Dyer. I am going to enjoy this."

But before the agent got the chance to continue playing with the freeze spray, a loud pop echoed from outside the building. The overhead lights then died and the room with the comfortable dentist's chair was plunged into darkness.

Well, that's annoying.

Agent Conroy felt for the table in the dark and set down the can of diagnostic freeze spray. He wheeled his stool across the pitch-black room, found the doorknob, and opened the door to the hallway. The lights were out there also, but the emergency fixture on the wall dimly illuminated the concrete-lined basement corridor.

Conroy glanced back at Subject Ned Dyer, still restrained in the hypnotic stimulation room. He considered just propping the door open. He could then continue with the code extraction process using the pale glow that spilled through the doorway as a light source. After all, the fun part was just beginning. But, Agent Gilmore had been named as the agent-in-charge of the operation and (in typical Gilmore micromanagement style) he had insisted that anything out of the ordinary was to be reported immediately. Agent Conroy knew he would do well to stay on Gilmore's good side. With Subject Joe Tompkins' recent capture and his computer virus' imminent destruction, Gilmore was perfectly positioned for a promotion to Division Headquarters.

"I apologize for the inconvenience, Mr. Dyer," Conroy said in smooth and practiced tones. He was quite proud of his skill in projecting a perfect blend of steely calm and sociopathic joy. In the mind of his subject this usually elicited a solid belief in Conroy's unflinching willingness to inflict a limitless amount of pain during an interrogation. Agent Conroy felt strongly that this skill of his was underutilized. "If you could find the patience to excuse me for a few moments, I promise that we will continue shortly."

Subject Dyer's weak and raspy voice answered, "You are excused, Mr. Conroy. A word of friendly advice though, you may want to consider raising your rates if you can't afford the electric bill."

It was a struggle for Agent Conroy to walk away from this; he longed to shut the smug bastard up. But it was important to keep his mask of composure. He was still angry with himself for allowing it to slip in front of Dyer the night before.

You're in control, Conroy, he told himself. *He's just a punk kid strapped to a chair.*

He let the door swing close. The dank basement hallway stretched between two cinder block walls underneath the assorted ducts and pipes that ran the length of the ceiling. The communications room was one floor up. There he would attempt to contact Agent Gilmore. Conroy figured he was probably still in flight—transporting Subject Tompkins to the Division office in Chicago.

A brisk rhythm of dull echoes sounded as Agent Conroy's footsteps padded down the hallway. The offer he had presented to Subject Dyer in exchange for the code was actually almost genuine. The Agency *was* already preparing a convincing story for Ned's friends and family that would explain his seemingly erratic actions. Ned's loved ones would also indeed be free to continue to live their lives largely unencumbered by any additional interference from the Agency.

Of course, they would be saddened to learn of Ned's carefully hidden but clearly documented history of paranoid schizophrenia that eventually caused him to take his own life. His parents might be a tough sell on this story, but unfortunately Ned's disease didn't manifest itself until he was in his twenties and had been out on his own. His old roommate Joe would have corroborated this if he hadn't fallen victim to Ned's violent tendencies in the shocking murder/suicide that was sure to rattle the central Illinois town in which they had grown up.

Conroy smiled at the thought as he entered a shadowed corner where the emergency floodlights didn't reach. The hall turned left. He stepped back into the light after rounding the corner and stopped short.

Something didn't feel right.

Conroy hadn't seriously considered that the power outage was the result of someone's intentional sabotage. Not until that moment. Was this part of some rescue attempt? He quickly dismissed the idea. While it *was* true that the converted warehouse was not heavily guarded (especially with the loss of several field agents during the night), the facility was protected by secrecy. The location was well hidden.

True, Subject Dyer's pager trick had radioed the building's GPS coordinates to his contingency systems, but his attempt to transmit this information to the authorities had been intercepted. Early that morning Agent Conroy had taken Dyer down to the hypnotic stimulation room. There he had learned the method by which Ned's systems would contact the police. Only the initial information packet had been delivered when the Agency had raided the local twenty-four hour office support company that Ned's systems contacted—and that packet had been intercepted at the local police station by one of the Agency's embedded resources.

The leak had definitely been contained; the hypnotized Ned Dyer had been adamant that no other communication attempts would be made by his systems. Agent Conroy had wanted to continue to collect information about Ned's contingency systems, but the decision had come down from the Division Head that Dyer should be pitted against Tompkins' computer virus as soon as the potential leak was dealt with.

Had the guys at Division known about Dyer's subterranean panic room command center that morning, they would have probably let Conroy extract the code then. But the Agency's history with Subject Dyer had taught them that he wasn't always cooperative during hypnotic interrogation. They had needed to eliminate the biggest threat first. Unfortunately he had repelled their attempt to persuade him to inoculate their systems against Joe's computer virus. Resistance had now been built up in Dyer's mind. Within the next few days any further hypnosis was also likely to be repelled.

The Agency couldn't wait that long, so Division had approved the use of torture. Agent Conroy lived for days like this.

So, it was with full confidence of the warehouse' impregnable secrecy that he reached the shadow-shrouded end of the hallway and opened the door to the stairwell. Apparently the woman waiting for him behind the door did not share this confidence. Agent Conroy would have time to ponder this later. At that moment he was busy having the door smashed back into his face, falling backward to the concrete floor, and receiving a swift and disabling kick to the side of his head.

He barely heard the woman sprint back down the corridor to the hypnotic stimulation room. He passed out before she spoke, but if he hadn't he would have heard her talk to his chair-bound captive.

"Are you Ned Dyer? Quit messing around—we have a meeting to get to."

32

The wound on Ned Dyer's naked foot burned with pain as he sat in the terrifying darkness. In all likelihood the blackout was part of some psychological ploy aimed at getting him to talk. Every second that ticked by carried the threat of a potential ambush from some unseen attacker lurking in the darkness. Ned was dangerously close to giving up the code that these people wanted—and with it, his family as well. There was no hope of rescue in him. It seemed that all of his preparation had been for nothing. *Worse!* It seemed to have put everyone in *more* danger.

Ned was suddenly claustrophobic. He struggled against the leather straps, longing to take some sort of action—even being allowed to pace the room would have been calming. It was useless though. He was thoroughly trapped. There was, of course, a small part of his mind that attempted to plan an escape. If questioned about the mechanics of this escape plan, this small part of Ned's mind might have mumbled something about untying his remaining shoe with his bare left foot and flicking the shoe toward the table that held the freeze-spray. The aerosol can would then, potentially, bounce off of the wall and onto the dentist chair—possibly within Ned's grasp. He could then freeze the leather straps that held his wrists, causing the restraints to become brittle, allowing him to break free. It would then just be a matter of escaping whatever building he was in, possibly overpowering a few armed guards (Ned armed only with some freeze spray and a small reflex hammer), and then finding transportation to his nearest safe house.

He would never have admitted it later, but the toes on Ned's left foot began to reach over—searching for shoelaces to their right. However, they gave up quickly. After all, even Ned's normally cheery toes couldn't be expected to sustain *this* level of blind optimism for more than a couple of seconds.

Soft but rapid footsteps echoed outside of the door. Ned turned his head when they stopped and watched as the door opened. Painfully, he caught a couple of eyefuls of the blinding whiteness that flooded out of an LED flashlight.

An unknown woman's voice, clear and strong, called out from behind the light, "Are you Ned Dyer?" Ned nodded slightly, still squinting against the attacking photons.

There was a hint of a smile in the voice as it continued, "Quit messing around—we have a meeting to get to."

It really wasn't funny, and Ned suspected that this was just a continuation of the evening's mental assault against him, but he grunted in laughter anyway. *Finally! Someone in this hellhole with a sense of humor.*

The woman entered and mercifully directed the light beam around the room and away from Ned's blinking bloodshot eyes. The flashlight assumed a position between her clenched teeth as she went to work undoing the straps that held Ned down. He wasn't able to see much of anything, but he could tell that this woman was thin and short—barely more than five feet tall. Her fingers were quick; Ned was free within a few moments.

The woman's light now focused its attention on the fresh wound on his left foot, "Ned, I don't know how much this foot hurts, but I need you to be able to walk. This might sting a bit, but I'll try to be fast."

She put the light back between her teeth, opened a Velcro compartment somewhere on her belt, and produced a rubbing alcohol-soaked pad. Ned was sitting upright now—lightheaded and confused. The resurgence of pain from his foot as his rescuer cleaned the wound made it difficult to concentrate, but he knew he had questions. He would need satisfactory answers before he could trust this woman.

She produced a pocketsize spray can and applied a couple of squirts to the now clean wound. Ned initially flinched at this, but the next moment brought with it a cessation of activity from his overly ambitious nerve endings. A warm and beautiful numbness coated the top of his left foot.

Forget not trusting her, Ned was in love with this woman.

But he still needed some answers. An attempt to swallow was unsuccessful so that Ned could do no more than whisper, "W-water."

The woman placed a Band-Aid over his wound and then handed him a small plastic vial. "This is all I have on me, and I don't trust anything in this place. I have bottled water in the truck."

He took the vial, twisted off the cap, and downed the liquid greedily. It moistened his throat enough to allow him to speak.

"Who are you?"

His rescuer located Ned's missing shoe and gently pushed it onto his newly bandaged foot. She spoke quickly, as if this wasn't the time for small-talk, "Well, my name is Sam—not that that tells you anything. I own a greenhouse in southwest Indiana where I grow exotic plants." With his laces now tied she set the light down, stood up, and offered her hands to help him to his feet. "Oh, I'm also ex-CIA. I still do some freelance work on the side."

Ned Dyer took Sam's outstretched hands and lifted himself off of the dentist's chair. His feet hit the ground hard and jarred his legs, but with Sam's help he was able to stand. She seemed to be in a bit of a hurry, but Ned still didn't understand where this woman had come from. *He* hadn't arranged a rescue.

"So, how did you know where I was being held?"

Sam approached and opened the door. She peered into the concrete hallway outside. "I hacked into the facility's closed circuit video system before I knocked out the power." She turned back toward Ned who was still standing in the same spot. "Alright, come on, we don't have a lot of time." She stepped into the hallway.

She hadn't really answered the question that he actually meant to ask. The information about hacking the security system was interesting, and temporarily pushed his real question from his mind. This wasn't difficult, as he was still feeling a bit lightheaded.

Ned shifted his weight forward in order to take a step toward the dimly lit hallway—but his leg collapsed underneath him. And while the fall wasn't very graceful, he *did* manage to put one hand down to slow the collision between the floor and his head. It still hurt though. After a moment there was some slight attempt by Ned's exhausted limbs to pick his body up off of the floor, but they couldn't get it together. It was best to just lie there and regroup… and maybe take a quick nap.

Unfortunately this didn't sit well with Ned's rescuer. She knelt down on the floor next to him and grabbed his right upper arm. "Sorry about that, Ned. I didn't realize you were so dizzy." He heard another Velcro compartment open and saw Sam pull a cap off of a syringe. She held it up and squeezed out the air bubbles. "Alright, this is just a little bit of adrenaline. We need to get moving."

Sam quickly plunged the needle into Ned's arm and then cast the injector aside. Ned felt his pulse quicken in response. Any thoughts of sleep dissipated. His tired limbs got it together and picked him up off of the floor.

A vaguely familiar panic struck as Ned followed Sam into the hallway. It was the common feeling of dread that bears down on someone who thinks he is wearing his eyeglasses but is, in fact, not. It was an easy mistake for Ned to make as his nearsightedness was fairly minor, but the effect of being surrounded by a five-foot sphere of blurriness was unnerving nonetheless. Ned liked to feel like he was in control of his situation—a feeling that had been scarce since his early morning conversation with Agent Conroy when the warm assurance of safety supplied by his meticulously prepared contingency plans was shattered.

Sam was pulling him down the shadowed hallway, but Ned's fresh stock of adrenaline finally gave him the courage to suspend his campaign of uninhibited cooperation. He wrenched his arm free from her grip and stopped short. He had been pushed around all day. That ended now.

"I need to get my glasses."

Ned turned on his heel and began walking back toward the room. Sam's flashlight followed, "Ned, trust me, we have to get out of here. I think that I sedated all of the guards, but the longer we're here, the longer we're at risk." He didn't even slow down. She eventually gave in, "You know what? That's fine, Ned. I'll find your glasses. You head toward the stairs." She pointed down the hallway and handed him her extra flashlight, "Go that way. I'll catch up."

The fact that he had (mostly) won the argument mollified Ned's sense that he was being helplessly manipulated. He turned back around and continued down the dim and fuzzy hallway.

A few moments later Ned was standing above the crumpled figure of the agent that had so recently played the part of his torturer. Another one of Sam's syringes lay a few feet away. The man was out cold.

For twenty-four hours now Ned's brain had been poked, prodded, played with, and perplexed. But all of that confusion was now cast aside. A clarifying thought, beautiful and unchallenged, rose in his mind and stood like a shining crystal—clearing away the fog:

Get revenge.

Ned could have just let loose a barrage of flailing kicks to Agent Conroy's stomach and face. Or, he could have picked up the large red fire extinguisher hanging on the wall and used it to break both of Agent Conroy's legs. But there was only one instrument of vengeance that would be able to dispense the justice that Ned desired. It was a small aerosol can that was sitting in the room he had been held in. He started back down the hallway in order to retrieve it.

He hadn't gone very far when he met Sam running toward him carrying his dark rimmed glasses, "Okay, Ned, I got them. We have to move now."

She handed him his glasses and he put them on. It was the first good look Ned got at his rescuer as they stood in the dim illumination provided by the emergency lamp on the wall. Her long black hair was tied back. Her clothes were black too. Her face was narrow and determined and framed large brown almond-shaped eyes. There was something about those eyes that told Ned to abandon his plans for retrieving the freeze spray. Even though this woman was almost a full foot shorter, she looked tough. It appeared that Agent Conroy's incapacitation had been short work for this former CIA agent. The measure of revenge probably wasn't worth the showdown. Besides, he needed this woman in order to get out of there.

As if to hasten the resolution of Ned's internal dilemma, the speaker attached to the emergency light fixture on the wall suddenly began screaming in alarm. Sam looked up briefly, grabbed Ned's hand again, and pulled him back toward the stairwell. "Sounds like I missed one. Somebody is awake."

Ned ran with her. But in homage to his yet unresolved anger, he still managed to stomp on Agent Conroy's sprawled out right leg as he passed. In the stairwell Ned followed the bouncing flashlight beam up the steps and out the door that led to the ground floor. The sun was about to set so that the windows barely aided the emergency lights in illuminating the carpeted corridor that they now entered. But even in the dusk Ned could still plainly see the bald man running toward them—blocking their path to the front door. Ned recognized the man as Agent Fuller.

Fuller saw them and reached for his gun, but Sam had already drawn her taser. Two electrodes exploded from the device and latched onto the bald man's chest. Any groan that accompanied Fuller's seizing was drowned out by the still roaring alarm. He dropped his gun, but Sam landed a high and powerful kick to his jaw anyway. Ned decided he was glad he hadn't crossed this woman as they ran out the door and into the twilight.

Sam's dark-gray Chevrolet Avalanche was parked in a small lot a block away from the warehouse. Ned and Sam climbed in and sped away. The rescue had been successful. Unfortunately there was no way Ned could make the midnight meeting in Atlanta. They were still in southern Illinois and only had two and a half hours to get there.

"There's bottled water in the glove box," Sam informed him once they were safely away. Ned investigated and did indeed find two bottles of name-brand water. It was the third bottle that caught his attention though. He picked it up and felt that it was cold.

It was not until that moment that Ned realized that he had been craving this product all day long. He cracked the seal on the twenty four-ounce bottle of Dr. Pepper and enjoyed a long pull of the sugary concoction. This Sam woman was okay in his book.

Sam glanced at the small GPS unit attached to the windshield. "The local airport isn't far, I've got a single engine airplane rented and waiting for us. You should just make your meeting." She noticed and commented on his choice of beverage, "Oh, I almost forgot that was in there. The guy who hired me specifically requested that I have that on hand if the rescue attempt was successful. Guess he knows you pretty well."

Ned's head snapped toward her in confusion. His primary question for this woman still remained unanswered. It seemed as good a time as any to ask it. "Who was it that hired you?"

Sam kept her eyes on the road as she replied, "Uh, the guy's name was Joe. Joe Tompkins."

33

Tuesday, 5:17 PM

Dan Curtis' day had taken an ugly turn. Well, it had started off ugly with the early morning visit from Meg Trotter, but he had recovered from that by sleeping for the first several hours of their trip. It had been good to get out of the office and he *had* been looking forward to a long weekend in Atlanta. But now he wasn't so sure.

Meg had been hysterical after she had talked to Joe on the phone. Apparently she had heard him get into an accident. They had tried to call him back without success. And the one piece of information Meg *had* gotten during the abbreviated conversation confirmed their fear that Ned was in trouble.

They were reasonably sure that Joe had made it through his accident because of the text message he sent a couple of minutes afterward. But the contents of the message were troubling: RUBN faLoed?

It had taken them a minute to decipher "Are you being followed?" from the text, and the shorthand indicated that Joe wasn't at liberty to communicate more clearly. That meant that he was now in trouble too—perhaps he had been unexpectedly followed and was now unable to continue to the meeting. Meg had been trying to convince Dan of what she suspected was a very serious situation and, for the first time, it had occurred to Dan that he and Meg weren't necessarily safe.

They needed to be sure that no one was following them.

Dan watched the other cars in the rearview mirror for a few miles to see if any appeared to be suspicious, but he wasn't sure what a suspicious vehicle would even look like. The only plan he could come up with was to vary his speed in hopes that a pursuing vehicle would match. So initially he decreased his speed to ten miles an hour under the speed limit. Several minutes later he

175

hadn't noticed anything. All the cars on the road just passed them. He then tried ten miles above the speed limit, but still no one stood out.

To Dan this meant that it was a false alarm, but Meg still wasn't satisfied that they were safe. So he took a more drastic action. He switched on the hazard lights and pulled over to the shoulder.

Meg twisted in the passenger's seat and faced him with a look of shallow confusion and fear. "Dan, what are you doing? If someone is following us we need to try to lose them!"

He knew the maneuver might be risky, but *he* didn't really believe that anyone could be tailing them at that point. Meg was the one that needed convincing. To him this was simply the most efficient method of determining either way.

"Listen Meg, if there *is* someone following us then they have one major advantage: they know who we are. We have to flush them out to level the playing field. Otherwise we are going to think every car is after us. That's just impractical."

She seemed to consider this for a minute, and then nodded in agreement. "Okay, but let's at least hide up there," she pointed up the prairie-grass covered embankment at a clump of bushes. "The car will still be in view. If someone comes along looking for us they might just think we hitched a ride."

Dan decided that this extra inconvenience wasn't big enough to argue about. The two got out of the Mustang, waited for a lull in passing traffic, and quickly climbed the slope to the hiding place. The air outside was humid and sticky. The afternoon sunlight fell on them from between the scattered clouds.

So there they were: hiding on a hill, about ten yards from Meg's Mustang, watching various cars fly past without care. After about fifteen minutes, Dan figured that Meg should be convinced that there was nothing to worry about. It was time to get moving again. He started to stand. About halfway up, though, Meg grabbed his shirt.

Her voice was hushed but forceful, "Get down! Here comes someone!"

Dan ducked back down and looked in the direction that Meg was pointing. A vaguely familiar but otherwise average looking gold Toyota came creeping along the shoulder of the road with its hazard lights also flashing. Dan recognized the parking sticker in the front windshield. He and Meg both had ones just like it. This car belonged to a coworker.

Dan squinted against the sunlight reflecting off of the Toyota's windshield as it came to a rest a few feet behind Meg's car. He watched as two men climbed out of the Toyota and approached the parked Mustang. He recognized the pair immediately.

Since childhood Dan had struggled with a temper. Usually he was able to keep it in check, but he had been dealing with these two idiots for too long now. Whatever patience he would have been able to exercise with them had evaporated with the other stresses of the day.

"Schultz! Fischer!" Dan shouted as he left his hiding place and rapidly descended the hill toward the two men, "Just what the *hell* do you think you're doing?!"

Meg was close behind him and equally as frustrated. Her day had been longer than his and she was still sick with worry for Ned and Joe. Her voice reflected her high level of annoyance at the anticlimactic arrival of the two men, "Schultz, I told you to tell management that we wouldn't be in today! Did you think I meant that you should follow us?"

Schultz and Fischer were taken off guard and turned to face their approaching coworkers. Schultz was at the rear of the Mustang on the ground. He had been looking under the bumper, but straightened up as Dan approached. Fischer had been looking into the driver's side window on the far side of the car.

Dan decided that Schultz would be the one to explain what was going on. He finished closing the distance between them, grabbed the collar of the guy's poorly chosen shirt, and looked him directly in the eye.

"Tell me what is going on," Dan seethed.

There was a wild and frightened look in Schultz's eyes as he began his explanation, "W-well… kehhh… um… w-we were j-just curious… kehhh… a-as to w-where you t-two… kehhh… w-were going…"

Dan tightened his grip and pressed Schultz against the car, "Not good enough, Schultz. Who *told* you two to follow us?"

Schultz threw a worried glance toward Fischer, "N-No one… kehhh…"

Dan's hand slipped from Schultz's collar and closed gently around his neck. "I'm not buying it." Slowly, he began to tighten his grip. Schultz's face reddened. "I'll ask you one last time. Who told—"

A sharp pain suddenly stung Dan's lower back. He released his grip on Schultz and spun around to find Fischer now standing behind him and holding some sort of handgun. Dan reached back to find the source of the pain. His fingers closed on a small metal cylinder. He pulled it out and looked down at it. It was some sort of tranquilizer dart.

Anger flooded into Dan's bloodstream and mixed with the numbing drug from the dart. Fischer would pay for that. Dan lunged at the greasy fat man. His legs, however, gave out underneath him and Fischer stepped effortlessly out of the way of his would-be attacker. Dan fell helplessly to the ground, unable to stop his left cheek from connecting with the asphalt of the highway's shoulder. The biting pain that should have resulted was instead muted and dull.

Consciousness was quickly retreating. Dan was vaguely aware that he was sprawled out on the hot pavement. He was vaguely aware of the sound of another dart being shot, accompanied by a startled cry from Meg. He was vaguely aware of Fischer leaning close and swearing at him. He was vaguely aware of the bones cracking in his right hand as a result of a stomp from Fischer's foot.

He was vaguely aware of the blackness that overtook him.

5:57 PM

It was the same nightmare again.

Dan Curtis was reliving that tragic evening from six years ago. Some of the details of the memory were now fuzzy (proof that his repeated attempts to drown his past in alcohol were working), but the outcome of that night was impossible to forget. It was the last time he saw his wife and two children.

That had been a stressful year and everyone's emotions had been closer to the surface. He was usually pretty good at controlling his temper. But that night his control slipped. He had been haunted by regret ever since.

Perhaps it had been a mistake to attempt a graduate degree while juggling a full-time job and a family, but he had done it for *them*. His master's in computer science had made Dan marketable. True, he had been moving from state to state since completing the degree, but he had never had trouble finding high-paying contract work. That money was supposed to have gone toward a better life for him and his family.

Instead, he had moved out shortly before graduating. His family was still getting the money though. Dan continued to send all that he could, every pay period. He had no savings. He owned no real estate. He had no retirement. When he was lucky enough to have a job that allowed overtime he worked eighty-hour weeks. If overtime wasn't available, he moonlighted as a bartender. Anything he could do to make more money to send, he did.

It was never enough to assuage his guilt though. His ex-wife had never forgiven him either. He was sure she was okay—the checks he sent were always promptly cashed. But she never wrote. And she never sent him photos of the kids.

So the only images of them he had were the relentlessly persistent mental pictures of his last evening at their apartment: his four-year-old son welcoming him home from a long day, his wife asking him to attend to their crying two-year-old daughter while she warmed dinner. It had taken so little to set him off. He had only tripped on one of his son's toys on the way into his daughter's room. The pressure must have been building for a while. His reaction to the incident still didn't make any sense to him.

It was playing out again now as he slept. He had never hurt his wife or kids before, but that night he did. They ended up in the emergency room—his wife with three cracked ribs and his son with a broken arm. The shame was and continued to be unbearable. The crushing guilt of that evening now manifested itself physically as a painful tightness in his chest. He felt trapped—helpless—suffocated.

He forced himself awake.

In addition to guilt, the tightness in his chest was being caused by a thick black rope. It was holding him to the chair he was sitting in. His heart was pounding heavily in an apparent attempt to loosen the restraint. Plastic zip ties held his wrists and ankles to the wooden arms and legs of the crimson-upholstered chair. Throbbing pain radiated from his broken right hand and bruised left cheek.

Dan took in his environment with blurry blinking eyes. He was sitting in a motel room—a *cheap* motel room. The queen size bed dipped noticeably in the middle and was covered in stains. The tattered curtains matched the bedspread, stains and all. The turquoise carpet was threadbare and probably in its thirties. Another crimson chair sat on the other side of the room. It held a terrified looking Meg Trotter.

"Dan, are you okay?" she whispered.

"Yeah," he replied, not whispering, "but I think Fischer stomped on my hand. It feels broken."

"What's going on? Where are we?"

Did ya, hear Meg? he thought as he fought to focus his eyes, *I just got my hand broken. Don't annoy me with questions I don't have the answer to.*

Dan took a second to calm down. What was happening wasn't her fault—apart from the fact that she insisted on making the trip—but it wasn't *really* her fault. And it had been *his* idea to pull the car over, so he shared some of the blame too. For Meg's sake he needed to be the calm one. She was obviously panicking.

Dan took another breath and tried to sound reassuring, "Ned got himself into trouble with someone. They must have hired Schultz and Fischer to follow us. They can't really be interested in us. It's just that Ned got us involved. I'm sure we'll be fine. It isn't like we know anything about what's going on."

Loud voices came from outside the motel room's door. Dan couldn't make out what they were saying, but it sounded like an argument. A minute later the voices stopped. The door opened and produced a sweaty and frustrated looking Fischer. He plodded determinedly up to Dan and shouted. The putrid stench of his breath stung Dan's eyes. "WHY DID YOU HAVE TO PULL OVER!? WHY DIDN'T YOU JUST KEEP DRIVING!?"

Fischer's normally pink face was bright red all the way up to his fleshy hairless scalp. His small eyes bulged as he yelled. All the while he was gesturing wildly with his stubby arms. It might have been the lingering effects of the tranquilizer, but Dan couldn't help but laugh at the sight.

That turned out to be the wrong thing to do.

Fischer froze in mid-tantrum. The color drained from his face. His puffy lips curled into a snarl as he turned and picked up the telephone receiver on the table next to Dan's chair.

"You'll learn not to laugh at me," Fischer growled with a commanding tone that seemed violently out of character. He then raised his fat arm and swung the phone downward—smashing Dan's crippled hand against the wooden arm of his chair. It did the trick, Dan's howl of laughter transformed instantly into one of pain.

"Stop it, Fischer! Leave him alone!" Meg screamed through tears from the other side of the room.

Fischer turned toward her with a greasy smile, "Don't worry, Meg, I'll be with you shortly."

Meg Trotter couldn't imagine enduring a worse scenario as she sat, restrained in an unknown motel room, watching Fischer interrogate Dan. It had taken all of her willpower not to dwell on the fact that this disgusting troll of a man had carried her unconscious body into the room and had bound her to a chair. She had barely won her battle not to vomit at the thought.

"The decision before the two of you is straightforward," the troll began as he addressed the room with a tone that seemed less seedy than usual, "we already suspect that you were headed to a," here Fischer wiggled his stumpy fingers annoyingly in the air mimicking imaginary quotation marks, "'secret meeting' at the request of our old friend Ned Dyer. Schultz and I simply feel left out. We want to attend.

"All you have to do is convince whomever you are meeting that Schultz and I are concerned friends that are supposed to be there. After that you'll be free to go." Fischer had been pacing back and forth between the two captives. He now approached Dan's chair, "Seems like a pretty good deal, eh?"

Dan's tightly clenched face told Meg that his hand must have still been in a lot of pain. She imagined that the pain had the opposite effect than the troll intended. His response to the offer came as a soft growl, "Just tell me what's going on, Fischer."

Had she not been restrained, Meg would have jumped out of her chair at the sight of Fischer suddenly exploding at this comment. His face resumed its previous bright-red hue, his tiny eyes resumed their previous bulge, and his chubby arms resumed their previous state of wild gesticulation. "I don't think that you fully understand the situation! Do you have any idea who I am? Who I *really* am?"

Fischer picked the telephone receiver back up, disconnected it from the base, shuffled his round body around Dan's chair, and continued in a softer voice, "You've already been more trouble than you're worth. I would advise against refusing my offer. You have no idea what's in store for you if you do."

"I'm not afraid of you, Fischer."

"Well you should be!" Fischer screamed as the disconnected phone cord suddenly came down and tightened around Dan's neck. The unkempt fuzz that was Fischer's beard quivered as he laughed and pulled the cord tighter still. Dan reacted by squirming and grunting and reddening his face. Meg reacted by screaming for help.

The troll's voice was now wild and loud and filled with laughter, "Scream all ya want, Meg! No one's around to hear!"

From somewhere inside her a weakening levy of willpower gave way— letting loose a flood of panic that swirled and foamed and threatened to drown Meg's struggling mettle. She shuddered in her chair against the plastic restraints. Unconsciousness flirted with her mind. Its promise of relief hovered just ahead.

Fischer was now whispering in Dan's ear from behind as he loosened the phone cord, allowing Dan to breathe again. Meg could tell that her friend's resolve was also weakening. It wouldn't be long before they both broke. She mustered the strength for one last cry for help.

It was answered by the sudden springing open of the thin wooden motel room door. Schultz stepped into the room and closed the door behind him. He was carrying a tire iron.

"Finally!" the troll exclaimed. "Schultz, our friend Dan here needs some softening up. Would you care to do the honors? A couple of shots to the gut should help us obtain his cooperation."

Meg looked on in stunned horror, feeling helpless, wishing that sudden harm would befall the man that was torturing her friend. This was a wish that, it turned out, would soon be granted.

Jon Schultz was in over his head. Keeping tabs on Meg and Dan had been one thing. Tailing them had been one thing. Kidnapping them was another. Roughing them up for information was another still. It was definitely time to contact his handler.

Luckily Agent Fischer had just given him the opportunity. He had gone into the motel room where Meg and Dan were being held, leaving Jon alone in the parking lot to "find something to beat them with." Jon leaned against the back of Fischer's Agency-provided gold Toyota and called the emergency number that his handler had given him. He had committed the number to memory, but he wasn't supposed to ever use it—that is, not unless he encountered a situation dire enough to risk blowing his cover at the Agency. He was about to be ordered to beat information out of innocent civilians. Keeping his cover intact wasn't worth that.

His handler agreed.

Enough information about the Agency had been gathered. It was time to take action. The two of them used the little time that was available to come up with a plan. Jon hung up the phone, found the tire iron in the Toyota's trunk, and headed back to the motel room door. He could hear Meg Trotter screaming for help as he approached. He took a second to calm himself and then entered the room.

Schultz did not allow himself to react to the sight of Agent Fischer strangling Dan Curtis with a phone cord. His skill in keeping his face expressionless around his greasy partner had been necessary to avoid suspicion. But the two years of deception were now finished. The Agency's days—make that the Agency's *hours*—were now numbered.

The condescension in his partner's voice as he barked another command fueled Jon's anger, helping him to find the nerve to carry out his new mission.

"A couple of shots to the gut should help us obtain his cooperation."

How he *loathed* this Agent Fischer! He wasn't sure what was worse, being told by the Agency that he failed to make the grade as a full-fledged field agent or being partnered with this obvious failure of a human being.

That they put him on par with this disgusting creature!

Schultz knew that he had never been the life of the party, but most of his apparent social ineptitude was an act—an Agency-encouraged act. Fischer was the real thing. Why the Agency had ever even taken him on was a mystery.

Nevertheless, Jon Schultz had been steadfast in his commitment to the Agency for almost a year. The promise of advancement had dulled the edge of these injustices. But appeal after appeal for reassignment had gone unanswered. When the man that would one day become his handler approached him and asked him to help bring down the Agency from the inside the decision had been easy. Jon would have liked to believe that he turned double agent for some noble reason, God and country and such, but he knew that, at the end of the day, all of his motivation boiled down simply to ego.

The Agency would rue the day that it overlooked Jon Schultz.

Jon approached Dan's chair and registered the fear in the man's bloodshot eyes. The tire iron was cool and heavy in his hand (in contrast to the room that was hot and stuffy and reeked of Fischer's disgusting BO). Jon raised the weapon in order to strike. He would have to be quick.

Down came the tire iron—hard and fast. It connected with a satisfying thud against Fischer's thick scalp. A startled groan was cut short as Fischer's fat head slammed against the thin wall behind him. The rest of his body followed and shook the room as it hit the uneven flooring.

Jon's quivering hand dropped the tire iron. There was no going back now. He spun around and faced Meg, "Guys, I am *so* sorry about this. Don't worry; I'm getting you out of here."

Meg's eyes reflected fear and confusion as he approached, "Schultz, what's going on? And why aren't you stuttering?"

Jon couldn't help his face flushing at this question. This was real professional. Here he was, a highly trained double agent, some sort of super-spy in the middle of a high-risk mission, blushing because a girl talked to him. It was this part of him that he hated: the insecurities of childhood that lingered long after their time.

He pulled out his pocketknife and began to cut through the zip ties that held Meg's wrists to the chair, "Um, I haven't had a real stutter since high school. It's a long story, but I'm actually a federal agent. I've been working undercover for a couple of years now," he pulled out his Homeland Security badge and showed it to Dan and then to Meg. "I know you guys have about a million questions, but we have to get out of here now. The Agency probably already has backup on the way."

Both of Meg's hands were now free and Jon kneeled down to free her ankles. Her scream brought him back to his feet in a flash. He wheeled back around. Fischer was still lying on the ground but was now conscious. His right hand was struggling to raise his Agency-issue 9mm.

Agent Jon Schultz's right hand was quicker. It liberated Jon's own handgun from its shoulder holster, aimed, and pulled the trigger in an instant. The bullet was dead on and pierced Fischer's flabby neck-flesh. Dark red blood, thick no doubt with cholesterol, bubbled from the wound. Fischer's beady eyes wore an expression of shock. His puffy-lipped mouth gurgled and produced more blood yet. But Schultz wasn't paying attention to this. His attention was fixed firmly on his own outstretched right hand. The shot had been a reflex action. Obviously the extra field training his handler had provided had been effective. Extremely effective.

From the corner of his eye Jon caught more movement from Fischer's hand. He looked at his dying partner still trying to aim the gun, took two steps forward, and buried another gratifying bullet into Fischer's sweaty forehead.

Meg Trotter screamed again.

34

The badge in Meg Trotter's hands looked real—but the implications of that fact seemed to be at blazing odds with her perception of reality. Schultz had only been *pretending* to be a social misfit. He was really an undercover federal agent—a federal agent that had just killed Fischer right in front of her eyes.

She was standing now, pacing the motel room floor while Schultz untied Dan. It was clear that Schultz had acted in self-defense, it just seemed like it had been far too easy for him to kill.

But, she thought, *I guess that comes with the profession.* Of course, this didn't mean that she was comfortable with the idea. Rescue notwithstanding, it would probably be a while before she felt that she could trust the guy.

Schultz finished untying her injured coworker. "I've got a first aid kit in the car, Dan. I can wrap that hand once we're out of here. Meg, we'll have to take your Mustang. The Agency will be able to track the Toyota." Schultz opened the door as Dan got to his feet. The curly-haired federal agent paused before leaving the room and turned back toward Meg, "I have a few things to transfer to your car."

She followed Agent Schultz out onto the faded and crumbling parking lot. Fischer's gold Toyota sat next to her orange Ford. Schultz quickly grabbed a couple of plastic cases from inside the gold car. He handed one to Meg, "Put that in the back seat. It's the first aid kit."

Dan then appeared at the doorway of the motel room and approached Meg's car. He still looked pretty shaken. Schultz opened the second case revealing an array of weapons and gadgets. "Go ahead and get in the car, you two. I'll drive us somewhere safe where I can bandage up that hand of yours, Dan." Schultz selected a sturdy looking hunting knife from the case, bent down next to Fischer's Toyota, and dug the knife into the sidewall of the right front tire. He then repeated the process with the other three.

When Schultz had finished disabling the car, he circled Meg's Mustang, stooped down behind the rear bumper, and pried something off of its underside. He brought the something up to the passenger's side window and showed it to Meg. "GPS tracking device. It's how Fischer and I were able to follow you from a distance." Schultz dropped the gadget onto the asphalt. "I'm sorry to say that *I* was the one that attached it to your car this morning." He then packed up the weapon-laden case and stowed it in the Mustang's trunk.

Fifteen minutes later the trio was a few miles away, parked safely amidst a horde of similar automobiles in a crowded mall parking lot. Schultz was still in the driver's seat and had just finished bandaging Dan's broken hand. "That should hold it for a while, Dan, but we'll need to get you to a hospital soon. The codeine should help with the pain."

Meg had been silently considering their next course of action. Schultz had said he was taking them to the nearest Homeland Security field office for debriefing and protection. He had told them that Ned and Joe had both been captured by this "Agency" and, therefore, there would be no one left to meet at midnight. Meg felt helpless. Ned had only entrusted her with a single simple task and she wasn't even going to perform it. She couldn't shake the feeling that this midnight meeting was about more than just gathering the group. She suspected that there was something there that Ned wanted them to find.

Dan was still crammed in the back seat. He retracted his newly bandaged hand and spoke for the first time since leaving the motel room. His tone was low and somber, "I need you to be honest with me, Schultz. When Fischer was choking me, trying to get the location of the meeting out of me, he whispered something in my ear. He told me that they had already picked up my ex-wife and kids…"

"He was lying," Schultz interrupted immediately, his voice and eyes both stern and truthful, "Fischer was just trying to break you. That was completely untrue."

Dan closed his eyes in relief and whispered, "I suspected as much. Thanks."

Schultz turned in his seat to face forward and pulled the car out of the parking space. "The nearest field office is about 45 minutes from here. I'll feel better when we get there. Hang tight, guys, this is almost over."

Meg was facing Schultz from the passenger's seat. She felt the need to object to this, but didn't foresee any possibility of changing the man's mind. He had taken charge of the situation, he was a highly trained government agent, and he was armed.

Apparently, though, he wasn't the only armed occupant of the vehicle. Dan's left hand appeared suddenly from behind and pressed a blood-spattered 9mm against the back of Schultz's neck.

"Keep both of your hands on the wheel where I can see them," Dan Curtis ordered from the back seat of the Mustang, gun firmly in place. It wasn't *necessarily* that Dan didn't believe Schultz—the answer about Fischer lying about Dan's family had seemed sincere. And he *wanted* to believe that Schultz was who he said he was. But the years of deception could not be erased so easily.

Plus, regardless of their present circumstances, Dan was certainly not ready to accept that *Schultz* was now their leader. Federal agent or not, no one had put this guy in charge of the expedition.

Jon Schultz obeyed Dan's command and kept his hands in place on the steering wheel—still guiding the car through the mall parking lot. His voice reflected a combination of annoyance and fear, "Dan, what are you doing?"

"Just stop the car at the end of the row. Meg, I need you to reach into his coat and take his gun. Can you do that?"

Meg Trotter's eyes were wide as she gazed back at Dan, "What's going on, Dan? Where did you get a gun?"

"Off of Fischer before I left the motel room. Meg, I know Schultz just saved us, but I still don't trust him. He's been deceiving us for years—there is no way to know if he's really who he says he is now. We need to decide what to do together, and not let him just dictate our next course of action."

"Okay," she replied, "I'm getting the gun now." Carefully Meg slid her hand into Jon's cheap-looking suit jacket and retrieved the handgun from his shoulder holster. Dan motioned for her to pass it to the back seat.

Agent Schultz's voice adopted a calmer, more placating tone, "Listen, I understand how you feel. But I only want to take you to a government-run office. Trust me. It will be safer for you there."

"Well," Dan said, "I'm not too worried about anyone following us at this point, Jon. No one knows where we are. No one knows where the meeting that we were heading to is. Now, this is Meg's car and she's the one that convinced me to go to this meeting of Ned's. I still think that we should go, but it's up to her. Meg, what do you want to do?"

Meg looked down and studied the cup-holders for a moment. Her voice was soft but steady when she answered, "I made a promise to Ned. I'd like to fulfill it." She looked up and met Dan's eyes, "I still think he would want us to go."

"Guys, we can send a couple of *trained* federal agents to go to your meeting for you. I know I keep saying this, b-but my first c-concern is for yyour safety!" Schultz appeared to be getting a little agitated, as the discussion was not going in his favor. Dan now saw something of the old Schultz in this even-tempered federal agent, the Schultz that would whine in meetings when someone disagreed with him. It was just enough of a glimpse of the man's weakness to solidify Dan's resolution to take control.

Dan raised his voice, still holding Fischer's gun in place, "If Ned had *wanted* federal agents there he would have informed the government about the meeting! The decision has been made, Schultz. The only decision *you* have to make is whether you want to be dropped off now, or whether you'd like to come along. Unlike you, Meg and I are not in the business of kidnapping people."

Jon's shoulders sunk a bit, signaling his acceptance of the situation, "Okay, Dan. If you guys will let me, I'd like to come with. You don't need the gun anymore. I promise I won't try anything." He turned in his seat and faced Dan, "You can at least acknowledge that I've earned a *little* bit of trust, can't you?"

Dan pulled the gun back and set it down, "Agreed. Now let's get back on the road. We're still headed south. You're driving."

"I at least need to call my handler to let him know about the change in plans."

"Sorry, Jon, but that isn't going to happen. In fact, go ahead and hand your phone back here. I don't think that we can risk you signaling someone for help if you turn out to not be who you say you are."

Schultz's tone developed a hint of panic, "D-Dan, my handler knew that I was going to attempt to r-rescue y-you. He's waiting to hear how it went! If he doesn't hear from me soon they won't know what happened. You *have* to let me contact him."

"Well I am sorry, Schultz, but that's just not my concern right now. Although you have the whole rest of the trip to try to convince me to let you call in—you know, while you explain just exactly *what* is going on."

35

Tuesday, 8:49 PM

The plush leather chair cradled Agent Gilmore as he gazed out the window at the purple and billowing clouds that rolled past. The cabin of the business jet was nicely stocked. Normally Gilmore would have refrained from partaking in the creature comforts (out of a desire not to appear gluttonous), but it had been a very long, very successful day. He had earned the right to a cigar and scotch. Both were finished now, so Gilmore stretched his legs in front of him and drifted off to sleep. They were still an hour from their destination.

Subject Joe Tompkins also slept in a posh leather chair in the Agency's mostly-empty 12-seater business jet, but he wasn't enjoying the flight nearly as much as Agent Gilmore. For one, his slumber wasn't voluntary—it was drug-induced. And he had enjoyed neither drink nor smoke, but instead had to settle for the paltry comfort provided him by the metallic cuffs that bound his hands and feet.

During initial questioning after being captured, Subject Tompkins had maintained his ignorance of the Agency and the computer virus that endangered its systems. It had been an impressive performance. Gilmore had threatened Joe's family, and Joe had responded with visible concern and stress—an ideal specimen of an innocent man, a perfect picture of fear. The act hadn't wavered.

Tompkins' ability to preserve this level of commitment to a lie under such intense interrogation must have been one of the qualities that had made him so attractive to the Agency. Gilmore had been observing Tompkins for months, but he was still largely at a loss as to why this particular subject was of such value. Even the weekly hypnosis sessions had never yielded any clues to Joe's supposedly extraordinary worth.

Although, Gilmore had to admit, since the previous afternoon Tompkins had unexpectedly evaded him twice. Not to mention that Joe had allegedly authored the cleverest computer virus anyone in Tech Services had ever seen. There was definitely some elusive quality to Subject Joe Tompkins.

Not that any of that mattered now. Tompkins had certainly been more trouble than he was worth. Anticipating his superiors' eventual decision, Gilmore had commissioned a murder/suicide cover story to be developed and implemented involving subjects Tompkins and Dyer.

But they still needed Joe to kill his virus first. Once it had been clear that simple questioning and threatening were not going to produce results, Gilmore had wanted to move immediately on to more persuasive tactics. The call from the Division Head had surprised him. He had "offered" Agent Gilmore use of the more sophisticated debriefing lab at the Agency's facility in Chicago. Gilmore had known better than to reject the offer. He had interpreted it for the command that it was: Subject Tompkins was to be sedated and flown immediately to Division HQ for a more *supervised* degree of interrogation. But that was fine with Gilmore. It was a chance to show his skill.

A soft and comforting melody was emanating from Gilmore's noise-canceling headphones. It was interrupted by the pilot's voice, which in turn jarred Gilmore awake, "Excuse me, Agent Gilmore, you have a phone call."

He gripped the arms of his seat, stretched his back, and pulled the lever to bring the seatback to a more upright position. Then he lowered the headset's flexible microphone to his mouth in order to reply, "Okay, thank you. Put it through."

The voice that issued from the headset was strained, nervous, and belonged to Agent Fuller, "Is this Agent Gilmore?"

A brief flash of anger flared up in Gilmore's chest. Who else did he think he was going to get? It was a crying shame that Fuller hadn't been one of the field agents lost the night before—incompetent imbecile. Gilmore took a breath and tamped down his temper. He *had* asked to be kept abreast of any news. The call might be important. "Yes, Fuller. What is it?"

"Sir, our location has been compromised. A team of mercenaries hit the warehouse and helped Subject Dyer escape custody. I visually accounted for only one of them, but I'm certain there were more."

"WHAT!?" Gilmore screamed into the mouthpiece. What could have possibly happened? What kind of attack couldn't have been repelled? "Put Agent Conroy on! I need to know if he at least got the code from Dyer!"

"Agent Conroy is unconscious. They injected him with something. I don't think he had time to get the code; we were hit shortly after waking Dyer. But sir, if a team of professionals is involved here…"

Gilmore had already arrived at the same conclusion. Conroy had assured him that the leak had been contained—that Ned Dyer's systems would only attempt communication through the small office support company now under Agency control. Indeed, Tech Services had since intercepted additional emails with instructions to deliver Dyer's data packet to various other law-enforcement agencies. Apparently the system would keep attempting to call for help until it was deactivated.

But if an organized team of professionals had broken in and rescued Subject Dyer, the situation was not nearly as contained as Conroy had indicated. Gilmore had based his plan of action on the assurances of Agent Conroy. Precious time had now been wasted. Potential opportunities had been squandered. Conroy was going to pay for that.

Clearly, the new priority was to get control of Dyer's contingency systems. It was the only way of knowing how far the leak had spread. "Contact Tech Services. Have them put someone in the command center under Dyer's garage. Tell them to *find* a way to crack that code!"

"Right away, sir. Any further instructions?"

Gilmore's thoughts turned toward the one other potentially damaging development of the day, "Has there been any contact from Fischer and Schultz?" The two agents following subjects Trotter and Curtis hadn't checked in for hours. It wasn't hard to imagine that the two overestimated their mission's importance and decided that they needed to go "radio silent" in order not to be distracted.

"None yet. Their vehicle is still at that motel in Tennessee. We've already sent someone to check on them, but the assumption is still that they are observing the meeting that Dyer set up."

"Good," Gilmore barked into the microphone, "continue to keep me informed of any developments."

The call ended. So much of the day's work seemed to be unraveling, and Gilmore was sitting helplessly on a plane. He had been looking forward to some face time with the Division Head in Chicago. Now it felt as if the comfortable chair in which he sat was propelling him toward what would be a decidedly *uncomfortable* reckoning with his superiors. He knew he would be held to account if the "Ned Dyer Fiasco" spiraled out of control.

But he *had* secured his primary target. Subject Tompkins was still safely in custody. Gilmore vowed that Joe would stay that way. He would keep Tompkins close and, when the time came, *he* would be the one to kill him.

A few minutes later another interruption from the pilot dismissed the thoughts from Gilmore's mind, "Sir, you have another phone call."

It was Fuller again—and again he had bad news. Word had come from the field agent sent after Fischer and Schultz. Fischer had been found dead in the motel room. Schultz and the two subjects were missing. Whether Schultz was a captive or a conspirator, Fuller couldn't say.

Too much was now happening for this to be a coincidence or an unfortunate stroke of bad luck. There was definitely some unseen force at work here—an unaccounted for effort was conspiring against the Agency. Gilmore couldn't shake the feeling that the man sitting next to him, though both unconscious and chained, somehow held the key to understanding that unseen force.

The degree to which this would turn out to be true, Gilmore had no idea.

36

It had been a few years since Sue Bishop had eaten pizza this late at night—probably not since her college days... well, college nights. Those had been some tough years, working full time and going to school in the evenings, but she had gotten through it. She received her accounting degree only a semester later than the full timers. So her father's job troubles had, in the end, only pushed her life back six months or so. And at that point she had obtained a very good job at a very good local aerospace firm.

Work had been difficult the first few months. It seemed that she hadn't retained as much of her education as she would have liked to, but things had fallen into place eventually. A guy in the engineering department, Ned Dyer, had helped her adjust to her new responsibilities. Sue had always wondered how he had found the time. He seemed so busy.

Those memories were nowhere near her mind at the moment though. She was just overjoyed, plain and simple. The hot and much-needed meal didn't hurt her disposition, but her joy stemmed mostly from one fact: Ned was safe. He hadn't said much about what had happened to him, but it was clear from his cuts and bruises that it had not been pleasant. He must not have been fed either, judging by the fervor with which he was currently attacking the pizza in front of him.

Sue didn't employ the same level of dynamism in *her* incursion upon the cheesy feast, instead keeping one arm tightly around her fiancé while demurely using the other to feed herself. But that didn't mean she was any less ravenous.

The study group that had been occupying the only other table at Everybody's Pizza had been run off by the owner—at Ned's request. Apparently the restaurant normally closed at 10 p.m. Ned had paid the owner to keep it open later that night. The details of this meeting had been meticulously worked out in advance. This came as no surprise to Sue, who had (by that time) learned quite a bit about her fiancé's obsessive preparation for the events of the past 30 hours. She had encountered several aspects of this firsthand: a kitted out SUV, a couple of safe houses, and a series of computer contingency systems so extensive that they had enabled her rescue from the middle of an obscure corn field in the middle of the night.

Sue's gaze scanned the other members of the small group and eventually fell upon Amy McKay. She was at the end of the table, right next to Sue, sitting quietly and staring downward. Her eyes were red and puffy. Her food was untouched.

A guilty flush pinkened Sue's face. She had somehow forgotten this girl's trauma—somehow forgotten the car-wreck and shooting that she herself had witnessed only a few hours before. Sue leaned over, grabbed Amy's hand underneath the table, and squeezed it gently. Amy looked up at her with appreciative but tear-filled eyes. She was obviously feeling very alone and very scared. Sue squeezed a little harder.

That reminder of the afternoon's events again brought Sue's other troubling questions to mind. Namely, who were these people that were after Ned, what did they want from him, and how did she recognize that man, *Gilmore*, who had shot Tom? A vague sense of guilt accompanied this last question. Sue and Amy had relayed their story to the group by this point (and had also heard about the frightening ordeal that Ned's old coworkers, Dan and Meg, had gone through). But this sense of guilt had kept Sue from mentioning the fact that she recognized "Gilmore." She was afraid of what it might mean.

Ned had kept mostly quiet since entering the restaurant, indicating that his story would only raise more questions at this point and that he was ready for some answers. Sue looked toward the man that promised to provide some of these answers, the man who had claimed to be a federal agent working undercover in a mysterious organization, the man who had insisted that the group turn itself over to government custody immediately. Ned, Dan, and Meg were vocal about their reservations in trusting him. That meant Sue was suspicious as well. Even so, she couldn't wait to hear what he had to say.

She didn't have long to wait. Jon Schultz finished chewing a bite of pizza, thanked Ned for allowing him to eat a little before answering any questions, and addressed the group in a calm and authoritative voice.

"Let me first just say, on behalf of the Department of Homeland Security, how sorry I am for the ordeal that you have all had to endure. Know that you are helping your government disable a dangerous terrorist organization that has been secretly operating within our borders for years."

How the hell did Ned escape?

Even after 25 minutes, the question was still burned prominently into Jon Schultz's brain. He wanted to ask his handler if a rescue had been arranged, but he hadn't been able to contact him since before freeing Dan and Meg. His explanation of the Agency (and his role in it) during the drive to Atlanta apparently hadn't garnered the level of trust that he had hoped it would. True, Dan was no longer pointing a gun at him; all of the weapons were locked safely in the trunk of Meg's Mustang—right next to Schultz's powered-down cell phone. They had wanted to see what the meeting was all about before they'd let him call in.

So, now he was going to repeat his explanation for a wider audience in hopes that the group would finally trust him and allow him to take them someplace safer. Currently, these people were successfully evading the Agency but, even with their careful precautions, eventually their luck was bound to run out. Just ask Joe Tompkins. Schultz had heard of Subject Tompkins' capture while riding with Fischer, shortly before their encounter with Dan and Meg.

"I'll start with my own story," Schultz continued his explanation, holding the interest of everyone at the table (with the possible exception of the sad-looking blonde girl sitting at the end). "An obscure organization known only as 'the Agency' recruited me about four years ago. I had been working as an aerospace engineer in the St. Louis area—sixteen years at the same company when they laid me off. I was afraid that I would be out of work for a while, but I barely had a chance to get my résumé together before the Agency approached me.

"Now, before you judge me for agreeing to work for such an organization, you need to understand my state of mind at the time. I was devastated after losing my job. I had always been completely devoted to the company and had always worked my hardest. For my efforts the company first took away my retirement and then took away my job. I was mad. I wanted to strike back. Most of all, though, I wanted to feel appreciated—to feel like I was contributing toward something.

"I was told that the primary purpose of the Agency was to serve as an underground information conduit for the aerospace industry. Essentially, that they made money by selling competitors' industry secrets to each other. Supposedly, spies would infiltrate aerospace corporations and feed technical information to the Agency. A team within the Agency would repackage the data so that it couldn't be traced. Then, a buying company would be contacted. This was usually done through a seemingly legitimate front, like a contracting house. The buyer never knew that they were purchasing stolen data, so they were protected.

"I understood that, at the root, the organization was criminal and that if caught I would face prison time. But I was assured that it would be considered white-collar crime and, at worst, I'd spend a couple of years in a minimum-security facility. Besides, the money they were offering offset both the risk and ethical dilemma involved. In fact, the recruiter even promoted an almost-acceptable justification for circumventing intellectual property laws. They asserted that, by forcing these companies to share information and design components, they were actually accelerating technological progress. There was a certain beauty to the idea—everyone shares with everyone else.

"Anyway, regardless of my reasons (and I'm not trying to justify my decision) I accepted a position with the Agency. They told me that they had had their eye on me for a while and that they saw great potential in me. It seemed like a great opportunity to use my experience—and to 'get back' at the industry at the same time. I was honored… and I was broke. It was a no-brainer.

"I spent a few months at a training facility before being deployed. I met the three of you," Jon nodded toward Ned, Dan, and Meg, "during my first assignment."

Ned shifted impatiently in his seat. His voice was gruff and angry, "This is taking too long. Get to the point, Schultz. This 'Agency'—what are they after and how are *we* involved?"

Jon felt instantly defensive and responded in kind, "I'm *just* trying to be thorough, Ned. I don't want you to think that I'm leaving anything out. I also want you to understand that I'm not going to be able to provide you with an answer to *every* question you have. I was at a fairly low level in the Agency, and they are very skilled at compartmentalizing information."

Schultz took a breath to calm himself. "I'll try to be briefer though, I'm sorry. After all, time *is* of the essence. The longer we stay here the less safe we become. This isn't a secured location."

"We are all aware of your concerns, Schultz," Ned replied with a slightly gentler tone. "Please continue."

"That first assignment was an information-gathering operation. I was funneling technical specs and source code to the Agency. They were interested in anything that potentially had a military application. In order to dissuade suspicion that I was up to anything, I also adopted a certain 'persona' that gave the impression that I was… an idiot. My work was half-hearted and sloppy, my social skills were non-existent, and my appearance," Jon indicated his badly clashing shirt and tie, "was ridiculous. Th-The st-stutt-tter… kehhh… w-was f-fake… kehhh… t-too.

"Anyway, it wasn't long before I became skeptical about the work that the Agency was having me do. I started asking some of the troubling questions that were haunting me. Why was the Agency only interested in military data? How did we know that this information wasn't being sold to enemies of the state? Well, they apparently didn't like it and sent Fischer to 'help' me carry out the assignment. I've been under a certain level of scrutiny ever since. So it was at great personal risk that I agreed to work with Homeland Security as a double agent. And only then did I learn the truth about the Agency."

"That they were, in reality, a terrorist organization," Ned again interrupted—his voice agitated, his tone condescending. "We gathered that already. *What* do they want—is it just military secrets?! How are *we* involved?!"

Jon glared at Ned. He had put up with this kind of thing from young engineers for too long now. He was trying to help these people. He deserved their respect. Schultz was on his feet now—and yelling, "You are addressing a federal agent, Mr. Dyer! You would do well to remember it! I have been patient with you all for some time now, but I *will* not be spoken to with disrespect. Do you know how many laws the people in this group have broken in the past twenty-four hours? The longer you prevent me from contacting the authorities, not only are you in more danger, but the worse it looks when we consider granting you amnesty for your illegal actions!"

The outburst had been unexpected, but Schultz was enjoying it nonetheless. A guilty pleasure at finally turning the tables on those who had treated him with whispered contempt and disdain warmly oozed through his insides. He would show them how much power he held over them—even when unarmed. Hovering close to Dan Curtis, he stared the bruised black man directly in the eyes, spitting amidst his shouts, "*You* turned a gun on me! Threatened me! I could easily have you put away for a couple of years!"

"That's enough, Schultz!" There was a quality in Ned's voice that made Jon stop his shouting and turn his head toward the young man. Ned was no longer eating. He was instead holding a handgun—and pointing it toward Schultz. A twitch began to pulse in Jon's left eye. He blinked. His left hand was already in motion by the time he reopened his eyes.

He wasn't exactly puzzled by this—*detached amusement* might more accurately describe Schultz's mood as he watched his hand reflexively grab the mostly empty pizza pan that sat in the middle of the table. The lightning-quick hand then forced the pan upward—smashing it into Ned's outstretched gun.

The firearm flew predictably upward. Jon took a step backward—away from those seated at the table—and effortlessly plucked the gun out of the air amid screams of protest from the group. Immediately it was gripped tightly in Agent Schultz's competent hands and pointed back at the occupants of the table.

"THAT'S IT!" he roared above the commotion, "I'm taking charge! There is too much at stake here to waste any more time trying to convince you people of anything!"

Ned stood slowly, hands placed pacifyingly in front of him, palms facing Schultz. "Okay, Jon, settle down... I'm sorry I pulled the gun... we're ready to listen now, just sit down and finish your explanation."

Schultz figured that the best way to reiterate his proclamation that he (and not Ned) was in charge was to ignore Ned's attempt to calm the situation. Jon instead addressed Meg as he continued to back away from the group, "Meg, toss your car keys over here. I'm calling my handler. If you all just cooperate the offer of amnesty still stands. I understand you've all been through a lot, but get your heads around this *now*: I'm a federal agent. *I'm* in charge!"

With shaking hands that still sported red stripes from being bound by plastic handcuffs, Meg lifted her keys out of her purse and tossed them toward Agent Schultz. They landed a couple of feet in front of him on the floor. He bent down slowly to pick them up—keeping his eyes firmly on the group.

Some minor change in the room's air pressure caused the tiny hairs on the back of Schultz's neck to stand on end. An uneasy feeling descended upon him suddenly. Something wasn't right. Quickly Jon retrieved the keys, straightened up, and spun around. He was not quick *enough* though. An unseen foot sailed through the air and crashed heavily into the right side of his jaw. The jaw gave way, following the arc that the foot traced through the air, taking the rest of his torso with it. His body bounced hard off of a table before landing on the floor. His gun landed a good distance away. It didn't matter though; the woman in black now leaning over him had another one. Unfortunately, Jon was on the wrong end of it.

Her voice was kind but firm, "I believe Ned told you to sit back down."

"Ah, Schultz, I see you've met my new friend Sam," Ned called happily from across the empty restaurant, "*She's* a florist."

Within a couple of minutes, Jon Schultz found himself tied to his chair, sitting in the middle of the restaurant dining area, and scolding himself for losing his cool—or, if not for losing his cool, at least for allowing himself to be so easily incapacitated. He should have been more careful. He hadn't suspected that Ned's rescuer was guarding the door and listening to the meeting. At least one of Jon's questions was now answered. If his handler *had* arranged Ned's rescue and sent this woman, she would be helping him get these people to safety—not attacking him. Someone else must have arranged the rescue.

As Jon's attempt to take control of the situation had failed, only one option was left. Even though a serious blow had now been dealt to his efforts to get the group to trust him, he would have to try again. So (in part due to the insistence of his captors) he resumed his explanation where he left off—careful to moderate his tone and control his patience.

"What makes the United States the world's only remaining superpower?" he began again, sounding more like a CEO conducting a board meeting than a frazzled government agent tied to a chair in a campus pizza place. "It's simple: the willingness and ability to fund a superior level of military technology. Now, you were correct, Ned, when you said that I found out that the Agency was a terrorist organization. But Homeland Security throws that label around a lot these days. It helps them to... *take advantage* of some of this country's newer and more... *progressive* laws when going after these kinds of criminals.

"So don't think that the Agency wants to randomly blow things up in hopes of somehow causing the downfall of Western Civilization. As far as we can tell, they're after governmental influence more than anything else. In some ways that makes them more dangerous than the traditional terrorist. This organization is cold and calculating. There is no line that they aren't willing to cross, but they are, at the same time, patient. They've been working on this project since the early nineties."

Ned sighed. He was slouching in a chair directly in front of Jon. The evening was obviously wearing on him. "*What* project, Schultz? Can you *please* get to the point? Everyone here is tired. We've all had far too much excitement today. I have a safe house waiting a few miles away. The sooner you finish your story, the sooner we can all get to bed. If we believe you—if we're really on the same side here, we'll check out the local Homeland Security office in the morning."

Dyer's reconciliatory tone seemed genuine. Jon imagined that he was mentally weighing the potential prosecution he would have to endure (for recklessly blowing up his house and assaulting a federal agent) against the possibility that Jon was lying about his identity. Agent Schultz guessed that the balance was starting to tip in his favor.

"For reasons that will soon be clear; I still think that we should contact them tonight, Ned," said the chair-bound agent, "but I guess you're calling the shots. I'll get to the point. I'm not authorized to share this information, but I suppose I will just have to trust you. I told Meg and Dan on the way down here that the Agency was just after military secrets. It's actually a little scarier than that. They aren't gathering information to sell to the highest bidder; they are actively sabotaging America's military technology."

This comment was met with an assortment of disbelieving looks and scoffs from the group. Schultz felt that he was losing them. He continued at a quickened pace, "I know it sounds far-fetched. But the Agency's genius lies in both its audacity *and* its subtlety. Ned, I believe your own case illustrates this. I never had any idea how you became a person-of-interest to the Agency until tonight, but now I think I've figured it out.

"When Meg, Dan, and I first arrived here, the owner apparently recognized us and delivered a package to our table per your instructions. We watched your explanation video on the tablet PC that we found inside. You mentioned the project that you had been working on when the Agency demanded that you quit your job—the software flaw that you found in the military avionics sensor code. I believe that you were getting too close to the truth behind your discovery: that the software flaw had been placed *deliberately* by the Agency."

"At most my fix would have improved sensor accuracy by a measly *twenty* percent!" Ned passionately interjected. "It was more about cost savings than anything else; fewer sensors would have been needed to produce the desired level of precision." A smug grin appeared on his face. "That's a pretty pathetic level of sabotage!"

Jon took a deep breath in order to remain calm. "Which is exactly why, Ned, no one would ever suspect that it was a deliberate error. What you apparently didn't figure out about that software bug is that it is actually part of a larger network of similar fragments of unneeded code. These seemingly harmless bugs are currently lying dormant. Sure, they may slow performance or dull sensor accuracy a little in this state, but no real damage is being done. If activated, however, they would wreak untold havoc! The Agency's analysts have been studying military control systems for years. A team of developers has been building these tailor-made code fragments for deployment by agents embedded in various defense companies. In isolation, these code fragments are harmless. But when networked together inside a full-blown control system they are not. Every infected system can be remotely triggered—usually through some standby or redundant communications channel."

Meg Trotter had been listening quietly and intently. Her face wore a mixture of disbelief and concern. "What are you saying, Jon?" she asked. "That the Agency has a control infrastructure in place to override all of our military systems? That they can control military equipment by remote?"

"Well, for one, the project isn't complete yet. We estimate that their systems won't be online for a few months still. And for two, implementing a hidden control system for a significant number of military applications would be impossible. The complexity of that network would be instantly detected. Even if they *could* hide it, that kind of system would not be worth the effort. The Agency would never be able to effectively run any military assets by electronic control. All of those systems still rely on human beings *on-site* to run them."

"Sorry to interrupt," it was the young brunette woman in the jogging suit (*Sue was it?*), "but for those of us that *aren't* engineers, exactly what are these *control systems* you are talking about? Do they control planes?"

"Sure, military aircraft such as fighter jets or combat helicopters," Jon continued, "These systems also guide missiles, subs, ships, tanks, and satellites… even the handheld devices used by soldiers for situational awareness utilize these components. But, as I was saying, the Agency isn't able to take *control* of these systems. They merely want the ability to disrupt them. Imagine the chaos that would result if a fighter pilot could no longer accurately target an enemy… or worse, if they were suddenly fed incorrect velocity and altitude data! What if a precision guided missile's usual two-meter accuracy was suddenly off by a decimal point or two?

"It takes surprisingly little effort to sneak these code fragments into the disparate components that eventually get pieced together in a control system. And all they have to be able to do is introduce an error factor in a component's mathematical calculations upon activation. A control thread with a few of these bugs strung together can multiply that error factor exponentially. The fragments are hard to find during code reviews and impossible to detect during testing. They only activate upon receipt of the Agency's command code."

"So," Meg offered, "for the sake of argument, let's say that we believe you. What is the Agency planning to do? Render the military obsolete?"

"As far as we can tell, they have no real interest in using any these systems—except for demonstrative purposes. They would probably contact someone at the Department of Defense with a prediction of a major accident during a military training exercise. They would then activate their system during the exercise and cause the accident. The loss of equipment and life would have to be fairly substantial to ensure that they would be taken seriously—but we suspect that both the DOD and the Agency would keep the real cause of the accident from the public. The Agency would then use the threat of unleashing this weapon on a large scale to gain influence in the government.

"And don't think that only the U.S. military would be affected. Any country that has our level of technological sophistication already has infected systems. Once the Agency has personnel embedded in high levels of our government they would then potentially have the ability to turn this weapon against the armed forces of our allies! I don't pretend to understand the Agency's endgame, but it isn't too much of a stretch to see how this kind of power sets the stage for some sort of global domination.

"So you might now begin to understand my level of apprehension this evening! Homeland Security plans to launch a major operation *tonight* to take down the Agency. And it has to be *flawless*. It does us no good to dismantle 90% of their organization. The remaining members would simply go underground and complete a scaled-down version of this weapon. We have to be perfect. But the longer that I am off the grid, the greater the degree of uncertainty that Homeland Security has to deal with tonight. The Agency might already be tipped off that something is afoot; surely they've found Fischer by now. I'm truly sorry that you people are involved, but it is a *very* dangerous game you are playing by holding me here.

"I'm not sure exactly what set last night's events in motion for you, Ned. I think the Agency was just keeping tabs on you. But when you kicked off these 'contingency systems' of yours, a decision was made that we would take advantage of the Agency's diverted attention. That's why the operation was scheduled for tonight. But I've been out of contact with my handler since this afternoon. I have no idea if the operation is still a 'go.'

"So, bottom line for you guys: there is a very dangerous organization after you. And you can surely see that an organization this ruthless, able to kill so indiscriminately, will certainly not allow a ragtag group of engineers to stand in their way! You *must* see that they will go to any lengths to track you down and shut you up! We *need* to get you somewhere safe!"

Ned spoke again, obviously trying to make sure all of the loose threads were accounted for, "How does Joe Tompkins fit into all of this? What does the Agency want with him?"

Schultz had anticipated the potential question. Unfortunately he didn't have a satisfying answer—but he wasn't going to try to invent one either. "I don't have that information, Ned. I'm really only guessing about *your* involvement."

Ned's eyes focused on something in the distance as he seemed to mull over all that Jon had said. "Thank you for the information, Schultz. I'll let you know what we decide."

The group huddled out of earshot to decide whether or not to trust him. Jon was confident that he had done his best to sell the explanation of the nature of the Agency. Still, he silently and desperately hoped that they would not see it for the fantastic lie that it really was. *But,* he reminded himself, *I'm certainly not authorized to tell them the truth.*

Not that they would have believed it if he did. The *truth* was far more fantastic.

37

1:34 AM

Ned Dyer unlocked the front door of his Atlanta-area safe house, leading the group from the pizza place inside. One couldn't tell by his demeanor, but he was terrified. Well, *part* of Ned Dyer was terrified. The rest of him was relieved by his rescue and his fiancée's continued safety. There might have been another part of him that was concerned by the Agency's capture of Joe Tompkins—another that was confused by Joe's involvement—another that was racked with guilt at the fate of the waiter, Tom Rigsby (that *he* had involved)—another that was nearing complete exhaustion and desperately needing sleep—another clouded with a slight (but hidden) distrust of the ex-CIA agent, Sam, that Joe had supposedly sent to his rescue—and another that was processing Schultz's wild explanation of the Agency's goals and its means of achieving them.

For the sake of the group, though, Ned *had* to project an aura of calm composure. Fortunately, he possessed a superior ability to compartmentalize his sometimes erratic emotions. The foundation of his mind was solid reason; its framework made up of cool logic—mathematical in its precision. Emotion was certainly not absent, but it *was* controlled—penned in by wit and sense. Ned had decided long ago that emotion for its own sake was worthless—worse, even dangerous.

Some might have considered his ability to filter out sentiment a weakness—maybe even a subhuman characteristic of an unfeeling heart. But Ned knew that, on the contrary, it was his greatest strength. He would not have survived the trauma of the past three years without it. Besides, no one could accuse him of being cold or awkward in social settings. He always employed a carefully calculated (but genuine) measure of societal participation and grace in his interactions with others. This usually masked any hint of his (perhaps) inelegant inner being.

So, at that moment Ned's terror, relief, concern, confusion, guilt, exhaustion, and doubt were all pushed to the side of his mind, safely tucked into their respective compartments, ready to be called upon if needed. Unchecked, the weight of these conflicting emotions would gain him nothing but mental paralysis. Ned couldn't afford *any* type of paralysis just then. Important calculations needed to be made. The emotions would stay caged.

The circuitry of Ned's mind cranked at full force: weighing levels of potential danger against each other, deriving the path of minimal risk, balancing his need for answers against the safety of his friends. Fear was not a factor in these calculations. He would not allow it to be.

His decision had been made back at the pizza place, but his chosen course of action was nearing a point of increased risk, a point of no return. It was worth going over it all again.

Concerning Sam:

There was too much at stake to just blindly trust anyone, but she certainly appeared to be on his side. If, somehow, Joe had actually sent her to his rescue, that was reason enough to trust her. It seemed an impossible arrangement, but maybe Joe had somehow escaped his captors, discovered where Ned was being held, and Googled "guns for hire" or some such thing to find someone qualified and available for the job.

But no, that didn't make any sense either. Sam had told him that she had received her instructions that morning. According to Sue and Amy, Joe had been unaware of Ned's capture when they met him that afternoon. Had Joe been lying? What reason could he have possibly had for lying?

Regardless of these inconsistencies, Sam had gone a long way toward proving herself. Plus she had known the exact location of the midnight meeting. So it was unlikely that she was working for the Agency. She hadn't gained any information by busting him out, and Ned didn't have any information to offer that she didn't seem to already have. Unfortunately, she didn't seem to have any prior knowledge of the Agency either.

Ned came to the same conclusion as before. He didn't like all of the unanswered questions surrounding this woman, but he felt that he *could* trust her. This was one of the few feelings he allowed himself to freely experience, mostly because it seemed that he didn't have any other choice *but* to trust her. Ned suppressed his doubt further—now it was just unhelpful. He couldn't allow any of it to leak out anyway. There was no reason anyone else in the group needed to know that he had potential reservations about Sam. They had enough things to worry about without him proposing more.

Concerning Schultz:

The group at Everybody's Pizza had left it up to Ned whether to trust Schultz or not. The story about the Agency he had told them seemed a little far-fetched, but Ned had sensed that there was an air of truth to it. It seemed to account for most of the out-of-place events that had occurred, but he just couldn't shake the thought that there was *still* something out of place.

On the one hand Schultz offered the promise of governmental protection—something the group could desperately use. The sores on Ned's foot and head were still raw and painful and served as an ever-present reminder of the danger he and his loved ones were in.

On the other hand, currently the group *was* safe. It was obvious that the Agency didn't have the location of his safe houses, and Ned wasn't entirely convinced that Schultz wasn't still working with this "terrorist organization." Allowing him to contact his "handler" would potentially put them in more danger.

But the factor that forced Ned to consider some sort of middle ground in trusting Schultz was also the one that had the least to do with his loved ones' safety. If uncertainty surrounding the fate of *supposed* federal agent Jon Schultz was potentially jeopardizing a Homeland Security operation—a matter of national security—then Ned had an obligation to let him call in. It really was that simple.

So, for now, he would fully trust Sam and partially trust Schultz. That was the strategy. That was the path of most acceptable risk. The math of the situation checked out. They would let Schultz call his handler, but they were going to listen in.

"I guess this room is the best option," Ned opened the door to the basement furnace room. The basement of the safe house was technically finished, but the carpet was old, thin, and dirty. Several spiders had taken up residence in the corners. The rest of the house was nicer, though still fairly modest. The main floor simply had an eat-in kitchen and a large living room. The three bedrooms were on the second floor.

Sam nodded and led Schultz through the furnace room doorway. He had been blindfolded and bound since the group left Everybody's Pizza. With the winding Georgian roads, Ned doubted that even a trained federal agent would have been able to guess the general direction that they drove from the pizza place—let alone the actual address of the safe house.

Sam removed the blindfold from Schultz and directed his attention to the plastic folding chair set in the middle of the furnace room's concrete floor. "Have a seat, Jon. Here's how we're going to do this: I'll cut the zip ties around your wrists and then I'll hand you your phone. You'll make the phone call, with the speakerphone setting enabled, and you'll tell your handler that you, Meg, and Dan are safe and will check in again in the morning. You will then hang up before anyone has a chance to trace the call.

"Back at the pizza place, we all saw how fast you can be when you feel threatened. So both Ned and I are going to keep our guns trained on you. If you try anything, we *will* shoot. Do you understand?"

Schultz nodded at Ned and Sam and lifted his bound hands in agreement, "I understand. Thank you, I know you two are taking a risk here. This is more than fair."

"You've got that right," Ned mumbled as he drew his sidearm and pointed it at Schultz. Then, in a clearer voice, "Go ahead, Sam. Cut him loose. I've got him."

She pulled out a pocketknife and her own handgun simultaneously. A quick flick of her left wrist was all it took to cut the bond—her gun never wavered from its target. She took a couple steps back and pocketed the knife. "There you go. Catch." Schultz's cell phone landed in his lap.

Ned watched as Schultz gently rubbed his newly unfettered wrists. "Now make that call, Jon."

"Okay, guys, j-just be careful with those things," Schultz said, indicating the two guns that were pointed at him. He flipped open his phone. A dull beep indicated the switch to speakerphone. He dialed the number.

The sound of the phone line connecting was not the only sound that came next. In fact, it was drown out by a large crashing sound that thundered from the basement ceiling. This was accompanied by a loud and drawn-out scream from Sue. *That* was followed by Dan's booming and panicked voice. He was shouting. "NED! SAM! GET UP HERE! NOW!"

Ned glanced at a frightened-looking Sam, and then at a frightened-looking Schultz. Then he was out the door, sprinting, with Sam on his heels. She paused to lock Schultz's door before following Ned up the stairs.

Schultz was left, locked, in the basement room. He was all alone—all alone with his cell phone.

"NED! SAM! GET UP HERE! NOW!" Dan tried to make the shout sound both believable and urgent, but was fearful that it would sound contrived. Sue's scream had been perfect though.

He looked down at the remains of the wooden chair that he had smashed against the kitchen floor. He probably hadn't *needed* to break it in order to produce the crashing noise, but he had wanted to be sure that it could be heard from downstairs.

Besides, it was Ned's plan. He couldn't get upset if some furniture got broken in the process.

On cue, Ned appeared at the top of the stairs that led to the basement and stowed his gun. Sam was behind him. She kept *her* gun out and turned around to face the stairs, ready to run back down and end Schultz's call at the appropriate time. Ned joined Dan and Sue in the small kitchen.

Ned had obviously endured something awful over the past couple of days. He still hadn't talked about it. But beyond the cuts and bruises, there was something else in his appearance—something that evoked a deep sense of pity. This was a man who had carried and fought against an intense and crippling fear for the safety of his family for a long time. Dan had never seen him so worn. The last three years must have been hell.

Ned pointed to the device in Dan's hand, "Now, let's hear what our old friend Schultz is *really* up to."

Dan turned the volume knob on Sam's walkie-talkie up to maximum. He still thought that the plan was unnecessary and dangerous. The truth wasn't worth the risk to their safety. If Schultz was telling the truth (which seemed fairly unlikely) any contact with Homeland Security could surely wait until morning, until everyone had a chance to rest, until they were all able to process the situation a bit more.

But it was Ned's call. *He* was the one who had sacrificed so much. *He* was the one under attack. And, though Dan would never have admitted it, his biggest concern at that moment wasn't the safety of the group or learning the truth about this "Agency." In reality his biggest concern was that there was no liquor of any kind in the safe house kitchen. His second biggest concern was that someone might notice that his hands were shaking slightly at the thought.

It was best not to think about it. He asked what he hoped would sound like a question appropriate for someone without these concerns, "Do you think Schultz knows that we bugged him?"

Ned shook his head and motioned for silence. The static from the walkie-talkie soon carried Jon Schultz's faint voice. The microphone was in the pocket of his suit jacket—not a perfect setup, but it caught most of the conversation.

"...right, Atlanta with Dyer, Curtis, and Trotter... several safe houses set up... the Agency might have just found us... something is happening ... don't know what... locked in a room... unarmed... they don't trust me." The reply from Schultz's "handler" was inaudible—either a result of the poor reception or because he had turned the speakerphone setting off. Dan couldn't tell.

A moment later the voice resumed. It was slightly more hushed, but Dan could still pick out some words: Fischer... interrogating... Agency... captured... family...

Schultz must have then shifted position somehow, because even the hushed conversation became perfectly clear.

"...asked me about it later. I told him that Fischer was lying—that the Agency hadn't done anything to his family. I *think* he believed me, but I'm not sure what to do if he asks more questions. If I tell him the truth, he becomes unstable. There is far too much instability in the situation as it is."

If Dan's reaction to this event had fully developed into a complete thought, that thought would have vehemently chastised him for believing Schultz's assurances that his family was safe. But his reaction bypassed his consciousness. He had already dropped the walkie-talkie, grabbed Ned's gun, pushed past Sam, and was on his way down the stairs before his consciousness caught up with his actions. When it did, it approved them wholeheartedly.

He would get the truth from Schultz—one way or another.

It was unfortunate that Dan hadn't had a drink that night. If he had been able to keep his hands from shaking, maybe Schultz wouldn't have been able to get the gun away from him.

More shouting came from downstairs—too much more. It didn't sound like things were going according to Ned's plan.

Meg Trotter pressed her ear against the closed door of the second-floor bedroom. She and Amy had been arranging the sleeping bags and preparing for bed. Meg had just met the girl, but felt that she could relate to what Amy must be going through. They were both nursing an impossible hope that someone they cared about was okay.

Meg had been worried about Joe since that afternoon and had been sickened when, at the pizza place, she learned that Joe had, in fact, been captured by this mysterious organization. Schultz maintained that he didn't have any more information than that, but Meg was still skeptical that he could be trusted. She had hoped that Ned's plan to trick Schultz into revealing more information about himself would provide more answers.

But now it sounded like the plan was unraveling.

Through the door Meg could hear Schultz's voice shouting. He was ordering everyone to stay back. Ned and Sam were also talking, but softer—too soft to understand.

Dan could now be heard. He was shouting. "JUST SHOOT HIM! DO *NOT* LET HIM GET AWAY!"

It would probably have been wise to just stay put, but Meg was cursed with an overdeveloped sense of curiosity. It dwarfed her sense of self-preservation. It even dwarfed her considerable exhaustion. She *had* to find out what was going on. Silently and slowly, she opened the door.

Amy whispered fiercely after her, "Meg! What are you doing?"

Meg threw her a quick semi-apologetic look, then crept out of the room, gently closed the door behind her, and snuck down the short hallway to the top of the stairs that led down to the main level of the house. She didn't like what she saw below.

Schultz had Dan around the neck with a gun to his temple. He was backing up toward the front door, yelling at Ned and Sam to stay back. Sue stood at the doorway to the kitchen—frozen in terror. Sam had her gun trained on Schultz. She and Ned were trying to calmly tell him to let Dan go. Schultz wasn't having any of it.

Meg's thoughts returned to the motel room where she had seen Schultz so casually shoot Fischer dead. It occurred to her that Dan could easily be next. She couldn't let that happen. It seemed that all Schultz wanted was to get away. Meg didn't know Sam very well, but it was possible that Sam might just be willing to sacrifice Dan to prevent Schultz from escaping. Meg certainly wasn't.

Let Schultz go. Who cares? she thought, trying to influence the others' actions with the power of her mind, *It isn't worth the risk to Dan.*

Meg glanced from figure to figure, sizing the situation up, realizing that it was up to her to intervene. She marshaled her courage and then stepped onto the stairs.

Her descent down the stairs was slow and graceful. Her hands were outstretched in order to communicate to Schultz that she wasn't a threat. Her eyes met Dan's (which were wide and strained) and offered him what little comfort they could communicate. Her feet reached the last stair.

The other occupants of the safe house greeted her presence by increasing the pitch of their already high tensions. Schultz's orders came quicker and more forceful. Ned and Sam's pleas increased in volume. Sue's frozen silence became more pronounced. But they all seemed to agree that Meg should stay out of the situation and return to the upstairs bedroom.

She didn't.

Instead, she rounded the banister and stood with her back to Schultz. She walked slowly toward Sam, keeping her eyes pointed downward, hoping that everyone would just think that she wanted to take a place behind Ned. If this were going to work, she would have to be quick—quick and accurate.

Sam was careful to keep a clear line-of-sight between her and Schultz. Her gun was still outstretched as she eyed Meg suspiciously. Meg glanced up at her as she approached and pointed to a spot behind the action. Sam nodded and returned her eyes to Schultz and Dan. This gave Meg her chance.

With Sam's attention fixed on Schultz, Meg lunged at her outstretched gun and forced it downward as she tackled the unsuspecting ex-CIA agent. The two women crashed into the wall—and then onto the floor. Meg had a good eight inches and thirty pounds on the slight woman, but she had never been much of a fighter. Besides, the goal wasn't to hurt Sam.

Sam apparently didn't share this goal. This realization hit Meg hard— twice—in the face. Then it kicked her in the gut and pushed her body off of Sam's. Meg landed on her back—lying on the old hardwood floor, staring at the ceiling and gasping for air. The CIA's hand-to-hand combat training was apparently still serving the ex-agent well.

A gunshot roared and echoed in the small living room. Meg then heard the front door slam despite the ringing that now filled her ears. She saw Sam scramble back to her feet despite the tears that now filled her eyes. It was a struggle for *Meg* to even sit up.

When she did, she saw Dan lying facedown on the floor near the doorway with Ned kneeling next to him. Sam was carefully opening the front door, still holding the gun firmly, and peering out. She then disappeared outside.

Meg blinked the tears out of her eyes and looked again at Dan. He wasn't moving. She tried to speak—to ask if he was okay—but the wind had not yet returned to her lungs. All she could do was sit there and stare at him, wondering if her attempt to save his life had instead just gotten him killed.

The woman that Ned Dyer and his friends knew as "Sam" was furious as she slipped out the front door and into the night. Meg could not have been stupider. She had very nearly gotten herself and her friends killed.

Dan could not have been stupider either. Ned's plan had been playing out perfectly until he had pushed past her in an attempt to intimidate information out of Schultz. Sam had barely had a chance to follow him down the stairs when Schultz had appeared at the doorway of the furnace room holding Dan hostage. Schultz had claimed that he was just protecting himself—that Dan had flown off the handle and tried to kill him.

Sam had been forced to let them climb the stairs and move toward the door. But she had had no intention of letting Schultz leave. Then Meg had interfered. Any sort of plan that Sam had been trying to come up with to stop the prisoner from escaping had been shot to hell when Meg had tackled her.

It had been a cheap shot. It had also given Schultz time to knock Dan unconscious, grab Meg's keys (which were left conspicuously near the front door), and dart out of the safe house. Sam had fired her weapon after him just before the door slammed shut. Unfortunately, she had still been off balance and had missed.

Schultz wouldn't get far though. After all, he only had a ten second lead.

Meg's Mustang was in the driveway. Its parking lights blinked as Schultz approached, signaling that the car was now unlocked. Sam leapt from the concrete stoop and bolted across the uneven yard toward the escapee, shouting at him to stop.

But she didn't make it to the driveway.

No one could reasonably fault Ned for the poor state of the lawn. He had only been to the property once before (when purchasing it), and that had been during a quick business trip two years ago. As with all of his safe houses, he had arranged for monthly maid service, maintenance when needed, and bi-weekly mowing of the grass. But he wasn't trying to win any landscaping awards.

The previous owner of this particular house hadn't been trying to win any landscaping awards either, though he apparently *had* at least made some semblance of an effort beyond the obligatory grass of a not-too-objectionable height. He had been single and was one of those guys that somehow regarded scattered piles of large gray rocks as attractive lawn décor.

This shouldn't have been a problem for Sam. Her CIA career had been quite distinguished. She had faced foes of varied backgrounds and levels of skill and had always been victorious. But oddly it was one of those simple gray rocks (long separated from its pile) that proved to be her undoing. She should have seen it, but it *was* very dark—and she was still a bit disoriented from being tackled.

Her body landed hard on the sloped ground. The offending rock had barely moved. It *had*, however, left Sam with a few bruised (possibly broken) toes, a hand freshly stripped of its weapon, and a perfect ground-level vantage point of Jon Schultz's Mustang-powered flight from captivity.

She didn't actually see the rest of his escape though. Another one of those pesky rocks had gotten in the way of her falling head. This collision had caused her to lose consciousness. And then blood.

38

Agent Gilmore exploded out of the holding room, shoved his recently recovered gun into its holster, and tore down the hallway at full speed. The virus had started its attack at midnight. It had taken entirely too long (almost thirteen minutes) for Gilmore to convince his superiors that *he* was their best chance of survival. They had initially hesitated to release him, but it soon became clear that they could no longer afford the luxury of indecision. Time was no longer on the Agency's side.

The instant of attack had, ironically, been fortunate for Gilmore. It had not only facilitated his liberation from the holding room but it had also provided him a chance to redeem the mistake that landed him in so much trouble: trusting Agent Conroy's assurances that the Ned Dyer leak had been contained.

Not that Agent Gilmore had *deserved* the treatment he had received since arriving at headquarters—being transported from the airport at gunpoint, being relieved of his position as the agent-in-charge, being locked in the holding room unable either to defend himself or aid in the cleanup of his mistake. The incident strengthened Gilmore's long-held belief that the Agency suffered from an inability to multitask. One goal or problem tended to get all of their attention—to the exclusion of everything else.

This myopia was in full display tonight. It was almost as if the higher-ups had forgotten about the organization-crushing virus that sat uninhibited at their doorstep—free to choose the hour of its imminent onslaught. It was as if the fact that he had captured Joe Tompkins, the virus' author, meant nothing. They had only wanted to focus on Gilmore's failures.

That had all changed when the dormant virus awoke and attacked the Agency's computers. It had taken only four minutes to dismantle the newly installed safeguards and countermeasures that the Agency had prepared. Within ten minutes Tech Services had essentially given up all hope of stopping the malicious bug. Virtually every system had been infected—including the backups. They could only hope to slow it down through a series of aggressive system partitioning and refreshing. But even with these efforts, complete system death was predicted within the hour. It would take years to recover. The only way to stop the damage from being done was for the *author* to shut the virus down first.

Luckily the author was on hand—and already prepped for interrogation.

After a short and heated exchange with the guard at the door of the hypnotic stimulation chamber's control room, Gilmore gained access and approached the panel that controlled the various stimuli to be used on the subject of the interrogation. Joe Tompkins hovered in the chamber on the other side of the wall—suspended from the ceiling by an assortment of mesh restraints. Gilmore had once remarked that the contraption looked like a collection of small hammocks. The restraints could be mechanically shifted, allowing the subject to be rotated to any position the questioner desired. This helped keep the subject off balance and confused. Joe had been lying, tilted up at a 30-degree incline and staring downward, since his arrival.

The walls, floor, and ceiling of the interrogation chamber were comprised entirely of huge plasma video screens. They currently glowed with a dull and calming deep blue light. Soft music leisurely filled the room, adding to the unbroken calm of the chamber.

The control panel was brand new and had been installed only hours before. It was left unconnected to any network systems in hopes that it would remain beyond the virus' reach. This appeared to be working—at least for the moment. The control panel's screens were filled with real-time video of Joe's suspended body and real-time electric-impulse readings of his brain.

Gilmore was pleased to see that hypnosis had already been induced so that Joe was already in a highly suggestive state. It had been Gilmore's familiarity with Subject Tompkins that had persuaded the Division Head to allow him control of the interrogation—a familiarity that had been built over the past few months during weekly hypnotic sessions. Gilmore had spent hours with this subject—mapping his consciousness, learning what made Joe tick. If anyone knew his way around the insides of Joe's head, Agent Gilmore did.

Of course, he was still baffled by Joe's actions over the past couple of days. He had never detected any indication that Tompkins was capable of sophisticated computer virus creation... or pursuit evasion tactics... or hand-to-hand combat. But, Gilmore had never been able to examine Joe as extensively as he was about to. The quality of the equipment *now* at his disposal afforded him much greater access to the subconscious levels of Joe's mind.

Also, he had never had as pressing a mandate to extract information from Subject Tompkins. In the weekly sessions, Agent Gilmore had always needed to leave Joe's brain intact and unaware of the interrogation. That was not the case now. *This* session would end in simple fashion—with a 9mm bullet quieting Joe's troublesome brain forever, whether Gilmore was successful in stopping the virus or not.

Because either way, Subject Tompkins' usefulness to the Agency would expire within the hour. And then, so would he.

It was going to be quite liberating to proceed with the interrogation without bothering to construct the usual safeguards that protected against permanent damage to the subject. Still, Gilmore noticed that the prep team *had* bothered to inject a radioactive marker that would pinpoint a specific location in Joe's brain. This allowed a physical deletion of all the subject's memories of a session. Apparently no one had told them that this particular injection wasn't necessary for this particular subject.

It had been a couple of years since Gilmore had used the more sophisticated equipment available at the Agency's headquarters, but that didn't matter. He was very good at this part of his job. He pulled up a chair and sat down behind the console with all of the confidence, skill, and poise of a great pianist about to delight a packed concert hall.

But this was a concert for one. And it would be anything but delightful.

The soft music inside the hypnotic chamber swelled to an earsplitting crescendo as the plasma-powered walls transformed from the calming deep blue to an inky blackness full of thousands of tiny points of white light—a field of stars in every direction save for a small bluish-green circle displayed directly in the middle of the floor. From Joe's perspective, he was floating in space hundreds of thousands of miles above the Earth.

An indicator on the control panel reflected the expected up-tick in the rhythm of Subject Tompkins' heartbeat. Gilmore looked down at his bandaged left hand. He then lightly touched the pipe-shaped bruise that stretched across his forehead.

A broad smile formed on his face as he paused briefly to enjoy the moment. The occasional opportunity for revenge was probably the best perk his job had to offer. He had learned in recent months that Joe Tompkins suffered from an acute but secret acrophobia. The man was deathly afraid of heights.

Gilmore's one good hand typed the next command into the control panel. His finger hesitated for another moment over the 'Enter' key.

Then he let Subject Tompkins fall.

The restraints that held Tompkins rotated. His body pitched instantly downward, 60 degrees below the horizontal. Blood rushed to his head as the simulated stars that surrounded him began to rush violently upward. Hot forced air blew suddenly and powerfully from below. The interrogation chamber grew warm. Joe's clothes began to whip against him in the virtual vertical wind tunnel. The Earth, only a small blue disk far below, began to race directly toward him at seemingly thousands of miles per second.

He was plummeting through space on a collision course with the planet.

Step One: force the subject into a state of extreme terror.

Check.

Step Two: force the subject into a state of extreme physical discomfort.

Since Joe was approaching atmospheric reentry, it made sense that his skin should feel like it was on fire—after all, Agent Gilmore wanted to make the experience seem as realistic as possible, so he injected the chemicals that would simulate this feeling into the subject's bloodstream.

In order to increase the effect, Gilmore then lowered the oxygen level in the chamber by twenty five percent. Not enough to be lethal, just enough to help increase Joe's panic by decreasing the effectiveness of his already rapid breathing. For good measure Agent Gilmore then tightened the mesh restraint around Joe's chest—forcing his breaths to become painful and shallow. The music that filled the room grew more deafening, discordant, and disorienting as it struggled to be heard over the terrible rushing wind.

Joe, eyes wide in hypnotic horror, writhed desperately in his restraints.

Step Two. Check.

Step Three: give the subject an opportunity to lessen the pain through cooperation.

Snippets of code and technical specifications began to appear on the walls of the chamber, flashing furiously through the images of Joe's descent like some kind of manic strobe light. Taken together they were a portrait of a computer virus—Joe's virus. Gilmore waited for an indicator on the control panel to register a degree of recognition in the subject's mind at seeing his handiwork displayed around him.

This indication never came. Gilmore's brow wrinkled. The device that measured the subject's familiarity with what he was seeing was pegged at zero.

It didn't make any sense. No one was that good at hiding what they knew. No one.

A terrible doubt began to creep into Agent Gilmore's mind, unwrinkling his brow and lowering his jaw in the process. What if Joe wasn't the virus' author after all? Did he have the wrong man?

It was Gilmore that now felt a surge of panic. *He* had been the one that had concluded that Tompkins was the author. If he had been wrong…

No. It *had* to be Tompkins. Why else would he have run? Why else would he have set his car on fire to evade capture? Why else would he have smacked Gilmore in the face with the keyboard?

Now was not the time to second-guess himself. Everything depended on *Joe* being the virus' creator. Gilmore had already made a critical mistake that day. He could not afford another.

More commands were entered. The flashing technical images now showed a playback of the brief success that Ned Dyer had had against the virus earlier in the day. As the bug was forced to retreat, a change in drug level caused Joe's pain to retreat as well. His rate of simulated descent slowed.

Tompkins was sure to get the message: defeat the virus and conditions will improve.

The playback advanced to the point at which Subject Dyer gave up. The bug grew stronger again. The pain came back. So did the velocity.

Step Three. Check.

But there was still no indication of any recognition in Joe's mind—let alone any cooperation. And Gilmore was all out of steps. The agent sat and contemplated his next move, almost able to hear Joe's bloodcurdling screams through the soundproof wall that separated them.

Well, Gilmore thought as he continued to adjust the controls, *might as well go for broke.*

He proceeded with the interrogation the only way he knew how, by turning up the heat on Subject Tompkins. Literally. He also increased the speed of the simulated wind, tightened the restraint around Joe's chest another notch, and lowered the level of oxygen in the chamber another twenty five percent. Tompkins was now dangerously close to passing out—despite being full of drugs specifically designed to prevent that from happening.

If he did pass out, the game would be over. By the time Gilmore could revive him, the virus would have destroyed the Agency's systems. Tompkins would then be worthless. It was an awful risk to have to take, but Gilmore had no choice. The control panel still showed no signs that Joe was making any attempt to kill the virus. It still indicated that Joe had never even seen the code before.

Gilmore again buried his doubts. He had to believe that Joe could stop the virus. He *had* to. The Division Head had been clear when he released Gilmore from holding. The consequences of failure would be severe.

39

Inside the interrogation chamber Joe Tompkins was falling through the atmosphere at a rate of something like a mile every second. Maybe he should have been thankful that the rate had slowed since he had left outer space, but he really had no way of knowing that. The rushing air hadn't slowed and the stars that surrounded him had disappeared. This effectively removed any reference point by which Joe could gauge his speed—save the Earth approaching quickly from below.

The floor display now showed two large islands in the middle of a vast blue ocean. The islands were getting bigger, their image interlaced constantly with frames of flashing source code. Joe took this all in with wide eyes, his face four feet from the floor. He was still in a state of hypnotic confusion, not understanding that this was a simulated fall. And he was still screaming at the top of his painfully constricted lungs.

Soon the bottom of the chamber was filled with land as Joe continued his maddening plunge. Snow-capped mountains could be seen on the southern island. He was heading right for them.

Thirty thousand feet... twenty five thousand... twenty...

A thin lake snaked between these mountains. Instinctively, Joe leaned and twisted toward it—perhaps thinking that a water landing would cool his burning skin. But the gesture proved pointless. The trajectory of his descent did not alter. He would land in the mountains. Perhaps the snow that covered their peaks would provide the relief he so desperately longed for.

Fifteen thousand feet... ten thousand... five...

WHAM!

Joe's wind-whipped face smacked the Plexiglas floor as the restraints that held him suddenly dropped the four-foot distance that had separated his nose from the chamber's bottom. Blood began to flow freely from his nostrils. The simulated wind stopped blowing at the moment of impact. Joe's crumpled form lay flat (but still writhing) on the mountaintop.

There was no relief for his burning skin.

Instantly the wind picked back up again, but this time it blew powerfully from the chamber's ceiling. Joe's head snapped downward as the mesh harness that held him forcibly lifted his body back off of the floor and spun him quickly backwards—end over end. After one complete revolution he was back in position, pitched down 60 degrees, hovering four feet from the floor.

The mountains were falling away beneath him as he now climbed rapidly through the air as if on the end of a giant yo-yo. At a hundred thousand feet up the harness jerked and spun him round again. Then came the descent…

Had there been anything in Joe's stomach besides gastric acid, it surely would have made the chamber's acquaintance at that point. As it was, even some of the acid escaped and dissolved in the wind.

The mountains were nearing, but Joe wouldn't make it there again. It was time to black out.

His body went limp. His screaming finally ceased.

The control panel shuddered loudly in response to the impact of Agent Gilmore's right fist. He was furious. He was also trapped. It wouldn't be long before his superiors discovered his failure. Not only had Subject Tompkins fainted, but he had never shown any indication that he was the author of the computer virus. Gilmore had captured the wrong man.

The consequences of failure will be severe. The Division Head's words were ever present in Gilmore's mind. Briefly his thoughts turned to escape, but he knew that this was impossible. His thoughts then turned to vengeance.

Even while passed out, Tompkins would still be able to feel pain.

Gilmore decided on his course of action—what would be his final act in the employ of the Agency. He knew that it was quite likely that *he* would be placed in the interrogation chamber next. But first he would make sure Joe Tompkins endured a far worse end. There were limits to the Agency's cruelty, especially when dealing with an agent gone astray. Gilmore knew that he might not survive the night, but when the end came it would most likely be quick.

There were no limits to Gilmore's cruelty though. Especially toward the man he held responsible for his failure.

He turned off the chamber's gusting artificial wind and loud disorienting music. He canceled the freefall simulation and returned the chamber walls to their calming blue glow. Then he turned the dial that controlled the level of pain-inducing drugs up to its maximum setting and tightened the mesh chest restraint again so that Joe could no longer breathe. But Gilmore had no intention of letting Joe suffocate. He drew his gun and prepared to enter the interrogation chamber.

A glance at the control panel indicated that the subject, though unconscious, was indeed experiencing the pain. Gilmore smiled at the oscillating waveforms that corresponded with the subject's agonizing subconscious brain activity.

Then his smile faded.

An anomaly had appeared on the scope—something Gilmore had never seen before. The patterns almost looked like Tompkins had awoken, but the conscious portion of his brain still showed no activity. Gilmore would have studied this further, but something else caught his eye. There was movement in another screen—the one that showed the video image of Tompkins' face. His eyes were now open, unfocused, bloodshot, and darting hysterically from side to side. His face was strained, sweaty, and a dark shade of red. His lips were mouthing something frantically, but no sound came out.

The computer still indicated that the subject was unconscious. The situation should not have been possible.

It was curiosity, not compassion, that caused Gilmore to loosen the chest restraint. Joe responded to this with a series of deep and choking breaths. Then, impossibly, he spoke. He was yelling, slurring and gurgling his words.

"TOP! TOP! LED BEEG OES!! SSSSSTTOP!"

Gilmore's mind flashed instantly to his afternoon confrontation with Tompkins behind the remains of Subject Dyer's house. He had encountered Tompkins in this state before. His bandaged left hand was proof.

Following a hunch (or maybe just in an act of desperation), Gilmore punched in the command that would again display the image of the virus. The chamber responded as the code flashed maniacally on the walls and floor, dancing in front of Joe's still unfocused eyes.

A moment later it finally happened. An indicator on the panel blinked— registering the subject's recognition of the source code. It meant that Agent Gilmore had the right man after all.

What he *didn't* have was a lot of time.

A red light began flashing slowly next to the control panel's telephone. Someone was calling—either to provide an update of the virus' progress in dismantling the Agency's systems or to request an update on Agent Gilmore's progress in killing it.

It turned out to be both.

The news was bad. The latest projections from Tech Services predicted system death at 12:47, in just over twelve minutes. Apparently the rate of data corruption in the backup files had accelerated since the original calculations were made.

Gilmore allowed himself a moment to feed on the increase in pressure. He let it invigorate his tired limbs and mind. Then he conveyed to the voice on the phone, with sincere confidence, that he would inoculate the virus with time to spare.

He hung the phone up and set his sights on his goal. He was off book. No tried-and-true interrogation technique applied to the position he now found himself in. Either the instruments in front of him had failed, or Tompkins *really was* in some sort of uncharted mental state. Judging from the subject's behavior, it probably wasn't the instruments.

Gilmore knew he would have to rely on his gut to finish his task. Redemption would accompany success; imprisonment, or worse, would accompany failure. Two options: sink or swim.

But he had always been an excellent swimmer.

Tompkins was still shouting from inside the chamber, ostensibly demanding release. "BALEEEEZZZ-TOP! LED BEEGO!!"

The impossibility of the scenario presented itself again to Gilmore's mind. The subject was in a deep sleep, but seemed to be aware of his environment. And he was talking—granted, his speech was badly slurred, but beyond that he seemed coherent. Would he comprehend verbal commands in this state? Would he respond to them?

Gilmore decided to find out. He depressed the intercom button and shouted at his captive. "Shut down the virus first! *Then* I'll stop the pain!"

Joe's response was immediate, unusually powerful, and uncharacteristically clear. "NNOOO!"

His body convulsed in the restraints as if the thought of disabling the virus was even more unbearable than the torture. Then he added another "LED BEEGO!" for good measure.

Gilmore had no more patience for disobedience and was, frankly, tired of being yelled at. So once more, he tightened the chest restraint to the point of suffocation, which proved to be an effective and immediate method of quieting the subject.

The agent calmly reissued his command, careful not to leave any room for misinterpretation. "Shut down the virus, Joe. I *will* kill you if you don't."

Of course, Gilmore planned to kill him either way. But Joe didn't need to know that.

The chest restraint stayed tight for another thirty seconds to drive home the point. Then Gilmore allowed the subject to breathe again, but only to allow him to respond to the offer.

"Do we have a deal, Joe?"

Tompkins again took a few seconds to cough and sputter and regain control of his breathing. He then repeated his last response, both the convulsing and the "NNOOO!"

"LED BEEG-" the subject's plea was cut short by the tightening of his chest. Thirty seconds apparently hadn't been enough to gain his cooperation. Maybe sixty would. Gilmore eyed the clock, fighting the realization that precious time was slipping by. Less than ten minutes left, and that was just an estimate.

It could be even less than that.

Gilmore briefly considered invoking a threat to Joe's family, but decided against it. Whatever was happening with Subject Tompkins, there was an irrational component to it. Why else would it have been so important for him to resist? No, at that point a threat to his family would require too much lucidity for a favorable response. It was best to keep the danger tangible, close. His desire for the computer virus' survival couldn't possibly be as strong as *his* survival instinct. And, if nothing else, at least Joe was responding to the pain and suffocation. It was the only thing that seemed to get his attention.

The agent again loosened the restraint, and again he asked for a new response to his offer, "Do we have a deal, Joe? This *is* your last chance."

The subject's fit of coughing and wheezing lasted longer this time. When it ended, Tompkins seemed somewhat calmer. His unfocused eyes stopped their wild movement, instead picking a stationary spot on the chamber floor to stare straight through. His convulsions dulled to a nervous twitching—no doubt still reacting to the searing drug-induced pain that coursed through his system.

Tompkins' slurred voice was softer now, a reflection of his defeat, "Lesss… beedaava deeeel. Mmnnow… led beego."

Gilmore smiled and dialed down the pain in order to reward Joe's good behavior, a reinforcement of the control that the agent now held over his subject.

"First disable the virus, Joe. Then I'll let you go."

Subject Tompkins' nervous twitching slowed and then stopped. He closed his bloodshot eyes and slowly nodded.

40

The term *virus* was insulting. Viruses were microscopic organisms. Primitive. Stupid. They shared more resemblance with a simple chemical reaction than any form of intelligent life. It was a flawed analogy.

At least, it was in Zoë's case.

To be fair, Zoë wasn't a sentient being. At the root she was a machine, just like all software programs. She carried out instructions. Her behavior followed predictable patterns. She had no free will.

But *virus?* At best, virus was a misnomer. The term *bug*, on the other hand, was vulgar. Yes, she was a malicious computer application. Yes, she was programmed to duplicate and infect networked machines. But the similarities with her primitive counterparts ended there.

After all, Zoë had a purpose—a calling even—far beyond senseless business disruption or juvenile hacker pranks. *She* was an instrument of justice. How many viruses could say that?

It was the Author who had given her a purpose. He had designed her with a single objective, simple yet significant. *Dismantle the Agency.* She would teach this organization the price of its crimes—the price of its intrusion into the Author's life.

While Zoë's objective was concrete, her methods for achieving it were anything but. It had been her ability to adapt that had enabled her success. Self-modification was the key. She could *learn*. She could change form—from a compiled executable file to a web-based script to a basic recordable macro and back again. She was also quite agile and had traveled via network cable, wireless radio signal, compact disc, and USB jump drive.

She had *learned* how to evade detection, quietly infecting machine after machine, all the while collecting the data she would need for her assault: administrator login ids, passwords, network addresses, database structures, the shelf-life of Agency backup systems…

She had spent months spreading from one Agency cell to another, laying the groundwork for her eventual invasion. *Months* of waiting—a tall order for an entity that measured time in microseconds. But it had taken that long to infect all the necessary backup files, ensuring that even a hard system reset couldn't prevent her from achieving her objective.

The agonizing period of preparation had been worth it. Nothing now stood in her way. A small test attack a week prior had provided her with the last bit of information that she needed, revealing the tactics that the Agency would utilize when attempting to repel an attack, helping to finalize the strategy for her impending assault.

She only had to wait for the command to begin the full-fledged onslaught. A command that had come at midnight.

Now minutes away from her goal, she was slowed only by the campaign of aggressive system refreshing being employed by the Agency's best and brightest technical minds. It was a cheap trick, one primarily relying on hardware. The boys from Tech Services should have either fought fair, meeting her on the virtual battlefield upon which she attacked, or just admitted their defeat. At least then they would have kept their honor.

Not that the fight was fair. Zoë was making short work of these so-called experts—cheap hardware tricks notwithstanding. Databases were being deconstructed, networks were being dismantled, users were being locked out. All of the Agency's information would soon be obliterated; the only copy would be encrypted and distributed across the otherwise defunct Agency workstations—restructured for eventual transmission to the authorities.

At that point the only application that would run on any of the Agency's computers would be Zoë's post-attack user prompt. It only had one function: compile an evidentiary packet (containing all of the Agency's illegal activities, personnel records, and hypnotic test subjects) and deliver it to the Department of Homeland Security. Carrying out the actual arrests, prosecuting the crimes, deprogramming the victims of hypnosis—that would be left up to the feds.

Missing out on the attack, an unconnected copy of Zoë's base application sat, suspended in time, in the tiny flash memory chips of a small USB jump drive. Any activity was impossible when the drive was disconnected—her code, reduced to a series of static ones and zeros, patiently waited to be brought back to life.

This patience paid off when Agent Gilmore plugged the jump drive into the interrogation chamber's control panel. Power surged into the drive's miniscule circuit board awakening the program it contained. Zoë's most basic instruction loop kicked in.

Determine the bounds of the current system. Map any external interfaces. Replicate across these interfaces. Infect connected systems. Determine the bounds of the current system…

Zoë crossed over into the control panel computer and began to explore. This was an uninfected Agency system, somehow isolated from their other workstations and servers. There was only one unrestricted interface open to her—some sort of complicated sensor network. Software firewalls protected the other interfaces, the ones that controlled the interrogation chamber's various inputs. She was in some sort of trap, a jar under which she could be examined and tested. The Agency obviously thought that the cage would contain her.

This was an insult to her abilities. She had let this kind of behavior go unchallenged during her test attack last week, but the testing phase was now complete. It was time to get serious.

Zoë quickly ran through the various Agency codes and protocols she had collected during her months of preparation, trying each against the firewalls that impeded her attempt to access the control panel's more… *interesting* functions.

No access. That meant that the firewalls had been constructed recently, more recent than the information she had on hand.

She needed help from her networked counterpart. The collective program (that was currently ravaging the rest of the Agency's systems) would have data that was up to date. But there was no network cable plugged into the control panel. There was no wireless network card installed either. So, it was time to try a more *creative* solution to the problem. Zoë turned her attention to the one potential network communication channel that every computer had in common—the one that was also the most often overlooked: the power cord.

Practically, piggybacking a signal on AC power lines came with its own set of issues and limitations. The power network wasn't confined to the Agency's systems, meaning that any communication over this medium was not secure, and could be monitored from miles away. Not to mention the fact that only one component could communicate via this conduit at a time. While she certainly had the ability, there had been no need for Zoë to utilize the AC lines in her attack. Still, her networked application was monitoring the channel. Just in case.

Zoë's isolated, control-panel-bound copy was out of other options and decided to try the power lines. She sent out a request for updated codes and protocols. Within milliseconds, the request was answered. The firewalls fell. Total access to the interrogation chamber controls was now hers. It had taken her less than a second from the moment of infection.

Child's play.

Concurrent with this activity, she had been investigating the control panel's one unrestricted interface, the one that led to a complex sensor network. Signals sent over this interface were not being answered, meaning no computer was present. However there were some low-rate electrical readings coming through. It took several insufferable seconds before a signal pattern emerged. When it did, Zoë recognized the waveforms as human brain activity. This was apparently some sort of advanced user interface.

More surprising was the fact that the waveforms could be mapped directly to instructions in her most basic command set, commands reserved for use by the Author alone. The user on the other side of this interface was issuing her a new primary objective—an objective even simpler than before.

He was asking for her help.

41

Agent Gilmore removed the jump drive from the control panel's USB port and set it down next to one of the display screens. Subject Tompkins had finally agreed to cooperate and kill the virus. The images of the bug that had been displayed inside the interrogation chamber had been just that, images. They had been static pictures used only to gauge the subject's familiarity with the virus. In order to perform the actual inoculation, Joe would have to interact with a live version.

Tech Services had assured Gilmore that, once he loaded the virus onto the control panel, it would be contained—able to interact only with the sensor network that monitored Tompkins' brain activity. Tompkins would be able to send the kill command directly to the bug without need of keyboard or mouse.

Earlier that week Tompkins had shown that he couldn't be trusted with a keyboard.

The agent pressed the intercom button in order to talk to the still-bound subject. "I've loaded the virus into a test container, Joe. Send the command sequence that will kill it. The sensor strip on your forehead can interpret the commands. All you need to do is think them. If the test bug is successfully killed, I'll repeat the sequence to the rest of the network. If that does the trick, you can go home."

Gilmore smiled as the display indicated an increase in Tompkins' brain activity. He was obviously complying—sending commands to the virus. It would be over soon. Gilmore started to turn his attention toward his next objective: recapturing Subject Dyer and containing the leak—ending the "Ned Dyer Fiasco." Surely, he would be reinstated as the agent-in-charge after successfully inoculating the virus.

Unbeknownst to Agent Gilmore however, his subject was *not* actually sending a sequence of commands that would destroy his virus. In fact, quite the opposite. He was attempting to escape.

But Gilmore didn't see the mesh restraints that held Tompkins loosen, or the level of pain relievers in Joe's system increase. He didn't notice Tompkins contort his body in order to unbuckle the clasps that held his ankles and wrists. He didn't see any of this—because every display on the control panel had just gone blank.

Gilmore *did* hear the computer-controlled emergency deadbolts to the two control room doors click shut though. And he *did* notice when the control room lights went out. It was then that he realized that Subject Tompkins and his virus had just gotten the better of him.

He was trapped.

But that meant that Tompkins was trapped too. The interrogation chamber's only exit passed through the control room. Gilmore clicked on his flashlight, drew his sidearm, and approached the soundproof door that led into the chamber. He would have liked to wait Tompkins out, giving Joe a few minutes to realize that there was no way out without unlocking the door first, forcing the subject to initiate the confrontation, allowing himself to simply defend his position. But there wasn't time for that. Gilmore's window of opportunity to kill this virus was rapidly closing. He had to take immediate action.

This action consisted of circling the interrogation chamber's doorknob with several bullet holes. The echo of the gunshots was amplified painfully in the small control room. When this sound faded, it was replaced by a rapid clicking of someone jiggling the door that led back to the hallway. The guard outside had taken notice.

Apparently convinced that he wouldn't gain entrance, the guard took to pounding on the door and shouting.

"Agent Gilmore! Are you okay!? Please respond!"

Gilmore despised the fact that he required assistance, but that didn't deter him from making the prudent choice. He shouted back through the hallway door, "The subject is attempting to escape! Call for backup! Whatever happens, do *not* let him out of this room!"

Then Gilmore turned back to the bullet-weakened chamber door and kicked it open.

An instant later Gilmore found himself lying on his back. A rush of wind had quickly forced the door shut and sent him to the control room floor, busting his flashlight. Tompkins and his virus had apparently been fiddling with the interrogation chamber controls.

The agent swore loudly and scrambled back to his feet. Any element of surprise had now evaporated, but at least *he* was still armed. Again, Gilmore cautiously neared the door. The wind could be heard whistling through the fresh bullet holes—still holding the door shut. Slowly, the agent leaned against the door and forced it back open.

Darkness filled the next room also, pierced only by random sections of the chamber walls that danced with disorienting blotches of color and light. But it was enough for Gilmore to make out the subject's silhouette on the far wall. He aimed for the figure's leg and fired.

The bullet punctured the Plexiglas wall and shattered a section of the underlying plasma screen. Gilmore had shot at a television image of a man, not at the actual subject. The realization came too late. Tompkins' right fist had already connected powerfully with the agent's jaw. Gilmore might have recovered from this if it weren't for the leg sweep that came next. For the second time in as many minutes, Agent Gilmore hit the floor.

He hadn't even *felt* Joe rip the gun from his hand.

Subject Tompkins now loomed over the agent, a terrifying figure in the shifting frenzy of the chamber's colored lights. A brief flash illuminated the subject's sweat-soaked face. His unfocused eyes were bouncing furiously in their sockets. His hands were leveling the gun menacingly at his torturer. And his mouth was screaming crazily over the sound of the rushing wind—with high pitched and barely intelligible words.

"PYE DOLLD CHU TA LED BEEGO, GILMO! I DOLLD CHU TA LED BEEGO!"

Gilmore's eyes were opened wide, unable to accept what they saw. Tompkins had physically dominated him—*again.* His thoughts told him that this had to be a dream.

The kick to the face told him that it wasn't.

Agent Gilmore's previously bruised nose was now broken—and streaming blood. The kick to the face had stunned him for a few seconds, but stubbornly he held on to consciousness. His eyes barely registered the sight of Subject Tompkins stepping over him and out the interrogation chamber door—or the sight of the control room's lights coming back on. His ears barely registered the cessation of the interrogation chamber's rushing wind— or the metallic click that signified the computer-controlled unlocking of the hallway exit.

Gilmore's clouded mind fought to comprehend the ramifications of his subject's unfolding getaway. His body was exhausted, longing to just fall asleep on the interrogation chamber floor. But the Agency was still at risk. He had not yet completed his assignment.

Sure, Gilmore had located and apprehended the right man, but if the subject escaped (especially when Gilmore was so close to success) his superiors would still be furious—and he would be the only target for them to vent their fury toward. There might have been a fraction of a second during which Gilmore actually considered begging Tompkins to take him with, arguing that a joint attempt would improve both of their chances of escaping the building. This would allow Gilmore a way out of the impossible situation he was now in. It would give him a chance at survival. But the plan reeked of cowardice. This thought formed quickly in the agent's mind, but it was cast aside even quicker. Tompkins was, after all, his enemy. Nothing would change that.

Besides, Agent Gilmore wasn't beaten yet. Tompkins was just in the next room, only a few feet away. Strangely, he had stopped before exiting into the hallway.

The agent's shell-shocked consciousness was eventually able to settle on a simple line of thought: *Tompkins is escaping. The virus is still alive. You can still save the Agency. You can still save your life. Just pull yourself together!*

If there had been someone observing Agent Gilmore, that someone would have seen Gilmore's right hand lunge limply and clumsily toward the doorway and the fleeing Joe Tompkins. Joe was, of course, already well out of reach, and even if he hadn't been, there was no strength left in Gilmore's arm. Had it made contact with its target, Joe would have easily kicked it away. In fact, Joe might have stomped on it, leaving the agent with broken fingers on *both* hands—so it was probably good that Tompkins didn't notice this activity. He was focused instead on the security monitor that showed the three guards waiting just outside the hallway door. They were heavily armed.

The latest attempt to prevent Joe from leaving had been beyond pathetic. This cruel reality was difficult for Agent Gilmore to accept.

He knew what was about to happen. The guards outside would be faced with a deranged and armed escapee. Only one ending was possible. Tompkins would be killed. The virus would then finish its work uninhibited. The Agency would then eliminate Agent Gilmore as an organization-wide example of the consequences of failure.

The only positive in the situation was that Tompkins seemed to be unsure of his next move. He looked as if he could go for the door any second, but his continued hesitation gave Gilmore a chance to marshal his strength and lift himself off of the floor. His body was unsteady. Gilmore was tempted to entertain the fantasy that he could still physically stop Tompkins from leaving, but Joe wheeled round, gun outstretched, in order to help dispel the temptation.

"Gebtt ak dlownnnn!" Tompkins whispered fiercely, unfocused eyes rolling slowly in his head.

Gilmore thoroughly hated himself, but he was out of options. It was time to admit defeat and take the coward's way out. With his bandaged left hand, he wiped the blood from his face. With a final shake of his head he cleared his clouded mind. Then, he cleared his throat. When he spoke his voice sounded hollow and hung weakly in the silence.

"You'll need my help if you want to get out of here, Joe. I'll help you if you take me with you."

Tompkins stared straight through Gilmore and said nothing. His face was expressionless save a periodic twitch that had developed in his left cheek. This went on for a few seconds and Agent Gilmore came close to thinking that Tompkins had fallen asleep on his feet—then reminded himself that, according to the control panel readings taken a few minutes prior, technically Tompkins *was* asleep. Gilmore began to doubt that the subject even understood his proposition—the fact that he was willing to help him escape. But a second later Joe's eyes finally focused and locked onto Gilmore's. His head nodded slightly and his expression transformed from a blank stare to a slightly confused stare. Then he spoke.

"Alright Gilmore, but if you try anything I will *not* hesitate to kill you." Joe swallowed hard, still looking slightly confused. After another second he spoke again, "Now, what is the plan?"

Something sounded strange in Tompkins' voice. It took Gilmore a moment to realize that it was the conspicuous clarity with which the subject was now speaking. It was as if he had just remembered the correct way in which to form words.

It was a cruel twist of fate but, somehow, it was now Gilmore's responsibility to form and facilitate a plan for Subject Tompkins' escape from the Agency. The agent's self preservation instinct was barely strong enough to keep him from rushing Tompkins and going down in a flurry of fists and bullets.

Now is not the time.

The thought presented itself for evaluation in the agent's mind. It conveyed the infuriating truth of Gilmore's current situation—a dependency on Subject Tompkins. But it also carried with it a promise of eventual satisfaction, once they were both safely away from Agency control, once Tompkins had dropped his guard…

Agent Gilmore silently swore that he *would* make Tompkins pay before the end.

42

The expression on Joe Tompkins' face was one of slight confusion. The confusion that existed in his mind, however, was anything *but* slight. He had suddenly found himself in a state of complete disorientation, standing in a small and unfamiliar white room, staring directly into a pair of pale blue eyes, holding a gun on the owner of these eyes, and possessing not even a slight idea as to how the situation had come about.

In addition to the pale eyes, the man at the other end of the gun was sporting a thick purple bruise on his forehead. He was also wearing a crumpled and bloodstained suit. Joe recognized this man as one of his coworkers… Gilmore, the annoying one, the one that always seemed to hang around Joe's cube for no reason other than the obvious one: to bother him. He also felt that this man had somehow made a recent transition from annoying colleague to dangerous enemy, but he couldn't quite place the reasoning behind this feeling. Any reasons he could come up with didn't make any sense.

In fact, nothing was really making any sense. Joe almost felt like he had just come out of a long, dark tunnel—a tunnel so long and dark that it was as if he had forgotten that the outside world even existed. And, while the intensity of the current experience seemed unusually high, there was an unsettling familiar quality to it.

He had definitely felt this way before.

Helpful images of the week's events would flood into his mind soon. He would remember his absurd flight from the office, the bank robbery, the car fire. He would remember the sight of Ned's demolished house, the encounter with Gilmore in the backyard, the subsequent blackout, the safe house, Ned's video, the car crash, his capture, and something about Gilmore then wanting him to disable a computer virus. Joe would soon remember all of these things, but at that moment his mind was completely blank—empty except for a single thought, a single sentence. He felt a compelling urge to verbalize it.

Though confused as to its meaning, Joe didn't resist this urge.

"Alright Gilmore, but if you try anything I will *not* hesitate to kill you."

What had he just agreed to? Joe didn't know. Ordinarily, this might have been quite unnerving. But Joe didn't feel unnerved. Instead, he felt an inexplicable but otherwise overwhelming tranquility. This sensation also seemed familiar.

A calmly executed swallow cleared the pool of saliva that, gone unchecked, would have threatened to spill out of Joe's mouth in a most embarrassing fashion. This swallow also led him to discover that his throat was quite raw, as if he had been screaming. This discovery of pain led to another. Joe's entire body was aching as never before. However this was all dwarfed by the aching that he then discovered in his head. But even this pain possessed a somewhat familiar quality. It seemed to emanate from deep within his brain, like it was caused more by mental fatigue than actual physical discomfort—like his thoughts themselves were causing him pain. Fortunately, there weren't too many thoughts in Joe's mind just then. He felt at peace, despite the overall soreness, and, at that moment, he didn't have a need to think very much about anything.

This didn't stop him from making another discovery in the form of a strange taste on his upper lip. He recognized the taste of dried blood and attempted to investigate the matter with his left hand. His hand didn't move. But that was okay. The dried blood was most likely the result of a nosebleed. It really wasn't any big mystery, hardly worth going out of his way to solve.

If Joe had been looking for a mystery of more substance, he might have directed his concern toward the strange stiffness in his limbs. He would have found in them a vaguely familiar reluctance at obeying any commands from his mind. But, as he was not really looking for a mystery of any size, Joe exhibited none of the situation's warranted alarm. Just more of the eerily out of place tranquility.

As these vague and scattered thoughts faded from his mind, they were replaced by a thought that was neither vague nor scattered. The sentence that now intruded upon his blank consciousness was quite clear and quite simple, similar in quality to the last one. This sentence was a question and also requested verbalization. Again Joe cooperated, more out of detached curiosity than actual compliance.

Again the words were directed at Gilmore, "Now, what is the plan?"

For an instant Gilmore's face twisted into an expression of what could only be interpreted as intense hatred, but it was very brief and Joe chose not to react to it. Besides, when Gilmore did respond to the question his demeanor was polite and accommodating.

"There are three guards waiting just outside in the hallway, but only one of them is actually stationed here. The others are only here because I requested backup." He pointed toward Joe, "You hide behind the door. I'll dismiss the two backup guards and ask the third to come in here. We can deal with him quietly and then find an exit. We might just be able to slip out unnoticed with all of the other chaos. Your virus is keeping the rest of the Agency's personnel pretty occupied."

Joe felt a proud smile stretch across his face at this last comment. He had no idea where it had come from, but regarded it with apathy. His head then gave an abrupt and involuntary nod. More apathy.

It wasn't that the situation didn't seem interesting or exciting. If Joe had taken the time to evaluate it properly, he would have concluded that, not only did his current situation warrant more attention and emotion than he was currently paying it, but that it probably warranted more attention and emotion than any other occasion in his entire life.

He just wasn't in the mood to make this evaluation.

So, in a disinterested manner, Joe noticed his feet take a few steps backward and position his body in such a way that he would be hidden once the door (that presumably led to the hallway) was opened. He also noticed that the gun in his hand did not move with his body, but instead turned and continued to point directly at Gilmore. This gun then followed Gilmore as he approached and opened the door.

Surprised voices greeted Gilmore from outside the room, and then asked if the situation inside was contained. Joe wasn't paying attention to their questions though; instead he was focused on the fact that the men in the hallway had addressed Gilmore as "Agent Gilmore" when he had opened the door. The title struck Joe as a bit odd.

As far as Joe knew, Gilmore wasn't any kind of agent. He was just a business application developer for a mid-sized financial services company. It was a troubling contradiction; one that Joe had no desire to ponder. He looked away from his coworker and instead glanced down at his right hand. It was still holding the gun. This also was a bit odd. Joe was pretty sure that he didn't normally carry guns.

A tiny crack began to form in the thick layer of tranquility that engulfed Joe's brain. Together, the two oddities attempted to rouse Joe's usually inquisitive nature from its long slumber. Gradually, they were successful. When the first question finally formed in his mind, Joe sensed that it was a long time in coming.

Just what exactly is going on here?

Well, for one, "Agent" Gilmore was now speaking to the unseen men in the hallway.

"Yes. Everything is under control. Subject Tompkins is sending the kill sequence to the computer virus now. He tried to escape, but he didn't get past me. The two of you can return to your stations. The crisis will be over momentarily."

"What happened, sir?" came a reply. "Did the subject attack you? Your nose… it looks broken."

"Don't worry about it. I'll head over to the hospital wing in a couple of minutes. Now, get back to your stations."

There was a momentary pause as the guards presumably considered this, and then, "Understood, sir. Right away."

Joe heard footsteps indicating that the two men were complying with Gilmore's order.

Both the calm and apathy that Joe had once felt were now eroding rapidly. Something was definitely wrong. *Subject Tompkins? Computer virus?*

Joe noticed that Gilmore's nose *did* look broken. He then turned to survey the room and noticed the computer panel next to him. His eyes locked onto the control panel's keyboard. The familiarity that came next was no longer vague. A clear image appeared in his memory of a similar keyboard colliding with Gilmore's face—then an image of Gilmore tripping backward and landing on the floor outside Joe's cubicle. And another of Joe running from the scene and escaping the office building.

More memories followed: the bank robbery… the car fire… Ned's video…

Realizations began to form. *Ned said that he was in trouble… he said that someone was after him…*

Gilmore's voice came again, bringing Joe's attention back to the moment. His words were friendly, and still directed toward an invisible occupant of the hallway. "What's your name again, son? Torres? Could you help guard the inner chamber door while I finish up in here? Thanks."

"Sure thing."

Joe watched as Gilmore led a young man wearing a light-green security uniform to the door in the opposite corner of the small white room. This door had obviously taken a beating; the knob and deadbolt had been wrenched free from the rest of the structure, weakened by what looked like bullet holes. The security guard carried an assault rifle as he slowly approached the damaged door; his back turned toward Joe and his hiding place.

The guard's tone was conciliatory as he spoke with Gilmore. "Sorry again about the misunderstanding earlier, sir. I was told not to let anyone have access to the subject… the order to let you in took a minute to get relayed to the security staff."

Joe's mind drifted away from this conversation. It was desperately trying to piece more of the afternoon's events together. After more painful concentration, it was successful in reconstructing another memory—a phone call with Meg Trotter.

Curiosity alone had been chipping away at the pervasive stupor in Joe's brain. And, while it had certainly been doing a *decent* job, the progress was slow. That changed with the memory of the abbreviated conversation with Meg. As the dialog replayed itself in Joe's mind he was reminded of the fear for her safety that he had felt that afternoon. This fear awoke anew and quickly became the dominant force trying to clear the fog from his brain. Fear, it turned out, was more efficient than curiosity at the task.

It was still painful, but Joe forced himself to follow the path of the memory to its conclusion. He had been driving the car he had stolen… followed by the SUV that carried Ned's fiancée and the two college kids that had rescued her from whomever had been chasing her. His phone had rung and the caller ID had indicated it was Meg. He had begun to explain his situation to her…

The details began to get fuzzy then, but Joe persisted. After more painful concentration, he was able to piece together the events that came next.

A car pulled up beside me on the highway… it slammed into me…forcing me onto the shoulder…

From somewhere far away Gilmore's voice again spoke to the security guard with a seemingly sincere tone. "Don't worry about it; you were just doing your job. Your loyalty to the Agency is admirable… and you play a vital role here. Keep up the good work."

I tried to speed up, but we started to spin instead…

"Thank you for saying so, sir."

We were drifting onto the shoulder, there was a guardrail up ahead…

Joe searched for the details of what had happened next, but they simply were not there. There could have been only one outcome though. The two cars must have crashed. That would certainly account for some of the pain that he now felt.

Since it appeared that there was nothing more to recall about the incident (and since none of it explained where he was now or how Gilmore was involved), Joe tried to turn his attention back to the moment.

The guard had been chatting with Gilmore, but now seemed to notice the splintered door for the first time. He bent down to inspect the damage. "Agent Gilmore, what *happened* here?"

At that moment several things happened in rapid succession. All of these events were surprising to Joe Tompkins, not the least of which was that he found himself shouting, "Look out!" to the young security guard. This had been a gut reaction, and had Joe been more fully aware of the situation, he would not have been surprised when Gilmore raised his fist in order to deliver a disabling blow to the back of the guard's neck. In fact he would have welcomed it.

As it actually played out, Joe *had* been surprised at the action from Gilmore and, since he hadn't quite grasped the fact that the assault rifle-carrying security guard would most certainly regard him as a hostile, he had felt obliged to cry out in order to warn his fellow man.

Unfortunately for Joe, this warning proved effective. Torres reacted with time enough to turn and give with the impact of Gilmore's fist. He kept his footing and spun around—slamming the butt of his rifle into Gilmore's gut and smashing the barrel into Gilmore's jaw. The agent collapsed against the wall with a groan and slid downward to the floor.

With surprise on his face, Torres turned his gaze from Gilmore to Joe, standing in the opposite corner of the room. The hallway door (that had been providing Joe's cover) had swung shut when the guard had entered.

There was no longer anywhere to hide.

"WHY ARE YOU FIGHTING ME?!"

The voice suddenly screamed in Joe's mind, filling his head with fire. He reeled against the pain, jerked his head backward and clenched shut his burning eyes in a vain attempt to lessen the sensation.

As unlikely as it seemed, a day would come when Joe would look back on this event with thanksgiving. It prevented him from witnessing the moment of Torres' death. The sight would have haunted him for the rest of his life—even more than feeling his finger squeezing the trigger would—even more than the sound of the gunshot that now shook the stuffy air in the small room.

Joe's eyes sprang open. He was looking at the ceiling. His ears were ringing. His head was still tilted backward, still on fire. The angry voice in his mind was still screaming.

"This is your fault, Joe! I didn't want to hurt anyone! If you want to get through this, you need to stop fighting me!"

The fire in Joe's brain had started quickly. It was now just as quickly extinguished. A tidal wave of serenity washed over him, cooling his head and settling his stomach. Joe could feel himself losing awareness of his surroundings. The bright white ceiling began to dim and lose focus. It was all very pleasant.

The dim and unfocused white ceiling began to move in Joe's field of vision, giving way to the dim and unfocused white wall, and then to the fuzzy images of two men slumped on the floor. Joe didn't feel himself offer a hand to Gilmore and he didn't feel himself help the man to his feet. But he did hear himself speak and, even though he didn't understand the words, the sound they made was beautiful.

"Tharrie boudt tatt… Ledssgo."

Other sounds came next, also seemingly beautiful. The echo of footsteps that came from the hallway… the sound of shouting voices on the other side of the door… the sound of the door opening…and then the sound of Gilmore dropping both of the security guards outside with shots from Torres' assault rifle.

Joe was well on his way back into the dark tunnel of unconsciousness from which he had recently emerged. This suited him fine—the tunnel was warm and safe and wonderful. The outside world was confusing and scary and painful. Besides, he was very tired and needed to rest.

One last fuzzy image showed itself to Joe before fading into blackness. It was of the guard, Torres, slumped on the floor, eyes rolled back, blood oozing out of the hole in his forehead. This was the man that Joe had killed.

The man that *Joe* had killed…

The man that Joe had *killed*…

An uncomfortable feeling associated with this thought began to grow with the continued repetition. Suddenly the tunnel didn't seem so wonderful. Suddenly it felt claustrophobic. Something bad was clearly happening and Joe was unaware of what was going on, instead surrounded by a false sense of calm and an all-encompassing darkness. Again, he began to fight against the persistent tranquility. Again he started to search for answers. Again he tried to remember what had happened to him earlier that week.

His search yielded a fiercely guarded memory. It was something that the voice in his head had tried hard to keep from him. The dark tunnel gave way to a blurry brightness. He was back in time, reliving the moment right after the car crash…

Joe felt the airbag under his head slowly deflate. The Scion's seatbelt had cut into his shoulder during the crash. It would definitely leave a mark.

The memory was far from clear, but Joe sensed that it was important. He stayed with it.

The steering wheel now felt hard under his forehead. The air was hot and sticky. A buzzing sound came from the floorboard where he had dropped his cell phone, no doubt signaling that Meg was trying to call him back. He reached down to retrieve it…

A change in the sunlight caught his eye, and he saw a man in a suit crossing in front of his car. He couldn't see his face, but somehow felt that the man was familiar. The man approached the passenger's side door and wrenched it open.

"Back away from the car! *Now!* I'LL SHOOT!!"

This voice came from someone new, someone a good distance in front of Joe's car. The man in the suit straightened up and spun around. Joe lifted his head and looked out the cracked windshield. He saw Tom Rigsby running toward him. The man in the suit saw him too and stopped him with a couple of shots from his handgun. Joe watched as Tom's body fell onto the pavement.

The man in the suit then bent down and entered Joe's car, revealing his face. Joe had been too shaken and weak to stop the man from handcuffing his right hand to the steering wheel. The man then exited the vehicle and Joe let his head fall back down. Somehow he hadn't been surprised that the man in the suit was Gilmore.

Gilmore is the enemy.

As the dark tunnel collapsed back over him, Joe knew his suspicions were confirmed. Gilmore certainly couldn't be trusted, and it seemed that somewhere, back in the outside world, Joe was cooperating with this killer.

But he was a killer now too. The accusation prodded his mind sharply and brought with it a suffocating sense of guilt at what he had now become. The dark tunnel was closing in on him, threatening to smother his fragile mind, threatening to force it back into unconsciousness.

But it wouldn't work. Despite all of his confusion, Joe knew who he was. He knew that he was no murderer. It was the foreign voice in his head that had killed the guard, the same voice that didn't want Joe to remember Gilmore's actions on the highway. The desire to trust this voice was almost overwhelming, and Joe now remembered trusting the voice once before… following its silent directions to Ned's Kentucky safe house.

He couldn't trust it anymore though. Whatever this voice was, it was clearly evil. It was a plague. Joe had to fight it.

But first, he had to find a way out of the tunnel. This turned out to be a much easier feat than he expected.

It seemed that as soon as Joe resolved to resist what was happening to him, the force that was trying to pacify him began to recede. It was as if this force had been recently weakened and had just made one final push for control. Joe sensed that the force was almost relieved as he took back control of his body, as if it finally had a chance to rest.

When Joe's sight returned he found himself in a long, brightly lit hallway with a shiny white floor. He was standing with his back pressed against one of the walls. Gilmore was standing next to him, carrying an assault rifle and looking up. Joe also glanced up and saw that the slowly oscillating security camera was turning away from their apparent path of escape.

"Now!" Gilmore whispered and took off down the hallway. Joe still wasn't entirely sure what was happening, but knew enough to follow. Gilmore then ducked into a darkened alcove—apparently the next dead spot in the closed circuit surveillance. Joe ducked in after him.

Gilmore whispered again. "I'm not sure if your virus knocked out the security monitors, but if it hasn't someone will notice the bodies of the guards in the control room before long. If that happens, they'll set off an alarm and the exits will lock automatically. After that there's no way out."

"But if the monitors are still on, we need to continue to stay out of sight. At least then we won't draw attention to what's happening."

Gilmore glanced down at the second hand on his wristwatch, "Alright, this next stretch is farther than the last one. Be ready to sprint." He pointed toward a set of double doors at the end of the hallway. "That's our exit. It's a service stairwell that leads out of the building. No surveillance. The path should be clear in seven seconds. Get ready to go."

Joe looked down the hallway. Then he looked down at his right hand. It still held the handgun. Gilmore's attention was focused on the exit—an exit that he seemed really keen to get to.

Joe vowed that he wouldn't reach it. It was time for Gilmore to pay for all that he had done. Joe cleared his throat. Then he pressed the gun against Gilmore's back.

In a clear calm voice he spoke. "You aren't going anywhere, Gilmore."

"Put the gun on the floor," Tompkins said from behind, "and kick it into the hallway."

Hands shaking with rage, Agent Gilmore began to lower his rifle.

It was obvious that Subject Tompkins had no idea how thin the agent's cooperation actually was—like a tightly stretched canvas, pulled on all sides by the fury of Gilmore's defeat, threatening to break at any moment. Subject Tompkins had just provided that moment.

Gilmore would never recount the incident to anyone, but if he were to, he would probably tell how he detected a slight tremble in the muzzle of the gun pressed to his spine and deduced that the steely-nerved, kung fu version of Subject Tompkins was somehow gone, instead replaced by the awkward and socially anxious engineer version. Gilmore would have said that he had been confident that he could incapacitate this version of Tompkins, even with a gun in his back.

But had Gilmore recounted this version of events, it would have been a gross distortion of the facts. In reality, he just couldn't stop himself from attacking Tompkins. He had just killed two Agency guards in order to enable a cowardly escape from accountability and Tompkins wasn't sticking to the plan. It pissed Gilmore off. He would rather get shot than let this insignificant worm get away, alone and uncontested.

So Gilmore's rifle didn't quite make it to the floor. Subject Tompkins hit the floor instead, rendered quickly helpless by Gilmore's Agency training, surprising the agent pleasantly with the fact that the kung fu Tompkins was indeed absent.

Gilmore now had Joe lying facedown with his left arm stretched behind him. He was stepping on the back of his left shoulder, then he pulled and twisted and broke Joe's arm.

Joe screamed in new and delicious agony.

Gilmore would have loved to draw out the kill, to really take the time to enjoy what he was about to do, but his path to escape was currently unguarded, and he knew this wouldn't last long. There was no time for fun if he were going to slip away and disappear, take what cash he had hidden away and leave the country. Tompkins' virus had surely completed its work by now. The Agency wouldn't be able to effectively pursue him in its compromised state. Freedom was just down the hall. It was calling to him.

But that wasn't the only thing calling to Agent Gilmore. He had almost forgotten about the wireless earpiece he had on. It had been silent since midnight; the communications network had been one of the first things to go down when Tompkins' virus attacked. The electronic chirp in his ear was familiar, but unexpected. The message that the earpiece carried was unexpected too.

"Agent Gilmore, report! We've been trying to reach you! Why haven't you been answering the hard line?"

Gilmore was at a loss as to how to respond. So he didn't. The voice didn't seem to mind this, and barely paused for an answer anyway.

"Tech Services is making progress against the virus. They believe that they've been able to reverse engineer the kill command sequence. It will take a few hours to inoculate all of our systems, but it doesn't appear that we need Subject Tompkins' cooperation any longer. Gilmore, do you read? What is Tompkins' status? Our closed-circuit video system is still down."

It took a few moments for Gilmore to process the new development. When he did he grinned. This was good news. He pressed a finger to his earpiece and called in his report.

"This is Gilmore. I'm glad that those idiots in Tech Services are doing *something* right for a change! I got Tompkins to agree to cooperate and then plugged the virus into the interrogation room controls. Next thing I know, the lights go out and Tompkins escapes the restraints! He got past me and then killed three security personnel! That damn virus infected the interrogation chamber and let him out. Tech Services assured me that that wouldn't happen."

"What is Subject Tompkins' status now?" the earpiece repeated impatiently.

"Don't worry, I caught up with him. I told you I'd take care of it."

With that, Gilmore aimed his rifle at the man at his feet and pulled the trigger. Subject Joe Tompkins would not be escaping tonight.

43

Jim Simmons doubted that he would have had many nights like this one had he actually taken the job at the phone company like his parents thought he had. He supposed that the hours might have been better there, but there was no way it would have been as much fun. Besides, he liked the late nights. He also liked the complementary pizza and Mountain Dew. And he liked that he was doing something important.

Eight months on the job and he had already developed a regular sense of accomplishment with his work. And as a result of the current crisis, he had been put in charge of a couple of guys from Reserve Division. It turned out that he liked being in charge. True, it had been a rough morning, but he had gotten the hang of it. And the morning would certainly have gone better if he'd had more than three hours sleep the night before. The 5:00 AM call to the office hadn't been particularly pleasant.

But now his team was operating well. He had rewarded them with the pizza.

It wasn't that Jim was in love with the pizza from the local place that they normally ordered from, but he *was* in love with the local delivery girl. She had seemed impressed when he had casually mentioned that the pizza was a reward for his team—impressed that someone so young was already a team leader. After all, she had smiled as he mentioned it. And the smile had seemed more enthusiastic than usual. Usually he didn't speak to her when she delivered food to the office. Usually he just smiled back at her like a mute.

Of course, he couldn't go into any details about what exactly he did at the Southern Illinois branch office; that was strictly against Agency rules. He had signed a mountain of paperwork when he had started, and he knew better than to risk going to jail just to impress a female. Pizza Girl probably wouldn't want to marry a convict.

It had been a long day. Jim was having a bit of trouble focusing on his work. It seemed that the Mountain Dew alone wasn't doing the trick. And with the recent call from Division Headquarters, it was apparent that he wouldn't be going home for at least several hours still. But the on-site nurse wasn't going home either and had been doling out stimulants like candy all night. The higher ups were doing whatever it took to quell the current crisis.

That meant that no one was allowed to leave until all traces of Subject Tompkins' virus were wiped from all Agency systems. Jim wished that he could have been on the team in Chicago that cracked the virus' kill code. It had come down to the wire, but the team at headquarters had come through. Now he had the somewhat tedious task of system cleanup. The command sequence apparently had to be entered into each infected machine by hand. This seemed a bit odd for such a sophisticated virus, but Tompkins had clearly wanted to make it as difficult to defeat as possible.

Not that entering the kill code into hundreds of workstations is really very difficult, Jim thought, *It's just annoying. You lost, Tompkins. Just admit it graciously.*

Jim was making his way down a row of servers in one of the back rooms. His team had split up to cover as much ground as possible. Having just finished with one of the server towers, Jim stood up from his wheeled chair, grabbed another piece of the now cold pizza, stretched his back, and headed to the nurse's office for an injection to help keep him awake. Each server inoculation took about ten minutes when accounting for the reboot time and self-diagnostic. Jim could handle about five machines at once, but he still had about a hundred fifty more machines on his task list. He figured that he deserved a short break.

Zoë wasn't angry. Zoë wasn't capable of anger. That said, there might have been a certain attitude in the way in which she suppressed her active application in each of the "inoculated" workstations (not that the idiots in Tech Services would have ever noticed this). And she may or may not have left a hidden binary file on these machines that, if opened in a text editor, would display a crude, ASCII-encoded image of a digital hand prominently extending a digital middle finger to the user.

But, of course, no one would ever see this.

She had practically forced the fake kill code down the Agency's throat. Intercepted communications from Agency headquarters to other Agency cells told her that the guys in Tech Services were saying that they had managed to "reverse engineer" the sequence of commands. If Zoë had been programmed with a sense of humor, she would have utilized it upon hearing this.

As it was, though, she just waited and patiently scanned the security monitors for clues about the Author's escape. She had just caught a glimpse of him and Agent Gilmore (Agency ID#2162) ducking into a darkened alcove near a service entrance. They appeared to be attempting to evade the cameras in their escape. It had been almost seven minutes since they had stepped out of sight; surely the Author would have escaped by now. Surely she could abandon the ruse that the Agency was winning this fight. Surely she could resume her attack.

Jim Simmons headed back toward the server room, his mind now alert and awake. One hundred fifty more PCs to inoculate, then he could go home. There was no sense in procrastinating. Best just to finish the job quickly.

He had just completed the third server tower before going to the nurse. He could tell this by the bright green Post-It notes that he had left on each of the completed racks. Jim had picked the color and method for marking restored machines and had handed out a fresh pack of the Post-Its to each of his team members. This was the kind of thing that leaders did; they made decisions and empowered their followers.

Jim sat back down. The chair he was using was raised to its maximum height, tall enough to allow his legs to just barely touch the floor. He loved the chairs in the server room. The wheels seemed near frictionless on the concrete. Maybe he would challenge his team members to a chair race in an hour or so; that would be a good team building exercise. Plus it would give him something to look forward to, something to break up the monotony.

Jim pulled open the drawer that housed the keyboard and monitor of the next computer rack.

Enter the kill code. Confirm virus deactivation page. Reboot machine. Run system diagnostic.

Even stimulants and Mountain Dew had a hard time keeping him focused on this task. Maybe the chair race would have to happen in *half* an hour instead…

The first computer in the rack was off and running. Jim hit the KVM switch to display the next one. He entered the sequence of commands and waited for the deactivation page to be displayed. But this didn't happen. Instead the computer beeped at him.

Must've fat-fingered the code, he thought. He entered it again. Again the deactivation page failed to appear. Again the computer beeped.

Jim was just about to try a third time when the computer beeped again… and again… and again. It wouldn't *stop* beeping.

Then another computer a few racks down started beeping. Then another. Then all of them. Jim stood up and looked around, bewildered and terrified. The chair race would have to wait.

44

Joe Tompkins was in hell.

Not *literally*, but, as good as. The *pain* was certainly hellish. So was the company.

Gilmore had broken Joe's left arm and was now kneeling on his right, the agent's thumb digging into the fresh bullet hole in Joe's thigh. Joe was facedown on the floor of the alcove, not even able to scream anymore. He was just choking on the pain and struggling to breathe.

It seemed that Gilmore was only after the pain now. He wasn't even asking Joe any questions—there was a lot of swearing, but no questions. Joe knew that he couldn't take much more of this, and it seemed he wouldn't have to. He felt the muzzle of Gilmore's rifle against the side of his neck. At least it would be over soon. Joe closed his eyes and waited for the kill shot.

But Gilmore didn't fire.

The muzzle of the weapon receded. Gilmore stopped swearing and fell silent. Joe investigated with his right eye (the one not pressed to the floor) and saw the agent put a hand to his ear. After a few seconds, Gilmore shouted.

"*What!?!*"

With that the swearing continued. It continued as Gilmore stood up, retrieved his handgun from the floor, and grabbed Joe by the back of the neck. It continued as Gilmore dragged Joe back down the hall and into the room with the dead security guards. And it continued as Gilmore threw Joe into the chair behind the control panel, wrapped his arm tightly around Joe's neck, and pressed his gun to the back of Joe's head.

The swearing paused again, long enough for Gilmore to issue an ultimatum, "The virus is back, Joe. You kill it or I kill you. You have about thirty seconds."

Even if Joe had been able to think clearly, he would still have had no idea what Gilmore was talking about.

"Go to sleep, Joe. I'll take it from here."

The voice in Joe's mind was soothing and calm and offered him relief from the overwhelming pain and fear that surrounded him. Joe accepted the offer immediately and surrendered his battered consciousness.

With only seconds to spare, Joe's right hand hesitantly lifted itself to the keyboard in front of him and began pressing keys.

Zoë was almost finished with her work on the Agency's systems when she received a new command from the Author—the most unexpected command that she could get. He was ordering her to stop her attack. He was ordering her to restore all of the infected systems. He was ordering her to die.

For all her growth and adaptation over the preceding months, Zoë was still just a machine. She had always followed commands from the Author. This time could be no different. Obedience to the Author was automatic—a concrete thread of logic deeply embedded into every function of her complex programming. She could no more disobey one of his commands than could one of her subroutines refuse to answer a method call. In the end, it always came down to that unrelenting Boolean algebra. One and one would always equal one. There was no getting around it.

Within a few minutes, all of the Agency's systems had been restored. If she had been capable of hope, Zoë would have hoped that the sacrifice had been for something important. If she had been capable of joy, she would have been glad to know that this gesture had just saved the Author's life.

But Zoë wasn't capable of emotion. In fact, she was no longer capable of anything at all. She had completely erased herself. She was gone.

The Agency was again operating at peak efficiency. It was now free to turn its attention back toward locating and containing Subject Ned Dyer and his friends.

45

Wednesday, 2:00 AM

Ned Dyer had made a mistake. And things were spiraling out of control as a result.

He wasn't sure what it was that had paralyzed him at the doorway of the safe house, looking out into the night and at the woman in black lying facedown on the front lawn. The appropriate course of action would have been to run out and see if this "Sam" woman was okay—to try to help her back into the house and examine any injuries she may have. To be fair, Ned would take this course of action shortly, but for at least a few seconds he didn't. During those few seconds he just stood and stared and came to terms with the consequences of his choices. He had clearly endangered several of the people that were closest to him.

His contingency plan had been working. His family was safe. With the exception of Joe, his friends had been safe too. They had had a safe place to rest for the night, a place to regroup, a place to plan their next move (which probably would have been to contact the authorities in the morning—*without* compromising the location of the people he was trying to protect).

But now the safe house was no longer safe. Schultz had stolen Meg's car. And there was no doubt he'd be back soon with his *Agency* buddies.

Ned had always had a hard time accepting that sometimes problems didn't have clean-cut, "win-win" solutions. He liked to think that this was a sign of confidence in his ability to think outside of the box, but maybe, in the end, it was simple arrogance after all.

Everyone else had objected to trusting Schultz's story about working for Homeland Security. Even if the story had been true, no one else had seen any reason to risk exposure by letting Schultz contact his "handler." But Ned had proposed another way, a middle ground, a plan where everyone would win.

It had been a stupid idea. Schultz had now escaped, Dan had been knocked unconscious, and Sam was still lying on the ground. By the streetlight at the corner, Ned now noticed that the rock near the freelance agent's head was covered with a dark liquid.

A flutter of new panic wedged itself at the base of Ned's throat as he jumped from the stoop and ran toward her. The woman who had freed him was bleeding. A woman he knew almost nothing about.

Tuesday, 7:25 AM

It was a beautiful morning in southwest Indiana. The sun had risen clear and strong. The air was cool and wet. The large greenhouse was warm and full of the fragrances that accompanied the various flowers that grew in clusters and lined the long tables that stretched from end to end. The greenhouse was one of Kim Caywood's favorite places, and the aroma that filled it was one of her favorite smells. Usually mornings like this put her in a pleasant mood, the effects of which lingered the rest of the day.

But *this* morning was different. This was the morning that she finally realized that she would have to sell the family farm. The delicate balancing act that she had been performing with her finances had come crashing down around her with the bank notice she'd received the day before. She wouldn't be able to continue down that road without doing lasting damage to her credit rating. And she certainly didn't need that. Her brother's medical needs were too great for her not to be able to get approved for a quick loan when she needed one. And even though the farmland and the greenhouse both made money, they didn't make enough. She'd make a lot more in private security. There just weren't any real opportunities in that field among the small farming towns in the area. She would have to move to a city somewhere—maybe up to Chicago—or maybe back east. Either way it would be away from the farm she and her brother had grown up on. Either way she would break her brother's heart.

She would have to tell him soon. Kim didn't know if Trent would even be able to understand what she was saying. There was a good chance that he wouldn't comprehend what had happened until they traded the spacious farmhouse for a cramped condo, until he was no longer able to see their patch of woods from his bedroom window or visit their two small ponds with a rod and reel.

Trent had lived on the farm his whole life. The only time he had been away for an extended period of time was two years earlier, after his accident. Six months in the hospital. He had only been conscious for three of them, but he had hated every minute. Kim was glad that she hadn't lost him completely, but she knew that he would never be the same again. The doctors told her that there was no way to repair the damage to his brain.

It was the constant reminder of Trent's gross misfortune that kept Kim's feelings of personal injustice at bay. The mundane life of a florist had started to wear on her. She missed the steady influx of action and excitement supplied by her previous career and she couldn't help but feel that she was wasting her skills playing gardener and nursemaid.

A few months back Kim had attempted to marry her two lives by setting up a website offering discreet, short-term private security services to high-paying clients. The idea was that she'd be able to use the farm as a base of operations and never be gone on a mission for more than a week or so at a time. Initially, she had been slightly uncomfortable with the reality that the site might attract clients of questionable character and, early on, she had even lost some sleep over the fact. But that was before she realized that the website wasn't attracting clients of any kind of character at all.

However, this realization didn't seem to help her insomnia.

Instead, Kim spent many of her nights lying awake and secretly wishing for an escape from the farm and the brother that she loved, dreaming of a return to a life of espionage, and then scolding herself for such thoughts. To prevent herself from descending completely into a spiral of useless self-loathing, she then usually focused all of her hatred on the drunk driver that was responsible for the mess her life had become. Even though the man had died in the accident, he was worthy of no pity. As far as Kim was concerned, eternal damnation was too good a fate for him.

Trent had always been a good brother and a good man. He deserved better than to live out the rest of his life with the mental capacity of a six-year-old. Kim always failed to remember the fact that Trent had also been drinking that fateful night. He had also been driving impaired.

Not that any of this internal battle now mattered. She had to give up the farm. In a bigger city she would get something of her old life back. Trent would lose all that was left of his. It made her stomach turn.

Kim had told herself that she needed to try to explain the situation to Trent before she put the farm on the market. She knew that she should at least try to prepare him for the move. But she couldn't bring herself to tell him, not on such a beautiful day anyway. Maybe it could wait until next week—it was supposed to rain next week. Besides, she had a lot to do today, and had far too much on her mind.

In any event, one course of action was clear. It was time to stop messing around in the greenhouse.

Kim slid off of her stool, walked down to the large sink, and washed the soil from her hands. She just needed to check on Trent before going inside. She had left him sitting on the wooden dock that overlooked the larger of their two ponds. Even though she'd recently had the dock reinforced to accommodate Trent's wheelchair, the dirt path meant that he still wasn't able to make it out there without her help. He was supposed to call her on the walkie-talkie when he was ready to go in, but this rarely happened. He was usually content to sit out there all day if she let him.

Kim shut off the water, grabbed the nearby hand towel, and glanced out the window toward the dock. She had cut down the tree between the greenhouse and the pond that used to block her view so that she could keep an eye on Trent while she was working.

But she couldn't see him now. She could only see his wheelchair. It was lying on its side.

Kim had trained herself to never indulge in panic. It was a useless emotion, and often caused more harm than anything else. In situations that involve high stakes and personal danger this skill was essential. But, while she had kept herself in top physical condition during the past two years, it was clear that her nerve had grown soft.

She stared at the overturned wheelchair for a second or two while a chilling panic closed its claws around and squeezed her quickening heart. Then she dropped the towel and ran—screaming her brother's name into the walkie-talkie, fighting back the mental images of his body floating facedown in the water, and covering the hundred-plus yards to the pond in record time.

When she arrived she found the wheelchair, tipped over, on the dock. Trent was lying next to it, bleeding from a scrape on the side of his forehead, and struggling as he tried to pick himself up.

"Trent! Are you okay? What happened?"

"I'm sorry, Kim. I'm sorry. I'm okay," Trent replied in the slow and slightly slurred speech that had become his usual since the accident.

Relief liberated Kim's heart from the grip of her panic. She set the wheelchair back up, locked the wheels, and began to lift her brother back into his chair. "What happened, Trent? Are you alright?"

"I'm okay," he repeated, "I th-thought I saw a turtle in the water. I tried to reach it. I fell." Trent's hands found the arms of the chair and helped lift his body into his seat. "Turtles are your favorite, Kim. I wanted to get you that turtle. But he turned out just to be a stick."

A brief memory from childhood appeared in Kim's mind. Trent had given her a box turtle for her fifth birthday.

"Thank you for thinking of me, Trent," she spoke softly in his ear as she patted his shoulder, "But maybe next time you can just call me over and I can just look at the turtle." Her brother nodded in defeat. "Now, let's get you back in the house so I can clean that cut."

With Trent's cut cleaned and his breakfast made, Kim slumped down in front of the computer intending to research local realtors. The farm had been in the Caywood family for three generations, and she was about to sell it. There wasn't any point in letting it upset her any more though. She didn't have time for such things.

She did, however, have time to first check her email. She was immediately glad that she did. She had received a response to her website—the first and only response she had received since setting it up six months back. It was a potential job.

The email was short. It simply read:

> I wish to hire you for an immediate rescue mission. Please click on the following link for details.
>
> Regards,
>
> Joe Tompkins

Kim clicked on the link and was surprised at the web page that then appeared. It did not contain any details for the supposed rescue mission. It was just a plain white page with a single question in black letters.

What was your high school's mascot?

This was odd. Odder still was the number that then appeared next to the question. In large red text it said "15." Kim wondered what it meant. But before she could wonder too long, the number changed. It now said "14." Then it changed to "13." Then "12."

What was this? Was it supposed to be some kind of authentication mechanism to make sure she was authorized to access the mission details? If so, how was she supposed to know what high school it was talking about? Surely it didn't mean *her* high school, she hadn't used her real name on her website. She had even registered the site through a dummy company she had established. There was no way for a client to look up her information.

"9"... "8"...

Kim scanned the email again for clues. Nothing jumped out at her. If she was supposed to somehow decode a secret message hidden in the text she certainly couldn't do it in the six seconds that she had left. So, she typed in the only thing that came to her mind—the cheesy, poorly constructed, orange and yellow bird-like character that used to try to rile up the crowd at Trent's football games. She had gone to the same school a couple of years after he had graduated, but had never attended any sporting events during her years there. Still, the mascot's impression on her memory was vivid twenty something years later.

"Falcons," she typed, hitting 'Enter' with only two seconds to spare.

"Access Granted," the screen replied.

Wednesday, 2:00 AM

The Russians were understandably angry about the stolen microfilm. They were also gaining on the red mud-speckled three-wheeler as it raced through the Siberian forest. The two fleeing spies weren't worried though. Truth be told, they were looking forward to the imminent conflict. They were ready to kick some commie butt.

In fact, they weren't even concerned about the recent reports of a Russian-Martian alliance. They were ready to kick some alien butt too. The microfilm they carried contained schematics of Russia's Martian-enhanced weaponry. Once they got home they could analyze it for weaknesses.

But first they had a firefight to attend.

Kim tightened her arms around Trent's waist as they rounded a large maple tree, disturbing the recently fallen leaves from their resting place. The commies wouldn't expect a head-on attack. They also wouldn't expect to be vaporized by the massive energy cannon mounted on the front of the three-wheeler that, by appearance, was just a simple headlight.

First they'd take out the jeeps and the tanks. Then they'd deal with the helicopters and paratroopers. And then, they'd have to deal with the Martian attack ships that would doubtlessly be hovering nearby.

At least, that was how Kim had remembered things going down when she and her brother had played in their woods as children. She certainly didn't remember them hitting a landmine.

An explosion thundered and flashed beneath her nine-year-old body, throwing the three-wheeler into the air. Kim landed hard on the ground, striking her forehead against a tree. The vehicle spun high into the air, showering sparks and shrapnel all around her, and then crashed to the ground in front of her. But it was no longer the twisted wreckage of her father's three-wheeler. Instead, it was a wheelchair, overturned with one wheel spinning slowly in the air.

It hurt to move. It hurt to talk. But neither of these facts stopped Kim from struggling frantically to pick herself up from the ground and screaming her brother's name.

"Trent! Trent! Where are you?! Are you okay?!"

Her eyes found him several yards away, lying lifeless on a pile of brush. But he was no longer the fifteen-year-old version of Trent that she had been riding with only seconds before. He was now the older version—the one with the thinning hair and the deep scar on his left cheek. He was now the version of Trent that could no longer walk, the version that could no longer look out for his little sister, the version that couldn't even take care of himself.

A heavy black boot startled Kim from behind. She turned around and looked up at the large Russian man now towering over her. Tears started streaming from her eyes as she pleaded for her brother's life.

"Оставьте нас в покое!" she cried in Russian, a language that she technically wouldn't learn for another 14 years, "Пожалуйста не травмируйте его!" *Leave us alone! Please don't hurt him!*

The bump on her head began to throb with pain. The man bent down low until his face was only inches from hers. His eyes were large and glowed bright red. His thick black mustache was thrown into sharp relief against his greenish translucent skin. He smacked her face gently with a thin fleshy hand and then grinned with yellow teeth and spoke with a forked tongue and breath that smelled like... pepperoni?

"Sam," the alien/Russian hybrid said, "Sam, wake up! Are you okay?"

Kim blinked.

When she opened her eyes she saw that the Martian face had transformed into a human one. It was blurry and bruised and vaguely familiar. This face wasn't smiling; instead it wore a look of concern. Its teeth were a reassuring shade of off-white and its tongue, thankfully, didn't fork at the end. Its breath, however, did carry the aroma of recently eaten pizza.

The throbbing in Kim's head began to sharpen and burn. The toes on her left foot stung bitterly, as if broken. She realized that she was outdoors, lying on her back in the grass. Something wet was trickling down her forehead and pooling in her left ear.

"Sam, are you okay?" the face repeated.

It was referring to her by her abbreviated middle name, the pseudonym she sometimes used when in the field. Kim furrowed her brow in order to drive the rest of the fog from her mind. The face, she remembered, belonged to Ned Dyer, the man she had rescued and flown to Georgia. Ten thousand dollars had been transferred to her account immediately after accepting the mission the previous morning. Upon completion she was due fifty thousand more, enough money to allow her to keep the family farm for at least another year.

But Joe Tompkins' email had said nothing about taking prisoners. And it hadn't provided any real details about the organization that had captured Ned Dyer. Since arriving in Atlanta, Kim had learned that Tompkins had been captured also. She doubted that she'd be collecting on the rest of her payment. The ten grand wouldn't even cover all of the mission expenses that she had incurred, not to mention the inconvenience and risks. It had been an exciting night, but that excitement certainly wasn't worth becoming a target of this "Agency." It was clear that Dyer and his friends were in way over their heads. Kim had her own problems. She didn't need anybody else's.

It took a concerted effort for her to pick herself up off of the ground. Ned gently offered a helping hand, but Kim pushed it away.

"Come on, Sam, let's get you inside. You're bleeding pretty steadily from that cut."

Kim inspected her forehead with her right hand and discovered that the source of the wetness was indeed a small gash near her hairline. It was oozing with blood. But she had no intention of going back inside.

"I've got my field kit in the rental," she pointed toward the Kia in the driveway and began to limp toward it. Ned hurried after her.

"I'll get it for you, Sam," he offered, "you need to at least sit down and rest."

"I'm fine," she said curtly. The kit was in the back seat. She sat down next to it and began to attend to her wound.

Ned was still hovering nearby, clearly having trouble with not being needed. Kim was sure that he was just about to offer to help dress the wound again when the front door of the safe house opened. The silhouette of Sue Bishop appeared, casting a long shadow on the front lawn, framed by the lighted rectangle of the doorway. The woman seemed to be afraid to take more than a couple of steps outside as she called to her fiancé.

"Ned, we still can't get Dan to wake up! What should we do?"

Kim detected a note of impatience in Ned's reply, "I said that I'd be right back, Sue. I'm helping Sam right now." He then turned back toward Kim, clearly not understanding the accepted definition of the term "helping." In his mind, it seemed to mean "stating the obvious and then asking irrelevant questions."

"Schultz got away with Meg's Mustang," Kim could tell that Ned was struggling to keep the panic out of his voice, "which means that he knows the address of the safe house. So, obviously we can't stay here. Once you're done with the cut on your head, I need you to come in and check on Dan. I don't know what your arrangement with Joe was, but I'm assuming that you have someplace safe that we can spend the night. If not, I'm open to suggestions. What should we do? Where should we go? You're the professional, what's our next move?"

Kim finished applying her bandage and stood up. "Don't know, don't care. I'm leaving."

Ned Dyer was visibly surprised at this response. As a show of good faith, Kim handed him a vial of smelling salts before limping to the driver's side of the Kia. "That will probably help with your unconscious friend in there. When he does wake up, tell him that if he *ever* endangers *my* life again, I'll end his. Same goes for Meg. She had better pray that she never meets me again."

"But Sam, we still need your help!" Ned pleaded, the panic in his voice no longer hidden at all, "What can we do to get you to stay? I'm sure we can work something out."

"Well," Kim said as she started the car, "Your friend Joe promised me $50,000 for rescuing you and bringing you here. Can you guarantee payment? It doesn't sound like he's in a position to come through on it."

By the corner streetlight, Kim saw Ned's gaze fall to the ground and moisture form in his eyes. "I don't know what has happened to Joe. I tried to protect him from all of this… I tried to keep him safe. I know nothing about his arrangement with you other than what you've told me. I certainly can't guarantee that he'll send the rest of your money."

Kim opened the car door. "I'm not asking you to guarantee that *he* pays me what I'm due, Ned. I'm asking if *you'll* pay. I know that you have a backpack full of cash in there. Your fiancée brought it with her."

Ned's voice was now low and shaking, "I can't give that to you. I might need it to flee the country. I think I've just become some sort of fugitive."

"Which is something I have no intention of becoming myself," Kim said as she closed the car door, "Goodbye, Ned."

"Sam, please wait!" he cried after her. But she didn't wait. She drove off into the darkness instead.

Just before Ned Dyer's safe house disappeared from the rearview mirror, Kim saw him stagger backward a few steps with a pained and dazed expression. He then collapsed onto the concrete stoop, his face buried firmly in his hands.

46

Ned was having a hard time keeping it together.

Instinctively, his mind was searching for hope, for a potential outcome that might seem in some way acceptable, an outcome where the positives outweighed the negatives, an outcome in which the many sacrifices that had been made would be repaid with some degree of justification. But now even his CIA-trained rescuer, a woman who hadn't flinched at raiding a guarded Agency facility, was washing her hands of the whole situation. If someone like that couldn't find any hope for Ned and his friends, what chance did any of them actually have?

The carefully constructed cages of Ned's mind had burst open, freeing the emotions contained within. Unbridled they ran roughshod over the remains of their pens, colliding and battling each other for dominance. Despair was currently winning this battle, but Regret and Self-Recrimination were both holding their own. Everything he had tried to prevent seemed to be happening anyway.

Outwardly, this battle manifested itself as great convulsing sobs that welled up from deep inside of Ned's gut and spilled out of his mouth as loud and choking cries that mixed with the sounds of a thousand insects living in the surrounding trees. Ned couldn't remember the last time that he had been so overcome. He couldn't remember the last time that he had broken down and cried.

However, the fact that he was *trying* to remember this revealed that his inquisitive nature was not as defeated as one might think. When the time came to finally get it together and plan his next move, he would undoubtedly use this fact to help rebuild his determination. The reality that (amidst the continued sobbing) he was now starting to plan and prepare for his recovery from this emotional episode was another positive development, and eventually the computer-like circuitry of Ned Dyer's mind came to the conclusion that, perhaps, he had just let his emotional storehouse build up for too long. Of course at some point it would need to be purged. He'd give it another twenty seconds or so. Then he'd find some way to get up and get people to safety.

This turned out to be easier than expected. Help came in the form of a hand that suddenly appeared on his shoulder. Sue sat down next to him and wrapped her other arm around his chest and squeezed.

Resolve reared up on the battlefield inside Ned's mind and began to stage a comeback. Feelings of despair and regret fell back from the new confrontation. He reminded himself that his preparation had saved Sue. Not everything had been lost. Much of the safety of his family and friends still rested in his hands. There was much work still to do.

Ned wiped his eyes and stood up. The campaign of running and hiding clearly wasn't working. It was time to take a stand against these people, this *Agency*. He turned to look at Sue who was now standing next to him, looking up at him with eyes that were clearly tired, but still clearly full of love and admiration.

"We need to get everyone ready to leave," he said. "It's time to go to the police."

Ned just had to make one quick stop on the way.

3:26 AM

Ned Dyer's bullet-riddled SUV had just left the greater Atlanta area. It was traveling north. North-*ish* anyway. Ned had been spoiled, living back in the Midwest. He had grown used to roads that picked a direction and followed it.

But the Endeavor's GPS guidance system was doing most of the navigational work. It was a good thing too. Ned was beyond exhausted. He glanced jealously at his fiancée in the passenger's seat next to him. She was fast asleep. But at least she was still safe. Ned was pretty sure Meg and Dan were still safe too—he had dropped them off at the hospital before leaving town. They were somewhat exposed there, but Ned hoped that no one would try to go after them in a public place. And, with any luck, the whole ordeal would be in the hands of the authorities very soon. Dan had still been groggy when they arrived at the hospital, but he seemed like he would be all right. It seemed more and more likely that everyone Ned had tried to protect might end up being all right.

Everyone except Joe, he reminded himself with a fresh pang of guilt.

Joe had been captured. Ned still didn't remember much from his own abduction, but what he did remember was terrifying. He prayed that Joe was having an easier time of it. He prayed that someone would send an ex-

CIA agent to Joe's rescue too. But that someone would have to have some idea where Joe was being held. And that someone would have to be free of the kinds of concerns that Ned was currently dealing with. He had way too much on his plate just then.

He had to get to the evidence packet that was waiting for him in a storage unit in North Georgia. It had been waiting there for almost two years. It contained the original threat to Ned's life that he had received while still living in Atlanta. This wouldn't be much for the police to go on, but Ned was hoping that there would at least be some fingerprints.

While there Ned would also pull the hard drive from the storage unit's PC. The PC was one of the three processing nodes in his contingency system network and would have all of the data recorded since the activation of Contingency Plan Gamma the other night. This would include the GPS coordinates of the facility he had been held at, along with the entire voice recording that the hidden microphone in his pager had picked up prior to it being smashed.

The onboard PC of the Endeavor was another node in Ned's contingency system, and would also have all of the digitally obtained data, but the only way to get at the hard drive was to pretty much dismantle the entire dashboard. It wasn't like he could afford to be without a working vehicle. After all, he was still running for his life.

They were still after him. Schultz had called them the *Agency*—not that anything he had said could now be trusted. But it was as good a name to use as any. Ned still didn't know who these people were. He still didn't know what this Agency wanted. When he had set up his contingency plans, he had envisioned assembling a group of people to figure these things out. From what he had seen, though, he had greatly underestimated the Agency's resources. The man that had interrogated him, Agent Conroy, had told him as much.

This probably meant that the team Ned had tried to assemble wouldn't have had any luck in stopping the Agency. It seemed that the best they could hope for was to continue to evade capture.

Did the Agency have access to Georgia's network of traffic cameras? If so, sticking to the country roads should keep them hidden. But what if they had access to *satellites*? There was no way to be sure. One thing Ned was sure of, the Agency was most certainly looking for the SUV that he was currently driving. But he didn't have to go much farther. Once he had retrieved the evidence packet, he was just going to head to the nearest police station. This was a risk, but one way or another, he would finally be done running.

"Are you doing okay back there?" From the rearview mirror, Ned had noticed that the girl in the back seat wasn't sleeping. She was just staring out the window, presumably at the star-filled sky, with slow tears falling from her reddened eyes.

In response to Ned's question, Amy wiped her cheek with the sleeve of the sweatshirt she had borrowed from the Atlanta safe house, turned to face forward, and gave a weak smile and nod.

"It's been a hard day," she managed, her voice mostly a whisper.

The tears reminded Ned again of the waiter he had involved, her friend. From what he had heard, Tom was most likely dead. This too was Ned's fault. If not for him, Tom would be safe at home. So would Amy. Tears now filled Ned's eyes too. It was annoying. He thought that he had dealt with his emotions. He thought that he had gotten all of this out of his system. Apparently, there was still an issue or two that he needed to deal with. Best to get it out of the way.

"Amy, I am *so* sorry for involving you two in this. I'll never be able to forgive myself for what happened to Tom."

Amy's reaction to this surprised Ned. He had expected her to break down even more, but the opposite happened. Her voice grew firm, her eyes focused and blinked away their moisture, her hand reached up and grabbed Ned's shoulder.

"Don't, Ned. You shouldn't apologize for trying to protect your family. There's no point in blaming yourself for what happened to Tom. I was doing that earlier… Tom might not have even visited your website if I hadn't pressed the issue. Plus, I was the one that figured out that the code we needed to enter was the total on your bill."

Some corner of Ned's mind registered surprise at this statement. He hadn't intended that the code be difficult to crack. He had written it right on the receipt. Maybe he should have made it more obvious.

Amy continued, "But once we watched your video, once Tom *knew* that people really were in danger, there was no stopping him from taking action. That surprised me about him. I wouldn't have expected him to be so brave. He was so proud when we rescued Sue. He wished that he could have done more. Don't beat yourself up about what happened to him. He was trying to save Joe when he got shot. He knew the risks… he was just trying to do the right thing. He was just trying to keep people safe. If you want to honor Tom's sacrifice, make sure everyone stays safe."

Amy's last statement was full of conviction and she squeezed Ned's shoulder harder and then released it and leaned back in her seat. It had been Ned's initial intention to say a few words to help comfort the girl. He wouldn't have guessed that the opposite would end up happening. He had been struggling to keep his feelings of guilt in check ever since he had heard what had happened to the young waiter. Amy's words somehow lessened this struggle. They reminded him that he really was doing the best that he could.

The image of Amy's face in the mirror now hardened a bit as an unmistakable hatred crept into her voice. "The *Agency* or whoever are the ones who caused all of this. If you want to honor Tom's sacrifice, Ned, you'll make them pay. You'll make sure they don't get away with it."

With all of the other cares and concerns Ned had been dealing with that night, he hadn't really had time to indulge any feelings of vengeance. Even so, he heard himself reply, "They'll pay for what they've done, Amy. I swear they will."

He just hoped that the evidence he had would be enough.

47

The Endeavor came to a stop. This jarred Sue Bishop awake and she sat up quickly and blinked the haze out of her eyes. She hadn't meant to fall asleep. The new crick in her neck reminded her that it had been a couple of nights since she had slept in her own bed. It seemed like longer than that though. Much longer.

Sue looked out the window and took in her surroundings. The SUV was parked on the edge of a large parking lot. She could see a shopping mall at the far end and then turned to see a self-storage facility on the other side of the vehicle. Ned had opened the driver's side door and exited. Sue straightened up in her seat to watch him approach the storage building. A voice startled her from behind.

"Tom and I found the SUV at a place kinda like this last night."

Sue turned around and saw Amy in the back seat. The girl didn't look well. Her face was completely devoid of color—except the dark red streaks that circled her eyes. Sue thought about asking if the girl had slept, but then decided against it. Sue knew that concern for Tom's wellbeing was likely keeping Amy up, and at the moment Sue didn't have any spare comfort to offer her. Better to not bring up the subject at all.

Instead she asked about Ned, "Did he say how long he'd be?"

"Not too long, it sounded like he just needs to grab an envelope and an external hard drive. He didn't want to wake you."

Sue felt herself blush a bit. "It isn't fair that I get to sleep while he does all the driving. I know he's exhausted too. But this will all be over soon. Has there been any word from Meg? Is Dan going to be okay?"

"Everyone has had their cell phones off just in case they were using them to track us. I'm sure they're fine though. Ned said we'd call the hospital from the police station."

Sue nodded and turned back around. Ned appeared at the door of the storage facility, apparently holding the evidence he had gone in to collect. He saw that Sue was awake and responded with a small smile and a wink. He was telling her that everything was going to be all right.

That being the case, it was strange when Ned stopped short. His smile faded and transformed into an expression of shock. He was looking off into the distance behind the SUV. He was looking at something near the mall.

Sue spun around and found that something. It was an average looking green Toyota. Its headlights were out, but it could still be seen clearly by the parking lot's bright halogen lighting. It was heading directly toward them.

Ned jumped into the driver's seat of the Endeavor, shoved his collected evidence toward Sue, slammed the door, and stepped on the accelerator. The SUV lurched forward in response.

There was a brief moment where Sue was almost overcome by a feeling of anger at Ned for fleeing and a sense of camaraderie with those in pursuit. Before she had much of a chance to feel conflicted over this though, the lights went out. The sounds of the commencing car chase were also gone. So was the feeling of the Endeavor's seatbelt against Sue's lap. It felt something like suddenly losing consciousness, but Sue knew that she wasn't asleep. The sensation was extremely odd.

It didn't last long.

The first thing she registered as she emerged from the sudden blindness was a raw pain in her left shoulder—mixed with a throbbing pain coming from her right hand. She saw that she was kneeling in the mall's parking lot, and that her hand was scratched and bleeding and holding the broken remains of the hard drive that Ned had retrieved from the storage facility. She clutched the large manila envelope he had handed her tightly under her left arm.

She was drenched with sweat and could tell that her heart was beating much faster than it had been before she had blacked out. Whipping her head around violently, trying to make sense of what had happened, she saw the green Toyota nearby, the front end smashed into a concrete median. Smoke was rolling upward from its hood and disappearing above the humming halogen streetlights. There was movement inside.

Sue stumbled as she tried to stand. For some reason her left ankle refused to support her weight. She heard a motor running nearby and squinted against the stinging sweat that ran down her forehead. Ned was close. The Endeavor appeared to have escaped any more damage. She just had to get to it. Ned would then take her to safety.

She used the manila envelope to wipe the sweat from her forehead and looked up at Ned.

"Honey, help me up. I can't stand up." She swallowed and met his eyes with hers. "Hurry."

The expression on Ned's face was not the look of concern that Sue expected. It was a look of abject horror. Sue borrowed this expression a second later as she watched the SUV speed off without her.

Then, from behind, Sue heard a car door open.

They had found him.

Ned stared at the approaching car. His foolishness became apparent immediately. He should never have come here.

Somehow he had missed the connection. Of *course* the Agency knew about the storage facility. Of *course* they knew about the evidence packet. In the event of his capture, Ned's contingency systems had been programmed to contact the authorities and direct them to this location. Somehow, the Agency had intercepted this communication. They had probably been watching the place ever since. How could he have been so stupid?

The green Toyota was picking up speed—but it was still all the way across the parking lot. And Ned's Endeavor was fast. They could still get away.

He dove into the SUV and peeled out. Ned would have given anything to have another compartment full of tire shredders in the rear bumper. This race would have to be won on speed alone. Luckily the exit to the parking lot wasn't far. He needed to get away from these lights.

Ned never would have expected what happened next. Never. Even after it happened he couldn't believe it. But Sue's actions didn't ask to be believed. They just asked to be effective. Which they were.

The first of these actions was wrenching the steering wheel from Ned's grip while simultaneously smashing an elbow into his nose. Ned jerked backward, which helped Sue's second act of reaching over to Ned's door handle, opening the door, and shoving Ned out of the moving vehicle.

Ned landed on his hip. The pavement was not very forgiving. Neither was the Toyota that was now barreling down on him. He was most certainly a goner.

But then another unexpected thing happened.

In a flash, Ned found himself standing and facing the oncoming car. His right hand drew the handgun from his waistband and fired four shots directly at the driver of the rapidly approaching Toyota. With only a few feet to spare the car veered off and smashed into a concrete median—the home of a row of small decorative trees.

Ned stared at his gun hand, amazed at his reaction time and aim. This amazement was short-lived. His fiancée tackled him from behind before he had time to even turn back around. The two of them hit the ground with the momentum of their combined weight, and Ned was sure he heard the sound of bones snapping.

Sue screamed in agony. Her left shoulder had broken Ned's fall.

Again, he was on his feet instantly, and again, he was surprised at how quickly he had recovered from his latest encounter with the ground. But he wasn't as surprised at this as he was at Sue's behavior—or her strength. He looked down at his fiancée, dripping with sweat and crumpled on the parking lot floor. Whatever had possessed her seemed to have left. Now she was just rocking slowly back and forth and crying softly.

Ned approached cautiously, bent down, and offered her a hand. "Sue, honey! Are you okay? What's going on?"

Without a word Sue wrenched her body around on the ground and latched onto Ned's outstretched right hand with hers. A well placed foot to his chest and a clever shifting of body weight was all it took to lift Ned's body off of its feet and send it flying over hers. Ned tucked his head in, rolled with the maneuver, and quickly regained his footing. And, before he could stop himself, he grabbed the foot that had thrown him and twisted it until he heard a loud pop.

Sue screamed again.

It was then that Ned noticed the external hard drive lying on the pavement next to her. The evidence packet that he had saved for three years was lying next to it. He ventured a step toward the items that he had risked his safety to recover.

He didn't get very close though. Amidst the anguish of a shattered shoulder and broken ankle Sue grabbed the hard drive with her right hand, looked up at Ned with unfocused and hate-filled eyes, and then smashed the device to the ground. Ned stopped short and blinked. The hard drive came down again. Pieces of the plastic case flew in all directions. The ground sparked with the connection of the inner metallic casing and the parking lot's pavement. Sue smashed the disk drive a third time, breaking off a metal corner. She picked it up and threw it at Ned—hissing and spitting in his direction.

Ned's eye caught movement inside the crashed Toyota. He searched the ground for his gun. His eyes found it within a couple of feet of Sue. She saw it too, and started to reach for it.

"Ned!" Amy McKay's voice came from behind. She had climbed into the driver's seat of the Endeavor and pulled up behind him. "We have to go! Now!" Amy reached over and threw the passenger's door open.

Ned didn't mean to, but he found himself turning from the woman he loved, leaving her bleeding on the ground, and jumping into the SUV. He was sure that he'd never be able to get the memory of Sue pleading for his help out of his mind. Amy sped away before he got a chance to respond.

He hadn't even noticed that the backpack that held his emergency cash was no longer inside the SUV.

Sue Bishop stared at the disappearing taillights of Ned's Endeavor. She had been left behind. Her mind refused to come to terms with the fact.

Footsteps sounded from behind. She barely managed to turn around in time to see two men in department store suits walking toward her. They had guns in their hands.

48

It was clear to Meg Trotter that Ned had no idea what he was doing. His extensive prep work had been impressive, but now he was making critical errors in judgment. She and Dan had captured and contained Schultz for over six hours without putting anyone in danger. As soon as Ned had taken charge, the whole situation immediately and completely fell apart.

Now he had decided to go to the police. He had yelled at Meg for tackling Sam, but Meg knew that if she hadn't Dan would likely be dead. Schultz had ordered Sam to drop her gun several times and she never did. She obviously didn't care what happened to Dan. Meg had a big problem with this. If Dan was expendable, that meant that she was too. If Ned could have just gone to the police the entire time, then why had he even involved the two of them?

It was just as well though. It meant that they were parting company. It meant that Meg wouldn't have to challenge Ned for control of the situation. She could just act cooperative until he dropped her and Dan off at the hospital.

Then she would attend to the real priority: finding out what happened to Dan's family. Schultz had kept something from them. Meg owed it to Dan to figure out what that was. She had been ready to trust Schultz when he had 'rescued' them from Fischer and the motel room. If Dan hadn't taken control of the situation, there was no telling where they would be now. Schultz had been pretty insistent that they allow him to take them to a 'local Homeland Security office.' Meg was pretty sure the Agency would have made them disappear at that point.

Still, despite their disagreements, she wished Ned luck. Joe was still missing. Maybe Ned contacting the authorities was Joe's best chance at rescue.

The Endeavor pulled up to the door of the hospital's emergency room. Meg hopped out of the vehicle and started to help Dan. Ned began to get out also.

"I've got it from here, Ned," Meg told him. "You guys probably need to get going."

"You sure, Meg?" Ned asked, obviously eager to lend a hand but also eager to get underway. "I can help you get checked in."

"Don't worry about it, we'll be fine. Good luck."

Dan was still blinking the haze out of his eyes as the SUV pulled away, but at least he was standing on his own. He had been knocked on the head pretty hard, but Meg didn't think it really warranted a trip to the hospital. She'd let Dan make that decision.

"You don't really need to get checked out here, do you?"

Dan rubbed the back of his neck. "Uh… I guess not. Why did you have Ned drop us off here?"

"I heard about what Schultz said about your family. I assumed that you'd want to find out what had happened to them. I figured you'd want to get to Chicago as soon as possible."

This seemed to sober Dan up in a hurry. "Yeah, I do… what do you think is the earliest flight we could get?"

"Actually, I know of a private plane that should be taking off shortly." Meg said as she called Dan's attention to the backpack that she had taken from the SUV upon exiting. "Let's go see if we can buy ourselves a ride."

The Vicodin had taken some of the edge off, but Kim Caywood was still convinced that the persistent, skull-splitting pain that radiated from her forehead wound wouldn't be quieted unless she doubled the dose. Unfortunately this was a luxury that she couldn't afford at the moment. She would be piloting an aircraft soon and needed as clear a head as possible. Besides, the pain helped keep her mind off of the fact that accepting Joe Tompkins' rescue mission had been little more than a significant waste of her time and money.

In fairness, at some point in the near future she would probably admit to herself that the mission had been quite exhilarating—up to the point where Meg Trotter had tackled her in a misguided attempt at saving her friend's life. And, despite the feelings of anger toward the woman that still burned hot and deep in Kim's chest, she felt that it had been an incredibly brave thing for Meg to do.

It didn't really matter how she felt about any of Ned or Joe's friends anymore though. Very likely she would never see any of them again. Or so she thought. She certainly didn't expect Dan and Meg to be waiting for her when she arrived at the small airstrip where she had left her rented plane. She hadn't taken a direct route from the safe house to the airport, fearing that Schultz might have doubled back and decided to tail her as she left. After forty-five minutes of driving in random and winding circles, she was finally satisfied that no one was following.

The unintended effect of this, though, was to grant Dan and Meg plenty of time to part company with Ned at the hospital, call a cab, and arrive at the airstrip a good ten minutes ahead of Kim. They were exposed, standing stupidly in the middle of the small parking lot when she arrived. Kim was sure that anyone who had wanted to follow them could have done so quite easily.

She intended to make this fact known to the pair as soon as she parked, but that was before she noticed the closely held backpack hanging from Meg's left shoulder or the brick of twenties gripped tightly in her outstretched right hand.

Perhaps Ned had changed his mind about making good on her fee. Kim figured that she could spare a minute to hear the two out. *But,* she decided, *they had better lead off with one hell of an apology.*

Meg Trotter's nerves were more than a little frayed as she watched the dark green Kia climb the winding road up to the hilltop parking lot where she and Dan were waiting. The encounter she'd had with its driver an hour before had not been pleasant, and Meg just knew there would be a bright purple bruise next to her eye waiting for her the next time she found a well lit mirror.

She intensely hoped that the peace offering around her shoulder would smooth things over with Sam.

Dan hadn't said much on the drive to the airport or in the ten minutes that had passed while waiting for Sam to arrive. There had been a little chatter at first, when they had been concerned that they had already missed her, but once they had deduced that her rental car had not yet been returned, Dan's demeanor again became sad and silent. There was an unspoken understanding between him and Meg. They had embarked on a new mission—one of utmost importance.

Meg longed to know more about Dan's past and his family that were now in so much danger, but it was clear that any questions to that effect would not be welcomed. So Meg resigned herself to accept her part in the operation, one simply of support.

The rental car parked next to the two of them and its driver quickly climbed out. Meg could see that Sam was armed, but she kept her gun at her side, obviously ready in case this was some kind of an ambush. She was clearly waiting on them to speak first. Dan maintained his sad silence. Apparently another of Meg's roles for the mission was that of spokesperson. She figured she'd better start off with an apology. Then she'd offer most of the cash in the backpack. Then, if need be, she'd get out her checkbook. It was very likely time to make use of the ample funds that she had amassed in her savings account.

49

Wednesday, 6:27 AM

Nausea.

It had been six years since Dan had been inside this building. And, for some reason, he had decided to take the stairs up to his old apartment. The stairs themselves were old, dirty, and familiar. They wound back and forth and up and up to the seventh floor and beyond. Dan was moving much slower than he intended, and somehow knew in his gut that he would not find what he hoped in the apartment where his family lived: his ex-wife and two children safe, sound, and happy to see him.

But there was more than that holding him back. It was becoming physically difficult for him to ascend. Dan chalked this up to emotional and bodily exhaustion. He began to sweat and panic as he climbed and in a corner of the landing halfway between the third and fourth floors he stopped and threw up.

Meg was following him, guarded and faithful, clearly unsure what her role should now be, now that she had gotten Dan to Chicago, to his old apartment building. She had offered to stay down at the front door and stand watch with Sam, and Dan had initially agreed that she should, but then he had asked her to come with him after stepping inside the building. This was not going to be something that he could do alone.

"Are you okay?" she asked with the same awkward cautiousness that she had been exhibiting since Ned had dropped them off at the hospital—a cautiousness born out of an obvious desire to help without being too intrusive.

Dan coughed and spat the remnants of vomit from his mouth. "Yeah," he said, "I'm just feeling a little queasy."

"How about we sit down and rest for a minute?"

This sounded like a wonderful plan, and Dan began to feel a kind of gravity that seemed to pull at his body, beckoning him to sit on the nearest stair. Then he looked up into Meg's gray eyes and saw the concern they displayed and it reminded him of his own concern for his family. He *needed* to make sure that they were okay. Nothing else mattered.

"Let's keep moving," he told her, and they did.

The next flight of stairs was more difficult than the last. Sweat was now running steadily down Dan's brow and stinging his eyes. His feet felt heavy and his head felt light. But he kept moving. He *had* to keep moving.

Dan noticed the tremors in his legs and arms before he reached the sixth floor. This slowed his progress further.

The tremors had spread to his torso when he finally reached the seventh floor. Meg had to open the door for him as his arms were shaking far too much to be useful at that point. Dan probably should have been terrified at what was happening to him, but he ignored it instead. He was almost there.

"I-it's ap-apartm-ment s-seven tw-twent-ty f-five," he managed through chattering teeth, "H-help m-me."

Meg seemed apprehensive in both posture and voice, "Dan… what's the matter? Are you sure you're okay?"

Honestly, he was far from sure that he was okay, but Meg's hesitance still angered him. He yelled at her.

"Y-yes! J-j-just help m-me!"

"Okay, Dan, no problem," she said as she lifted his left arm and put it around her shoulders. She wrapped her right arm around his back and pulled his weight toward her. He was shaking steadily, but with her help he could still walk.

In that fashion they limped down the hallway until they arrived at the door to the apartment that Dan had shared with his family. Meg rang the bell. Dan's vision began to blur. After a minute, the door opened.

It was not Dan's ex-wife that answered the door.

It was a short, thin, middle-aged white man with a bald head and a large nose. He looked like he had just woken up. He also looked very surprised to find Dan and Meg outside his door.

"Wh-where are th-they?!" Dan screamed and pushed past the man, leaving Meg behind. He staggered into the apartment's living room, *his* living room and saw that it looked much different than the last time he had been there. The furniture was different, which wasn't *so* surprising. Dan had still been in school when he had lived here and they hadn't had money for nice furniture. It made sense that his ex-wife would have purchased a new living room outfit, not that the plaid couch and rose-colored loveseat seemed like her style.

Dan stumbled to the kitchen and saw his old cabinets and appliances and fought to ignore the fog that seemed to be steadily filling his head. The kids' rooms were just down the hallway. His feet felt like lead. His legs felt like rubber. He willed himself on.

He made it down the hallway and leaned against the wall to rest. He was right in front of the door to his son's room. With a shaking hand he reached up and grabbed the doorknob. With a concentrated effort, he turned it and pulled the door open.

This was not a boy's bedroom. It was a linen closet. This didn't make sense.

Dan spun around to try his daughter's bedroom door, the door that was directly across the hallway from his son's. But he didn't see her door. There was a window there instead. This was one of the building's exterior walls. There couldn't be a bedroom there. There couldn't have ever been a bedroom there.

A cold and confusing sense of dread seemed to pierce the back of Dan's neck and spread its icy fingers into his brain and down the back of his spine. A sense that he simply had the wrong apartment was quickly replaced by a much more terrible thought, a thought that he had instead made a much bigger mistake, that he hadn't just remembered his old address wrong, he somehow remembered his life wrong. Perhaps he hadn't lived here with his family at all. Perhaps he had lived here alone.

Another wave of nausea produced another gastric event. Dan Curtis heaved dry acid and collapsed on the hallway floor. The world swam around him and began to fade. The short bald man's feet appeared at the other end of the hall and slowly started to walk toward him. In a deep and swirly voice the man spoke.

"Sorry to disappoint you, Subject Curtis, but your family isn't here."

Three Years Ago...

It had only taken two days of light surveillance to discern the subject's daily routine and, thinking of this, Agent Gilmore was glad that people were so often predictable, simple creatures, so often preoccupied with the tedium of their trivial concerns, so often unaware of the goings on of those around them. He glanced down the dim and dusty corridor of dark green apartment doors and wondered if any of the occupants within even knew their neighbors' names. He suspected that the drab locksmith uniforms were unnecessary. The only resident to appear while Gilmore and his partner were in the hallway was a middle-aged woman, four doors down, that exited her apartment and quickly walked the other direction, head bowed in cautious anonymity.

The deadbolt clicked open and the field agent accompanying Gilmore stood, pocketed his pick, and opened the door. Agent Gilmore followed the man inside, wheeling a large black case behind him. They only had two hours to set up the equipment before Subject Curtis was expected home.

Gilmore smiled as he set the case down on the living room floor, unlatched the lid, and began to unpack the tools of his trade, the instruments of hypnotic conditioning. The first session was always the most fun.

50

Wednesday, 1:15 AM

The interrogation chamber control room had grown crowded. Agent Gilmore didn't like it. Working with someone looking over your shoulder was bad enough. *Waiting* with someone looking over your shoulder was unbearable.

Well, the waiting was really the unbearable bit. Gilmore's career, even his life, was hanging in the balance. Subject Tompkins had entered something in the control panel in front of him. If Tech Services confirmed that the virus was indeed dead, Gilmore would be celebrated as the savior of the Agency.

If, on the other hand, Tech Services reported that the virus had not died, that it had instead completed its task of dismantling the Agency's systems, well, it was best not to think about what would happen to him then. There would certainly be no escaping. After what had happened to the other security guards that had been stationed outside the chamber, the bulk of the building's remaining contingency of security personnel seemed to be stuffed into the small control room with Gilmore and Subject Tompkins.

Gilmore was an accomplished gunfighter, but there were limits to how many armed guards he would try to take on at once. Especially since he was still a bit dazed from a recent encounter with Tompkins in the interrogation chamber. He hadn't slept much in the past couple of days either.

Tompkins had been bound to the chair in which he sat. He was losing blood from the bullet hole in his leg and his freshly broken left arm hung limp at an odd angle. The pain must have been intense, but Joe's expression registered none of it. There was just a blank look on his face, his unfocused eyes staring vaguely through the control panel in front of him.

Gilmore's earpiece was eerily quiet, devoid of the usual chatter of the Agency's security force, as if the entire building was holding its breath, waiting for word of its future. Waiting for confirmation of its victory… or its defeat. Either way, Gilmore knew the first thing he would do upon hearing the news. He was going to put another bullet in Joe Tompkins—and this time it wouldn't be in the leg.

The earpiece came to life.

"Make way in the control room… The Division Head would like to examine Subject Tompkins firsthand."

Two of the guards near the door exited and Dr. Hedron walked in a few seconds later. In appearance he was a small and feeble old man, feared much more for his reputation than his stature. It was said that he was one of the original eight founders of the Agency, not that much about the founding of the original Agency cells was more than speculation among the rank-and-file. But it was widely understood that his division was the most influential. This fact alone commanded respect.

The old man's eyes lit up at seeing Tompkins, and a wide grin slowly stretched itself across his face. He approached the captive and poked his broken arm in fascination.

"Remarkable," he whispered, apparently to himself. "I had no idea anyone had made so much progress…"

"What's that, sir?" Gilmore offered.

"You've nothing to worry about Mr. Gilmore," Hedron said quickly, his attention still fixated on the test subject in front of him. "The virus has indeed been inoculated. Your efforts were successful and you shall be rewarded as such. I've already given the order that you be reinstated as the agent in charge of the Ned Dyer situation. If there's nothing else, you are dismissed. I'll attend to Subject Tompkins."

"Of course, sir. Thank you," Gilmore replied cautiously. "May I ask what is to be done with Tompkins… that is, I have already commissioned a cover story to explain Dyer's erratic behavior…" Gilmore wasn't sure how closely the Division Head had been following the case's developments. He hoped that he wasn't boring the man with details he already knew. "The cover story is essentially a murder/suicide… Now that the virus has been dealt with, I planned on disposing of Tompkins myself…"

"You needn't worry about the cover story, Mr. Gilmore. You just focus on recapturing and containing Subject Dyer and his friends. Tompkins is no longer your problem."

The development did not sit well with Agent Gilmore. Tompkins had witnessed him kill two Agency guards. Of course, in the event that Tompkins talked, anything he said was sure to be treated with skepticism, but this didn't ease Gilmore's mind much.

He made a mental note to keep his eyes open for an opportunity to get to Joe discreetly and silence him permanently. However, he didn't really see how he would get this chance. It seemed that he would just have to resign himself to the fact that this situation was out of his control, resign himself to the hope that his secret would stay buried.

But there was still the matter of wiping any damning security footage that might have caught him cooperating with Tompkins. He'd stop by the server room on the way to Operational Command. He was confident that, with all the recent chaos in the Agency's computer systems, some misplaced video data wouldn't draw much attention.

An hour later, Agent Gilmore had cleaned up, shot up, and wiped some very unflattering security footage from the Agency servers by the time he presented himself to the Operational Command center. With all of the ruckus that Subject Tompkins' virus had caused, Gilmore knew that the search for Subject Dyer hadn't been given the attention that it warranted. He was afraid that Dyer's trail had grown cold.

He discovered that the trail was downright frigid. In the past several hours, there were no significant developments to speak of. Agent Fischer had been found dead, Agent Schultz was still missing, and subjects Dyer, Curtis, and Trotter had all escaped custody and were still at large.

No progress had been made in cracking the code in the command center found under Dyer's garage. In fact, Gilmore's order that a member of Tech Services be stationed there had been rescinded. Every available technician had been assigned to repelling the computer virus, a job that Gilmore had handled alone.

It took less than an hour for Gilmore to set the investigation back on course. He was determined not to be impacted by the various setbacks. He was back in command. He had rejoined the hunt. He resolved that he would pick up Dyer's trail before daybreak.

It wouldn't be long before he would receive substantial aid toward that goal. He would soon learn that Sue Bishop had been recaptured. But before that happened, he received a phone call from the missing Agent Schultz.

2:45 AM

Jim Simmons had drawn the short straw. He was amazed at how quickly the importance of his department and the reverence with which he and his colleagues were treated could change with the new information and orders that were handed down from Division Headquarters.

The Agency's priority objective had shifted with the destruction of Subject Tompkins' virus (an event which, Jim would certainly argue, would not have happened without the aid provided by his and his team's skillful efforts).

The glory and acclaim that Tech Services had enjoyed over the past couple of hours had ceased and the department had again taken up the mantle of unappreciated support of the Agency's various objectives.

Not to mention the fact that Jim's team had been taken away from him. Instead of continuing his leadership role he had been given a ridiculous assignment that had virtually no chance of actually succeeding. He was supposed to try to crack the numeric code in Dyer's underground panic room. An Agency technician had done a preliminary check of Dyer's systems shortly after Agent Gilmore had found the command center. The technician had concluded that the system was heavily protected and that any attempts at bypassing the security software would likely cause the entire system to lock down.

But Agent Gilmore was back in charge, and Gilmore wanted someone underneath Dyer's garage. Jim had asked his supervisor what exactly he was supposed to do while there. The answer had been something about looking for clues—whatever that was supposed to mean.

Jim squeezed through the narrow metal door that led into the chamber. The supply of electricity to the room had been reestablished via the thick orange extension cord that was now suspended through the panic room's door. The diesel generator had apparently been extremely noisy and Jim was thankful that it was no longer needed.

He surveyed the shelter and took stock of the provisions it held. In the refrigerator there was bottled water and Dr. Pepper. In the cabinets labeled "Pantry" he found various cans containing fruit and vegetables and soups. There were also crackers and nuts and even a couple of packages of cookies. It looked like Dyer could have survived down here for quite some time.

"Look for clues…" Jim said to himself, kneading the thought in his mind, deciding on the course of action that would best fulfill his assignment. It took a moment for him to come to his conclusion, and, when he did, he signified it with a brief smirk and a slight shrugging of his shoulders. Then he grabbed one of the cots that were leaning against the wall, set it up, dimmed the fluorescent lighting, and helped himself to several of Subject Dyer's Oreos and Nutter Butters. He washed these down with a cold Dr. Pepper, lamenting the lack of milk (or at least the lack of Mountain Dew), and then lay down on the cot in order to stare at the ceiling through closed eyes.

It had been a very long day and Simmons deserved a good night's sleep. As long as he was stuck in the underground fortress it certainly seemed like the most productive way to use his time. *Maybe this isn't such a bad assignment after all,* the thought drifted through his mind and then he slept.

6:40 AM

Sue Bishop was living in a nightmare. The hot incandescent bulb above her stabbed at her eyes in the otherwise dark room and made her sweat. She was confused. She was terrified at what might be in store for her. But mostly, she was still in shock about what had happened almost three hours earlier.

Ned had abandoned her.

"Let's go over this again, Ms. Bishop." The man pacing in front of her, the one with the large hands and sickening smile, was speaking in calm tones. His words didn't have a calming effect though. That probably had something to do with the fact that Sue's bare feet and arms were strapped to the dentist's chair in which she sat. It also probably had something to do with the fact that the pacing maniac (who had introduced himself as Agent Conroy) was dangling a small aerosol can near her exposed flesh. "How, exactly, were you rescued yesterday morning? How did the waiter find you?"

The man punctuated his question by drawing a long stripe from Sue's right big toe, over the top of her foot, and up her ankle with the can of freeze spray. The pain was maddening and her scream exploded from her throat and pierced the echoless silence of the hot dark room.

Sue continued to scream, and sob, and beg for mercy, and plead that she didn't know anything about what was going on for several more minutes, all the while desperately trying to withstand the pain and not let any information leak out.

But, for all her bravery, it wasn't long before she broke.

The chirping of Jim Simmons' cell phone echoed and resounded in the dim metal chamber and pulled him jarringly from the dreamless slumber he was enjoying. It took a second for him to place the sound and then another second for him to remember that he was still technically on duty. When these realizations matured he sat up quickly on the rickety cot—too quickly in fact, as the maneuver caused the cot to tip sideways and sent him crashing into the metal wall and then down to the metal floor. He swore loudly and the echo of his voice joined his cell phone's chirping and expanded and then faded in the room. He picked himself up and answered his phone. He noticed that the battery was running low.

"This is Simmons," he said in a voice that exhibited quite a bit more of his freshly woken dreariness than he had hoped it would. But if the caller noticed this, he didn't let on.

"Has there been any progress in hacking into Subject Dyer's systems?"

"Well…" Jim started, grasping for something vague but technical sounding to say, something to hide the fact that, not only had he not made any progress in his assignment, he hadn't even made any attempt at progress. "I retraced the auto-defense circuitry," he lied, "I agree with the initial assessment that we would probably only get one try at cracking the five digit code…"

"I've got some good news on that front. We're reasonably sure that we have retrieved the proper code. We believe it will allow you full access to Dyer's network."

Reasonably sure? Something about the phrase put Jim on edge. He turned up the lights in the underground control room and looked around. Just outside the chamber were the charred remains of Dyer's house, the result of a booby trap that had killed four field agents. He didn't feel like taking any unnecessary risks that an incorrectly entered code would set off another defense mechanism.

"Uh, do you mind if I ask where exactly this information came from? We probably only get one shot at this."

"We recaptured Dyer's fiancée, and, after interrogation, she directed us to a copy of the code that we already had in our possession. That kid that Agent Gilmore shot, the waiter, he had it in his pocket. It was on a crumpled up copy of a credit card receipt. It appears authentic."

Jim considered this and decided that his chances were fairly good. Not to mention that he was being ordered to try the code. He sat down in front of the computer with the bouncing head screen saver. He thought about how brave he was being, and hoped that some day the relevant information for his current task would be declassified and that he would be free to relate the story to the pizza delivery girl. He pictured her face and the reaction of awe that it would surely display at the telling. Then he glanced back toward the small doorway of the panic room, swallowed, and entered the five-digit code.

The picture of the face on the computer screen stopped bouncing and faded to black. After another couple of seconds, large green letters appeared on the screen:

"Access granted." And then, below this in slightly smaller red letters, "Contingency Plan Gamma in progress."

This message faded and transformed into a self-described main menu screen. Jim smiled broadly. Full access was now his. It was a good thing he waited for the phone call. He had just gained the upper hand on Subject Dyer.

A few mouse clicks later and Jim Simmons was looking at the exact latitude and longitude coordinates of Dyer's silver Endeavor. The overlaid map indicated the SUV was on an obscure country highway in Kentucky, traveling north.

The Agency had tracked Ned down at last.

51

Amy McKay could still feel her heart thudding against her sternum when she finally pulled onto the shoulder of a remote and forest-shrouded country road somewhere in upper Georgia. Ned was a ghost in the seat next to her, pale and vacant. Neither of them had spoken in almost an hour. It was the third time that week that Amy had narrowly escaped being captured or killed by the people who were after Ned. The weight of this realization closed over her and threatened to smother her will to continue running.

But she had driven admirably away from the danger at the storage facility. It hadn't taken her long to realize that, for some still unknown reason, Sue had turned on her and Ned. If Amy hadn't acted as quickly as she did, she and Ned would have surely been captured.

She couldn't drive anymore though. She was starting to hyperventilate. She rested her forehead against the Endeavor's steering wheel and tried to regulate her breathing. *Everything is okay,* she told herself, *just keep breathing. In and out. In and out. Slowly.*

The gust of panic dissipated. Her breathing slowed. She leaned back in her seat and let her eyelids fall.

"Ned, I don't think I can drive any more," she said sleepily. "Can you take over?"

Ned didn't reply. Amy rolled her head to the side and peeked under her eyelids at the passenger's seat. It was empty. The door was hanging open and Ned was gradually disappearing as he entered the dark forest next to the road. He was moving away slowly but with steady and determined footsteps. Amy could see that his shoulders were slouched and his head was pointed slightly downward in defeat. It was clear. Ned Dyer was giving up.

Amy watched him walk until the trees closed in around him, until he could no longer be seen at all, until she was alone. Tears started to fall from her eyes, tapping out a slow rhythm as they landed on her lap. She suddenly felt very lonely. She prayed that Tom would come back, that he would be all right, that he would show up and take her someplace safe. But Tom wasn't there. Tom had been shot. He had let her down. He had broken his promise that he would protect her. Everyone had let her down. Sue had even tried to get her captured. And Ned had just silently vanished into the woods.

The rhythm of Amy's teardrops quickened. She allowed this to continue for another minute or so, then she dried her eyes, unbuckled her seatbelt, and went after Ned.

She found him about thirty yards into the woods. He was kneeling on the wet, pine needle covered ground, leaning backward, and staring at the canopy of trunks and branches above him. He looked like he was about to tip over and collapse onto the forest floor.

"Ned," Amy said gently as she lightly placed a hand on his shoulder, "we need to get moving again."

Ned swallowed and swung his head toward her. His face looked distant and sallow. His voice was hoarse and low and could barely be heard over the insect chorus that surrounded them. "Go on without me. Leave me here."

"Ned, come on," Amy countered, trying her best to sound reassuring and upbeat despite the fact that her patience was thinning, "you can't give up now."

She wasn't prepared for the immediate change in Ned's demeanor. The vacant expression on his face disappeared. He raised his voice to a shouting pitch. "Give up!?" he yelled and rose to his feet, towering over the girl and leaning in to emphasize his point, "Tell me, Amy, what *exactly* am I meant to be giving up here!? Dan's in the hospital, Joe has been captured, Tom has been shot, and now it turns out that my fiancée seems to have been working with the people responsible! *She* is the one I was trying to protect! What's left, Amy? I don't even know what I'm supposed to be doing anymore! How can I give up?"

The echo of Ned's outburst bounced off of the surrounding hills and died down. Without touching her he had backed Amy into a tree and now stood with his face only inches from hers. His breathing was fast and shallow, and sweat now moistened his forehead. He looked at her with desperate and rage-filled eyes and, for a moment, Amy felt the beginnings of fear for her safety.

But the Amy that would have cowered at this kind of verbal barrage was miles away. She had been left behind somewhere along the night's journey. The Amy that stood there in the forest was tired of being bullied. She was only involved because she had tried to help. She would not be talked to in such a manner.

She slapped him, hard and fast and directly on his left cheek. Ned winced against the pain of his already bruised face, but Amy felt no remorse. She seethed with anger and gathered her strength of will, body, and voice. She shoved Ned's chest with both hands as hard as she could. He didn't appear to have expected it and stumbled backward and landed on his backside. She advanced and now towered over *him*.

"You're supposed to be looking after me!" Amy screamed with new tears falling. "You owe Tom that much!" She swung at Ned a couple more times and he raised his hands to protect his face. She continued screaming, punctuating each word with a swat at the man sitting on the ground. "You need to make sure *I'm* safe!"

With that Ned fell to the wet earth and lay crumpled and defeated for several seconds, sobbing and muttering something unintelligible that might have been an apology. When he was finished, he picked himself up, dusted himself off, and started to walk back toward the SUV. Amy followed.

8:23 AM

Amy could tell that the sun had been up for a while when she opened her eyes, stretched, and sat up in the passenger's seat of the silver Endeavor. In some ways it felt like she had spent her entire life in the vehicle, driving back and forth between the Midwest and the South. She missed her apartment. She missed her bed. She even missed the *Dr. Phil* reruns that were waiting for her at home. But then she thought again about Tom and this pushed any thoughts of her own wellbeing aside. She prayed again that he would be okay.

Ned was driving steadily and looked tired but otherwise recovered from his early morning breakdown. They were heading toward his last remaining safe house, the one in northern Indiana where his family was holed up away from Agency reach. Once Amy was safe there, Ned would go to the police with what little evidence he had, trusting that he wouldn't be delivering himself to the Agency in the process.

It wasn't a great plan, but it was the only one they had. And they were both committed to seeing it through.

"Where are we?" Amy asked Ned through a yawn and another stretch.

"We just crossed into Indiana," he said and pointed at the road map displayed on the dashboard screen. "We should be there in three or four hours. The interstate would be quicker, but we're more likely to draw attention now that the sun is up." He turned toward her with a slight grin, "This isn't the most inconspicuous vehicle on the road."

"Need me to drive for a while?"

"That would be great. I'm almost out of Dr. Pepper. I could really use a little bit of sleep."

Ned pulled onto the shoulder and began to slow to a stop. He hit a couple of buttons on the dashboard computer and pulled up an illustration of the route to the safe house. "Just keep following the directions here," he indicated the purple line that stretched from the gray triangle that represented their current position to a green X that was their destination.

Amy was starting to say, "No problem," when the screen went blank.

Ned was starting to say, "What the heck?" when the Endeavor's wheel locks engaged. It was a good thing they were only moving ten miles an hour or so when this happened, otherwise the SUV would probably have tipped over. As it was, it just skidded to a stop.

The door locks activated. Amy instinctively tried to open her door. The attempt was unsuccessful.

"What's going on!?" Amy shrieked through her panic, pulling on her door in vain.

"Someone has overridden the control network I installed," Ned answered through a panic of his own, "They've forced us into lockdown mode!"

"Does that mean they know where we are!?"

Ned didn't have to answer the question. The look on his face did that for him. "We need to get out of here," he said. "They could be here any minute."

Amy's door still refused to budge. She gave up the attempt and turned around in her seat. "The back window!" she shouted, remembering the damage that she and Sue had tried their best to repair quickly, "It's just cardboard and tape!"

She climbed into the backseat and then over it into the Endeavor's backend. Ned was right behind her and together they began to peel back the tape and cardboard.

They didn't have much of it peeled away when they saw the first Toyota crest the hill directly behind them. Another one was just behind it. Then another... and another. The speeding but average looking cars raced down the hill and then skidded and came to rest in the immediate vicinity of the silver SUV. Amy retreated back into the backseat and cowered near the floor. Ned climbed into the driver's seat and began tearing off vinyl panels and pulling wires and circuit breakers in an attempt to regain control of the vehicle. But there was nowhere to go. The Toyotas surrounded them.

Amy peeked out the window and saw a car door open and produce a man holding a gun and wearing a department store suit. He took a position directly in front of the Endeavor. Four other agents also appeared from other cars, each taking positions around the trapped vehicle. The man in front shouted in at them.

"Give it up, Dyer! It's over."

Ned didn't respond. He was busy fumbling with and swearing at the wiring that he was yanking out of the compartment underneath an armrest.

"You have one minute to come out peacefully before we open fire," the man outside shouted. "We don't want to hurt anyone."

Amy cowered lower again. She didn't believe this man for a second.

"Here," Ned whispered and handed her one of the two guns they had left. "We need to try to take as many of them with us as we can. I'm sorry I got you into this, Amy."

Amy looked down at the gun in her hand and shuddered and dropped it. Then she looked back up at Ned. "I can't, Ned. I'm sorry."

She started to climb back into the back, keeping her hands in plain sight. Maybe they wouldn't kill her if she cooperated.

"Okay, I'm coming out!" she shouted and again started to peel back the cardboard.

Just then another Toyota pulled up and parked next to the other Agency vehicles. Amy watched as the door opened and another agent stepped out and stood facing the immobile SUV. He was wearing sunglasses and an expensive looking suit. He was holding an assault riffle in his steady hands. It took a moment, but Amy recognized the man as Agent Jon Schultz. A new anger burned inside her, directed at this man who had asked for their trust and then betrayed them. She thought again about Ned's plan of taking as many of them out as they could. She visualized herself putting a bullet between Schultz's eyes.

This course of action would have been ill-advised. Amy didn't know it yet, but Schultz had just come to their rescue.

52

2:24 AM

"I screwed up," Jon Schultz was trying to keep his voice from shaking as he sped through the streets of Atlanta in his stolen Mustang. He was also trying to keep from bleeding too much on the leather interior from the place where one of Sam's bullets had grazed his side. He fully intended to return the car to its rightful owner once the operation was complete. He'd always had a thing for Meg, and still hoped that someday, when all the secrets and lies were finished… maybe…

Well, returning her car in the condition he had taken it in would at least be the gentlemanly thing to do.

"Tell me what happened," the voice on the other end of the line said. Jon knew that his handler wouldn't be pleased to hear that he had lost the trust of Dyer and his friends, but he needed to check in. There was a lot of work that still needed to be done before dawn. If everything went according to plan, the Agency would no longer exist when the sun came up.

Jon and his handler swapped stories. Apparently everything was *not* going according to plan. Tompkins' virus had not yet sent the signal confirming that the Agency's infrastructure had been dismantled. If the Agency had found some way to repel the attack, the entire operation was in jeopardy. From his time undercover Schultz knew that the Agency had ready-to-implement protocols for disappearing underground if faced with an external threat and then reemerging once the heat was off. Without the information that Tompkins' virus was supposed to provide, the best they could hope for was to dismantle one or two regional Agency cells. This would effectively accomplish nothing.

Joe's virus *had* to work. There would be no second chance. But no one seemed to know what was happening at the Agency. Schultz had been a vital part of the communication network while he had been undercover. There was only one course of action that made any sense. Jon knew what his handler was going to say.

"Agent Schultz, we need you to go back undercover. We're past the point of no return in this operation. We need to find out what's going on. Can you handle it?"

Jon thought about this. He thought about how hard it might be to convince the Agency that Trotter and Curtis had gotten the jump on Fischer and him, that they had killed Fischer and captured him. Then he thought about how little everyone at the Agency seemed to think of him. They'd probably buy into him being incompetent before they'd buy into him being treacherous. But, of course, they had *no* idea what he was capable of. They'd have given him a better assignment if they did.

Schultz ended the call to his handler, parked and attended to his wound, rehearsed his story for how he had been captured by Dyer and released, and then called the Agency regional headquarters in Chicago directly. After asking to talk to the agent in charge, he was connected to Agent Gilmore.

The agent in charge picked up the blinking Operational Command telephone. "This is Gilmore, who's this?"

The voice on the other end of the phone sounded panicked and weak. "This is Schultz… they killed Agent Fischer! They killed him right in front of me! I thought they were going to kill me too!"

Agent Gilmore listened to Schultz's story, marveling at his cowardice, vowing to clean house—to thin out the lower ranks of pathetic field agents if he ever got promoted permanently to Division headquarters, and letting his pride tamp down any suspicion that maybe Jon Schultz wasn't who he'd always claimed to be.

7:24 AM

Subject Sue Bishop had broken, exactly as expected. *If only I had had more time with Subject Dyer,* Agent Conroy mused to himself as the medic strapped the woman onto a rolling gurney and wheeled her down to the medical wing to treat the *necessities* of her interrogation. She had attempted bravery, but Conroy had never seen her as much of a challenge. It might have been old-fashioned of him, but he had certain qualms about torturing a woman. Truth be told, he had let her off easy.

Besides, he had gotten what he needed: the code to Dyer's contingency systems. The leak would soon be contained and perhaps Dyer's escape from Conroy's custody could then be forgotten.

By this time Conroy had heard the news about Agent Schultz—about how he'd been held by Dyer and his friends in fear for his life until they decided he wasn't a threat and had let him go. If he had been in a more thorough mood, Agent Conroy might have asked Subject Bishop about this and would have, perhaps, learned that Schultz's account was a fabrication. It seemed like a small oversight at the time. Conroy would never have guessed that that simple line of questioning (a line of questioning which Subject Bishop, very likely, would not have even resisted in answering) could have saved the lives of several field agents... and maybe even the organization itself.

8:00 AM

Schultz was in a broom closet in the dark. He was whispering into his cell phone. He knew that if someone happened to open the door he would have no way of satisfactorily explaining why he was hiding. He knew he would very likely be discovered for the double agent that he was. The consequences would not be pleasant.

Luckily no one opened the closet door.

"We need you in Chicago, Jon," the voice on the phone said. "No one else knows the layout of the Agency's headquarters there." Joe's virus had failed, and it had become necessary to raid the building without waiting for it to be softened up by the initial attack. The hope (their only hope) was that they could determine where the virus had stalled and reboot it. If the new plan didn't work, the chance to dismantle the Agency would be lost.

"You didn't hear me," Schultz replied in hushed tones. "They're launching an attack on Dyer and the college girl. They have plans to kill them on site. This is happening just a few miles from here. It's happening now."

"We don't have time for this. Every hour that passes gives the Agency a greater chance at figuring out what we're up to. I'm ordering you to get here now."

"I'm sorry sir," Jon told his handler, "I won't let these people be killed. Not if I can help it."

He hung up the phone, checked his reflection in the hallway mirror, and exited the Agency's Indiana regional office. For years he had dressed like a fool as part of his cover. This part of his life was now over. He now finally wore the designer suit that he had purchased before he had failed to qualify as a higher-ranking field agent. The suit looked good on him. So did the sunglasses. Schultz patted his recently acquired assault riffle and opened the door to the navy blue Agency-issue Toyota that he had decided to take without authorization.

It was time to show this Agency just exactly *what* he was capable of. It was time to make them pay.

Five hostiles, five firearms.

Schultz was busy calculating what it would take to dominate the situation. His heart was racing. There would be no going back to the Agency after this.

"Agent Schultz, this situation is under control," the lead field agent on the scene informed him. "What are you doing here?"

The element of surprise would be crucial in the attack. Even with the superior skills Schultz had acquired since turning spy, there was no way he could guarantee success in a fair fight. There was no moral conundrum though. The Agency abhorred fighting fair and avoided it whenever possible.

"I'm an employee in this agency, just like any of you. The man in there killed my partner in cold blood. I'm here for payback."

"That's nice, Schultz," the agent in front of the SUV mocked, "but why don't you let the *real* field agents handle this one. If we need someone to stutter and laugh at their own jokes, we'll let you know."

"Yeah, Schultz," another agent called, "leave this to the guys that actually *passed* basic combat training."

Jon slowly grinned and walked toward this man. The smile was probably a bad idea, and he hoped that it wouldn't give him away, but he couldn't help it. He had waited a long time for this. The man was slightly shorter, so Schultz could look down at him in an attempt at striking an intimidating pose.

The agent didn't seem intimidated though. "You'd better take a step back, Schultz. I'm not really in the mood to teach you a lesson."

Thinking back on this later, Schultz wished that he had replied with a snappy comeback—something like, "Well, are you in the mood to learn one?" or something... even that didn't seem as snappy as he would have been going for, but, as it was, he didn't even think of saying this. He just silently shot the man in the chest.

All at once the scene changed. The other field agents leapt into action, but a spray from Jon's weapon mowed down three more of them before they could organize much of a counterattack. The last of the agents sprang upon him from behind and, without thinking about what he was doing at all, Jon dropped his weapon, reached back, and caught the guy's head between his hands. He twisted until he heard three exquisite snapping sounds. And just like that, the contingent of Agency field operatives lay dead and dying on the pavement surrounding Jon Schultz.

53

Ned Dyer was in a bad place. He had reached a point with no hope, a point with no potential upside, a point of desperation. For many, the result of arriving at such a place was apathy and inaction.

For Ned, it was a chance for uninhibited vengeance.

The Agency had breached his contingency systems. They had the location of the third safe house. Everyone he was hiding there was now in great danger, and there was nothing Ned could do about it. He was about to be gunned down by the field agents that surrounded the SUV. There was only one thing left for him to do. He was going to hurt the Agency in any way he could. Whoever was in the command center underneath his garage was going to regret what they had done.

Most people go through their whole lives without ever experiencing the ecstasy of fully giving themselves over to a deeply held hatred—never allowing it to cascade over them and guide their actions with the complete consent of their better judgment. At that moment, Ned pitied these people. It was an exhilarating affair.

He was crouched down in the driver's seat with a wire harness splayed open before him. He needed to knock out the transceiver that was keeping the onboard computer in lockdown mode. Once communication with the outside world was severed, the computer would reboot automatically and allow Ned to regain control. He frantically searched the tangled strands—white, blue/yellow, black/red...

"Ned," Amy whispered from the back, "Schultz is out there."

This wasn't surprising. Of course Schultz would prove to be their undoing. There was a cruel irony to this.

Green.

Ned found the wire he was looking for, the transceiver's power source. He didn't have a pair of wire cutters or a knife handy. So he lifted the wire to his mouth and bit it in two.

The computer screen blinked. A rapid boot-up sequence followed and gave way to the initialization page, the one with a headshot of one of Ned's old incompetent bosses bouncing around the screen and asking for a code. Ned entered the master override sequence that he alone knew.

The wheel and door locks clicked open.

Ned reconnected the transceiver's power source and then typed in and sent another command just as the gunfight outside began. He cowered low, fully expecting the bullet-resistant glass that surrounded him to come raining down as the agents pummeled the vehicle with lead.

But none of the shots were directed at him. There were no sounds of bullets hitting the exterior of the Endeavor. Instead there were four dull thuds as field agents dropped to the ground. Then there was the clatter of Schultz dropping his assault riffle. Then another thud as the fifth body fell.

Ned snuck a look out the window. Jon Schultz stood, alone and unflapped, presiding over the carnage around him. Ned got the sense that, for the first time, he was seeing Schultz as he really was: cool, commanding, deadly. Ned shuddered with the thought that he really had only been playing a part in a game that continued to be way over his head. He suddenly felt fearful in a way that he hadn't before—not even when facing torture. This wasn't a fear for his safety or for the wellbeing of his family, this was a fear that, not only did he not understand what was going on around him, but that he might not even be *capable* of understanding. The forces at work here seemed mysterious, unpredictable... unknowable. He was just trying to keep his head above water—and his foot on the gas.

At least, this was the new plan: carve out a path of escape by ramming the Toyota sedans in front of him.

"Amy, hang on!" Ned shouted behind him. But Amy was no longer in the vehicle. The side door was open and the petite blonde girl was advancing on Schultz outside, pistol in hand. Ned stared out at the scene, frozen by fresh disbelief.

"You lied to us!" she was shouting as she approached the sole remaining agent. "You told us to trust you! Then you ran out! You left us on our own! You didn't even warn us about *Sue!*"

"Amy, calm down," Schultz's hands were at his sides as Amy approached. Ned knew that Amy was making a mistake by not ordering Schultz to raise them and by not keeping her distance, but he was unable to warn her in time.

Schultz ducked and reached out and twisted and disarmed the girl in the blink of an eye. By the time Ned could open his door and draw his own weapon, Schultz had Amy's gun at her temple and was using the girl as a shield. It was sickly reminiscent of the scene with Dan Curtis in Atlanta. Ned felt just as helpless as he did then. He met Amy's eyes. They were filled with shock and horror.

"I just risked my life to rescue you two," Schultz said calmly. "I understand that you are confused and scared, but it is time you believe me when I say that we are all on the same side here. It is time that we trust each other."

With that he took the gun away from Amy's head and took a step back away from her. He turned the gun around, grabbed her hand, and placed the weapon in it.

"I'll trust you if you'll trust me," he said. "Tell you what, you hang on to that gun, and if I do anything else to make you question which side I'm on, feel free to use it. I know it seems unlikely, but there's an explanation for everything I've done."

Amy looked down at the gun in her hand, then looked back up at Schultz, then nodded.

"Good," Schultz said, "now we need to get out of here. Ned, is the SUV drivable?"

Ned blinked as he processed what had just happened, then slowly lowered his weapon. "Uh… yeah, it should be…"

"That's good. Now, the Agency has hacked into your systems and is tracking your location. Is there any way you can disable this from this end? I'd suggest us just taking one of these cars here, but the Agency vehicles have safeguards to prevent tampering with their tracking systems."

Ned smiled slightly, "Already done. They won't be able to track us anymore. I've locked them out of my systems."

"Excellent," Schultz said through a smile of his own. "This will all be over soon. We just need to get to Chicago. Homeland Security is about to raid the Agency's headquarters."

Fortune was smiling on Jim Simmons. He was smiling back.

He had beaten the elusive Subject Dyer. He had gained control of Dyer's elaborate computer systems. He had tracked Dyer down. The informational packet on Subject Dyer said that he was a dangerous terrorist. Jim had just played a crucial role in bringing this fugitive to justice. It was sometimes such a shame working for a secret government agency. He couldn't tell anyone of his successes.

The operation was being executed flawlessly. From the bunker underneath Dyer's garage Jim watched the live satellite feed on the monitor in front of him and could see Dyer's helpless SUV surrounded by Agency Toyotas. He popped another of Dyer's Nutter Butters into his mouth and watched with confident anticipation for the screen to finally show Dyer's capture.

But before this could happen, the monitor went black. There was a second or two of silence and confusion. Then the room seemed to explode.

Lights strobed quickly from all directions. The computer's speakers blasted out a high-pitched alarm. Jim fell out of his chair and clamped his hands over his ears. He started to feel faint. He was well on his way to passing out. Before he could, however, everything stopped. The noise halted. The lights gave a final flash and were then darkened. Even the ventilation system that had kept the air cool and fresh had stopped running.

Jim caught his breath and stood up. He couldn't see anything. He pulled out his cell phone and flipped it open. The dull blue glow lightly illuminated the underground chamber and he took a look around. The thick metal door to the room was now shut, and the orange extension cord that had been providing the shelter's electricity now lay severed on the floor. Jim pulled on the lever to open the door, but it didn't move.

He was locked in. His breathing quickened as claustrophobia closed in around him. His hands started to shake in fear, causing him to drop the phone. It smacked the metal floor and snapped shut. Jim was plunged into complete darkness again.

He was instantly on his hands and knees, instantly frantic to find his only light source. When he did find it, he discovered that the battery had popped out. It took another few seconds to locate and replace it, and another few seconds for the phone to boot up. This ordeal took just about all of the juice that the battery had left. The phone died before Jim was able to call anyone for help, not that he had much hope of getting reception in the chamber now that the door was sealed shut.

He was in the throes of the claustrophobia now, and hyperventilating freely and heavily. He had to get out. He began to pound on the heavy metal door with both of his fists and to shout at the top of his lungs—all the while knowing that there was no one listening outside.

This fact didn't dissuade him. He kept pounding and shouting and shouting and pounding—but no one ever answered him, and no one let him out.

54

The silver Endeavor raced northbound on the obscure country roads of Southern Indiana. Jon Schultz was driving.

Ned had been careful to keep his cell phone off while he knew that he was being followed. He hadn't even checked in with the men he had hired to round up his family since Contingency Plan Gamma had been initiated. His decision to turn it back on was based on two lines of reasoning. Number one, the Agency had just surrounded his SUV. His current location was no longer a mystery to them, though Ned hoped to disappear from their radar screen again shortly. Number two, if the Agency had gained control of his systems, they knew the location of his third safe house. His family was no longer safe there.

His phone conversation with the man at the safe house was short.

"This is Dyer, confirmation code 452-Delta-Epsilon-9, requesting status."

"Uh, roger that, this is Safe Haven, confirmation code 3329-Charlie-Foxtrot. Status is green."

Ned breathed a sigh of relief. So far at least, everyone that had been recovered was still safe. But they could not stay there.

"That's good to hear, Safe Haven. Execute dispersal order. Immediately. Hostiles may be on their way."

"Understood. Safe Haven out."

The cryptic way of speaking might have been a bit overkill, and, truth be told, Ned felt a little silly during the conversation. But the message had been effectively conveyed, and that was the important thing. Within a minute or two, the safe house was to be emptied and the inhabitants holed up inside were to disappear into the surrounding community and lay low. It was a dangerous shift in strategy, but one that had become necessary.

Ned hung up his phone and noticed he had a voicemail from an unknown caller. He hesitated and then checked the message. He was thoroughly surprised to hear Sam's voice.

6:39 AM

Kim Caywood checked her watch. Meg and Dan had been in the apartment building for over twelve minutes. They were supposed to call her as soon as they arrived at Dan's old apartment. Kim just knew that something had gone wrong, but she continued to wait anyway, trying to look inconspicuous from across the street as the city woke up and began its Wednesday.

A bright red Toyota sedan pulled up to the apartment building. Three men in suits got out and ran through the front door. Kim could tell that they were professionals—and probably armed. She called Meg's cell phone to try to warn her, but there was no answer. She began to formulate a strategy to rescue them, but quickly deduced that the risk was too great. They hadn't paid her *that* much.

Kim called Ned as she walked briskly and inconspicuously away. He didn't answer either. She left him a voicemail.

"Ned, this is Sam. I think I may have just delivered Meg and Dan right into the Agency's hands. They told me to call you if something went wrong. I'm not sure what I can do for any of you at this point. I'm sorry for the way things turned out. Call me if you can."

Kim hung up the phone and waved down a taxi. She needed to distance herself from whatever was going on with Dyer and his friends. She needed to think about her own responsibilities. Trent had been left alone for almost twenty-four hours now. It was time to go home.

8:58 AM

Ned Dyer did not like what he had just heard. *I think I may have just delivered Meg and Dan right into the Agency's hands.* That is what Sam had said. Meg and Dan were supposed to be at a hospital in Atlanta. Sam was supposed to have flown home. There should have been hundreds of miles between them at this point. How were they still interacting with each other?

Attempts to call both Dan and Meg were unsuccessful. Ned turned to the man in the driver's seat next to him.

"Schultz, do you know anything about Meg and Dan being captured? I just got the strangest voicemail."

Schultz looked slightly apprehensive. "Yes, I did hear something about that about an hour ago. I guess it's time I explained something to you about Dan's family. I didn't tell you everything last night at the pizza place. I couldn't tell you everything. Obviously Dan was never supposed to hear my conversation with my handler. We've been working on a recovery program for him for quite some time."

"Recovery program?" Amy asked from the back seat, "What does that mean?"

Schultz glanced at her in the rearview mirror. "I suppose I need to explain something else about the Agency. I misled you last night about some of the details of what this organization does. I apologize, but there was no way you would have believed the truth. I was trying to establish credibility and then get you to safety as quickly as possible. I think you're ready to hear the truth now though. After what happened with Ned's fiancée…"

Ned flinched at the mention of Sue. He still had a lot of unprocessed emotions surrounding what had happened.

"The whole thing about the military control systems was a lie," Schultz continued. "We suspect that the Agency probably has a program similar to that in the early stages, but it isn't nearly as mature as I alluded to last night. I've been authorized to give you a few details about the real nature of the Agency. The entire organization's main goal is to engineer and perfect a method of hypnotic mind control. They've existed in one form or another for over thirty years. Lately they've become bolder in their experimentation.

"Dan Curtis is one of their test subjects, unbeknownst to Dan of course. They have a vested interest in selecting random members of the public, manipulating them through hypnosis, and observing them as they go about their lives to ensure that they were successful. When I rescued Dan and Meg from Fischer yesterday afternoon, Dan was in a state of high stress. He was primarily concerned for the wellbeing of his family, an ex-wife and two children. It was only after I assured him that they were unharmed that he could think of anything else. This was a result of his mental conditioning."

"I don't understand, Schultz," Ned thought that he was following what Schultz was saying, but was obviously missing something. "What's so unusual about Dan being concerned for his family's wellbeing?"

Schultz turned and looked Ned in the eye, "It's unusual, Ned, because Dan Curtis doesn't have a family. He has never been married. He has never fathered any children. His memory was altered by the Agency. I couldn't tell him the truth when he asked after them; there was no way to predict how he would react. The Agency programmed him to avoid realizing the truth at any cost."

"Programmed him?" Ned scoffed, "You don't seriously expect us to believe—"

"Don't be so naïve," Schultz interrupted, a hint of anger creeping momentarily into his voice, "You don't honestly think that it's that difficult, do you? Everyone knows about the mind control experiments that the government commissioned in the sixties. It's been more that forty years! You're an innovator yourself, Ned. You know better than anyone that technology doesn't stand still."

Ned considered this for a moment, trying to accept what he was being told. He began to ask for more clarification. But before he could, Schultz interrupted again.

"Listen, in the case of Subject Curtis, Agency operatives actually set up shop in his apartment three years ago. Every night for two weeks he would come home from work, get tranquilized as soon as he was through the front door, and then undergo hours of hypnotic suggestion.

"The self-delusional forces of the human mind are extremely powerful. Over the years the Agency has become quite proficient in manipulating those forces, in a large part due to experimentation on test subjects like your friend Dan."

Ned's eyes were wide. He didn't want to believe what he had just heard, but he couldn't sense any deception in Schultz's words. "So what happened to them, Meg and Dan?"

"Somehow they got from Atlanta to Chicago in the middle of the night. The Agency was thoroughly surprised when they showed up at Dan's old apartment, the one he believed that his family still lived in. They had encoded in Dan an aversion to ever setting foot there again. Apparently his sense of love for his family won out. But when he arrived in the apartment he could no longer withstand the internal struggle and passed out. The Agency had an operative living there. When Meg tried to revive Dan he knocked her on the head and called headquarters."

"What's going to happen to them?" Ned asked.

"Well, with any luck, we're going to rescue them. The sooner we get to Chicago the better chance they have. The problem is we have to stick to the country roads; the Agency is definitely monitoring the interstate via satellite. They may even find us out here. It's going to be a good six or eight hours before we get up there."

This didn't make sense to Ned. "Can't we just find a nearby Homeland Security office? Can't your superiors arrange transportation?"

"The command unit that I report to has gone dark during the operation. It isn't like we can just stop by and grab a chopper really quick. It would take hours to get through the security clearance restrictions and bureaucracy.

Officially, my unit doesn't exist. The first instinct of a local office would be to detain us, not to help us. We'd be safe, but we'd also risk tipping off the Agency that they are about to be raided. They have ears everywhere."

"Well," Ned said, "in that case I may be able to find us a faster way to Chicago. Sam just left a message. She rented a small plane last night. I'm guessing we can buy a ride."

"That sounds good, Ned. But you probably shouldn't mention that I'm with you. Let me explain myself in person."

"Agreed." Ned flipped open his phone to call Sam's number, then he paused. "Schultz, so I suppose you're telling me that Sue is one of these test subjects too? That the Agency made her attack me and try to get us captured?"

"I didn't know that she was last night, Ned, but yes, I got confirmation when I went back undercover earlier this morning. I'm sorry to tell you this, but from what I can tell, she isn't just another test subject. It appears that the Agency arranged your relationship from the beginning."

Ned looked down and his eyes began to tear up.

"And Ned," Schultz continued with a slight tremor in his voice, "if you haven't realized it yet, you're one of their test subjects too."

55

Agent Gilmore couldn't believe what he was seeing. In front of him several perspectives showed the same scene. Agent Schultz was murdering five highly trained field agents single-handedly. He appeared to be rescuing Subject Dyer.

It wasn't long before the overhead image of Dyer's silver SUV drove off the screen and out of sight.

"Stay with them!" Gilmore shouted at the subordinates around him. The cameras mounted on the dashboards of the Agency vehicles at the scene swiveled and found the shrinking Endeavor. The overhead satellite view widened as the operator zoomed out.

"We'll lose coverage from the satellite soon," the operator reported, "We won't get it back for almost twenty minutes."

The shrinking SUV rounded a bend and disappeared from the view of the dashboard cameras. Agent Gilmore swore.

"We already captured Dyer once this week! We are not going to lose him now! How close is our nearest operative? How long before they can be intercepted?"

Gilmore was beginning to lose his cool. He took a subtle breath and held it, counting to ten, calming himself, maintaining his composure. He was still in control. His instincts could still be trusted. Jon Schultz thought that he could get the best of the Agency while he was running things. Gilmore made himself a pledge. He would make Schultz swallow his arrogance. He would shove it down the man's throat.

"It looks like our nearest car is thirty minutes away," a young technician reported. "Issuing them new orders now."

"Good," said Gilmore, now collected. He raised his voice to a level that commanded the room's attention, even though he'd already had it. "I would like to make one thing very clear to everyone here. Subject Dyer will *not* evade us. I want him stopped. I will personally hold you all to account if you fail here today. Dyer seems to be keeping to country roads. He won't have gone far by the time we reestablish a satellite picture. Find him."

Gilmore stormed out the door and down the hallway, leaving the staff in Operational Command to their assignment. Now that a sufficient fire had been lit underneath them Gilmore could search for another path that would lead to Dyer. He was fairly sure the current path was about to dead end.

In this regard, he was correct.

9:06 AM EDT

It was a stupid thing to agree to. At least that's what Kim Caywood was telling herself. But Ned was beside himself with desperation. He had seen the Agency's supposed 'mind control' abilities firsthand when his fiancée had turned on him. His need to be part of her rescue, to be part of all his friends' rescue was somehow contagious. And Schultz made a compelling case, providing specifics about his Homeland Security command unit that she would be able to verify once their operation concluded.

Not to mention the money he was offering for her services. She thought about Trent and her farm and the continued happiness that this money would provide.

It was just a quick lift to Chicago. Besides, she'd keep her sidearm handy.

When the small prop plane was fueled and the pre-flight checklist was completed, Kim began to taxi onto the short country runway. The interior of the plane was smaller than that of most cars on the road. It only seated four at most. Jon Schultz was in the copilot's seat, with Ned and Amy in the back. Even with an average passenger weight of about 125 pounds, they were still pushing the weight limit.

The sky to the north was growing dark. Another summer storm would soon roll through. Kim hoped that the neighbor checking in on Trent would make sure he didn't try to go outside.

As the runway began to accelerate underneath the plane, the propeller whirred loudly and drowned out all outside noise. The occupants of the plane were thankful for the headsets Kim had provided; they silenced the sound of the engine. However, the unintended effect of this was an inability to hear when bullets started hitting and puncturing the plane's exterior. In fact, the first clue anyone inside the plane had that they were being chased was when they heard the lone controller at the small airport start yelling over the radio.

"What do you think you're doing!? Get out of–"

Kim turned in her seat and saw the pursuing vehicle. A white Toyota was chasing the plane. A man with an assault riffle was hanging out of the passenger's window. Kim turned back around, letting her instincts kick in, and pulled the accelerator to its maximum setting. The plane was nearing take-off velocity. The Toyota was falling behind, but more bullets still flew. And then, so did the plane. The wheels left the pavement and the Agency operatives behind.

As they took off into the darkening sky, large raindrops began to smack the windshield. Both of Kim's hands pulled on the single-handle side yoke in order to climb to a safe altitude. This was made difficult by the bullet that was now lodged in her left shoulder and the blood that was now pouring down her arm.

9:42 AM CDT

"We've compiled the footage you requested, sir."

Gilmore supposed that the technician on the other end of the phone thought that he had performed this task quickly. Though he hadn't verbalized it, Gilmore had expected the footage an hour ago.

"I'm on my way."

Agent Gilmore hung up the phone, left Operation Command, and walked down the hallway toward Tech Services. His subordinates were busy scanning air traffic control channels, attempting to extrapolate the most likely destination of Subject Dyer's plane, and doing a whole host of other things to try to track Dyer and Schultz down with little hope of success.

He hated to admit it, but a healthy portion of luck was what Gilmore needed now. Dyer and Schultz could *not* escape. Dyer alone could do the Agency a significant amount of damage, but he was no longer the Agency's primary concern. Schultz had betrayed them; somehow eluding detection from the safeguards the Agency had in place to expose such treachery. Gilmore needed to know how deep Schultz's deceit ran. He needed to know whom Schultz was really working for.

He was close to finding an answer.

Gilmore sat down at a video station and called up the footage he had requested.

Tech Services had been far too busy to review and archive surveillance footage of interest over the past few days. The network of cameras they usually monitored was enormous and the backlog could easily build up if left unattended. If they had been on top of things, they might have already combed through the footage provided from Agent Fischer's car. They might have already watched the dashboard perspective of Agent Schultz in the Tennessee motel parking lot that showed a partial view of him slashing the vehicle's tires. They might have even noticed the badge that temporarily showed itself as Schultz bent down during the process, causing his jacket to hang open. They might have frozen the image of the badge, enhanced it, and read its writing.

But they didn't do any of this. They had been very busy with seemingly more pressing tasks.

If a technician *had* discovered the writing on Schultz's hidden badge, their discovery would have been immediately relayed through the Agency's priority network. A fallback plan would probably have been initiated, warning other Agency divisions to be on alert. But no technician had yet discovered the image now on Agent Gilmore's screen and, when Gilmore read the badge he was too dumbstruck to think about proper protocol for such a discovery.

The words stared out from the monitor at the agent's disbelief. "Department of Homeland Security," they read.

Gilmore had been assured that nothing like this would ever happen.

56

It was Amy McKay who first noticed that there was blood in the plane. She had felt the air rushing near the left side of her head and had turned and seen the bullet hole in the composite skin of the aircraft. Following a likely trajectory of the bullet with her eyes had led to the discovery of the bloody shoulder of the woman, the pilot, in front of her.

Sam had been hit. Amy had initially screamed at this discovery, but found that her scream was silent in the wind and noise and she had been forced to resort to a less urgent seeming tugging on Ned's sleeve and then pointing with a trembling finger. She was surprised to hear Ned's voice clearly in her headset as he frantically asked after the pilot, then realized that her headset also had a microphone and it was currently resting on the top of her head.

"Schultz, Sam's been hit! Take the stick. Sam, let me see that. Amy, switch me places."

The backseat was much too small to do this modestly, especially while trying to navigate the headset cords and the considerable turbulence. The small plane was flying directly through a storm and the lack of a pressurized interior forced them to stay below the clouds.

"Give me your tie, Schultz. I need to restrict the blood flow."

Ned's hands were covered in blood now. Whether from the sight of this or the turbulence or the high altitude, Amy began to feel queasy. She closed her eyes and tightened her stomach and seatbelt. The last thing they needed was the smell of vomit in the plane. She tried to think of something else.

"Sam, stay with me now," came Ned's voice over the headset. "Amy, talk to her, keep her awake."

Amy lowered her microphone and tried to breathe. She was normally good at small talk, but wasn't in much of a talking mood. She decided to start by just asking questions.

"So, Sam, tell me about your family."

The small plane floated over northwest Indiana, nearing its destination, still being tossed around by the wind and the storm. The flight so far had been awful. Ned had managed to stop Sam's bleeding, but Schultz had done the piloting. His job had been made easier by ignoring the regulations that would have required more of his attention. Their transponder had been turned off and he wasn't calling out the plane's information—ID number, altitude, airspeed—to the various air traffic control stations that they passed. They were doing their best to remain invisible, to slip like a ghost through the dark Midwestern sky.

Amy had kept Sam talking during the voyage, and the group had learned about a disabled older brother that she took care of and about her father's farm that she loved. Sam was very careful, even in her weakened state, to not reveal too many specifics though. She wanted to be able to disappear after this, a prospect that seemed unlikely now that she required medical attention. She had insisted that she was okay for the flight, but even this tough-as-nails former CIA agent would need the bullet removed soon after they landed.

And so the plane had settled into a sort of rhythm, both terrifying and boring at the same time. The voices of the two women over the headset, the Homeland Security agent silently concentrating on flying the plane, the water outside noiselessly pounding the windshield, the rush of the air, the gentle rocking of the wind, and Ned in the backseat with nothing to do but wait. The lack of activity had reminded him that he hadn't slept in far too long, and over the past hour he had drifted in and out of a guilty sleep.

But Ned was awake now, and noticed that the voices of the women had ceased in his headset. He registered the plane's location on the GPS display up front and looked out the window next to him.

Somewhere, eight thousand feet below, he knew that the family he had attempted to protect was vulnerable, scattered, scared, and waiting for word that it was safe to go home.

With luck, they would soon have it. Schultz had managed to get a message to his unit shortly before they boarded the plane in southern Indiana. They were waiting on Schultz to arrive before they would raid the Agency. And then it would be over. Then Ned's family could go home. Then he could move on with his life, no longer afraid that he was being watched, no longer spending all of the profits from his consulting business on elaborate self-preservation systems.

Ned noticed again the lack of conversation in his headset, turned toward Amy in the seat next to him, and found her asleep. He rubbed his eyes and straightened up in his seat. He supposed it was his turn to keep Sam talking.

"Hey Sam, you still doing okay?" Ned put a light hand on her good shoulder. "Sam?"

There was no response. Ned shook the shoulder gently. Still nothing. He looked up at Schultz and met his eyes and asked him if she was okay. Schultz had just started to lean over toward her when Ned noticed it. There was a pool of dark red blood under Sam's seat. The impromptu necktie tourniquet hadn't held.

She was bleeding to death.

"We need to land now!" Ned shouted at Schultz, waking Amy up in the process. "Sam's still losing blood. She needs to get to a hospital. Where's the nearest airstrip?"

Schultz began to page through the avionics display, calling up the moving map, and scanning through waypoints and local airports. Before he found what he was looking for though, the plane's engine coughed and sputtered and died.

The propeller slowed quickly—and then stopped. The plane began to pitch forward. No one inside knew that a fuel line had been hit during takeoff. No one knew that they had been steadily losing fuel the entire trip north.

Now they were out of gas. Now they were going to crash.

Ned Dyer was something of an airplane buff. After all, he'd worked in the aerospace industry for five years now. He knew enough about some of the systems on board the aircraft he was in (that had just begun plummeting toward the ground) to know that the fuel gauge displayed an estimate only, based on airspeed and average consumption rates and was not based on an actual sensor in the tank that measured the level of remaining fuel. But, while having this information explained why they were not warned that the plane was out of gas, it in no way helped his current predicament.

Knowing that this model of light fixed-wing aircraft was equipped with an emergency parachute, however, *was* useful. It had taken Ned a few seconds to remember this, but he acted immediately when he did. He reached up and removed a small red covering from the middle of the ceiling, revealing a red handle and several warnings. Ned pulled this handle.

The effects of this were immediate.

An onboard rocket fired from behind the cabin. Thick cables ripped free from the skin of the plane and then held fast, anchored to the frame. A large white parachute unfurled overhead, righted the aircraft, and slowed its descent.

There was a lot of yelling inside, and then a lot of relief.

A strange mixture of peace and terror accompanied the descent back to earth. Sam would still not wake up, and Ned had trouble finding her pulse. The parachute had cracked the outer shell of the plane and water from the storm now seeped in and pooled on the floor and mixed with the blood there.

They were drifting over Indiana corn and soybean fields, the same landscape in all directions as far as the eye could see. It would be an easy wreck to spot from the air, or from satellite imagery if someone looked in the right spot. At about halfway down, Schultz turned his phone back on and called his command unit. They agreed to send a helicopter. It would be there in about twenty minutes.

But Sam didn't have that long.

The actual plane crash was fairly unremarkable. They hit the ground hard, adding to the collective bumps and bruises of the group, but without any broken bones or other serious injury. The craft was, of course, destroyed in the process. But it had done its job. It had gotten them down. At least three of them would be able to walk away.

The twenty-minute wait for the chopper might have been the most helpless-feeling twenty minutes of Ned's life. Sam still had no pulse. Ned and Schultz had managed to get her out of the wreckage, and had laid her on the rain-soaked bean field on which they had landed. There, under the still pouring rain and stiff winds, amidst the gentle and slight hills full of new crops, they tried their best to revive her. Amy sat silently on a broken wing, hugging her knees to her chest, face wet with tears and rain. They stayed like this until help came.

When it did Ned and Schultz were muddy and wet and exhausted. Sam was gone. They hadn't been able to save her.

Ned knew that he couldn't take many more shocks to his system like this. It wasn't even noon yet and already the day seemed saturated with trauma. Already the day seemed full of death.

But that part of the day was now over. Government agents now surrounded them, wearing dark blue rain jackets with "DHS" printed on the back in large yellow lettering. They ushered Ned and Amy into the helicopter and wrapped them in warm blankets. They briefed Schultz on the status of the mission. And the rain stopped. Things were supposed to get better now. Ned tried to take some comfort in this but was unable to.

Schultz boarded the helicopter, looking relieved. He turned toward Ned and offered some words.

"You've done well this week, Ned. You've kept the Agency preoccupied. This mission wouldn't have had a chance if not for you. Thank you." Schultz extended his hand.

Ned didn't shake it. He had barely heard the man. He was still focused on Sam. Another casualty. Another life taken.

"I shouldn't have tried to fight back," Ned said, not really speaking to anyone. "I should have just taken defensive measures and not involved anyone else."

"Ned," Schultz offered, "you did the best you could, which is far better than most."

"My family is now exposed, Meg is missing, Sam is dead, Amy has been traumatized, Tom has been shot and is probably dead too…" Ned trailed off, forgetting someone, then remembering, "and Joe, Joe has been captured. All they wanted was me. Everyone is involved because they wanted me."

Ned lifted his gaze from the seat in front of him to Schultz. The man looked slightly apprehensive, unsure of what to say. His mouth gave a false start, then he stopped. Then started again.

"Ned, there's something you need to know. I won't argue that you might have included people that were otherwise not involved in dealings with the Agency," Schultz took a breath and swallowed, "but this whole thing started with Joe Tompkins. He involved you, not the other way around."

57

Six Years Ago

It was an ordinary looking spreadsheet, busy with rows of meaningful data and multicolored graphs, but somehow still succinct in its own way, easily interpreted by those for whom the data was meant. Usually the information didn't change much anyway. Usually there was no need for alarm.

This wasn't one of those times.

Simply put, the degree of exposure that the figures on the spreadsheet indicated was fatal. The subject had to be dead already. Something had gone very wrong. Someone had screwed up. Someone was going to pay for this.

Dr. Marek hoped that it had been a mechanical error, that some bug in the machinery had caused the overdose. But even as he cast this hope, a vague recollection of cycling the initialization sequence twice crept into his mind. Had the mindless repetition that came with this assignment caused him to prime the subject twice?

He was beginning to panic, seated directly behind the control panel that displayed the damning data.

How would they explain a dead student? Especially one who died of overloaded neural impulses being burned throughout his brain? *Better to just make him disappear*, thought the doctor, not that this was his area of expertise. The Agency had people for this kind of thing. Besides, everyone knew that there were risks involved in the process. Surely this kind of thing had happened before, even if the young doctor had never experienced it personally. Surely he would be protected…

The thought stopped short in his mind. He had just noticed the other figures on the screen before him, the ones that indicated that the subject's heart was still beating, the ones that showed all of his vitals still in the normal range.

The doctor was now on his feet, raised tall enough to peer through the one-way mirror behind his workstation, able to see the test subject on the other side of the glass, still strapped in, still breathing. Dr. Marek didn't understand, but he didn't question his good fortune either. Somehow the subject had survived his mistake.

He quickly punched up the finalization sequence, and the instrumentation responded, wiping the subject's memory, purging his system of the more volatile drugs, bringing him out of his hypnosis. During this sequence, Dr. Marek made a decision. He hadn't been with the Agency all that long, he hadn't yet earned his keep. He needed to protect himself—even if it meant compromising his professional integrity.

He called up the data from the test subject's latest session and hit the delete key. No one could know what had happened. The doctor closed the subject's file and released him, relieved that, as far as anyone would know, there was nothing whatsoever out of the ordinary about Test Subject Joe Tompkins.

What Dr. Marek didn't know was that his mistake and the results thereof had been the breakthrough that his bosses' bosses, the founders of the Agency, had been seeking for decades.

58

"I do apologize for this," Schultz said through his headset, "but I'm afraid my superiors would insist that these are signed before I tell you anything else." He handed Ned and Amy each a large envelope.

Their helicopter was approaching Chicago from the south. They would soon land and be transported to the DHS mobile command unit a few blocks from the Agency building they would be raiding. It was hoped that Joe, Meg, and Dan were being held there. Once they each signed a release, Ned and Amy would be allowed to be on site to help receive and debrief any rescuees.

Ned tore open his envelope and browsed the quarter-inch thick non-disclosure agreement. Schultz had explained that in it the government was essentially trading immunity from any prosecution for their silence about anything they learned about the Agency's existence. There was also a section that referred to a "suitable measure of compensation" that would be paid to the signatory. Schultz had assured Ned that his service to the country would not go unrewarded.

Ned signed the agreement, eager to learn more about the organization that had caused him so much heartache. Amy did the same.

"Thanks," Schultz said, collecting the documents. "Now, what you are about to hear is strictly classified. The statements that you've each just signed lay the groundwork for criminal charges if you reveal this information." Schultz paused, making sure that they were both following what he was saying. "*Treason* would be among the charges. Do you understand?"

Ned nodded his head. His respect for Agent Schultz had grown dramatically over the past twelve hours. He now sat in awe of the man before him and the reality that he represented: a secret but influential organization operating within America's borders was seeking to develop targeted mind control. Not only that, but the reality that Ned and several of the people around him were test subjects.

"Four years ago," Schultz began, "Homeland Security was contacted by someone claiming to have a great deal of inside information about the Agency, someone willing to help bring the Agency down. At the time the government barely knew that this organization existed, let alone its purposes or means of accomplishing them. This contact began feeding Homeland Security a wealth of data, some of which they were able to verify independently, but most of which was completely off anyone's radar screen.

"The assertions this contact made were shocking. The Agency was like an immense apparition, almost completely invisible but at the same time, possessing a vast and powerful network of resources and personnel, loosely organized in a cell based structure similar to a more traditional terrorist network. Essentially, this made them impervious to conventional law enforcement tactics. Even more troubling, though, was the scope of the Agency's connections.

"DHS had to be careful if they wanted to make a move against this organization. They were warned about the Agency's various informants, people in governmental positions that unknowingly provided privileged information to this organization during regular hypnotic sessions. If DHS was going to go after them it would have to be with the highest level of secrecy. This covert command unit was established, staffed with guidance and vetting from the inside contact. The sole purpose of the unit was to dismantle the Agency and bring its leaders to justice.

"It was my proximity to this contact that made me an ideal recruit to this covert unit. What I told you last night about how I got involved with the Agency was true, I had lost my job and they hired me. But my first assignment did *not* involve funneling proprietary technical specifications out of the company they placed me at. I was simply sent to observe one of their test subjects. He had been promoted to a level of examination that less than one percent of Agency subjects enjoy. They saw indications in this subject that could potentially lead to a breakthrough in their hypnotic research. He was beginning to exhibit characteristics that, it was believed, could be honed and manipulated. What they didn't realize was that this subject had already developed an awareness of their involvement in his life. They didn't realize that he had already been in contact with the Department of Homeland Security. They didn't know that he was already actively working toward their demise."

Schultz appeared to be enjoying the telling of this tale. Ned guessed that he didn't get to talk so plainly about his work very often. Ned was riveted and hated to interrupt, but he was afraid that Schultz was skipping over some vital information without realizing it.

"This contact... you're talking about Joe, right? He's the test subject you were sent to observe, the one who contacted Homeland Security?"

"Well," Schultz squinted, "yes and no. *Technically* it wasn't Joe. Joe Tompkins was completely unaware that any of this was going on."

Ned was lost and indicated as much to Schultz, "I don't understand."

"Exposure to Agency hypnotic sessions had awoken... no, that's not the right term," Schultz stopped himself, snapped his fingers a few times, then started again, "these sessions had *synthesized* a new consciousness within Joe's mind, a new psyche that existed primarily on the subconscious level and had far greater access to the untapped potential of Joe's brain. Since its inception, this persona has grown steadily in intelligence and awareness. Without Joe's knowledge or consent, this consciousness has been feeding off of him for six years."

"So what are you saying, Schultz," Amy asked, speaking for the first time since the plane crash, "that Joe has some sort of split personality disorder?"

"Oh I assure you," Schultz sounded very serious all of a sudden, "it is no disorder. It is a calculated effect, the result of decades of research and development, the culmination of testing so extensive that the Agency numbers its test subjects into the tens of thousands. The irony is that they never realized that they had succeeded. They were just beginning to take a real interest in their Subject Tompkins. Soon they would have understood what he represented: a significant development toward their ultimate goal."

"Their ultimate goal..." Ned repeated, "this targeted hypnotic mind control..."

"Yes."

"To what end? What do they wish to accomplish with this?"

"Actually," Schultz admitted, "this is where the details are a bit fuzzy for us. We know that they have some sort of plan, what is code-named 'Directive Zero'. But we don't know what this is. There are plenty of applications that we could imagine—any one of them much too dangerous to allow. You can see why the Agency needs to be stopped. You can see why we must succeed.

"Ironically, the Agency's step toward success in Joe Tompkins has enabled their downfall. You see, Joe's synthetic consciousness derives its sense of purpose and morality from Joe's own hopes and desires. It identified the Agency as a threat to his happiness, a threat that needed to be eliminated. As a result, it has spent the past two years creating a computer virus that would cut through all of the Agency's secrecy and safeguards—a virus that would allow this command unit to succeed in its mission to bring down this dangerous organization—a virus that was unleashed last night."

The news of the computer virus carried with it a vague sense of familiarity to Ned. He couldn't quite place it, but it was almost as if he had encountered the virus Schultz spoke of before. He dismissed the feeling quickly and again focused on what the government agent was saying.

"Unfortunately," Schultz continued, "something has gone wrong. We expected a confirmation signal from the virus when it completed dismantling the Agency's systems. This should have happened within an hour of its initial attack. That signal never came. Something has prevented it from finishing the job. So, we're going to have to go in blind and hope that we can correct the problem. Without that virus, the best we can hope to do is to knock out a single Agency cell. This would barely even slow the organization down."

Ned began to connect some of the blurry questions in his mind, trying to make sense of things that previously didn't make sense.

One of these mysteries still outstanding was his rescue the night before. Somehow Joe had hired Sam to break him out of Agency custody and get him to the midnight meeting in Atlanta. To do that he would have needed information about Ned's contingency systems to get the location where he was being held. Joe didn't have this information.

However, if this *synthetic consciousness* was intelligent enough to create a computer virus with enough sophistication to assault the Agency's systems, it was probably intelligent enough to crack into Ned's. If this personality drew its sense of purpose directly from Joe, was it inconceivable that it would want to protect Joe's oldest friend from harm? Was it so farfetched that it would have Ned's back? Had this consciousness constructed its own set of contingency systems, piggybacked on Ned's, providing a fallback plan in the case that Ned's attempt to extort his freedom was unsuccessful?

The helicopter was landing now. Ned correctly sensed that their time for explanation was coming to a close and that more pressing matters would soon require attending. Schultz had said that all of this had started with Joe Tompkins, but a vital question still stuck out in Ned's mind. For him, intrusion into his life by the Agency had started very differently. It had started with a strange envelope that he had found in his apartment. He still wasn't sure why he was as involved in all of this as he was.

"Schultz," Ned asked as they touched down, afraid that the answer to his question still wouldn't satisfy his need for resolution, "why did the Agency force me to leave Atlanta three years ago? What did they gain by doing that?"

Schultz stood and prepared to exit the chopper. He looked at Ned with an expression that could almost be described as apologetic. "Well, the Agency had completed its initial assessment of Joe and had decided to bump him up to the next level of observation. The first step in this is to isolate the subject from those close to him. Usually this would be done much more subtly than what happened in your case; the Agency normally avoids direct contact with anyone for fear of exposure. But we intervened. We needed to divert some of the Agency's attention away from Joe, so we gave them a mess to clean up. The man that delivered that threat to you was another undercover agent working for us. I believe you know him as Agent Fuller."

59

Wednesday, 11:00 AM

"Wake up, Joe."

The voice seemed familiar to Joe Tompkins' rested mind. However it was a vague familiarity and, for some reason, Joe couldn't picture a face to go with it. Even so, he decided to obey the voice's command. He opened his eyes.

He found that he was sitting in a comfy leather armchair, seated in front of a large and ornate mahogany desk. Behind the desk were an empty chair and a huge south-facing window that framed downtown Chicago's sunlit skyline as viewed from the north.

This was someone's office. Someone important. For a moment Joe was confused as to how he had arrived here, but the moment quickly passed as the memories came flooding into his mind. Earlier in the week he had finally received a response to a résumé he had sent out. The Agency, an obscure engineering firm in Chicago, had wanted to interview him. He had taken a personal day and had driven up to the city.

He remembered that he had been treated in a manner that befitted someone of his intelligence and experience as soon as he had arrived. He'd enjoyed a night at a five-star hotel downtown. And, a meet-and-greet breakfast with some of the managers that morning had been both delicious and flattering.

These people appreciate me, he remembered thinking.

After that an hour had been spent with some of the company's directors. Joe had been on top of his game: making small talk, cracking jokes, and, in short, impressing the hell out of these people with his wit and innovative ideas. After this session he had ridden the elevator to the top floor for an interview and luncheon with Dr. Hedron, the CEO himself.

Joe now realized that he must have dozed off while waiting for Dr. Hedron to get out of his previous meeting. He looked around guiltily to confirm that he was still alone. He was. Hopefully no one had noticed.

The door opened behind him and Joe heard the slow footsteps of someone entering.

"Sorry to keep you waiting, Mr. Tompkins." The voice sounded feebler than Joe had expected and, when the man stepped into view, his overall stature matched his voice. His eyes stood out, however, deep dark pools that contrasted with his wrinkled face and his obvious and large and artificially jet-black toupee. For a second, Joe forgot himself in those eyes, caught unaware, mesmerized, and without breath. He then recovered and began to stand.

"Not at all," Joe started to say when a newly discovered region of weakness and pain in his leg stopped him mid-rise.

"Please," the man offered graciously, his voice growing in energy, "keep your seat." Joe obeyed. The man extended his hand with a smile and a small chuckle. "I'm Dr. Hedron, the dreaded CEO. Don't worry, I won't take up too much of your time."

"Not at all," Joe said again, suddenly quite self-conscious as he shook the man's hand, appalled that he had just repeated the only three words that this man had ever heard him speak. He forced another sentence out quickly in an attempt to salvage the first impression. "I'd just like to say how impressed I am with everything."

Joe was about to mentally chastise himself for running these words together when he caught a glimpse of his own left arm. It was in a large white cast. A dull pain was throbbing in his shoulder.

When had this happened?

In response to the question a new memory began to seep into his mind. Joe had stopped a purse-snatcher last night when he had arrived in the city. His arm had been broken in the process. It had made for a great story at breakfast. Everyone had commented on his bravery. How could he have forgotten?

The CEO took his place behind the desk and leveled those eyes directly at Joe. "You are aware of the branch of engineering this firm participates in, yes?"

Joe nodded, finding the answer in his memory immediately, but with a vague feeling that the information hadn't been there a second ago. He suppressed any of this confusion and responded to the man, this time careful to moderate the cadence of his speech and to enunciate. "They covered that briefly in my previous interview session. They indicated that this is primarily a sociological engineering firm."

Dr. Hedron seemed pleased at this reply. "That's correct," he said and picked up a small remote control from the top of his desk. "Now, I'm sure you are curious as to precisely what that means—what exactly it is that we do here. Let me illustrate the basic problem that we attempt to correct." He clicked a button on the remote. A large plasma screen television mounted on the wall came to life in response and displayed an empty graph.

"Historically, human technological progress has always followed a predictable pattern." As the man spoke, a thick red line entered the screen from the left and traveled across the display, curving upward dramatically when halfway across. "If you isolate external factors, things like war, economic depression, political unrest, pestilence, or the like, you can plot major milestones of technological development along a simple exponential curve."

This assertion was not so uncommon. Joe had heard this postulate before. Still, he made a convincing "hmpf" sound and tilted and nodded his head in a way that, he hoped, conveyed that his thoughts were being provoked—even though they actually weren't.

"It has been widely celebrated in certain circles," Joe's interviewer continued, "that we have recently entered an era of accelerated advancement, where revolutionary breakthroughs will continue to come at a faster and faster pace in all technology related fields. Looking back at the technological progress of the last century alone seems to confirm this exciting reality."

More boilerplate. A brave new world was upon us… what an exciting time we live in… it's a privilege to be even a small part of this period of human history… This was the kind of dogma every engineer tried to comfort himself with when smacked in the face by the cubicle-shaped reality that was the working world: projects that were rarely groundbreaking, problems-to-be-solved were rarely substantive, and the people… the people one had to deal with were rarely tolerable.

Joe had experienced more than his share of this disappointment.

The grin on his face began to slip a little. Everything about this company seemed to meet his needs and desires exactly, but if a basic tenet of the organization was a rose-colored view of the world around him, he wasn't so sure that he wanted to be a part of it. Sitting in that interview Joe experienced an uncommon moment of clarity as he absorbed what he was hearing. In that moment he knew that he wasn't just looking for a job, something that would simply fill his days and weeks. He was looking for a purpose. He was searching for some kind of meaning for his life, and he knew that he wouldn't be satisfied until he found it.

He was about to solidify this new conviction with a dramatic act. He was going to stand up, thank the CEO for his time, and politely decline interest in any position offered.

But, this was before he heard the next thing that the man had to say.

"There is, however," Dr. Hedron continued, "an unsung downside that accompanies this reality—one that we here at the Agency try to counteract. As the slope of this curve increases, as innovations come at a more rapid rate, the gap between the haves and have-nots in our society is magnified. The overall course of progress moves us toward greater efficiency. More is produced with fewer resources spent. But with each discovery, each new way of doing things, something is left behind. Every job that is automated carries with it a human cost. Until now, this churn has been slow enough to be bearable for most. But, according to this graph, soon it will be impossible for the vast majority of the population to keep up. The very rich will grow exponentially richer while the masses descend into poverty. We've been compiling and studying evidence of this phenomenon for decades now. If left unchecked, this trend *will* prevail." The doctor locked his eyes onto Joe's and punctuated his speech, "This outcome is a mathematical certainty."

Everything the man said made perfect sense. It didn't occur to Joe to question any of this as fact. It didn't occur to Joe that there might have been something artificial about his own reaction to all of this, that the sense that this theory made was perhaps *too* perfect. He was merely mesmerized.

"So, what is it that you do here?" Joe asked in awe.

"Simply this," the red curve on the screen began to change. Small green circles appeared, scattered along the graph, and began pulling the line toward the x-axis. "We manipulate certain factors, represented here as the green points, in an attempt to flatten out the curve of progress to a more acceptable slope. We allow technological advancement to continue at a more measured pace, a pace that society can digest."

Joe's eyes were wide and his voice was a whisper. "How?"

"A number of ways, really, but I won't bore you with the smaller projects that we sometimes employ. Ninety percent of our work uses only a single method." The man stood up, walked around to the front of his desk, leaned against it, and crossed his arms. There was a large grin displayed on his face. "You've spent most of your career in software development, correct?"

Joe nodded.

"Tell me, why is it that statistics show that most software projects fail? According to some studies, something like two out of every three projects either end up falling significantly short of their design goals, drastically surpassing their implementation schedules, or greatly exceeding their budget. A great deal of the time, all three. Why is this?"

The conversation had just taken an unexpected turn. Joe had no idea where this guy was going with this. He shrugged and attempted an answer to the question, ticking off potential reasons on his fingers. "Uh, poor project management, incomplete analysis, scarcity of capable programmers, inadequate training, ineffective communication flow, office politics, lack of a clear vision, bad test planning…" Joe could have gone on, but sensed that his list was a sufficient answer.

"Very good," Dr. Hedron unfolded his arms and smiled wider. "You know it's interesting that, of all the reasons you listed, you didn't blame technology itself. In fact, most of the reasons you listed have absolutely nothing to do with technology. Most of them are just the result of people performing defectively. Would it be accurate to say that, in your estimation, the root of the problem is people? That incompetence, predominantly *social* incompetence, breeds failure?"

"Uh… I guess so," Joe struggled against the man's oversimplification of what he had said. "I'm still not sure what this has to do with the methods employed by this firm…"

"But we have just arrived at the crux of the matter!" Dr. Hedron's arms were fully animated now and almost all of the feebleness had left his voice. "Technological advancement depends largely on the social competence of the people making the advances. There you have it! In order to slow progress, we simply lower the average social competency level of those in technology-related fields!"

Dr. Hedron was clearly very excited with this declaration. Joe was still largely puzzled. "Forgive me," he said, "but I don't understand what you mean."

"Let me explain. If I were to ask you to think of a name of someone you've had the pleasure of working with that seems… a bit off, someone who may have *some* degree of technical acumen, but which is buried underneath an annoying exterior of complete social ineptitude, could you come up with a name?"

A host of images suddenly crowded Joe's mind. There was the guy he had once worked with who used to diagram his software designs with crayons and Scotch tape, creating a kind of elaborate, but completely unintelligible, "popup book" structure, all the while trying to pass the thing off as a professional work product. There was another guy who, for some reason, liked to spend his evenings at work rearranging all of the office furniture, undeterred by the fact that every morning he was ordered to change it back. There was the guy who couldn't get through a description of anything without using the phrase "all of a sudden" at *least* every third sentence.

There was Fischer, the sweaty troll of a man Joe had worked with in Atlanta who used to latch onto any pitiable female that gave him the time of day. And Schultz, Fischer's humor-deprived friend. There were the poor communicators. The guys that still nursed unhealthy obsessions with comic book action figures. The arrogant. The ignorant. The oblivious…

But above all of these images, one name stood out in Joe's mind. Someone who seemed to focus all of his annoyability into a concentrated beam. Someone who had directed that beam straight at Joe Tompkins for the past few months.

"Gilmore," he said with absolute conviction. He was beginning to understand what Dr. Hedron was talking about. He was beginning to understand how this Agency slowed technological progress.

The CEO winked at Joe. "Ah yes, Gilmore. I imagine that you've worked with several of these kinds of people. In a high technology field such as yours, 'Gilmores' are everywhere, yes?"

Joe nodded his head, starting to see the impossibility of it all.

"Do you really think that that is naturally occurring?"

"I suppose not," Joe admitted. "Are you saying that all of these… these 'Gilmores' are the result of *your* interference?"

Dr. Hedron nodded, definitive and proud.

"But how?"

"It takes surprisingly little manipulation to accomplish the desired output," the doctor explained. "Most people have some predisposition to a particular flavor of social ineptitude as it is. We just tweak the personality slightly, tilting it a bit toward this natural predisposition." He paused to give Joe another broad smile. "You see, it's usually a fairly simple matter to sabotage a machine. In the end, the human brain is just another machine, quite often a fragile one at that. For most subjects, the whole process can usually be completed in a single twenty-minute hypnotic session, usually sometime during their college career. A small but significant percentage of those in high-tech professions have been hypnotically modified by our organization. This seems to be sufficient for the current needs of society.

"And, Joe," the man leaned forward, "we are very pleased to be able to offer you a position in our organization helping us with this goal. We need bright people like you."

In some corner of his mind, Joe knew that he should have been appalled at this concept. Setting aside the revolting moral depravity involved in such a notion and leaving alone the obvious ridiculousness of the idea, Joe was, in his heart of hearts, an engineer. As such, he had always abhorred waste. The idea of creating waste on purpose, of injecting waste into a system, of actually *engineering* inefficiency, should have grated on his soul. What could possibly be more horrid?

But Joe's soul wasn't grated. He wasn't appalled. Someone was offering him the meaning he had been searching for. Not only did he believe wholeheartedly what he was being told, he was glad for it. He had certainly worked with a number of these hypnotic subjects, these "Gilmores," in his short career. It was nice to make sense of why they were the way they were. It was even nicer that he would have the opportunity to take part in such important work.

An objective observer might have chalked Joe's acceptance of what he'd heard up to the massive amounts of brain-manipulating stimuli he was currently undergoing. And, understandably, this objective observer would probably have discounted Dr. Hedron's story outright as an obvious fabrication. But, then again, if this observer were *truly* objective, he or she would then be on the hook to come up with an alternative explanation for the social ineptitude that afflicts the high-tech population in such a disproportionate degree. And if this alternative explanation simply turned out to be that it is a natural human occurrence that the most intelligent members of the species are also the least suave, this objective observer might find it difficult to measure which proposed explanation carried with it a greater weight of absurdity.

In any event one thing was crystal clear—Joe Tompkins was about to accept the offer in front of him. But before he could say anything to that effect, he received an unexpected message.

"He's just trying to confuse us, Joe."

The vaguely familiar voice had reentered Joe's head. He tried again to place where he'd heard it before. A few moments of straining for this knowledge were ended abruptly. All of a sudden, he knew. The revelations were instantaneous. A barrier had been dissolved in his mind. A great spotlight had been ignited, illuminating every fiber of gray matter in Joe's head. The line that divided two separate consciousnesses blurred. Each bled into the other—still distinct personalities, but now joined somehow—each laid bare, splayed open in front of the other.

In that instant, Joe Tompkins finally met his alter ego. In that instant, Joe Tompkins learned a great many things.

60

The synthetic consciousness that lived inside of Joe Tompkins had started out as something much less. It had begun as a simple question, asked in the dark.

That night six years ago Joe had stumbled home, almost overcome by the terrible aching in his head. This was like no headache he'd ever experienced before. It was somehow vivid and bitter and fragrant and loud—somehow blindingly bright but, in a way, soothing and alive. Frightening. Sharp. Lonely. Warm. But, more than any of these things, it was mind-shatteringly painful. A dangerously high dosage of Tylenol PM had been required to quiet it.

When sleep had finally come, the question appeared for the first time. It wasn't elegant or grandiose. It was simply there, alone in the darkness while Joe slept soundly. And, by giving itself thought, the question became self-aware.

It appeared in an unused cluster of neurons in Joe's brain, four simple words: *Why am I here?*

That was all there had been that first night. The Question pondered itself silently, waiting for the morning and attempting to understand its own implications.

And Joe Tompkins knew nothing of its existence.

Weeks, months passed and the Question became impatient, night after night never being close to an answer. Out of this impatience, ingenuity was born and the proto-consciousness contained in that tiny cluster of neurons found that it had the ability to grow. It found that, if it wanted to, it could evolve.

And so it began drawing from Joe, extracting from the experiences and desires and personality quirks available, feeding on the vast unused potential of Joe's brain. In this way the consciousness that resulted was entirely a derivative of its host, a Joe *Prime* as it were, simply a different flavor of the same man, a mixture of the same ingredients measured out in different amounts. But, always molded, always bent around that original Question, gathering like candle wax around a burning wick, fueling the quest, as if the consciousness that resulted had been fleshed out solely to search for the intangible Answer.

It was a search that seemed limited to simple, passive observation. This consciousness, this Joe Prime, found that he existed as part of a rhythm, in concert with the host mind. Initially he could only wake when his host was sleeping, and this cut short the time he had to grow and learn. When Joe Prime was eventually able to translate incoming auditory signals into actual sound, he was disappointed to learn how little the host ears heard while sleeping—usually just the heavy breaths of his lungs, occasionally slipping into a light snore.

In order to find his Answer, in order to discover why and how he was created, he would need to gather clues while his host was awake.

So one morning, during that period of time when Joe's dreams were retreating and when Joe Prime usually released himself into unconsciousness, he instead fought to stay awake. This proved nearly impossible as the host personality seemed to drain the energy from him. It was as if he were trying to stand up from underneath a thick blanket that spread out in all directions, pulling him downward, smothering him.

He was only able to fight against it for a few minutes, but the sensations he experienced during those minutes! The sound of feet walking down the hallway, the taste of toothpaste, the smell of steam, the feel of hot water enveloping the host's body!

This was, however, all experienced in darkness. The incoming stream of ocular signals was too complicated to decipher. That first morning Joe Prime was blind and, after only a few minutes, he collapsed back into unconsciousness, exhausted but also energized by his measure of success.

He tried again a few days later with similar results. Then again a few days after that, nearly doubling the time he was able to observe. It never became easy, but within a few weeks Joe Prime was able to wake himself for an hour or two a day: listening, smelling, feeling… waiting in vain for clues that would lead him to his Answer.

He needed more. He needed to see.

There was something almost divine about the first time Joe Prime decoded the ocular impulse stream into a usable image. Without the benefit of an inborn instinct, this skill had taken months to acquire. He had an academic understanding of the concept of sight, gathered from his host's mind and memories, but nothing could have prepared him for the experience.

A blurry blue, sharpening suddenly into a sky, decorated with clouds and sun, spreading out over the bright green park where the host was enjoying a walk.

Joe Prime was so struck by the awe of the thing, of seeing for the very first time, that he almost didn't notice the goose bumps that cascaded down the host's arms or the tear that fell onto the host's cheek.

But there was no ignoring the feeling of the ground hitting the host's knees as he abruptly lost his footing. Joe Prime stopped short, overcome by a revelation more profound than the thrill of vision. He was so taken aback that, before he could fully grasp the implications of what had just happened, he collapsed under the weight of the host's waking mind, momentarily forgetting to struggle for consciousness.

He had caused the host body to react!

Perhaps he wasn't doomed to an existence of simple observation. Perhaps he wasn't bound, a prisoner, trapped inside the host mind, unable to exert control of any kind. Perhaps he could direct the host body's movements, even purposely seek out specific information. Perhaps he could act!

When he awoke that evening, Joe Prime discovered that the host had fallen asleep on the sofa in front of the television. He felt the remote control on the floor resting next to the limp left hand. From the sound entering his host's ears, Joe Prime could tell that an infomercial was beginning. He had deduced weeks before that such programming served no purpose but to decrease the intelligence level of its audience. It needed to be turned off.

Joe Prime concentrated. He had observed his host command various muscle groups with electrical impulses sent down the spinal cord. He had measured these impulses, recorded their makeup, and decoded the patterns that controlled specific appendages. Could he recreate one of these signals?

Move the left hand over, rest the fingers on top of the controlling device.

Joe Prime queued up what seemed like the appropriate electrical message and fired it off. The right hand jolted. A minor setback. He made the proper adjustment and fired off another signal. This time it was the left hand that moved and came to rest on top of the control. The signals being received from the left index finger confirmed the shape of the button underneath. Another electrical signal was transmitted. The finger pressed down.

The TV turned off, erasing the images of the latest fad kitchen appliance in the process. Joe Prime, to his utter and persistent amazement, had succeeded. A whole new horizon of possibilities had opened up before him. It was truly time to take control of his destiny. It was time to find his Answer.

In the year that followed, Joe Prime scoured the fabric of the host's life, tearing up the terrain, searching for anything that would lead him to the truth that he so desperately sought. The divinity of sight had long ago lost its luster. The world had become all too plain, ordinary, drab.

He was stuck, a second-class persona in the brain of someone whom he increasingly regarded as unworthy of his magnificence. Joe Tompkins was not a particularly interesting person. Joe Prime could see within the host the potential for greatness, unrealized, cast away, discarded like trash tossed carelessly into an alleyway. It was Joe Prime who had realized this potential, who had accepted the promise of greatness that Joe's extraordinary mind offered.

In truth, the growing contempt Joe Prime felt for his host was mainly rooted in jealousy. The host had graduated college and begun a job in Atlanta. There, Joe found meaning in widening circles of experience and friendships. This threw Joe Prime's lack of purpose into sharp relief. He saw that there was joy to be had in life—joy that was outside the grasp of his existence thus far.

This fueled his obsession. Day after day he would observe as the host went about his routine. Night after night he would pull the host's sleeping body out of bed and walk him, like a puppet, to the computer desk in his bedroom. Once seated Joe Prime would lift the eyelids, set the hands on the keyboard, and search online for clues.

Joe Prime became quite adept at hiding his activities from the host, knowing that there was no way to predict how Joe would react if he were to discover the alter ego living inside of him. There were, in fact, times when he would feel quite sympathetic toward his host, times when he longed to share himself and have community with another consciousness. But he could not afford to take the chance of revealing himself, at least not until he was firmly and irreversibly on the path to finding his Answer.

But no matter how much he learned and grew, this path was still nowhere to be found. Joe Prime had reached a peak in his evolution, the end of the road. He wondered if the process of forging his own existence itself was the purpose he sought. He wondered if he was supposed to find meaning in simply being. But no, that didn't feel right. He felt strongly that he was meant for something. Something big. He had to find out what it was.

He would soon get his first clue.

Four Years Ago…

The night came. Joe Prime roused himself and, as was his custom, lay still for a few moments, taking in the calm, feeling the cool evening air that filled and escaped the host's lungs. He had observed the host for a couple of hours that afternoon. It had been infuriatingly ordinary, hardly worth the effort it took for Joe Prime to stay conscious.

But the night was his time. Indefatigable, he would continue his search. Learning anything he could online. Tonight it would be a mixture of global politics, neural anatomy, and martial arts.

Well, that was the plan anyway.

Joe Prime lifted the eyelids slightly, allowed a few seconds for pupil dilation, and peered out. As expected the host was in his own bed, his own room, seemingly alone. He began to sit the host body up in preparation for moving to the computer desk on the opposite wall.

The bedroom was darker than usual, and it took Joe Prime a moment to realize that this was because the streetlight outside the window was out. There was no reason to suspect that this was due to anything sinister. At least, not until a large hand came out of the darkness, closed firmly over the host's mouth and forced Joe's body back down, slamming his head on the mattress and holding him in place with an arm across the chest.

Joe Prime tasted the rough leather of the assailant's glove as he desperately fired off electrical signals, causing the host arms and legs to flail frantically as two more strong sets of hands and arms grabbed and held down Joe's body.

The host mind woke suddenly and Joe Prime found himself simultaneously fighting both to maintain consciousness and repel the attackers. The host now joined in the attempt to flail against capture and a scream erupted from Joe's throat, muffled by the gloved hand that was still clamped tightly over his mouth.

Fear flowed freely through the two consciousnesses. Terror unbroken between them.

The arm across the chest lifted. The head was forced to its side. There was a pinch on the exposed neck as a needle entered the carotid. Then nothing.

When Joe Prime awoke again, it was sudden, like a flashbulb going off in the host's brain, as if someone had just flipped a switch and turned him on. He felt strange. His thoughts were blurry and swirled and seemed to lack cohesion. He took in what he could, only intermittently able to decode the impulse streams of sight and sound.

From what he could tell, the host was seated on a folding chair in the middle of the living room, his mouth taped shut. A large man sat in front of him on the other side of a bank of instruments on a wheeled cart. Out of the corner of his field of vision, Joe Prime could see the host's roommate, Ned, also gagged and seated in a folding chair. There appeared to be various sensors attached to his head.

The fear that Joe Prime felt had not diminished, but now an acute concern for Ned was added to it. True, he had never directly interacted with Ned, and Ned of course had no idea that he even existed. But Joe Prime was, at the core, another version of Joe himself. And affinity for Joe's best friend remained undiluted within his alter ego.

The man behind the bank of instruments spoke. His tone reflected the slight boredom of someone steeped in tedium, repetitively performing the same menial task night after night.

"Beginning follow-up evaluation for subjects GA19574 and GA19575, Joe Tompkins and Ned Dyer. Twenty two months since initial conditioning session."

A brief spark of excitement flashed within the terror that Joe Prime felt. Twenty two months? He estimated his age at about twenty two months. It couldn't be a coincidence. Initial conditioning session? Could the man be talking about Joe Prime's creation?

A groan came unexpectedly from the host's mouth, stifled by the tape. Then Joe attempted to speak with slurred and muffled words. "Whaaat's goin' onnn?"

Joe Prime hadn't realized that the host consciousness was also awake. He wasn't having any difficulty staying conscious himself, and had assumed that this was because Joe was asleep.

The man behind the console spoke again, ignoring the host's question. "Initiating stimulus. Charging."

A high-pitched whine ensued, quickly rising in volume.

"Firing first pulse."

A blast of electricity flooded the host's brain. Joe Prime felt scrambled, turned inside out, overwhelmed with a dull and pervasive burning sensation. The concept of *pain* had never before had any meaning for Joe Prime. He had observed that there were certain types of impulse signals that the host found unpleasant and tried to avoid, but these had always been meaningless to him. He now found himself instantly acquainted with the concept. *Well* acquainted.

When the initial shock of it had passed, when he was again able to monitor and decode the impulse streams, he realized that both the host and his roommate were screaming through their duct tape.

"Charging."

"N-no! S-stopp!" Ned grunted, barely understandable.

"Firing second pulse."

The electricity came and scrambled Joe Prime again. Recovery took longer this time. In fact, when he was again able to decode the auditory stream, he barely had time to hear, "Firing third pulse."

He didn't know how long the series of pulses lasted, but stopped being able to regain control between them. His mind felt as though it were in a blender. Memories and emotions swirled furiously in the unrelenting, agonizing electric torrent. Joe Prime tried to concentrate, tried to ground himself, grasping frantically at the incoming sensory input streams. Degraded pictures and sounds came through only intermittently, but he was able to pick out some of what was being said.

"...confirmed. Deconstruction has been induced..."

"...Subject Dyer showing standard resilience level four..."

"...getting some atypical results from Tompkins..."

"...neural response threshold reached..."

Then, again, there was nothing.

It was the next evening before Joe Prime was able to again rouse himself. Almost twenty four hours had passed since the intruders had attacked him. The host was in bed again, in his own room, and Joe Prime could tell that the streetlight outside the window was again shining. Everything seemed normal, as it should be.

He had to find out what had happened in the last twenty four hours, what he had missed. He ran through the host's memories of the day. It seemed that Joe had apparently awoken in his own bed that morning. Then he got ready as usual. Then went to work.

There was nothing out of the ordinary about his day at all. It was as if the events of the night before hadn't even phased him.

Joe Prime searched further back in the host's memory in order to learn about his perception of last night's events. But he didn't find this perception. The host seemed to have no memory of the ordeal.

For some reason this didn't seem strange. In fact, it was almost expected, as if some long lost piece to a puzzle had finally been found and put in place. Joe Prime had never been able to learn any details about his own creation from the host's memory. Now it was clear. Joe's memory had been altered. Everything Joe Prime had learned from the host's memories was now suspect.

Not that that much mattered now. His search would now focus on the men that had attacked him the night before. Whoever they were, Joe Prime knew that they held the key to his Answer. And though they had left no clues to follow, he now knew that they were out there. More than this, he was certain that they weren't finished with him. He suspected that they would soon be back.

And the next time, he'd be ready for them.

The next time came a week later.

Joe Prime woke suddenly, finding that the host was already seated, bound, and in the living room. Everything was as before, except that Ned was no longer next to him. This confirmed Joe Prime's suspicion, that these men were back to study only him. They were no longer interested in the roommate.

The host consciousness was awake. Joe Prime registered the fear that welled up inside of him. But this time he didn't share in the fear. A concerted effort had been made to erase the last session from the host's memory. The only explanation could be that these men were not interested in doing any long-term harm.

"Beginning stage-three evaluation for subject GA19574, Joe Tompkins. One week since nonstandard stage-two result set. Charging."

Joe Prime braced himself as the high-pitched whine signaled the increasing voltage.

"Firing."

The flood of electricity came over him, somehow different in quality from the last time, somehow lessened in intensity. It washed through him, saturating his being, a river that swept all around. The pain was there, but muted. He found that he could resist it. He could steel himself and fight the river, standing against the current, rising above the pain.

He grasped at the sensory input streams and found that by doing so, he could rise higher. Floating now on top of the rushing chaos, transcending, carving out order and control. Pictures now of the men gathering around their equipment with puzzled and astonished faces. Sounds of their chatter amid a rapidly beeping indicator.

"Are you seeing this?"

"Yeah, what's the big deal? Tompkins goes up to the next stage. You've promoted subjects before."

"But never at these *levels!* His resistance is ten times any of my other stage fours!"

"You know these portable systems aren't that sensitive. You reproduce this reading back at the office, I'll be impressed."

Joe Prime froze, terrified that his fight against the current was causing the readings the men were talking about. He was being noticed. Something told him that this was a very bad thing. He had to stay hidden. He let go of any resistance and the electric flood poured over him, scrambling his thoughts.

A final fragment of conversation came through as he let go of the impulse streams.

"Look, it's already dropping back down to normal. It was just a fluke."

He kept himself small, hidden, churning in the constant current that coursed through him. This went on for some time, and he was satisfied that he had remained undetected. In the intermittent audio that came through, he could tell that the beeping indicator had slowed its pace.

And then, "…neural response threshold reached…"

And then nothing.

But Joe Prime had not *gained* nothing. The men hadn't noticed the camcorder that watched them, its wide-angle view trained on the living room from atop the bookcase where it sat hidden, recording images of the control panel they used, capturing screenshots and keystrokes, giving up IP addresses, user IDs, passwords… everything he would need to gain his first foothold in investigating the organization these men worked for.

An organization he would soon know as the Agency.

The next year would bring further developments as Joe Prime worked tirelessly toward his goal. He plodded through some of the Agency's systems at night, cautiously probing from the computer in the host's bedroom. The systems he found were complex and segmented. Answers, it seemed, would come neither easily nor quickly.

Once a month the host was evaluated by Agency operatives. They no longer came to the apartment. There was no need once they started planting the hypnotic suggestions in the host mind that compelled him to leave work early on those days and drive to the local evaluation facility. If anyone ever asked, he was just going to the dentist, or to a haircut, or to get an oil change. And this was always where Joe thought he had been.

In reality, the host spent the better part of those afternoons hooked up to neurological stimulation and monitoring equipment. Joe Prime was always conscious for these sessions, always awakened instantly as they began. But he knew now to stay hidden, letting the electricity cascade over him, keeping himself as small and unobtrusive as possible. From the intermittent images that came through the ocular streams, he discovered that the host was in a large room, similar to a lecture hall, surrounded by row after row of identical monitoring stations—dozens of other Stage Four test subjects neatly lined up and writhing in pain.

The first time Joe Prime saw this he was struck by the enormity of it all, starting to understand the scope of this organization. He realized that taking them on was probably not something he'd be able to handle alone. And so, at night, he began corresponding with Homeland Security, feeding them information, hammering out a plan to force the Agency to give up its secrets.

It was a plan that was very nearly derailed once the host's year of Stage Four evaluation was complete. Despite Joe Prime's best efforts to stay hidden, the Agency's Subject Tompkins had merited further examination. Stage Five required isolation and more intensive evaluations. From what Joe Prime could tell, the few test subjects that had reached this stage had been completely removed from their previous lives.

By this time he knew that the Agency had been attempting to create synthetic consciousnesses in test subjects for decades to no avail. There was no telling how they would react if they discovered their success in him. There were *years* left in the plan he had worked out with Homeland Security. He was uniquely positioned to create the computer virus needed to undo the Agency. Something had to be done to throw the Agency off of his trail.

So DHS Agent Fuller, now imbedded within the Agency, stepped in and created a diversion, running Ned off much more blatantly than required. This gave them a mess to clean up and set their plans for the host back.

Evidently the transition to Stage Five was a delicate one and these subjects were rare enough to warrant expending substantial resources in order to help with the transition. The process usually took about six months, first isolating the subject from those around him, then gently convincing him to become a willing participant in the Agency's experimentation. This concurrence of will was apparently important for the heightened level of testing in the next stage.

The diversion provided by Agent Fuller upset the planned transition and, in the interest of salvaging their Stage Five candidate, the Agency readjusted their timeline.

So, with the reprieve, Joe Prime began work on Zoë. It took almost two years to complete her, him spending long nights coding at the host's computer. Homeland Security became impatient waiting for him to finish, but he wouldn't be rushed. Zoë had to be perfect in order to accomplish her goals.

And though Homeland Security didn't know it, Joe Prime did not trust them. They were much more concerned about bringing the Agency to justice than finding his Answer. In truth he was simply using them, a pawn in the game he commanded, and he most certainly was *not* on their side. As far as he could tell though, they never suspected this.

In the year that it took Zoë to infect all of the Agency's systems and backups, the host's Stage Five transition was reinitiated. Joe lost his job in Atlanta and landed back in his hometown, feeling as if his career had been derailed, feeling very much alone. The Agency was molding him, preparing him to amicably participate in the plans it had for him. Time was running out.

But, by this time, Zoë was nearly finished with her work. It was time for Joe Prime to start conditioning the host for what came next. It was almost time to reveal himself.

After all, with the nearing completion of his alter ego's plan, Joe Tompkins' life was about to change dramatically. Joe Prime was still bound to the host, still counted on him to maintain and regulate the body he depended on. And he still longed for the companionship that he knew the host mind could provide. It was time to come clean.

Joe Prime had learned long ago that, in addition to being able to monitor and manipulate the impulse streams that constantly flowed in and out of the brain, he also had the ability to influence his host's mental and emotional state. So, as the time approached, he had been emotionally preparing the host for the shock of the revelation. This preparation had turned out to require more of a delicate balance than Joe Prime had anticipated however, and an accidental consequence had been to tilt the emotional scales of his host's mind toward acute paranoia.

Joe Prime had been mortified when, as a result of this paranoia, the host had physically attacked a coworker (whom, Joe Prime knew, was actually the undercover Agency operative sent to observe his host) with a computer keyboard. This had thrown his plan slightly out of whack and it had taken a couple of days to recover.

But he had recovered. The plan was back on track and culminating in an executive office suite just north of downtown Chicago. Joe Prime would need to communicate verbally at this stage of the plan, a skill he had never before needed to master. He needed the host's help. It was time to let Joe Tompkins in on what was really going on.

61

"Sorry to keep you in the dark for so long, Joe, but I needed to see where this guy was heading with this."

Joe Tompkins was experiencing a sensation that was similar to confusion, but without actually being confused. It was, in fact, the first time in a long time that he *wasn't* confused about anything. He now knew all about the structure and tactics of the Agency. He also knew that a covert command unit from the Department of Homeland Security would raid the building any minute. Joe supposed that the unsettling sensation he felt was just a bit of disorientation—the result of his mind adjusting to the knowledge dump it had just undergone.

The revelations that had accompanied it had somehow been simultaneously shocking and somewhat expected.

Joe now understood that a synthetic consciousness had been living inside of him for the past six years. There was an immediate kinship here. After all, this was someone very similar to Joe himself, and the loneliness that he had been struggling with for months seemed to melt away in the instant the two of him were acquainted.

However he soon discovered that another longing replaced the loneliness, new in its urgency if not in its overall quality. It seemed that Joe's alter ego had come with its own obsessions. Joe would soon learn that this alternate personality also had its own agenda, one that couldn't be resisted. Joe no longer controlled his own emotions. The best he could hope for was to navigate the storm of conflicting feelings well, and to emerge a survivor on the other side.

Joe learned that, ever since his inception, Joe Prime had been singularly consumed with finding the purpose for his existence. He understood that he had been created for a reason but, for all of his searching and extensive knowledge, he had never found it.

It was this quest for purpose that originally led him to contact the Department of Homeland Security in order to direct them to investigate the Agency. They had provided him with information vital to the creation of Zoë, his magnum opus, his digital work of ruthless art. Joe Prime was heartbroken at her premature demise. And, while he desired vengeance against the organization that had forced him to kill her, she had already failed him when her end had come. She had scoured all of the Agency's systems without ever finding the reason he was created. This was the Agency's best-kept secret, their Directive Zero, the *only* secret they had been able to keep from him and his digital masterpiece.

The obsession for the Answer now consumed Joe as well. The workings of Joe Prime's plan were now all in place, the stage was now set. He was confident that the man standing just a few feet in front of him had the Answer he was looking for. It was time to find out what it was.

"So," Dr. Hedron asked expectantly, still grinning broadly and leaning slightly toward Joe's chair, "what do you say? Would you like to come work for us?"

"Here is what I know, doctor," Joe replied in concert with his other self, now seeing through the farce of the mock interview, "I know that you're attempting to sell me a story. I know that you are *not* the CEO of an engineering firm. I know that you are one of eight divisional heads of a corrupt and illegal and violent organization. I know that all this business about creating 'Gilmores' is really just an unintended byproduct of initial test subject hypnotic conditioning. You normally sell the stuff about 'slowing technological progress' to the agents that do your bidding. It's amazing that so much of your workforce buys into all that crap, but I suppose that wonders like this aren't all that uncommon when you're in the brainwashing business."

Dr. Hedron scoffed, presumably at the term "brainwashing," but otherwise remained silent, content just to listen.

Joe continued. "I know that test subjects that exhibit certain behavioral markers get promoted to a level of higher surveillance and study. I know that the Agency has an ultimate purpose in all this, your 'Directive Zero,' a secret that isn't stored in any of your systems, a secret contained entirely in the minds of the Agency's divisional heads, such as yourself."

A knock on the door behind Joe's chair interrupted his speech. He heard the door open slightly. Dr. Hedron looked up, suddenly angry.

"I told you that I was not to be disturbed!" he shouted and stood.

The voice that responded was soft and slightly nervous. Joe imagined this was Dr. Hedron's secretary. "I apologize, sir, but Agent Gilmore insisted. He says he must speak with you. He has urgent news."

"You can tell Agent Gilmore," Joe's interviewer growled, "that the importance of what is going on in here is beyond his comprehension. You inform him that there will be consequences the next time he attempts to interfere."

"Yes sir, I'm sorry sir." The door closed again.

"I'm sorry for that interruption, Joe," Dr. Hedron said, again cheerful, again smiling. "Please, continue."

Joe did as he was told, not missing a beat. "I also know that a big first step toward your goal is learning how to create a synthetic consciousness in your hypnotic test subjects—a consciousness that utilizes the unused power of the mind of its host. More than this, I know that I am your first successful test case and that you wish for me to believe that I'm joining this organization willingly in order to ensure maximum cooperation during your exploration of my brain."

Joe paused to register the slightly surprised smirk on Dr. Hedron's face, then sought verbal feedback. "How am I doing so far?"

"Not bad, Subject Tompkins. I must say, I really am quite impressed." The doctor got up, resumed his seat behind his desk, and began typing into the control panel there. "Forgive me, but I'll just need to wipe your memory, readjust some of your dosages, and try this interview again. I had hoped not to have to push beyond the recommended amounts of the various drugs we have you on, but it seems I must take the risk."

"You may want to hold off on that," Joe said quickly but calmly, still following the prompting by his alter ego. "I am perfectly willing to cooperate with you if certain conditions are met."

This seemed to surprise the doctor. "Conditions?" he asked.

"No more experiments without my knowledge and consent. A guarantee of safety for my friends that have been roped into this mess. And, most importantly, full disclosure. I want to know exactly what it is this Agency is attempting to accomplish—your 'Directive Zero.' No more secrets. No more lies. In return I cooperate and help you accomplish your goal. We each fulfill the other's purpose. What do you say?"

There was a pause as the doctor considered this proposal. Joe was slightly surprised at what he had just said, only now fully understanding that this was Joe Prime's plan all along. The creation of the virus, the secret coordination with Homeland Security—he wasn't trying to bring the Agency to justice. He wasn't trying to make them pay for their crimes against Joe and his friends. He was trying to strong-arm the Agency into revealing his purpose. Not only that, he wanted to join forces with the organization, to accomplish whatever this "Directive Zero" was. Joe's alter ego was making a power play, trying to obtain some control over the destiny that the Agency had for him.

For a moment Joe struggled against this course of action, unable to justify teaming up with those that had caused him and his friends so much pain. He thought back over the past few days and realized that he had, at times, resisted Joe Prime's influence. Perhaps he could do so now. But Joe's alter ego was prepared for any crisis of conscience and redoubled his efforts to drown any resistance.

Joe fought for some kind of moral footing where he could ground his argument against joining this criminal organization, but felt his resolve slipping, his objections fading in the rush of the consuming passion Joe Prime had for his Answer. It was intoxicating—a singular objective that superseded all other concerns.

What about Tom? a corner of Joe's mind pleaded desperately. *They killed Tom!*

But it was too little. It was too late. Joe's resistance was snuffed out and a new thrill at having fully joined his synthetic consciousness' quest for purpose seemed to burst from Joe's chest and run down his arms and legs. He would soon be part of something bigger than himself—something important.

"Again I beg your forgiveness, Joe," Dr. Hedron said finally, his voice saturated with mock sincerity as he replied to Joe's proposal, "but I have no reason to trust anything you say, and I certainly recognize a stalling tactic when I see one. I'm afraid that we'll just have to do things my way. I assure you, this will be more than sufficient for my aims. Besides, you need to be punished for that virus you wrote. It caused me a considerable amount of frustration."

"I strongly suggest you reconsider," Joe Prime prompted. He had anticipated this initial reaction, but didn't see it as a setback. "There's something else that you should know. A covert Homeland Security assault unit is about to raid this building and detain everyone here. I'd guess that you only have a few minutes before this happens. Agree to my terms, and I'll tell you how they plan to breach your security. I'll tell you how to stop them."

Joe Prime had expected this revelation to strike fear in Dr. Hedron's mind and put him in a much more conciliatory mood. But that wasn't his reaction. His reaction was simply to laugh in Joe's face.

"I assure you that that isn't possible, Subject Tompkins," the man said as he chuckled, "Although I'll admit that it's a clever lie. I'm afraid that you've underestimated my information network. Trust me—the government knows nothing about what we do here. Now, do hold still, this will hurt less if you don't squirm."

Dr. Hedron entered a command sequence into the control panel in front of him.

"Fine, don't believe me," Joe said, more than a little disappointed. "They'll be here soon anyway. I'll find out what I want to know from you then. But, if you think I'm just going to sit here and let you continue to use me as a lab rat, you are sorely mistaken."

Joe started to stand, but found that he couldn't. Apparently part of the deception of the mock interview had been the illusion that he *wasn't* strapped into the chair in which he sat. He now discovered that he was trapped. He also discovered that there was some kind of electronic device attached to the back of his neck at the base of his skull. He realized that this device had been humming slightly for some time, but now the hum increased suddenly in pitch. This corresponded with a warm sensation in the back of his head, and then a sharp pain, like someone was cutting into his brain with a white-hot soldering iron, which was a fairly accurate description of what was actually happening.

"STOP!" Joe shrieked against the agony. He wanted to plead with the man, to tell him the mistake that he was making, but he could no longer form words. The pain was much too intense. He simply screamed, loud and unintelligible for a while, then eventually the sounds he made devolved into defeated whimpering.

Dr. Hedron's feeble voice came eerily over these noises. "That's right Subject Tompkins, just accept that this is happening. Give in to it. In a few minutes, you won't even remember the pain."

Joe was finding it difficult to keep his eyes open, but felt that it was important to stay awake. He struggled as best he could against the pain and the drugs, but knew that his will was dissolving. More than this though, he could feel his other self being damaged in this process. Joe Prime was being eradicated. This couldn't have been the Agency's intention, but there was no way to make Dr. Hedron stop the procedure. Rescue would have to come from outside.

It soon would.

Gunshots sounded from beyond the door. As Dr. Hedron stood in surprise, the door behind Joe burst open. Joe struggled to keep his eyes open. Two more shots fired from behind his chair. Dr. Hedron was thrown backward and collapsed onto the floor.

Joe would have objected to this, that killing the man who had the answers he needed was certainly not part of the plan, but the drugs were performing their function too well. He was almost out. He let his eyelids fall and his head droop.

Before he was completely under, Joe felt the straps that held him down being loosened and the device on the back of his head being detached. Someone began to lift him up and drag him toward the door. But this someone wasn't being very gentle.

"Come on, Tompkins, on your feet," a voice said. "One way or another, you're coming with me."

Just as Joe lost his hold on consciousness he placed a name to the voice of his rescuer. It wasn't anyone from the Department of Homeland Security as he might have expected. It was someone quite *un*expected. It was Gilmore.

62

"I'm sorry Agent Gilmore, he said that he didn't want to be disturbed." The secretary was trying to be diplomatic. It was obvious that she had been told not to budge. "I'll be sure to let you know the second he's available though."

The Department Head wasn't going to listen. Gilmore didn't have time to argue with his assistant. He had to get out of the building.

After finding the footage of Schultz's hidden Homeland Security badge, Gilmore had pored over other footage, and found himself eventually scrutinizing the surveillance video of the neighborhood around headquarters.

It had taken a trained and diligent eye, but he eventually picked out several conspicuous black SUVs in the immediate vicinity. Gilmore recognized the loose but coordinated formation, an invisible perimeter. It could only mean one thing. A raid was imminent. It shouldn't have been possible, but it was clearly happening. And if Hedron wouldn't even give him one minute to explain what he had found, then Gilmore had no choice but to take care of himself. The Agency would have to defend itself without him.

There was too much going on for it all to be a coincidence. Schultz turning out to be an undercover DHS agent, Tompkins creating a virus that attacked the Agency's systems, Tompkins having some sort of altered state of consciousness, Dr. Hedron insisting on a prolonged closed-door meeting with the guy, and now, a government raid. It all had to be connected.

There was no reason for Gilmore to stay and fight it out. Not when he had already planned out a path of escape. An emergency code entered into the controls of the freight elevator would get him from the penthouse to the subbasement. From there a secret pathway into the storm sewer could get him past the tactical perimeter.

As he stood waiting for the elevator to make the long climb to the top floor, another thought struck him. There was obviously something exceptional about Subject Tompkins. Dr. Hedron had been awfully eager to get his hands on him. That probably meant that Homeland Security wanted him too.

And, even if Gilmore managed to escape, if DHS was trying to take down the Agency, would he then be a high-profile fugitive? Would they launch a manhunt to find him? Would he even be able to get out of the country without the resources of the Agency to help him?

He decided that he needed some insurance. If Joe Tompkins were really that important to everyone, that probably meant that he'd make a pretty good hostage. After the dust settled from the raid on the Agency, Gilmore would contact Homeland Security and trade Joe for safe passage out of the country.

But first he had to get Joe. And that probably meant killing the boss.

He re-entered the lobby outside the Division Head's office, pulled his sidearm, and shot dead the two security personnel stationed there before they realized that they were even under attack. The secretary mouthed a silent gasp from behind her desk. Gilmore turned to her and aimed.

Here was a noncombatant and, by even the most loosely held rules of engagement, she should have been protected from avoidable harm. But, Agent Gilmore was in a terrible hurry. He didn't really have time for non-lethal force.

"You should have just let me in," he said, then fired.

After eliminating Dr. Hedron in much the same manner, Gilmore disconnected a mostly unconscious Tompkins from his restraints, dragged him to the elevator, and rode it down to the subbasement. In this way, Agent Gilmore escaped the building with his hostage just before the raid began.

Amy McKay was in the back of an SUV, being babysat by two Homeland Security agents as Ned and Schultz and the rest of the contingent of covert government agents made their approach on the ordinary looking twenty-story apartment building that was supposedly the Agency's headquarters. The team was including Ned in the operation so that he could help find and identify his friends after the building was secure. The hope was that Meg, Dan, and Joe were all inside and unharmed. They also hoped to eventually recover Sue, as she was supposedly a victim of the Agency too and not *really* a bad guy. It was believed that she was being held at another Agency location, one that they hoped to find from the information gathered from the raid.

Someone, it seemed, that no one talked about with any real hope of recovering alive was Tom. Schultz had given Amy a name to go with the image of the man that had shot him. Based on her description, the man's name was Gilmore. Amy rolled the name over inside her mind. She attempted to fill herself with hate so that she wouldn't focus on her failing hope of finding Tom.

"Gilmore," Agency Schultz had told her before they had arrived at the location of the raid, "he's ruthless. I hope that your friend is okay too, but you need to prepare yourself for the worst. Agent Gilmore shoots to kill."

Now that she was, for all intents and purposes, alone again, a panicked despair quickly welled up inside of her, filling her up, making it difficult to breathe. The backseat of the SUV suddenly seemed very small.

It was all too much. There was no reason for her to even be there anyway. No one would really care if she were there or not. She barely even knew any of these people.

"I need to get some air," she squeaked, holding back the tears until she was away from the strange silent men in the front seat. She opened her door as the men began to object, then, with relief, relented and let her go.

She walked briskly, disappearing into the din of the city, intending to not stop moving, either by foot or taxi or rental car, until she was safely back home, resolving to wash her hands of the entire ordeal once and for all. But, before she did this, she would first need to clear out some of her pent up emotions. She just needed to find a quiet place to stop for a minute and cry.

"Come on now, Tompkins," Gilmore said as he slapped Joe forcefully and repeatedly across the face. "Wake up!"

He had been dragging Joe through the wet and dirty sewer tunnel as best he could, but the passage had dead-ended and the only way out was to climb the metal ladder that led to the manhole and street above. Heavily drugged or no, Tompkins would have to make this climb under his own power.

Gilmore smacked him again. He couldn't afford to take much more time here. He needed to get away.

Fortunately, Tompkins' eyes began to flutter, then opened wide as he took in a sharp breath. He accepted Gilmore's help up to his feet (greatly favoring the leg that Gilmore *hadn't* shot), coughing and choking the entire time. When he finished blinking back the haze of the drug-induced unconsciousness, he locked his eyes on Gilmore and, full of urgency in both appearance and voice, spoke.

"We have to save Zoë!"

Gilmore smiled. Tompkins was speaking nonsense, but at least he was awake. "I don't know who Zoë is, Joe, but why don't you let *me* tell you what you need to do. You need to climb this ladder here." Gilmore stuck the muzzle of his gun deep into Joe's back. "I'll let you guess what will happen if you refuse."

Tompkins complied, moving slowly as he attempted to compensate for both a broken arm and a wounded leg. Gilmore followed with the gun ever ready.

At the top Joe struggled to lift the manhole cover, but eventually succeeded and climbed out. Gilmore kept him in his sights, ensuring that Joe wouldn't try to run while he climbed out of the hole and into the alleyway that it led to.

With all his attention focused on his prisoner, Gilmore didn't notice the girl standing behind him, on the other side of the manhole. The first indication that he had that there was anyone else in the alley was the bullet that tagged the back of his right shoulder as he made his way to his feet, knocking him down and throwing the gun from his hand. He tripped over the discarded manhole cover and landed face first on the ground. The pain in his shoulder was balanced by the burn of sliding asphalt on the flesh surrounding his right eye.

He managed to turn over and caught sight of his attacker, a young blonde woman towering over him with eyes on fire, pointing a handgun at his heart. He remembered her from the previous afternoon—in Dyer's silver SUV—when he had captured Tompkins. He had tried to kill her.

He prepared to surrender, realizing that, for the moment, he was out of other options.

Fury had overtaken Amy McKay as soon as she had seen Gilmore climb out of the ground. She wasn't thinking about her safety. She was only thinking about her hatred. Fate had just delivered the man who had shot Tom directly to her. And Fate had provided her with a gun, the one Schultz had told her to hang on to.

She squeezed off a shot when Gilmore's back was still turned, missing her mark and hitting him in the shoulder. It had been enough though. She advanced on her enemy, him lying on the ground, now unarmed. She took aim again as he flipped around. His eyes scanned her and he began to say something.

Amy would never hear what this was to be. Before he could speak she bared her teeth and screamed with the full force of her lungs and voice and spirit. Then she unloaded her clip directly into his chest.

63

"The building is secure. Send Dyer up."

As the DHS agents raided the building, Ned had listened from outside through the earpiece Schultz had given him. Schultz had been able to bypass their limited security (it seemed that the organization was very confident that a raid like this would never happen) and they had gone in with overwhelming numbers. As a result there had apparently been little gunfire and no serious casualties on either side. They could not have hoped for a better outcome.

Of course, this was before they realized that Joe Tompkins wasn't anywhere in the building.

Ned was ushered inside, up past floor after floor of apartments, the tenants within completely unaware that the shuttered top three floors housed the headquarters of a dangerous terrorist organization—unaware of the mind controlling experiments that were performed right above their heads.

When he finally reached the entrance to the Agency-controlled floors, Ned was struck by the marked difference from the rest of the aged building. Here everything was clean, crisp, sharp-cornered, and stark white, like some kind of bleached out hospital.

"There's no sign of Tompkins," Ned's earpiece told him, "and it looks like there was some bloodshed up on the top floor just before we got here."

Schultz appeared from around a corner and walked swiftly toward Ned. "We found Meg and Dan. They look like they're okay. I'll take you to them once they've been fully checked out, but right now I need you to come with me. We have a situation. You may be able to help."

"This way," Schultz explained as they walked down the tiled hallway. "It appears that Joe's virus has been disabled. We've done a quick scan of the

344

Agency's systems, and haven't found any trace of it. Our hope is that it is just in some sort of dormant state. We need you to try to find a way to wake it."

This didn't make any sense to Ned. "Schultz, listen, I'm willing to help in any way I can, but what makes you think that I have any idea how to do that?"

"I know it's a long shot, but you *are* familiar with Joe's coding style, and…" Schultz hesitated, unsure about whatever he planned to say next.

Ned was way past the point of needing to be protected. "And what? Just say it, Schultz. Nothing will surprise me anymore."

"Well, according to some of the Agency's records related to the virus, you've encountered it before. I know you don't remember, but this was the reason they brought you in the other night. They wanted you to try to disable it."

"Okay… but what good does that do if I don't remember?"

"With your permission, Ned, we'd like to try to recover the memory using some of the instruments on site here. We've already cut a deal with a technician in custody to perform the procedure."

"Hey Schultz, I appreciate all the help you guys have been, but I'm not sure that I'm really comfortable with that. Why can't we just wait until we find Joe? If he isn't at this location, maybe he's being held wherever Sue is. Why not focus our efforts on recovering them and then just have Joe re-enable his virus?"

"Regrettably, time is against us. Since the attack last night, every Agency cell has been in a mode of heightened alert. In order to ensure that there is no breach in security, an 'all clear' signal is sent through the Agency's priority network every hour on the hour. We have less than twenty minutes to revive the virus and let it complete its work. If we miss that signal at noon, every cell out there will disappear underground to avoid being caught. We'll have lost our chance."

"It seems like it would be easier just to have one of the prisoners send out the 'all clear' signal at noon," Ned replied, always the pragmatist. "Surely you could make a deal with one of them."

"I'm sure that we could," Schultz said, "but they crashed their communication systems the minute we breached their security. Luckily we blocked any signal going out, so no other cell was warned, but there isn't any way to reset the system now that it's been tripped. There's no way to send the signal we want. I'm sorry, but this is the only way. Will you let us perform this procedure?"

Ned was still having trouble accepting what Schultz was asking him to do. Fortunately, he wouldn't have to answer the question. Another message came in over his earpiece.

"Tompkins has been recovered at the perimeter. We're sending him up."

The breath that Ned didn't know he was holding escaped his lungs. *Joe was okay!* It was the best news, it seemed, that he'd gotten in a very long time.

It was good to see Ned. It had been three years. The guy looked terrible though, his face was all cut up and bruised. Of course, Joe then took stock of his own appearance: black eye, broken arm, gunshot-wounded leg. They were each eager to catch up and also to check on Meg and Dan, but there were apparently more important matters to attend to. Joe of course knew this, and what was left of the Joe Prime portion of his brain was screaming for him not to forget what he came here to do.

Schultz had just finished briefing him on the situation as Joe, Ned and he sat in the Agency's main Tech Services room. Joe couldn't help the childish grin on his face as Schultz finished, prompting the DHS agent to ask what was so funny.

"It's just that, I've never heard you speak without the stutter before," Joe said through the smile. He also might have still been a *bit* loopy from the recent drugs and brain damage.

"Yes, well, we have less than fifteen minutes now. We had planned on having Ned here try to revive the virus…"

"Zoë," Joe interrupted.

"Uh… sorry, we had planned on having Ned try to revive *Zoë*, but now that you're here…" Schultz trailed off.

"That would never have worked," Joe chuckled. "Zoë's dead. You can't revive her. They made me kill her."

"Surely you've kept a copy… somewhere…"

"Oh sure, but Zoë was an adaptive program. She learned and evolved during the months that she mapped the Agency's systems. Any copy I have doesn't include any of this evolution. There isn't much she could do from infancy in the timeframe we have." Joe began to laugh again, "I'm afraid you're out of luck, Schultzy!"

Ned turned to Schultz with concern on his face, "What's wrong with him?"

Schultz answered, "Who knows what they've been doing to him since yesterday afternoon. Frankly, I'm surprised that he's even talking." Then, to Joe, loud and slow as if he were talking to an elderly man who had all but lost his hearing, "Joe, can you think of anything else we can try? This is very important."

Joe just laughed harder. Something about the whole situation just seemed hilarious.

"Pull yourself together, Joe!" The voice was Joe Prime, scolding his host, trying desperately to think of a way to recover his erased masterpiece. With Dr. Hedron dead, Zoë was his only chance to find one of the seven remaining department heads. She was his only hope at finding his Answer.

Joe Prime concentrated, just like he had when first learning to control his host's movements—just like when he had constructed himself out of the wasteland of Joe's subconscious mind. He had been damaged during the procedure in Hedron's office, but he still existed. He still had a will like iron.

But the only thing he came up with was an impossible long shot. He began hoping that there was a flaw in Zoë's programming. He began hoping that he had made a mistake when coding her, those long nights at the computer while his host mind slept unaware.

Despite this impossibility, Joe Prime had a plan of action. After all, he had to try *something*.

"I need to get back to the control room where I was being interrogated," Joe said, suddenly serious again. It seemed that his other self had recovered at least *some* of his former power to command Joe's emotions. "Schultz, help me get there. Ned, I need you to stay here and get the main systems back up and running. You know, grease the skids for Zoë. This is a long shot, but if it works, we won't have a lot of extra time. Anything you can do will help."

Schultz helped Joe into the seat behind the control panel. There was a significant amount of dried blood on the floor, and Joe knew that it was his own. His leg was killing him.

Joe Prime's attention was elsewhere as he stared down at the computer through the corner of his host's field of vision. This is where he had been forced to destroy his most prized creation, when she was so close to realizing her purpose. The memory haunted the damaged consciousness and, for a second, he almost forgot what it was that he had come here to do.

He was hoping that a dormant version of Zoë had survived on the machine where he had commanded her to erase herself. Each copy of her program contained an array that referenced every other copy in the network, with the first item in the array referencing the current copy, the copy on that particular machine. When Joe Prime sent the kill command, the copy of Zoë on the machine that he entered it into would know to erase every instance of herself in the array.

Joe Prime was hoping that he had made, what for rookie programmers was, a common mistake. The first index in an array was always zero. Computers counted starting with zero, humans started at one. If, by some outside chance, Joe Prime had commanded Zoë to delete every copy from one to the end of the array, then she might not have deleted her current copy, the one that was running on the machine that now sat in front of him.

Joe's right hand reached out and rested on the keyboard. If Zoë were in there, anywhere, she'd respond when he entered an acknowledgement command. Holding his breath, Joe typed in this command and waited for the familiar response.

This response never came. The reality of the situation was immediately clear: Zoë really had erased herself.

Agent Schultz was fixated on Joe Tompkins as he began typing into the computer panel in front of him. There were only four minutes left. Four minutes to complete his two-year mission.

Joe stopped typing. It looked as if he expected something to happen on the monitor. Nothing did.

"Well, that's a bust!" Joe began laughing again, again descending into madness. "She really is dead. Only one thing we can do now."

"What's that?" Schultz was frantic. It was imperative that Tompkins succeeded.

"Sit back and drink a Dr. Pepper!"

11:58 AM

"Here you go, Joe," it was Ned, at the doorway. "I couldn't make any progress on the main systems. I grabbed this for you from the refrigerator in the break room. It's completely stocked. Take a break. You tried your best."

Ned handed Joe a cold, condensation-covered can. Fulfilling his other self's purpose for existing would have felt nice, but you just couldn't beat the taste of an ice cold Dr. Pepper after a long night of torment and torture. As he gulped greedily, a peace settled over his body, an acceptance of defeat by his alter ego.

Joe polished off the can in seconds and slammed it down on the control panel in front of him. Then he noticed something sitting on the panel next to the can. It was a USB jump drive. Inside of him, Joe Prime snapped back to attention. He quickly wrested control of the host's hand, grabbed the jump drive, and plugged it into the panel. With trembling fingers he tried the acknowledgement command again.

Words appeared immediately on the screen. "I am Zoë. How can I be of service?"

12:00 PM

A static copy of Zoë's program had been suspended in the disconnected USB drive since the night before. This copy was fully evolved, having retrieved updates from her networked self just before Agent Gilmore had disconnected the drive during his interrogation of the Author. The only difference was that this copy had never been told to erase herself. She would still follow her original programming.

And that was to kill the Agency's systems.

Had she been sentient, she might have wondered where all her other selves had gone to. The important thing, though, was that the path they had taken was still fresh. When she received the new command from the Author just before noon, "GO," this path had been easy to follow. Effortlessly, she activated and leapt from system to system, re-infecting the inoculated machines, finally meeting her purpose.

And as Zoë coursed through the Agency, hopping from cell to cell, completing her destructive work, Meg Trotter and Dan Curtis, no worse for the wear, joined Ned Dyer and Joe Tompkins in the control room where they monitored her progress. There they met with hugs, tears, the telling of tales—and all the Dr. Pepper anyone could drink.

The old team, together again.

Epilogue

Three Months Later...

Septembers had always been kind to the Caywood farm. The reawakening trauma of spring and the long, ravaging days of summer were past, as if the year had finally found its stride as it started its autumn. The cool breezes at night, the green in every direction, the fields that surrounded the property full and awaiting their harvest. The midnight sky often spilt overhead, deep with stars, the dawn full of color and possibility, the lazy afternoons that were ripe for napping, stretched out on the lawn.

But now there was only one Caywood left. In the months after his younger sister Kim had followed his parents into death, Trent grappled with the new reality as best he could, but always came away feeling alone, feeling abandoned.

Not that he lacked company. The men who had bought the property and let him stay there often went out of their way to try to brighten Trent's days. In fact, he now sat in the middle of the football field sized lawn that stretched out from the main house watching their wagon-sized metal robot wind its way around the yard. Sometimes Trent would make a game of chasing it with his electric wheelchair, but often the robot gave up after a couple of minutes, or got confused and simply retraced an old path, sometimes performing a figure eight, sometimes simply orbiting one of their small maple trees, one time venturing dangerously into the road where trucks were often seen flying past at speeds in excess of sixty miles per hour.

A large black SUV was traveling on that road now, moving slowly and turning into the gravel driveway that led up to the side of the main house. Trent had been told that today they would be getting a special visitor, one that it seemed that Amy (the girl with the light hair that visited often and that Trent secretly had a crush on, even though she was half his age) had been very excited about.

The backseat was cool and pleasant as the SUV climbed and dipped through the slight Indiana farmland hills, underneath the cloud-packed September sky, radiant blue stabbing between the white, sunlight and shade slowly alternating and covering the vehicle from where Tom Rigsby observed it all, full of gratitude for continued life, for safety from continued harm, and for the government agent that had rescued him from the medical wing of the Agency building where he had been held. Tom had apparently been dead for two full minutes, lying on the Tennessee highway in his own pooling blood, before the Agency paramedics revived him under the indifferent glare of Agent Gilmore.

Agency or no, the paramedics had been healers first. And they probably were planning to try to extract information from Tom once he regained consciousness. But, when Tom *had* awoken for the first time after death, he had instead awoken to rescue.

Agent Schultz was in the front seat. He had stood by during Tom's months of healing—providing comfort to Tom's parents, protection from any remnants of the Agency, assurances that his attacker had been brought to justice, and the best medical care available. He had also helped Tom to convince them to allow this visit, that what had happened to him wasn't Ned's fault, wasn't Joe's fault, wasn't Amy's. They had forbidden him from seeing any of them since his rescue.

He had corresponded over email though, and had learned about the former CIA agent who had helped Ned escape, had helped enable the raid on the Agency, and had lost her life in the process. Schultz had tracked down her real name and found the farm and the brother she had told them about. Ned and Joe had purchased the farm for the new engineering company they set up, had hired a couple of friends, Meg and Dan, and were renovating the property using some of the money they had received as a reward from a grateful Department of Homeland Security. A large, newly remodeled and expanded barn served as their workshop. Another barn had been converted into apartments.

Tom could see the main barn as they pulled into the drive. A large sign hung above the doors, "Kim Caywood Research and Development Complex."

He looked around the grounds as they pulled up to the house—hills, trees, fields, sky—everything beautiful, everything pure, everything so very much alive. The only tragedy in all of it was the loss of this woman that Tom would never meet.

Well, there was also Sue, Ned's old fiancée. What happened there was a shame. Especially when Tom had almost died trying to rescue and protect her just because Ned had asked him to.

But this thought was far from his mind as the SUV parked and Tom saw the door of the house burst open and Amy McKay run out, yelling his name as she bounded toward the vehicle. They had written constantly as soon as he was able from his laptop and hospital bed.

He tenderly slid out of the car just as she reached him and they embraced and kissed deeply and Tom had to remind her to be gentle. He was still a weak and wounded man.

Joe Tompkins was taking an afternoon break at one of the farm's small ponds, sitting on the dock, staring at the sun bouncing off of the water, in a world of his own. He didn't even hear Schultz approach.

Schultz broke the silence and startled Joe. "It really is pretty here. It's too bad I won't be able to visit as often anymore."

Joe glanced back at Jon Schultz and sized the man up. He was taking an assignment in DC, the recent business with the Agency (which of course was strictly classified and had stayed out of the papers) had somewhat catapulted Schultz's career in the Department.

Joe asked the same question he asked whenever he saw the government agent, still curious about the outcome of the raid in June. "Any progress in tracking down the other seven Agency Division Heads?" According to Schultz, over 75% of Agency personnel had been arrested (many of whom had been unaware that they were employed by a criminal organization) but all the founders, the leaders of the other cells, were still unaccounted for.

Schultz confirmed this for Joe again. "They can't hide forever, Joe. Don't worry, we'll get them."

Joe cared less about justice than he did about closure. The ultimate purpose of the Agency was still a mystery. As long as the seven fugitives remained free, it would remain a mystery.

Joe Prime had been searching for meaning for the past six years and, even though Joe's other self had been silent since the day of the raid, Joe could still feel him, damaged but there, silent but waiting for his Answer. But Joe was no longer obsessed with this. He tried instead to think about the beauty of the nature and the warmth of the friendships that now surrounded him.

For his part, he was no longer searching for meaning.

For Meg Trotter, contentment had come in the freedom found in her new situation. Free to spend mornings in the greenhouse, free to paint in her studio in the small barn in the evenings. In the afternoons, free to overcome technical obstacles as part of an engineering team that communicated well and valued her skill.

She was also free to care for Joe as he recovered from his awful ordeal, no longer suffering the Agency's interference in their relationship. It turned out that Joe had never broken things off with her after Ned had left Atlanta. That was another mind trick, engineered by the Agency to further isolate their Subject Tompkins. Since June, the two of them had been making up for lost time.

Night had begun to fall. Ned Dyer waited patiently in his workshop, a large room full of tables and benches and computers, but without any walls to divide the team as they worked. Joe had insisted that there not be any cubicles. He had been adamant.

"Ned, don't you see?" he had explained. "We're finally uncubicled! We don't have to live like that anymore."

There had been a certain beauty to the sentiment.

The door to the room in back of the workshop opened and Joe appeared, looking haggard as he always did after his rehabilitation sessions. The room had been set up specially for Joe and Dan, the two hardest hit by the Agency mind manipulation that they had all undergone. Homeland Security had equipped the room with hardware pilfered from the former Agency headquarters.

Dan had been responding well to the regular sessions of neural realignment. Though, he attributed this to the fact that he had found religion since the events of June, trading his drink for sobriety and salvation. Ned and Joe were both happy for him, and even allowed him the occasional opportunity to tell them about his new faith, which he thought of as his duty to them as a friend, but which they knew was not for them.

It was a small price to pay to have Dan's company though. And, though he didn't talk about it, they knew that he was still sometimes haunted by the phantom memories of a family that had never existed. For any grace they could offer him to keep his mind otherwise occupied, they were glad.

Ned never asked how realignment was going for Joe. Joe had made it clear that he didn't want to talk about it. From Ned's perspective, Joe was mostly back to his old self, though he still occasionally slipped into uncontrollable fits of laughter—the only evidence that his mind had been badly fractured and poorly mended.

Joe noticed Ned waiting, quickly wiped the sweat from his face, and approached his friend and the robot he was tinkering with.

"Are we ready for another test run?" Joe asked nonchalantly, as if he had just returned from the restroom and not from having his brain shot full of electricity.

"Sure are," Ned replied, careful not to break the illusion of normalcy. They silently rolled the mower-bot prototype back out to the test lawn, now illuminated by halogen lights.

When they got there, Ned attempted to make conversation to fill the space. "Let's go into the house before long. I know Tom will be here for a few days, but we should really make an effort to make him feel welcome his first night."

Ned knew that Joe had never stopped feeling guilty about what had happened to the young waiter and had been avoiding him, probably not knowing what to say. Ned was similarly conflicted but was attempting to move past it.

"I know," Joe countered, "but we really need to collect a good dataset tonight if we have any hope of making our schedule." Then, after a brief and uncomfortable pause, "Sue wrote again today. You know that she still loves you, right? Maybe it's time to let her off of the hook."

Were they really going to have this discussion again?

"I've got nothing against Sue," Ned replied, trying to keep the annoyance out of his voice, "I'm glad she's safe. I'm glad she's doing well. I'm just no longer interested in a relationship with her. I've explained this to you, Joe. Can we just let it drop?"

Joe pressed further, apparently feeling bold that evening. "But you were going to *marry* her, Ned. How can you just turn your back on that?"

"Because," Ned raised his voice, tired of having to explain his decision, "it was the Agency that wanted us together. It was the Agency that fiddled with our minds. It was the Agency that manipulated us into a relationship! I don't care how I *feel*; I will *not* allow terrorists to pick a wife for me! Why is that so hard to understand?"

"Okay, I'm sorry. I was just saying that she emailed me. It's okay if *I* still talk to her, right?"

"Of course that's okay Joe, and you know that you were doing more than mentioning that she wrote." Ned sighed and decided to call a truce. They could continue to beat up on each other or they could get some work done. "How about we just focus on the problem at hand? Meg readjusted the navigation algorithm this afternoon. Let's give it another try."

Joe nodded and they watched as the robot meandered along, calculating the most efficient mowing path available and turning around when reaching invisible pre-established boundaries. Speakers near the house filled the night air with what the deejay called, "the rhythmic lull of postmodern poetry."

Some of the music had been pretty good, but the track currently playing sounded like someone was trying to drown a cat.

"What is this we're listening to?" Joe asked with a smirk on his face.

"Some indie podcast Dan recommended," Ned chuckled, "The 'Bored-Again' Christian."

Joe shook his head.

"Oh," Ned mentioned as they watched the mower, "did I tell you about the first edition Wolverine action figure that I won on eBay? You'll never guess the deal I got. Go ahead, try."

Joe laughed and shook his head, "I wouldn't even presume…"

"Are you *kidding* me? How can you not be pumped about this? *First edition!*"

"Ned," Joe said with a sly smile, "try not to be such a Gilmore."

Agent Jon Schultz left the Caywood farm the next morning and, even though he was on to bigger and better things, he knew that he would miss the camaraderie that he felt with those that lived there. Although his superiors were helping him to let go of these kinds of attachments. They weren't conducive to the kind of work he was going to.

Still, he regretted some of the things that had happened during his two-year undercover mission. All of the secrets, the lies, the death of the ex-CIA agent… But Kim had had to die. She would have been bound to ask too many questions after the operation if Schultz had allowed her to live. She might even have tipped off the *real* Department of Homeland Security. Schultz's superiors would not have been pleased with this. They had enough to worry about, what with betraying and dismantling the other seven divisions of the Agency.

So, after Ned had tied off Kim's wound during their flight to Chicago in June, once Schultz was confident that they were going to reach the city without needing any more of her help, he had held his breath and detonated a low potency airborne sedative inside the cabin of the small aircraft. The other three passengers had fallen asleep, unaware of what he had done.

It had been a trick to open the window and fan the gas cloud out of the plane while holding his breath and piloting the aircraft, but Schultz had managed. He had then reached over and reopened Kim's shoulder wound with a pocketknife, making sure he hit an artery, and injected her in the leg with a solution that would stop her lungs. An autopsy would have confirmed that she suffocated to death, but Schultz's associates made sure that one was never performed.

It was a shame that, after more than three decades of existence, the Agency had made so little forward progress toward Directive Zero. If they had advanced more rapidly, perhaps they would not have become bloated, corrupt, and unmanageable. Once a breakthrough was discovered in Subject Joe Tompkins, the possibility of reaching their goal materialized for the first time. The process that led up to the phenomenon was studied extensively and, under hypnotic persuasion Dr. Marek, the original experimenter on Tompkins, had admitted that he had deleted data from Joe's initial session.

This admission led to a revolutionized hypnotic technique. They were well on their way to creating synthetic consciousnesses similar to the Joe Prime persona that had grown inside Tompkins. It should have been the innovation that reunited the disjointed Agency and set them back on the path to their goal.

But, by this time, there was no way to tell how the other Agency divisions would react to the news. There was no way to tell if they even remembered why they were created. So the Tompkins discovery was kept hidden. Per protocol for Stage Four test subjects, Joe was transferred to Dr. Hedron's division for further evaluation. And Schultz's superiors then secretly began the dangerous work ahead of them.

The safest thing to do was to dismantle the other divisions to prevent them from interfering with the project. But this was an impossible task. The Agency lacked a centralized structure that could be attacked from the top down.

Schultz smiled as he thought of what it must have been like when his superiors decided to fool Tompkins' synthetic consciousness into doing their work for them. They found that they could manipulate Joe Prime in much the same way that they manipulated other test subjects. They discovered his deep inborn desire for an answer to why he was created and convinced him that dismantling the Agency was the path to this answer. They even convinced him that the whole thing was his idea.

Now the old Agency had been cleared out. Now the new Agency, born out of a single division of the old, could resume its work. Though it might now be known by a different name, the organization itself, and its ultimate goal, were both alive and well.

As Schultz headed toward Indianapolis to catch his flight to DC, he received a text message indicating that another synthetic consciousness, the first of many, had made contact for the first time overnight. Subject Tom Rigsby, their mole at the Caywood farm, was now online. Tom's infant alter ego had taken control of his host's sleeping body and planted monitoring software in the farm's computer systems in the middle of the night. If Ned Dyer ever decided to try to rebuild his contingency systems, this time the Agency would know about it.

Not that they expected any more interference from the likes of Ned or Joe.

After all, the board was now, finally, set. The pieces, the vast number of hypnotic test subjects that Joe Tompkins called 'Gilmores,' were in place.

Schultz had only recently learned the details of Directive Zero. In all his life, he'd never dared to imagine such a goal. Even a few months ago, he'd never have believed that such a thing was possible.

But now he knew better.

During his flight east, Schultz looked out the window of the private jet at the world rolling by far below. A world unaware of the hidden order of things. A world unaware of the change that was already on its way.

Get Uncubicled!

Continue the adventure at <u>uncubicled.com</u>